PUBLIC MORALS

PUBLIC MORALS

THE DEVINE TRILOGY

TOM COFFEY

Once again, to Jill

"Everything is money and power and how to
use them both."

—Diana Vreeland

Praise for Public Morals

"New York City is much more than the glitz of Broadway and the glamor of Seventh Avenue. There's also the grimy, seamy, dirty, disreputable, cutthroat underside—the fun and interesting side. In *Public Morals,* Tom Coffey slam bang drops us into a society so corrupt you might have to slip a buck or two just for giving you the time. We're not in Kansas anymore. We're in a city where it's almost impossible to tell the good guys from the bad. And that's what makes this such a compelling, fun read."—Charles Salzberg, three-time Shamus Award nominee and author of *Man on the Run*

I

Part One

1982

Chapter One

Paco, the pimp, voice hoarse from smoke and aggravation, told Devine he could make some money.

"How much?" Devine asked.

"She owes me two thousand."

"That's unlike you. What happened?"

"She's got ways."

Devine could imagine what they were. "I've never done anything like this."

"Sure you have. Just not for me."

That hurt, but it was true. Devine asked what his cut was. He'd just delivered the pad but could always use more.

"Ten percent," Paco said.

"Not even close."

They dickered over the phone before settling on thirty.

Terence Devine paced the corner of West 73rd and Amsterdam Avenue while junkies spilled from Needle Park before beginning their drug-induced stagger/float toward the SROs lining Upper Broadway. Lincoln Center glowed six blocks south. Do-gooders kept saying it would brighten the neighborhood, and things were starting to turn around, just you wait, but anybody with any sense knew that New York was too far gone, and the smart play was picking what you could from the city's carcass.

He saw the woman who owed Paco quick-stepping from the 72nd Street subway station. Her shoulder bag was slung across an animal print winter coat, and her pissed-off expression looked permanent. Doubtless she had charged her client the cab fare home and pocketed what was left over.

Although the streetlights were busted, Devine tried to read her as he tailed her past the derelict Ansonia building. She wore heels, and he estimated she was five-foot-four out of them. Dark brown hair stretched halfway down her back. She was in her mid-twenties but, even across the darkened street, Devine noticed lines creasing her forehead. She called herself Nadine LaFleur, but if that was her real name, he was Robert Redford.

A small iron gate had been wedged onto the sidewalk in front of her walkup near West End Avenue. Those things were beyond useless, but the landlord could jack up the rent by fifty a month.

The woman unzipped her bag before reaching into it without breaking stride. Her key was in the gate's lock in a split second, and then she was through and rushing up the steps to the front door. From across the street, a guy who sounded Puerto Rican shouted that he wanted a blowjob. Nadine never slowed and never turned, but she did raise her middle finger.

A minute later, the lights sputtered on in her third-floor apartment, which faced the street.

Devine stepped over the trash-strewn curb before heading to her building. He needed two seconds to pick the lock on the gate. As he headed up the stairs, the Puerto Rican guy asked if he was gonna get a blowjob. Devine raised his middle finger and pressed the buzzer for 3A.

No answer. Nadine was wary. Living in Manhattan was like being part of the food chain on the Serengeti.

Devine blew on his hands. It was cold, and he wished he'd worn something heavier than his leather jacket. This time he pressed the buzzer hard before putting his mouth close to the intercom.

"Ms. LaFleur."

Still no answer.

"I'm with the police, Ms. LaFleur."

"Horseshit."

He adopted the don't-make-me-stop-this-car voice he sometimes used on his kids.

"I'm not here to arrest you, but there's something we need to discuss."

"I'm not gonna buzz you in."

"Then I'll give you thirty seconds to get down here. We can talk face-to-face."

He timed her with his watch. Twenty-eight seconds later, the tall and narrow door that separated the foyer from the staircase jerked open. Now that he could see her under the harsh overhead light, he figured she had eighteen months left to make money off a beauty that had once been effortless.

He pressed badge and ID against the glass but made sure his thumb obscured his name.

"Finger down," she said.

He lowered it. She peered at his identification before cracking open the front door. She kept her arm wedged against it.

"My guy's supposed to take care of shit like this."

"Can I come inside?"

"I'd rather talk here."

"It's cold, and this could take a few minutes."

She opened the door wide enough to let Devine slip through, then led him up the stairs.

"Are you staring at my ass?"

"I'm here on business, Ms. LaFleur."

The door to her apartment had four bolts, which she unlocked in five seconds. When they walked in, Devine was struck by how ordinary it was. A beige rug covered most of the hardwood floor. The sofa, easy chair, and coffee table were all brown and looked straight out of the Sears catalog. The black-and-white TV was tuned to "Dynasty." The only unusual thing was her bookcase, which was lined with novels by Faulkner, Hemingway and Fitzgerald—stuff Devine was supposed to read in high school. An ounce scale served as a bookend.

"What's this about?" she asked.

"Paco."

"Never heard of him."

Devine closed the door. "Don't make this any more difficult than it needs to be."

"I should call my lawyer right now. His name's Ortega. He'll eat you alive."

She headed for the phone, but Devine was across the room the instant she began pressing the numbers. She shook him away when he clamped his palm around her wrist.

"Nobody touches me until they show some cash," she said.

"You're the one who has to show some cash, Ms. LaFleur."

She stared at him blankly, like a pedestrian in a crosswalk who couldn't believe she was about to get run over by the speeding yellow taxi.

"Paco wants his money," Devine said. "You've been holding out on him. That's why I'm here."

"What kind of cop are you?"

"Nobody can make a living on a Civil Service salary. Sometimes I have to freelance."

She put down the phone, stared straight at him, and came close to smiling. "I don't have it."

Hookers lied. So did pimps. Johns, too. Everybody lied all the time, and years ago Devine had learned there was no reason to believe anything anybody told him.

"You owe Paco two thousand dollars," he said. "When you give me the money, I'll get outta here. Otherwise, you'll be stuck with me all night."

She dropped her voice to a tone that was husky and alluring, then rubbed her hand over his chest with a warm and assured touch. "My apologies, Officer Devine, but I'm flat broke."

I wish she hadn't seen my name, he thought, but now I understand why Paco didn't come here himself.

"I'm gonna meet my girlfriend later, Ms. LaFleur. I've been in this line of work a while, and I know how to save my bullets."

She pointed to his wedding ring and shook her head in disappointment.

"That's why I need a girlfriend," Devine said.

He kept his eyes fixed on her face. He liked to watch people think. The more their eyes darted, the more outlandish the stories they invented.

She looked aside, walked into the bedroom, and yanked open the top drawer of her nightstand. Devine noticed a copy of "L'Etranger."

"I can give you four hundred," she said. "It's all I've got."

She shoved some green paper at Devine, who began counting. It actually came to four hundred and twelve.

"Where's the rest?" he asked.

She let out a snort that he assumed was an attempt at a laugh. "You cleaned me out. Happy?"

A glossy leather handbag the color of ivory lay on her bed. Devine grabbed it by the strap and snapped open the clasps.

"That's mine!"

She swooped toward him with nails ready to scratch and claw, but he pushed her aside before opening the bag all the way. Inside were rings and bracelets and a roll of cash. Devine held the money between his thumb and index finger while she stood against the door to her closet and rubbed the back of her neck.

"How much is in here, Nadine?"

"You have no right—"

He was tired of this woman. He wanted a beer and a cheeseburger. Then he'd see Gina.

"You have no rights," Devine said. He wanted to keep his voice from rising, but sometimes it was hard to control. "This is a kangaroo court, and I will hop all over you until I get what I came for."

She rushed toward him with her hand drawn. He grabbed her wrist before she could swing her arm. They stood there like high schoolers about to begin an awkward dance.

"You're a goddamn shakedown artist," she said.

"We're not here to talk about my failings. We're here to talk about yours."

He pushed her away and counted the new money.

"There's two hundred and thirty-one dollars here. That leaves you—" He paused while he did the arithmetic. "—thirteen hundred and fifty-seven short."

"Good math skills," she said.

"Not as good as yours."

Devine sat on the edge of her bed, reached into his waistband and pulled out his gun. He hoped she didn't realize the safety was still on.

"I've been in hundreds of places like this. Girls like you—"

"I'm not a girl," she said.

He smiled without mirth. A trick every cop learned. "Professional women like yourself always have money stashed in spots most people would never look. But I will, because I know. I will ransack this apartment if I have to, but I am not leaving until I get all the money you owe your employer."

"Dream on. You wouldn't believe the men I do business with. If I call them, they'll boot you off the force so fast you won't know what happened."

Devine understood. Nadine LaFleur regarded herself as a courtesan, so she was paid for more than sex. After the act, still on the clock, she engaged in pillow talk with power brokers whose wives and kids had tuned them out years ago. Women in the life often told him it was the worst part of the job.

He put her leather bag in his lap. It looked like an accessory a Sutton Place society matron would purchase in a boutique on Madison Avenue.

"If you don't have the money," he said, "I'll take this to a pawn shop I know in Hell's Kitchen."

"You can't do that."

She reached for the bag. He pointed the gun at her.

"I can do what I want."

"It was a gift, you bastard."

With his free hand, he shut the bag, jerked open the top drawer of her dresser, and began hurling socks and nylons to the floor.

"Is it in here?" he asked. He was shouting. By now, he didn't care. "Is the goddamn money in here?"

Bony fists smacked into his upper back.

"I'm gonna do this to every drawer in the apartment."

He whirled around. She slapped him, stinging his cheek. He shoved her onto her bed. She writhed as he pinned her.

"Get off me!"

"I'm tired of this shit!"

"Leave me alone!"

"Where's the money?"

"Go fuck yourself!"

He pressed the gun to her head. The safety was still in place. He told himself everything would work out.

Chapter Two

Devine strode into Clarke's, brushed past suits and models, motioned to the barkeep. At the counter, a pint of Harp, ice cold, was ready. He downed most of it in one chug. This was his favorite bar. Sinatra always took Table 20 when he was in town.

"Tough night?"

The tender's voice reeked of Galway. Sometimes Devine felt like asking for his green card.

"They're all tough."

"Quinn's here."

Devine left a fiver and straightened his back. He was a bit over six feet and weighed nearly two hundred. His hair was dark and full and wavy, his eyes were deep-set and blue, and by now he believed all the women over the years who had told him he was good-looking.

When you're in the pub you fancy, Da liked to tell him, always act like you own the joint.

Jamie Quinn, columnist for the *Daily News*, sat in his regular booth in back. Opposite him were two fellas in their early twenties with smooth faces slack from alcohol. Cigarette butts quivered on their lower lips.

Quinn jerked a thumb at his companions. "Beat it. I gotta talk to this guy."

Devine slid in as they stumbled away. A couple of nights a week, Quinn dragged in the cub reporters to see how much they could handle.

"You a grifter, Terry?" Quinn asked.

"Everyone's a grifter in New York."

Quinn reached into his stained jacket and took out the small notepad he always carried. He looked like he'd been wearing the same suit for forty-eight hours.

"I'm gonna use that," he said.

In his column, one of Quinn's recurring characters was a plainclothes cop he called St. Francis, who rousted skels in the worst parts of the city. Devine was one of the inspirations for what everyone assumed was a composite. He and Quinn had met in Brooklyn in 1973 at the site of an armed robbery turned deadly. Devine was still in uniform then. As they talked over the body of the store owner, they formed a bond that revolved around alcohol and information.

Quinn knocked back the last of his beer. Devine raised his arm without turning. In less than a minute, a freckle-faced waitress set a mug of Schaefer and a shot of Bushmills in front of Jamie Quinn.

"You got anything for me?" the columnist asked.

"We have a new captain," Devine said.

"Name?"

"Adrian Lynch."

Quinn's bushy brows shot up as he pushed a cowlick out of his eyes. His hair was turning gray. Soon, it would match his skin color. "I've heard about him. Rising star."

"That's the rumor."

"I wanna meet him."

"I'll see what I can do."

Time for the quid pro quo. Quinn had sources everywhere in the department, even in sections Devine had never heard of.

"Waddya hear?" Devine asked.

"Whispers. Rumors. Innuendo. I believe all of them."

"Go ahead."

The boozy film faded from Quinn's eyes. The man was lucid whenever he wanted. "It makes sense you got a new captain. Big investigation's coming up. They're targeting Public Morals."

Devine remembered what Da had told him shortly after he joined the force: about every ten years, the department made a show of cracking down on the gifts and favors that made life bearable for New York's underpaid police officers. The only cops who ever got caught, Da went on, were either stupid or careless.

"Thanks for the heads-up," Devine said. "I'll keep my ears open."

Quinn pointed to a long red scratch on Devine's cheek. "She go a little overboard tonight?"

Devine winked at the freckle-faced waitress as she slipped fries and a cheeseburger in front of him.

"Sometimes I like it rough."

A moment after Devine parked his Lincoln in front of Paco's white brick building on Second Avenue, the doorman rapped on the passenger window and motioned him to move. Devine shut the ignition and slid the keys into the pocket of his leather jacket.

Louder rapping on the window.

Devine looked into the glove compartment, just to dawdle, before getting out on the driver's side and locking the door. When he set foot on the sidewalk, the doorman got in his face.

"What the fuck's wrong with you?"

Devine reached into his back pocket, took out his badge and pressed it as close as he could against the man's eyes.

"I'm here on city business, so unless you start talking nice, I'm gonna haul you in for interfering with a police officer. Then I'll lose the paperwork. You'll be in Rikers three months before anyone notices."

The doorman backed away and mumbled something that sounded like "sorry" before opening the door to the building as wide as he could. Devine slowed to look at his watch. It was a few minutes before midnight. He should call Gina to tell her he was running late.

Paco opened his door just across the elevator bank as soon as Devine stepped onto the twelfth floor. It was the first time he'd seen the pimp's apartment. Devine expected lava lamps and shag rugs, but the couch and carpet were straight out of the Ethan Allen showroom.

Paco motioned to the window, which looked out on a slice of the East

River and part of the Triborough Bridge.

All this agita for a view of Queens, Devine thought.

"Nice, huh?" Paco asked.

"Not bad."

"It goes to show you," Paco said.

"Goes to show what?"

"You come to the mainland, you work hard, you can get ahead. A lotta people piss all over that idea, but I believe, man. Red, white and blue all the way."

Devine suspected that Paco voted Republican.

"What you got for me?" the pimp asked. "Everything go okay?"

Devine took cash from his pockets. The bills were crumpled because Nadine had stuffed them in dozens of hiding places. Paco leaned forward so far he almost fell to the floor.

"Waddya so worried about?" Devine asked.

"I need the money, man. I can't go outside till I pay my bookie."

Like every gambler Devine had ever met, Paco believed he knew way more about sports than he actually did. The pimp lit a Lucky Strike with a shaky hand.

"That shit's gonna kill you," Devine said.

"Women are gonna kill me," Paco said.

"The betting, too. The only people who make money off gambling are the guys who run the games."

Devine smoothed the bills before spreading them on the coffee table. He'd also found a piece of notepaper shoved into a plastic shell that once contained nylons. He'd stuffed it in his wallet without looking. Now he opened it while Paco counted his money.

"Fourteen hundred dollars," the pimp said. "Thanks, man. You took your cut?"

"Of course I took my cut. I'm not an amateur, and I trust you as far as I can throw you."

The writing on the paper was cryptic. In a woman's hand, it gave an address in the East Thirties, as well as three phone numbers with initials after them: "DA, AG, AF." Devine folded the paper and stuck it in his wallet.

"I need your phone," he told Paco.

"Claro. Mi casa es su casa."

"No it ain't."

But the pimp had reminded him of something, so Devine's first call was home, where his wife answered sleepily on the fifth ring. Before he could speak she said, "You're not coming home."

"Something's come up. How're the kids?"

"They asked for you at dinner."

"I'm working."

"You're always working."

"I'll be home tomorrow. Tell them I love them."

"It'd be better if you told them yourself."

Devine hung up and began dialing Gina's number, but he noticed a loopy grin on Paco's face.

"You're Ward fucking Cleaver, man. I had no idea." Paco dropped his voice and tried to sound Anglo. "'Tell them I love them.' What're their names? Wally and Beaver?"

He was laughing so hard his eyes were rolling, and he failed to see Devine's quick strides across the room. The cop threw a punch while he still had momentum, and his fist hit hard and flush against Paco's cheek. Tingling pain ran through Devine's wrist and up his arm while Paco let out a yowl. Devine kicked the pimp's right knee, and his cries turned to the type of baying that sounded like a dog under a full moon. Paco dropped to the carpet, but Devine picked him up and shoved him against the wall, then proceeded to slug him in the ribs and stomach a few times.

"Don't you ever—"

"What I do?" Paco gasped. "What I do?"

By now he was slumping, so Devine propped him up by grabbing his cashmere sweater.

"I swear to God, you scumbag, if you ever say anything about my kids again—"

Paco wriggled like a worm in wet dirt. The sweater began to slip from

Devine's grasp.

"Lo siento, man."

"—I'll fucking kill you—"

"Lemme go."

"—and then I'll go out to dinner to celebrate."

Blood covered Devine's hands and jacket. He figured there was blood on his face, too. He'd check a mirror before he left, but he wouldn't clean up all the way. Sometimes Gina liked to hear about how physical he'd been.

With one great turn of his body, Paco wrenched free. Devine heard a tearing sound followed by screams of pain, but what bothered him most was the sensation of something he felt just for a second. It was hard but flexible, long and thin, and in a flash he recognized what it was, because he'd worn a wire a few times himself.

Chapter Three

"In certain ways," Eamon Powers said as he rubbed a Pall Mall in the ashtray, "this really fucks up our investigation."

Terence Devine said nothing.

"You taking the Fifth?" Powers asked.

The conversation was being recorded. Three other Internal Affairs dicks were observing the interrogation on the other side of the soundproof glass.

"The department's a lot cleaner than it used to be," Powers said. "Narcs arrest dealers instead of working with them. Evidence stays in the property room, where it belongs. But there's still one big cesspool."

Devine had been listening to this crap for hours. Although he had yet to invoke the Fifth Amendment, he was thinking about mentioning the Eighth.

"Did I say something funny, Officer?" Powers spit out the last word. "We've got enough to strip your badge and your pension and put you away for at least ten years."

Powers took another drag on his cigarette. He was six-foot-three but bone thin, one of those men who preferred smoking to eating.

"I talked to my inspector," he said. "Woke him up at two a.m. You can imagine how happy he was about that."

Devine thought about Gina. He had never called.

Powers went on. "My inspector talked to the DA's office, and he told me it's gonna go down like this: you'll work for us."

Devine blinked a few times.

"If we get a dozen indictments in Public Morals," Powers said, "you stupid fucks might finally realize we're serious about keeping the department clean."

Devine stayed silent.

"You just gonna sit there the rest of your life?" Powers was close to shouting.

"I should call the union and get a lawyer."

"We got you on tape."

"I was conducting my own investigation. My methods are unorthodox."

"You expect anybody to buy that?"

"It'll be my word against a pimp's."

Powers stroked his chin. Devine needed only one member of the jury to believe him.

"I'm authorized to make you an offer," Powers said. "You've got a minute to make up your mind."

Devine glared. If he looked intimidated, they'd push him around forever.

"When the investigation's over," Powers said, "we'll let you plead to a couple of misdemeanors."

"No charges at all," Devine said.

Powers looked like a man sucking a lemon. "I can do that. But you'll be dismissed from the force as soon as it's done."

"I need time accrued."

"You're kidding."

"I've been in the department long enough to get half my pension. I never kid about money."

Devine called Gina at seven-thirty.

"What happened to you last night?" she asked.

Nadine, he felt like saying. I heard about a call girl named Nadine, and my life turned to shit.

"I was detained."

"You shoulda detained me."

He pictured himself sliding her panties down to her ankles. She always sighed with easy pleasure before asking for his handcuffs.

"I wanna see you," he said.

"You ran outta time. I'm working today."

"I'll be there in fifteen minutes." He hung up before she could say No.

Gina Galante was a twenty-three-year-old aspiring artist who did temp work as a steno to make ends meet. Devine met her while she was preparing the paperwork in the DA's office for one of his cases. She had transformed a barren day worker's desk into an explosion of color that was dominated by a twisted piece of metal shaped like a vagina. He pulled up an empty chair, waved his hand over her stuff, and said, "This should be in MoMA."

She focused on her typing. Fastest hands he'd ever seen. "It's better than that," she said, and right away she intrigued him.

They worked late and ate dinner in Chinatown. He insisted on walking her home. The city was dangerous, and she lived in the desolate area near Fulton Market. Everyone but the fishmongers had abandoned the area decades ago, so the buildings rotted and rusted until artists started squatting. Devine thought it was weird to live in an old warehouse. Gina explained that she needed space and light and low expenses.

Most of her loft was occupied by canvases, easels and industrial-size cans of paint. She had glossed the colors of the walls to a soft yellow. The place glowed whenever the narrow windows caught a sliver of light.

"You shouldn't have done this," Devine said.

She handed him a glass of rough Spanish wine. "Why not?"

"You put a lot of work in, but you don't own it."

"Nobody owns it. That's what's great about it."

She looked straight at him. She was the only person he'd ever met who concealed nothing.

"I'll leave if you want," he said.

"I don't want," she said.

They went at it a while and everything was fine, just as it had been hundreds of times with dozens of women, but after a while she bit his ear and told him he could tie her up if he wanted—gently, lightly, a bit of kinky fun—and as the night went on, and she urged him to explore her as deeply as he could, he kept telling himself, with the power of revelation: I never realized it could be this good.

At seven-forty-five, after she buzzed him in, the first thing she said was, "You look like hell."

"I've been up all night."

"Looks like you were in a fight."

"More than one."

He reached for her, but she moved away. She told him she'd made extra coffee.

"I don't want coffee."

"That's all you're getting."

She finished assembling herself in front of a full-length mirror she'd found in a Dumpster. She had polished and shined the thing until it gleamed.

He walked up behind her, put his hands on her hips, and brushed his mouth against her ear. She had long dark hair that she usually let fall straight down her back, nearly to her waist. Today, in a concession to office grooming, she had parted it in the middle and tied it into a ponytail.

She pressed her palm against his stomach. Pushed him back. Told him to take a cold shower.

Devine woke at noon and reheated the coffee Gina had left before walking to Powers' office in the basement at headquarters, where he was introduced to a prosecutor named Adam Fishman. The lawyer was in his early thirties, with thinning hair and the skeletal but toned look of a man who ran marathons. His eyes were dark and merciless, and his face was marked by the nicks and blemishes that indicated he had hurried his morning shave.

"It's too early to go to the grand jury," Fishman said, "and you were one of our biggest targets. The stories we've heard about you ... "

"Your interest in me is flattering," Devine replied.

"That's why you're perfect for this," Fishman said. His voice was clipped. Devine pictured him logging miles with no wasted motion. "You're as dirty as they come. Nobody will suspect you're working for the good guys."

Devine wanted to get out of there as quickly as he could, so he stayed quiet.

"You'll wear a wire most of the time," Fishman said. "We want you to tape the other detectives and plainclothes while you're handing out the pad. When do you do it?"

"Thursdays," Devine said.

"Why Thursdays?"

"So everyone has money for the weekend."

Fishman made a note on one of those long yellow pads lawyers liked to use. His hands were bruised, as if he'd punched out a wall. He probably did, Devine said to himself, when he found out about the deal I made.

"What about my superiors?" Devine asked.

"What about them?" Powers replied.

"We've got a new captain. Adrian Lynch. I dunno anything about him. We haven't talked about money yet. I dunno if he's there to clean house or to grift."

Powers and Fishman exchanged glances. Devine was surprised they hadn't worked this out beforehand.

"He's not a target," Fishman said.

"What if he asks for a cut?" Devine said. "Most captains get twenty-five percent. They keep ten percent for themselves and kick the rest upstairs."

Fishman put more notes in his pad. "I didn't realize it was so organized."

"I organized it," Devine said.

Everyone has needs and wants, and Devine's centered on his three-bedroom house on Staten Island and the bungalow down the Jersey shore, where he also kept a small boat. Every year he bought a new Lincoln and gave his wife the old one. During school breaks in the winter they always went to Florida, where his parents had moved after Da left the force.

Devine owned a dozen suits from Barney's, and he wore one every Sunday to church at St. Clare's. He had planned to spend seven more years in the department before retiring with a full pension and moving to Florida. Now they'd have to go earlier. Devine figured he could live near his parents and work with Da on the fishing charter he ran into the Gulf of Mexico.

Now he tried to avoid thinking about what he was doing as the IAD nerds strapped the wire. He had worked with some of his colleagues for years. They drank together, and sometimes they spent nights at the Garden. There was a lot of talk about brotherhood, but he was the guy who'd taken the risk by running the pad. Everyone else was happy to let him. So when he asked himself what they would do if they were in his position, his answer was simple: Exactly what I'm doing.

His first stop was Lynch's office. A note on Devine's desk had said the captain wanted to see him.

"What's this about, sir?"

Without looking up from his paperwork, Lynch told Devine to come in and close the door.

Devine rocked on the balls of his feet. The wire was running, so he started thinking of ways to talk about money, but before he could say a word, Lynch posed a question in a surprisingly nervous voice.

"Ever hear of a girl named Nadine LaFleur?"

Chapter Four

No one had seen her for days, and a stench wafted from her apartment. Everyone in New York knew what that meant, so her landlord called the cops rather than look in himself. Now Devine found himself in an airless room with Mulligan, a Homicide detective whose face ranged in color from crimson to scarlet.

"Her pimp's name is Jose Almonte," Devine told him. "Street name Paco. Runs a high-end operation and insulates himself, so we've never made anything stick."

"He hit his girls?"

"Beat-up workers can't earn. Paco's a businessman."

"The vic was knocked around pretty bad. Died of head trauma. Place ransacked. Medical examiner says she was dead three days before we found her."

"Burglary gone bad. Happens all the time."

Mulligan shook his head. "No sign of forced entry and a savvy chick like her wouldn't have let in some cretin off the street."

Devine glanced away. The squad room had six other desks, all occupied by glowering detectives bleary-eyed from overwork. Keeping up with all of New York's murders was a killing job.

"Ever arrest her?" Mulligan asked.

"No."

"Ever fuck her?"

"What kinda question is that?"

"The kind I'd ask anybody in Public Morals. We all know what you guys are like."

"I never fucked Nadine LaFleur. Did you?"

Mulligan looked like a guy who had just seen his least favorite in-law swipe the last beer in the fridge. "The pimp's our best bet. They waste their women all the time. Where do I find this Taco guy?"

Devine thought of all the places he'd look, then told Mulligan the tenth most likely one.

He slipped into a phone booth in the back of a candy store on Sixth and laid a half-dozen dimes on the counter. No answer at the first number. The second one sounded disconnected. He let the third one ring twenty times until he finally heard the voice of a tired Latina.

"Hola?"

"Donde es Paco?"

"No aquí."

I think that's bullshit, he felt like saying. I wish I knew how to say bullshit in Spanish. Mierda de toro?

"Tell your chulo it's Terry. Tell him it's urgent. Tell him it's so fucking urgent his todo el mundo will explode if he doesn't call me in cinco minutos. Here's the number I'm at. Escríbelo, chiquita."

He read off the number on the phone in Spanish to make sure she got it right and was pleasantly surprised when the callback came three minutes and forty-two seconds later.

"Fuck, man, fuck."

Devine sensed Paco's flop sweat coming through the phone.

"You kill her?" Devine asked.

"What kinda pregunta is that?"

"The kind Homicide is gonna ask you."

"You think I'm gonna say something to you over the phone? You think I'm stupido or something?"

Despite the situation, Devine smiled. Paco had the survival instincts of a subway rat. Devine gave him a location to meet in person and told him to be there in half an hour.

"What if I don't show up?" Paco asked.

"I sent Homicide on a wild goose chase," Devine said. "If you stand me up, I'll tell them exactly where they can find you."

The ground was muddy despite the cold. As the sun slid below the tops of the buildings on the west side of Central Park, Devine heard the squishing sneakers of grim-faced Manhattanites plodding around the reservoir. The next sound he heard was hard breathing beside him.

"This is fucked up, man."

"Murder is always fucked up, Paco."

"That ain't what I mean. All these people running around and shit. Why they doing that?"

"Exercise."

"Waste of time. We're all gonna die anyway."

"Homicide's asking questions, Paco."

"You tell them anything?"

"I told them you were her pimp."

"Why'd you do that?"

"I'm in Public Morals. I'm supposed to know stuff like this. They'll find out sooner or later, and if I give them information, it looks like I'm cooperating."

Devine leaned against the chain-link fence. He had one big question, but he didn't want to sound overly concerned, so he let it float like a wispy cloud.

"Did you tell the IAD guy and the prosecutor where I got the money I gave you?"

Paco shook his head. "I said you got it from one of my workers. I didn't tell them which one, and they didn't ask."

"If they find out I was in Nadine's apartment that night, both our deals are fucked." Devine paused. "The murder investigation's being run by a detective named Mulligan. You're gonna see him."

"You're outta your mind."

"He's gonna find you eventually," Devine said. "If he has to look all over the city, he'll think you're hiding from him. And if he thinks you're hiding from him, he'll think you did it. In fact, he already thinks that."

"I didn't kill her, man. Did you?"

"That's a helluva question to ask a police officer."

"Nadine was good-looking, smart. She could be nice when she wanted. Fantastic in the sack, too. But she was a pain in the ass. And she did drugs." He shrugged. "I could see you getting mad at her. One thing leads to another. You know how it goes. I wouldn't blame you."

Devine ran his hand over the metal. The water in the lake was black. Nothing inside was alive.

"There's one great thing about New York," Devine said.

"The business opportunities?" Paco asked.

"People are killed every day, and new cases crowd out the old ones. A week from now, nobody's gonna remember Nadine LaFleur. Until then, we just hafta look like we're doing what Homicide wants."

The lights were out, and the house was quiet. Devine let himself in through the kitchen and opened a Heineken before turning on the TV. A news blonde chirped about the city's latest surge in crime.

The noise on the stairs was too heavy for the kids. Devine brought bottle to mouth. Bridget, smelling of tobacco, sat beside him and folded her arms across her stomach. TV showed the swirling colored lights of an ambulance.

"I never know when you're coming home," she said.

"I'm involved in something."

"You're always involved in something."

"It's deep undercover. Could take a while. I can't say anything more about it."

He didn't want to look at her, but he turned anyway. Her face was puffy, and he asked himself if it was from sleep or worry or eating or crying.

"You never wanna talk about anything," she said.

On TV Devine saw Paco coming out of a station house where he had been questioned about the murder of Nadine LaFleur. The pimp looked better than Devine had ever seen—clean shirt, pressed pants, hair slicked and combed and parted. His lawyer, the young hotshot Rolando Ortega, wore a three-piece suit and did all the talking.

Bridget lit a Parliament and pointed at the screen. "You know that guy?"

"Yeah."

"He do it?"

"I'm not sure."

"I bet he did something."

Most of the men in Devine's family were cops so he enrolled in the Police Academy right after high school. The work was steady, and when he reached his forties he'd be eligible for the pension. After a few years on the force, everyone told him it was time to settle down. He met Bridget at a bar. In six months they were married. Michael came along in twelve months, and Sheila three years after that. It was what you did. You landed a job and got married and had children and worked a while and got a place down the shore and then traded it all in for the move to Florida.

"You coming to my game?" Michael asked.

Devine tried to snap to the present. He'd drunk one Heineken too many the night before. He tried to remember if he had left Bridget all the cash she wanted.

"Don't you remember, Dad?"

Bridget put pancakes in front of the kids and warned them about using too much syrup.

"When's the game?" Devine asked.

"I told you."

"I forgot."

The game was Saturday, Michael said.

Two days away, Devine thought. I should be there.

Michael cut his pancake in half, then quarters, then eighths. He was a deliberate child, and his Catholic school uniform suited him. Devine turned to Sheila, who was in kindergarten. She squeezed out syrup in a zigzag pattern that made Devine think of the stuff in Gina's loft.

"What're you doing today, Cupcake?"

She was dreamy. Usually it took her thirty seconds to answer a question. For a while he thought something was wrong with her, but by now he understood that she needed time to gather her thoughts, which were always roaming.

"We're gonna practice drawing."

"That sounds nice."

Sheila made a face. "Sister Immaculata is gonna give us homework. She says we hafta draw a picture of the Baby Jesus with His Mother."

"I wanna look at it when you're done," Devine said. "Maybe we can frame it or something."

"But what if I don't wanna draw a picture of the Baby Jesus?" Sheila asked.

Your mother does not want to hear this, Devine said to himself. "What would you rather draw?"

Sheila chewed a bite of her pancake. Syrup dribbled from the corner of her mouth.

"Trees and sky. Regular people. Maybe a doggie."

Bridget whisked away Sheila's plate and juice cup. "Do what Sister Immaculata tells you," she said.

Chapter Five

Of all the shitholes in the city, the West Side piers were the worst. With port traffic long gone to Jersey, the docks were falling into the Hudson River, and with no longshoremen around, the area had long been conquered by queers and rodents.

"You want some, Mister?"

The question came from a slender Black kid, maybe sixteen, with a tiny voice and soft almond eyes.

"Why aren't you in school?" Devine asked.

"You a cop?"

"Waddya think?"

"I'm not particular. I'd do a cop."

"Why are you doing this?"

"I'd rather work in fashion, but those people are awfully prejudiced."

Children like him are thrown away like pieces of litter, Devine told himself, and I'm supposed to pick them up.

"Where's Erik?" he asked.

"I dunno who you're talking about."

If the kid looked stronger, Devine would have shoved him against the wall and kneed him in the nuts. Instead he glanced around to check out the other hustlers. Business was always slow before lunchtime, so the men lounged and preened.

"If you don't tell me where Erik is," Devine said, "I'm gonna go over to one of those guys and beat the crap out of him. Just because I can. Then I'll tell all your buddies it was because you wouldn't tell me where I could find

Erik. How do you think they're gonna react?"

The kid gave Devine an address on Twelfth, just across West Street.

Erik had set himself up on the second floor of an abandoned sweatshop in a wide and high room with a desk, a chair, a phone, and a couple of mattresses. Most of the window glass was shattered. His gray-streaked hair stretched to his shoulders, and his fingers had turned brown from Marlboros, which he smoked because he lusted after the cowboys in their ads.

Devine shivered from the river wind. "Nice digs you got."

"I need to cut expenses, and it costs me money every time I see you. Who told you I was here?"

"Your Black kid. Affirmative-action hire?"

"Randall. I'll hafta talk to him. I was trying to hide from you. I'm short this week."

"You're short every week. How old is he?"

"He said he was eighteen."

"If he's eighteen, I'm George Burns."

"Arrest him. Arrest me."

Erik laughed. He ran the largest gay hustling operation on the piers. Some guys in Public Morals wanted to crack down on it, but as master of the pad Devine overruled them. Being virtuous, he informed his colleagues, interfered with making money.

Devine sat on the desk's edge. "We've got a new captain. I'm trying to get a read on him."

Erik lit a Marlboro. "I remember getting busted once on Christopher Street. Back in my younger days. Before I became a businessman."

Devine and Erik met during Stonewall—the young cop's first big action. They got to talking while Erik was in the holding pen. He said he wanted to run guys the way madams ran brothels, and Devine told him he had to make sure the authorities let him operate in peace. The only reason the NYPD busted Stonewall was because the cheap Mafia bastards who owned the joint refused to pay for protection.

"Lynch ran you in for tricking?" Devine asked.

"I remember thinking he had a good name for a cop."

"Anything memorable about the bust?"

"I offered him twenty bucks to let me go, and he turned me down. Then I offered him a blowjob, and he said he only took them from girls."

Devine extended his palm. "Just for that tidbit, I'm not gonna get mad when you short me today."

Erik reached into a drawer and took out an envelope that Devine stuffed in one of his inside pockets before taking out the piece of paper he'd removed from Nadine's apartment.

"What's at Thirty-One East Thirty-Seventh Street?"

"That's the high-rent district." Erik swept his arm around. He had squatted in one of the city's Bermuda Triangle areas, where nobody owned anything. "Do I look like a high-rent kinda guy?"

"You didn't answer my question."

Erik blew smoke. "Why do I hafta tell you?"

Devine squeezed the envelope in his pocket. "Because even by your standards, you're being cheap. My guys have families to support, and I sense a chance to earn."

Erik cast his eyes skyward. Concrete dust flaked off the ceiling. Devine wondered if asbestos was up there, too.

"I hear stuff on the Q.T.," Erik said. "I dunno how much I believe."

"Tell me what you hear. I'll figure out how much is real."

"The place is like Oz—everything your heart desires, as long as it's illegal. But it costs. As I said, it is the high-rent district."

"Who runs it?"

"The mob. I think it's the Gambinos."

Devine shook his head. "Those guys never wanna spread their money around, but that's the only way capitalism works."

Wind gusted off the Hudson. Devine wrapped his arms across his chest to keep some body heat.

"One last thing," he said as he rose to his feet.

"I love it when you're dramatic."

Devine resisted the urge to roll his eyes. Every transaction with Erik resembled the third act of "Carmen."

"Nothing happens to that Black kid."

East Thirty-Seventh between Park and Madison Avenues was a quiet block of townhouses and low-rise apartment buildings, although the Morgan Library took up a big chunk of the street's south side. J.P. Morgan had been a cutthroat businessman, but in his will he turned his home into a museum, and now he was remembered for philanthropy. The history classes he endured had taught Devine one great thing: If you have enough money, you get away with every crime you commit.

He hopped on numb feet and blew on his fingertips. Devine had been under a dry cleaner's awning for half an hour watching a stream of prosperous middle-aged white men enter the townhouse catty-corner from where he stood. The door to the place was opened by a six-foot-two gorilla in a Brooks Brothers suit. The white men nodded at him as they entered. Everything seemed businesslike. Devine checked his watch when he noticed two short-skirted women in their twenties clicking up the steps in heels.

Four in the afternoon. Time for a shift change.

The door opened again, and Devine pressed himself as far as he could against the dry cleaner's facade. He was unsure how much longer he could stay there without being spotted by the gorilla, although the guy seemed serene about the palace of sin's operations—an attitude that made Devine increasingly pissed off. An enterprise like this was supposed to deal with Public Morals, and he'd been unaware of its existence until his encounter with Nadine LaFleur.

A sandy-haired man with a round, unlined face stepped onto the stoop and said something to the gorilla before taking out his wallet and removing a bill, which he pressed into the goon's hand. Sandy, as Devine silently named him, then gripped his shiny briefcase as he headed down the steps with a dreamy half-smile on his face.

Sandy looked in his forties and moved easily, like a former jock. He had the beginnings of a double chin and a gut. His beige overcoat was straight out of the Sears catalog, and his black oxfords were from Thom McAn. Devine guessed he was a striver from the big flat states who backslapped his buddies at the Rotary meeting on the first Wednesday of every month.

Just the guy I need, Devine said to himself. He'll wet his pants when a New York City cop confronts him.

Sandy checked his watch as he sauntered west. Devine noticed a wedding ring, and now he could see the man's life in full: ad rep for the biggest company in Peoria or Dubuque or Oshkosh, married to his high school sweetheart, four or five children back home, a good-natured fella who traveled a lot for work and now he was on his way to an afternoon meeting with the Madison Avenue guys handling his firm's latest campaign.

Devine jaywalked across Thirty-Seventh and loped toward the rube. Near the corner of Madison, directly across the street from the Morgan Library, Devine fell in beside him, flashed his badge, and summoned his cop-in-a-hurry voice.

"Excuse me, sir."

Sandy blinked a few times. He had the distracted look of a man still enjoying postcoital bliss.

Devine identified himself and asked, "What were you doing in that building?"

"I, uh, I, uh, I—"

"That place is under surveillance," Devine said. "We know what goes on in there."

"I have a wife and kids back home."

"They'll hate to hear that Daddy's been arrested."

Sandy worked his mouth before blurting, "I've got a meeting in ten minutes."

"Then, for the next nine minutes, you better tell me exactly what goes on inside."

Which he did. The first floor had a coat room and lounge, where customers could have a drink or three before moving on to the higher floors for some action. There were girls on the second floor—"That's where I spent my time," Sandy said, "I get lonely on the road"— gambling on the third, drugs on the fourth, and boys on the fifth.

Sandy shuddered when he mentioned the boys. "That stuff's perverted. I'm glad they keep it out of the way."

"How'd you hear about the house?" Devine asked.

"From the people I'm working with," Sandy said. "They send everyone here."

And they probably get a kickback, Devine said to himself. Everybody's making money off this place except me.

"Who runs it?" Devine asked.

"A fellow named Angelo. He wears nice suits. Makes sure everybody's happy and having a good time." Sandy thought a second more, convinced he had to add something. "He's Italian."

"I appreciate your cooperation," Devine said. "Now beat it."

"I'm sorry if I caused you any trouble, Officer." Sandy reached into his wallet. "I'd like to make it up to you."

He extended a ten-spot.

"For something like this," Devine said, "I usually get twenty."

Clarke's was packed belly to elbow with people getting a head start on the weekend. Devine squirmed into Quinn's booth. The first slug of Harp felt good.

"Nadine LaFleur," Quinn said.

Devine told himself to keep his poker face. "I've heard the name."

"I talked to her parents," Quinn said.

Devine focused on taking deep breaths. Nothing to see here. Just move along.

"Why'd you do that?" he asked.

"Nadine was a source. She gave me the working girl's point of view."

Devine ran his mind over Quinn's columns. In his gallery of sinners he sometimes referred to a woman named Michelle, who spent much of her time servicing the needs of Manhattan's rich and powerful. Like everything Quinn wrote, Devine suspected most of it was malarkey.

"The parents' phone number was in the apartment." Quinn was still talking. Devine had zoned out and was afraid he'd missed something important. "So I called 'em. They're from Dublin, New Hampshire. Her father's a doctor. Norman Rockwell shit."

"Let me guess," Devine said. "Nadine LaFleur was not her real name."

"Martha Owens."

"Her dad's like Marcus Welby, and her mom ran the PTA, and they have no idea how any of this happened."

"Right on the first two. Wrong on the third. I already filed my column. It's running tomorrow."

Oh shit, Devine thought. Oh shit oh shit oh shit. He lifted mug to mouth so he could obscure his face while he thought of something to say.

"You shoulda talked to me first," he said as he put the pint down hard on the table. "The case is a loser. Working girls get killed all the time. Anybody coulda done it."

"That's not what the mother says."

Devine threw Gina onto the bed as soon as he walked into her loft. By the end she was on all fours and screaming, and he was shouting as well as he pounded into her from behind, and since no one was around for blocks they could let out everything they felt.

In the morning he woke up first. The nearest newsstand was on Fulton Street near the subway. He read Quinn's column on his way back. The goddamn thing was plastered over Pages One and Three, which were filled with pictures of the victim and her parents and the town she grew up in.

Martha Owens had come to New York to attend Barnard College. In New Hampshire she was a good student who wanted to do something with her life, but in the city temptations were all around. Like so many others, she gave in—to drugs and booze and sex, an existence given over to indulging her worst impulses. She left school and sometimes fell out of contact with her family for months.

Recently, it got better. Martha wrote letters home twice a week and called every Sunday. She was thinking about re-enrolling and said she was involved in ventures that had led her to meet a number of influential men.

She was exploring sides of life she had only imagined—discoveries that alternated between dispiriting and exhilarating—and she kept notes about all of them in a journal. Some people in the literary and media worlds had encouraged her to write a book. Suddenly, life was full of possibilities.

The parents told Quinn they'd like to see Martha's journal. There might be information in it only they could figure out, details that could point them to the person who had perpetrated the crime. They did not believe she was murdered by a stranger.

Quinn wrote that he had tried to talk to Mulligan in Homicide about the case, but neither the detective nor anybody else in the Police Department had returned his calls.

The column ended with the parents telling Quinn about their plans to take their daughter's body back home, where they would lay her to rest in the family plot at the Congregational church. It was mud season, so grave digging was difficult, but the New England air was crisp and clear and clean.

Chapter Six

Michael had the ball, but he was trapped in the corner by a kid three inches taller and twenty pounds heavier. As the bigger boy waved his arms like a member of a flight crew directing a fighter jet onto an aircraft carrier, Devine silently urged his son to lean into him so he could draw a pity foul.

Michael raised his hands as the other kid swiped at them, then threw the ball down as hard as he could on his opponent's shin. The ball bounced out of bounds, Michael's team retained possession, and a light round of applause rattled the overheated gym.

As Devine silently congratulated his son for making an intelligent play, the bigger kid shoved Michael on the shoulder and spun him around, then threw a punch. Michael ducked; shouts echoed over the wooden bleachers; players, coaches, and referees swarmed the scene.

It took a few minutes to sort out the situation, but when it was, the kid who had tried to hit Michael was tossed from the game. He was the other team's best player, and without him Michael's side came back to win.

"That was a smart move," Devine told his son as they drove back home.

Michael said nothing for a few seconds. He liked to consider his words before uttering them. It was a rare trait in an adult, let alone a child.

"That guy is a hothead," Michael said at last. "I knew he'd screw up."

"Here's my picture, Daddy."

Sheila walked toward him with her arm outstretched and a piece of yellow construction paper fluttering in her hand. It was Monday morning, so Bridget slept in while he took the kids to school. Devine had left an inch-thick wad of bills on the dresser so his wife could go shopping, then wondered if that was enough. Everything cost more every day.

He put down the *Daily News*. Spring training was in full swing in Florida. Da loved going to exhibition games.

"Lemme see that, Sweetheart."

It was the Nativity scene Sister Immaculata had told the students to draw. Devine expected to see stick figures, a small barn and a few animals, but Sheila had filled in every space of the paper. The manger and the buildings surrounding it looked grimy and sagging. A crescent moon peeked over an eave and the sky blazed with stars, but there were no angels and none of the people wore halos—omissions that silently pleased Devine, who had met plenty of sinners, but never a saint.

He looked more closely at what his daughter had done. The line of the buildings showed a nice perspective, and the faces of the animals and people were as close to realistic as a five-year-old could manage. Devine remembered spending hours on pictures when he was young, obsessively happy as he filled in details, until one day Da told him that he was wasting his time with drawing and needed to focus on something important, and Ma said he would have to make a living at something and she'd be goddamned before she supported a starving artist.

"Do you like it, Daddy?"

Devine pointed to the faces of the Holy Family. "They're kinda brown, don'tcha think?"

"But that's how people in that part of the world look."

He nodded, then motioned to Mary. Every picture he'd ever seen of the Blessed Mother had portrayed her as smiling, unruffled and beatific, but Sheila had drawn her as haggard, with a cross look on her face.

"Jesus' mom doesn't look happy," Devine said.

"But that's how moms look," Sheila said.

Especially if they've given birth in a manger, Devine said to himself. He nodded at Joseph, whose eyes were drooping. "What's his problem?"

"He's tired. Daddies are always tired."

Devine went with his family to eleven o'clock Mass at St. Clare's every Sunday. He believed in rituals, and it was important for a man to devote one day of the week to his wife and children. So the Devines attended church and ate an early dinner of roast beef and mashed potatoes and if husband and wife were going to make love, this was the night they did it.

Michael plopped his book bag by the door. He was always ready to go five minutes early. Devine waved him over and said, "Look at this drawing your sister made."

The boy scrunched his face.

"Whatsa matter?" Devine asked. "Don'tcha like it?"

"I like it fine," Michael said.

The kids got along, which pleased their father. While growing up he had argued all the time with his siblings. Now they lived deep in New Jersey, so he rarely saw them, which pleased everyone.

"You look like you're smelling something from the landfill," Devine said to his son. "What's your problem?"

"I don't have a problem," Michael said. "But Sister Immaculata might. I doubt she's gonna like it."

Devine examined the picture, which struck him as nontraditional but respectful, although he noticed that Baby Jesus' face was contorted in a fit of infant rage. "What about Him?" he asked Sheila.

"It's a She," his daughter said.

Devine looked closer. The blanket that snuggled around the Baby was pink, and Her hair was adorned with a bow.

"Jesus was a boy," Devine said.

"Why does Jesus have to be a boy?" Sheila sounded defiant. Devine was unsure if he should admire his daughter's moxie, or worry about it.

"Historical accuracy," he said.

"But boys are icky," Sheila said. "Jesus wasn't icky."

Chapter Seven

Jamie Quinn loved causes almost as much as he loved alcohol, so Devine figured he'd better come up with one that would halt the columnist's effort to turn Nadine LaFleur's death into a crusade.

"People," Devine said over beers at Clarke's.

"What about them?" Quinn asked.

"Waddya they need?"

"Food. Sex. Sporting events. You know I got my start covering the Dodgers?"

Devine did not want to hear again about Quinn's first days in the business, when he followed Duke Snider around Ebbets Field for the *Brooklyn Eagle*.

"People need something to believe in," Devine said.

Quinn shivered with disgust. "Sounds like that godawful Streisand song."

Devine went on. "It all started when the Dodgers left for California. Tore the guts outta the city. Ever since then, crime's been rampant, garbage is everywhere, and on those rare occasions when the subways work, they're filled with graffiti and muggers."

"Tell me something I don't know," Quinn said. He looked around to see if anybody more interesting had entered the room. Like most journalists, Quinn had the attention span of a three-year-old on a sugar rush.

"The new captain we've got. Lynch."

"What about him?"

"I'm getting a read on him. I think he's the real deal."

"Why do you say that?"

"He wants to turn things around. Street-level stuff. He's trying to clean up New York even though no one at headquarters gives a shit. Sometimes we gotta break the rules."

Quinn, who liked rules-breakers, stroked a few of his chins. "Can you set something up?"

Devine nodded, knocked back his Harp, and rose from the table. All I have to do now, he said to himself, is convince Adrian Lynch to become a knight in shining armor.

Mulligan called from Homicide. Because of the newspapers, Nadine LaFleur was his top priority.

"Give it a week or two," Devine said. "It'll pass."

"Maybe, but right now someone high up has a bug up his ass about this. We gotta sweep up every hooker and john who knew her."

One column from Jamie Quinn, Devine said to himself, and we're all jumping through hoops like seals in a circus act.

"We need names," Mulligan said. "Locations, too. Where did she work?"

She might have free-lanced at a place on East Thirty-Seventh, Devine thought. I wonder if Paco knows anything about that.

To Mulligan, he said: "I dunno. I've run across her pimp a few times, but I never heard of her until she died."

"Then find out," Mulligan said before slamming the phone.

Devine coughed while he knocked on the doorframe outside Lynch's office. Without looking up, the captain asked, "What is it?"

Lynch liked to keep the door slightly ajar—one of those managers who stressed the appearance of approachability.

"Got a minute, sir?"

"Come in."

Devine slipped in. Lynch kept his head down, jotting bold and confident notes on typewritten sheets before shifting them to his outbox. Devine had never seen anyone move so much paperwork so quickly. No wonder the brass loved him.

"A situation's come up, Captain."

"Go on." His head was still down.

"You're new here, sir, and I'm not sure you're aware of all the informal procedures we have."

"What do you mean by 'informal,' Officer?"

"Well, sir, Public Morals has its own way of doing things. If we went by the book all the time, nothing would get done."

"Procedures are in place for a reason, Officer."

"I view them as guidelines rather than straitjackets."

Lynch finally looked up. "That's a good line, but I'm not sure how it'll play in the long run."

"I handle a lotta things around here that don't end up in our reports."

"What kinda things, Officer?"

"Lemme give you an example." Devine cleared his throat. "There's a place in Murray Hill. East Thirty-Seventh. Quiet, off the beaten path. It's a five-story townhouse with girls, boys, drugs and gambling. A man could break most of the Ten Commandments there in one afternoon without even trying."

"You've surveilled the place?"

"I have. But there's a catch."

"What is it?"

"I believe the guys running it are in the mob."

Lynch's next words were half statement, half question. "So they've spread some money around to make sure they can still operate?"

"If they did, I haven't heard about it."

"What exactly are you proposing, Officer?"

"There are couple of ways to go. We can try a straightforward bust, but there are problems with that."

"Such as?"

"If we get a warrant, there's a good chance they'll hear about it from people in the courthouse. By the time we raid it, the place will look like something out of Edith Wharton."

"You've read Edith Wharton?" Lynch was a Fordham graduate.

"I know who she is," Devine said. "I make references like that so I sound smarter than I am."

"What do we do if we don't get a warrant?"

"We can still raid the joint. You and me and a couple of guys I trust."

"Without a warrant? The department's not gonna like that. Neither is the DA."

"We'll say we didn't have time. We received an urgent complaint from the neighbors."

"Have we?"

"Not that I know of."

"So we roll the place? Then what?"

It was the question Devine had been waiting for. He leaned closer to Lynch and dropped his voice, though he directed his words toward his chest so the wire would pick them up. "Well, sir, there'll be plenty of money, in cash. And plenty of girls, ready for action."

Lynch brought his head close to Devine's ear before glancing at the door. No one was there.

"Tell me about the girls."

Devine gazed at the streetwalkers and hustlers and junkies and dealers and muggers teeming in Times Square. Even if he was inclined, it would be impossible to arrest them all.

Most of the restaurant booths were empty, although a few were occupied by whores who had grown tired of working in the cold. Devine drummed his fingers on the Formica table while he reached for an enamel mug filled with stale coffee. Caffeine at one a.m. was a bad idea, but he planned to meet Gina.

Paco slid into the seat opposite him. "Why are we meeting here?"

Devine waved his arm around. "Because I love this place. Middle America meets total depravity."

"Howard fucking Johnson's—let's get outta here."

"There's a gay strip club right above us. We could go there."

Paco shuddered. "Maricons make me sick. Those are the guys you should arrest. Put 'em in prison and get 'em away from decent people."

"We gotta talk about Nadine."

"If I'd known all that wholesome crap about her, I woulda made her charge more. Dress her up like Dorothy in 'The Wizard of Oz,' make her wear pigtails and say 'gosh' and 'golly'—"

"She ever work at Thirty-One East Thirty-Seventh Street?"

Paco blinked a few times. "Mob guys run that place. I steer clear of them."

"You didn't answer my question. Ever loan her out?"

"My girls work strictly for me."

"I wouldn't be so sure, amigo. I suspect she worked there or was thinking about it."

"She never told me nothin' 'bout that."

"What would you have done if you'd found out?"

"Nadine's dead. That question's hypodermic."

"Humor me."

Paco shrugged. "When somethin' like that happens, you knock some sense into her."

"So that's what you woulda done, if you'd found out."

"Which I didn't, like I said."

The men glared at each other. As usual, Devine was unsure about believing what Paco had told him.

"Homicide wants this case closed pronto," Devine said. "So they want you, as her employer, to fork over a list of Nadine's clients, as well as the locations she worked at."

Paco stared out the window. It was twenty degrees in Times Square, and most of the women were barely dressed.

"You sure you want me to do that?" he asked.

"I'm sure I don't. But Homicide does. Or at least they think they do." Devine rose to leave. "You've got two days."

After an all-nighter with his lover, Devine strode into Eamon Powers' office at eight a.m., tossed an audiotape on his desk, and watched the IAD guy's face fade from gray to ashen while he listened to the conversation in Lynch's office.

Adam Fishman pressed his fingertips to his chin and pursed his lips before saying, "The golden boy has a weakness."

Powers responded with a series of "fucks."

That's the problem with these schemes, Devine felt like telling him. Once you start casting a net, you're bound to bring in some fish you'd rather leave in the sea.

"I'll tell the head of my division," Fishman said. "But I doubt he'll have a problem with making Lynch a target."

Powers uttered some blasphemous comments about the Holy Trinity.

"You're gonna bag a captain," Devine said. "This is gonna make your investigation."

"Not this captain," Powers mumbled. "Anyone but him."

"Who's his rabbi?" Devine asked.

"All the way up." Powers was still mumbling.

"The commissioner?" Devine realized he sounded stunned, but putting a satyr in charge of Public Morals struck him as a terrible idea, even by the frequently ridiculous personnel practices of the NYPD.

But when Powers nodded, Devine suddenly understood the department's plan. Unlike everyone in the long-corrupt Public Morals squad, Adrian Lynch did not take money. He would preside over the troubled division for a short period, during which all of its many shenanigans would be exposed. After being hailed as the man who had cleaned things up, Lynch would get a transfer and continue his ascent up the slopes of the bureaucracy.

Devine leaned back in his chair. Time to go all in.

"I just had an idea," he said.

"I don't wanna hear it," Powers said.

"I do," Fishman said.

"Jamie Quinn wants to meet him," Devine said.

"That blowhard on Channel Four?" Fishman asked.

"That's his night job," Powers said. "Mostly, he writes swill for the *News*."

"I read the *Times*," Fishman said.

"Goddam buncha Commies," Powers said.

Devine ignored them. "I know Quinn, and I know how he works. If Lynch makes a good impression, which I'm sure he will, Quinn will write some columns that'll turn him into Sir Galahad. When you bring Lynch down, the investigation will look like an even bigger deal than it already is. And it'll be good for you guys—you weren't afraid to go after the department's favorite son."

"And Jamie Quinn will look like a chump." Powers was mumbling again, but Devine could tell he was warming to the idea.

But Lynch won't take the fall all by himself, Devine said to himself. He'll point his finger higher up, nobody will wanna go there, this whole thing will end, and I'll slip off to Florida.

Chapter Eight

Adrian Lynch pushed himself away from his paperwork and began pacing his office.

"Before I got here," he told Devine, "people told me you were crazy. Now I know they're right."

"Jamie Quinn is a black-and-white guy," Devine said. "Heroes and villains with nothing in between. Usually, he writes about villains. That's the way the city is right now. But if he can find a hero ... " Devine let the idea linger.

Lynch stopped in front of the small mirror he had nailed to the office wall and adjusted his Hermès tie. "Why should I be a hero?"

Devine approached his superior and spoke just loudly enough for the wire. "Because by the time he's done writing about you, everyone will know you're not some deskbound cretin who collects hemorrhoids while he's waiting for his pension to kick in. You're a man of action ridding New York of the vermin eating it from the inside."

"I'm gonna tell you something I never told anybody," Lynch said.

This might be good, Devine thought. "Go ahead."

"Sometimes I think, when my time with the force is over, I'd like to try writing. Some cops have done that."

"Quinn could help you there."

Monday night at Clarke's—low-level hum, room to move and breathe. Devine made the introductions at Quinn's regular booth in back.

"You've been tough on the department," Lynch said.

"I've been tough on the brass," Quinn replied. "Never on the guys in the street."

Lynch lifted his drink. Courvoisier on the rocks. Beer made him feel bloated.

"Tell me about this raid," Quinn said.

"Officer Devine has put the place under surveillance," Lynch said.

"East Thirty-Seventh, between Park and Madison," Devine said. "Nice neighborhood. Low-key."

"This house has everything," Lynch said. "Girls, boys, drugs and gambling. One-stop shopping for degenerates."

Quinn jotted some notes. "I might use that. I like people who gimme stuff I can use."

"If we do something like this," Devine said, "we're supposed to get approval up and down the chain of command. Dot every i. Cross every t. You know how long that'll take?"

"Bureaucrats," Quinn snorted. "Nitpickers. The banes of my existence."

"I've been a by-the-book guy in my career," Lynch said. "But I'll tell you something about Public Morals—it's different. If you go by the book, you'll never get anything done."

Quinn kept scribbling. "Tell me more, Captain."

At two p.m. the next day, five men in suit jackets huddled in the doorway of a vacant Murray Hill storefront while grains of sleet slithered past.

"I'm thinking of calling you guys the Four Musketeers," Quinn said. He blew on his hands before stuffing them into the pockets of his trench coat. "Or maybe the Four Horsemen. I haven't decided yet."

"Four Musketeers makes us sound queer," Lynch said.

The other cops nodded. Devine had enlisted the plainclothes guys Finley and Burke, who were looking forward to their cut.

"Then I'll make it the Four Horsemen," Quinn said. "The cavalry riding to the rescue of the city, whether New York wants it or not." He nodded as he spoke. Like most writers, he loved the sound of his own words. "When are you guys going in?"

"When we get an opening," Devine said.

"When will that be?" Quinn asked.

"Maybe five seconds," Devine said. "Maybe five hours."

Quinn's face nearly collapsed in disappointment. For ninety minutes, they watched tides of men ebb in and out of the townhouse until Quinn uttered a string of excited obscenities.

"You see that guy standing on the sidewalk, looking over the place like he's a tax appraiser?"

The cops nodded.

"Appeals court judge. Federal bench. Rumor is he's on the shortlist for the Supreme Court."

"This just keeps getting better and better," Devine said.

The cops and Quinn reached the building just as the judge mounted the steps. Finley and Burke hid behind some trash cans as Quinn called out, "Judge Roper."

The man turned slowly. Quinn stood on the sidewalk. Devine and Lynch flanked him.

Roper tried to smile, but Devine had rousted hundreds of men in situations like this, and humor was the last sense they could summon.

"Quinn," Roper said. "Didn't expect to see you here. Why aren't you on the mean streets?"

"All the streets are mean these days, Judge."

"Better come down here, Your Honor," Lynch said.

Roper did. He carried a briefcase. Devine never understood the fondness people in the legal profession had for their goddamn briefcases.

Quinn introduced the men to one another—Captain Lynch and Officer Devine of the Public Morals Squad, Judge Andrew Roper of the United States Court of Appeals for the Second Circuit—and they all exchanged small nods.

Lynch spoke first. "You're a long way from Foley Square, Your Honor."

"Sometimes I have to meet people," the judge said.

"In a brothel?" Lynch asked.

Roper licked his lips. "I guess I should walk away."

Lynch shook his head. "You're gonna get us in there."

Roper blinked a few times, as if he couldn't believe what he'd just heard.

Lynch went on. "You're gonna tell that moose at the door that we're with you. You've told us great things about this place, and we wanna check it out for ourselves."

"Show the moose your warrant," Roper said.

Before the judge could step away, Devine said, "It'd be a shame, Your Honor."

"What was that, Officer?" He spat the last word, like a Shakespearean king addressing a commoner.

Devine kept his voice steady. "It'd be a shame if word got around about this."

Roper looked like an aggrieved citizen who wanted to call the cops, except he was dealing with the cops.

"It's like this, Judge," Quinn said. "If they show a warrant, the scumbags inside will call their lawyers, and they'll be able to keep the door closed half an hour while they destroy the evidence."

"And then the lawyers will get here, which will fuck up everything even more," Devine said.

Roper looked at them dubiously, as if they were trying to plead down a murder charge to shoplifting.

"You do this, Judge," Quinn said, "and I'll do you a favor—I'll leave you outta the column I'm gonna write about the raid on this place."

Roper pulled himself up to his full height. Like most men in authority, he could summon deep wells of dignity at moments of abject humiliation. Jerking his head toward the townhouse door, he motioned for the police to follow.

Lynch told Quinn to stay outside until the place was secured. Things were likely to get rough.

The door opened slightly when Roper and the cops reached it. Devine caught a sliver of the gorilla's face.

"What was that bullshit down there?" the gorilla asked.

"These fellas are friends of mine," Roper said.

The door remained in the same position. "Nobody comes in without an appointment," the gorilla said. "You know the rules."

Devine leaned toward the gorilla and did his best to adopt a flatland accent. He doubted the gorilla had ever been west of Newark.

"We're colleagues of this gentleman from Omaha, and we just got in town for a conference. We've heard that this place is one of the best things in New York City, and that conference is gonna be mighty dull."

The gorilla laughed. "Sheep fuckers."

Every wise guy Devine had ever met went wild at the sight of cash, so he opened his wallet as wide as he could. "We'd really like to check out your merchandise."

The door creaked open. Massive oak job, probably original to the building.

"Once you try us out," the gorilla said, "you'll never have sex with a farm animal again."

Devine reached into his waistband, took out his gun and smashed it across the gorilla's face. Roper fled while Finley and Burke charged up the steps. The gorilla staggered back. The cops pinned his arms. Devine slugged him in the ribs, but he suspected his own hand had sustained more damage than the gorilla's midsection.

Lynch put his mouth close to the gorilla's ear. "We're NYPD."

"Where's your warrant?" the gorilla asked.

"The judge was our warrant," Devine said.

"You need a warrant," the gorilla said.

"You're running an illegal operation," Devine said. "What makes it even more illegal is this: You've been holding out on us."

A dark look of confusion came to the gorilla's face. He was about twenty-five and had nothing going for him except muscle.

"I dunno nuttin' 'bout that," he said. "I just watch the door."

"Where's Angelo?" Devine asked.

"I dunno who you're talkin' 'bout," the gorilla said.

Lynch bent one of the goon's fingers back so far it snapped. The gorilla winced but emitted no sound as he wriggled in the cops' arms. Devine reached inside his suit jacket and felt for his switchblade. He nodded to

Finley and Burke, who let the gorilla's arms swing free. The guy's frown was deep, serious and sincere, and he swung his arms in front of him as if he was surprised they could move.

In one swift motion, Devine slashed the blade over the gorilla's right wrist. The guy looked startled as he raised his hand to eye level while blood spilled out.

"Where's Angelo?" Devine asked.

"Shit," the goon said. His pupils began to dilate.

"I'm gonna slash your other wrist in a second," Devine said. "Or maybe your carotid artery. You'll bleed to death."

The gorilla blinked a few times. "My arteries ain't corroded."

"You need to get to a hospital. But first, you've gotta tell us where Angelo is."

The goon balled his fist and swung at Devine, who ducked. Lynch whipped his service revolver on the back of the guy's head. The goon wobbled, tried to turn around to throw a punch, slipped on his own blood. After he crashed to the floor, Lynch put his revolver next to the guy's ear and clicked it into firing position.

"I'm gonna shoot you if you don't tell us where Angelo is," Lynch said.

"Second floor."

"Good. Now get your ass to a hospital."

The goon stumbled out while the cops headed for the stairs. As they started to climb, they encountered a silver-and-black-haired man wearing an Oleg Cassini suit and Ferragamo loafers.

"What going on here?" he asked in a velvet voice.

Devine had expected the usual mobster gravel.

"Angelo?" he asked.

"Who wants to know?"

Devine flashed his badge. "We're raiding you."

"Where's your warrant?"

Devine was always impressed by professional criminals' understanding of the Constitution. "We don't need a warrant. You know why? Because you opened this place without telling us. I've got kids in parochial school, so I need to earn."

"I don't think you gentlemen understand the situation," Angelo said.

"What do we need to understand?" Devine asked.

"Can we talk in my office?"

Devine and Lynch exchanged glances.

"Quinn's still outside," Devine said to the captain. "He's expecting something to happen. Better bring him in here and complete the raid."

"Quinn?" Angelo asked. "Jamie Quinn?"

"Friend of mine," Devine said. "We brought him along. He's looking for a column."

"That was a mistake."

"We've gone too far now," Devine said.

They went down the stairs to the first-floor foyer. Angelo pointed to the gorilla's congealing blood.

"What happened here?"

"We had an altercation with your doorman."

"He better be all right. Paulie is a valuable member of my organization."

Angelo pushed open a mahogany door that revealed a high-end cocktail lounge lined with bookcases and filled with comfortable furniture that looked imported. A long and deep coat room was beside the bar, which was tended by a neatly groomed man in his thirties who wore a bow tie and a white ruffled shirt with studs.

Finley and Burke both had a foot on the bar rail as they sipped Johnnie Walker neat. Lynch jerked his thumb toward the street and addressed the two plainclothes.

"Get Quinn in here and finish this thing. Arrest the hookers and the guys running the gambling. Let the customers go with a warning. We never wanna see them here again. Like that'll do any good." Lynch turned toward Angelo. "Officer Devine will finish questioning you, Mr.—?"

"DiNapoli." The bordello master looked straight at Devine. "Would you like a drink, Officer?"

"Jack Daniels and water."

DiNapoli turned to the bartender. "Bring Officer Devine's drink to my office."

"Certainly, Mr. DiNapoli."

The whoremonger pushed open another mahogany door. The room was smaller than the lounge but just as well-appointed, with deep upholstered chairs and a maple desk that gleamed. DiNapoli sat behind it and motioned Devine to a chair.

"The question confronting us," the mobster said, "is how we turn this mountain of shit into a landfill."

"Why is it a mountain of shit?"

"We service a high-end clientele. Our customers expect confidentiality and discretion. They certainly don't expect to be disturbed or distracted."

"Sorry we ruined their day," Devine said. "But Public Morals can't allow a place like this to operate without being cut in on the business."

The bartender brought in Devine's drink and placed it on a coaster within arm's reach. When Devine sipped he expected swill, but it really was Jack Daniels, 90 proof and tempered with a splash of ice-cold New York City tap water.

"We have clearance," DiNapoli said. "All the way up."

"I call bullshit."

"And if I call the people I know, I could end your career right now."

Devine felt like saying, That might be a blessing. Instead he squinted hard at the man at the other side of the desk. Something was familiar about him and his manner.

"We've met," Devine said. "You ran Stonewall."

DiNapoli nodded.

"You didn't take care of us then, either," Devine said. "That's why we raided the place."

"The situation was similar," DiNapoli said. "We thought we had protection all the way up. You may recall that none of the men who led that raid ever got promoted."

"I was a rookie street cop back then," Devine said. "Just following orders."

"The Nuremburg defense won't cut it this time."

"Who's protecting you?" Devine asked. "Who did you talk to instead of us?"

"I can't tell you that."

"You can't shut us out."

"You guys are expensive."

From the floors above Devine heard the angry cries of working girls losing opportunities to earn.

"This is gonna be all over the *Daily News* tomorrow. We have to close this place down. Can you find another location?"

"We have a backup spot two blocks away."

"Perfect. Same neighborhood, but you'll put some distance between your business and the Morgan Library. This block has way too many tourists, schoolkids, and matrons from the Upper East Side."

"You gonna arrest me?"

"I'm afraid I have to. You know your rights?"

"When this conversation is over, I'll call my attorney."

"After you reopen, you'll cut us in. I don't care what kind of deal you have with whoever is supposed to protect you. They can't protect you from us."

"I can have you sent to Siberia, Officer Devine. Someplace where you'll have no chance to grift."

"In that case, I'll tell Jamie Quinn everything, and he'll create a media circus. None of us want that, Mr. DiNapoli." Devine paused. Drank some more. The bourbon soothed his nerves. "Work with me here. You'll find that I'm reasonable."

DiNapoli gritted his teeth like a guy in a dentist's chair. "How much do you guys want?"

Devine ran figures through his head. "Five floors means five thousand a week."

"One thousand."

Devine was being lowballed, but his time on the force was limited, and he needed a new revenue stream. "Two thousand."

"Fifteen hundred."

"Okay, but there's a catch."

"There always is."

"Captain Lynch. The man who led the raid."

"What about him?"

"He doesn't want money. He wants girls. After you've reopened, he gets complimentary privileges."

DiNapoli nodded. "If you fellas leave a few women behind, he can get started right away. As a sign of my good faith."

Devine extended his hand. He always appreciated straightforward business discussions.

"There's one more thing I need to ask you about," Devine said as he and DiNapoli stood and shook.

"What is it?"

"How long did Nadine LaFleur work here?"

DiNapoli blinked a few times. "You're talking about that girl in the papers."

Devine tried to hide his surprise. He had expected DiNapoli to deny ever hearing of her. "That's right."

DiNapoli shrugged as if her life and death were matters of no importance. "A few days here and there. Free-lance thing."

Nadine would have split her earnings with the house, not with Paco, who was notorious for keeping a high percentage of his workers' earnings.

"You're not Homicide," DiNapoli said. "Why are you interested?"

It was an intelligent question. Like the best wise guys, DiNapoli intuitively understood matters of turf.

"The brass wants her case resolved ASAP, so I've been working with Homicide."

"I run a tight ship here," DiNapoli said. "Anybody gets outta line—employees or customers—they're not allowed back in. Simple as that."

"Was anyone stalking her? Getting clingy about her?"

"I didn't hear anything about that. And I woulda heard."

Devine took his final slug of Jack Daniels and enjoyed the newfound lightheadedness. He walked with DiNapoli toward the office door.

"What was she like?" Devine asked.

"She had problems. They all do. I didn't concern myself. I'm running a business."

"How did she wind up here?" Devine asked.

"Referral."

"By whom?"

"Nobody here uses their real name. I'm sure you understand."

"I'm sure I do. Thanks for the drink."

Devine stepped into the lounge while DiNapoli closed his door to begin an evidence-destroying binge. A few feet away, the barkeep was reading Quinn's column about Nadine. Devine approached the guy, pointed to the courtesan's picture, and told himself to keep his voice even and uninflected. He didn't want to sound as if he knew too much or too little.

"I understand she worked here."

"I don't concern myself with what goes on upstairs." The barkeep flipped the page. More crime on Page Five.

"You didn't answer my question," Devine said.

"You didn't ask one."

Devine snatched the paper off the bar and flung it in the air. Sheets of newsprint fluttered around the book-lined space.

"Your boss and I just had a good conversation," Devine said. "You know why? Because he didn't jerk me around. I can run you into Rikers and keep you there six months if I feel like it. Or I can just beat the crap outta you and claim you were resisting arrest."

The tender gulped. "I thought everything was taken care of."

"This operation has to relocate. After that, you'll be okay. But I've got an immediate problem—Nadine LaFleur. Her murder is the department's top priority, so you better be honest with me when I ask questions about her."

The keep nodded meekly. Would-be tough guys always wilted in the presence of authority.

"I'll start from the beginning," Devine said. "I know she worked here."

The tender nodded again.

"What was she like?"

"She did tricks."

"That doesn't tell me anything I don't already know." Devine hoped his impatience was showing.

"Demons," the keep said. "All these women have them."

"What were hers?"

The tender tapped the side of his nose. Paco had mentioned drugs, and now Devine knew which one she indulged. Cocaine was an expensive habit, even for a top-of-the-liner, though it explained the ounce scale Devine had seen in Nadine's apartment.

"Was she a ball buster?" Devine asked.

The keep nodded. "Tightly wound, you know what I mean? Just about anything could set her off."

Devine made mental notes: Nadine LaFleur, high-strung cokehead but fantastic in the sack, free-lancing at Manhattan's most expensive brothel while holding out on her pimp. It should be possible to pin *somebody* for her murder.

"She have any regular customers?" Devine asked.

"Two guys in particular," the bartender said.

"Describe them."

"First one is skinny. Thinning hair. Early thirties. Intense. Kinda quiet. Really fierce eyes, like he was X-raying everything. He wears off-the-rack suits, so he looks a little outta place here. But he must be able to afford our prices, or Mr. DiNapoli wouldn't let him in."

"What about the second guy?"

"A coupla years older than the other one. Blustery. Has a combover. Looks like a jock who stopped exercising—big frame, but everything's sagging. Definitely has money. Wears Brooks Brothers all the time."

"They have names?"

"Smith and Jones, just like everyone else around here."

"Nadine have a preference for either one of them?"

The barkeep thought for a second. "She liked the thin, balding guy." He pointed to a small table in the corner of the room, underneath some leather-bound books that Devine guessed were first editions. "They used to sit over there and talk. Sometimes, she'd pull down a book, and they'd leaf through it while they split a bottle of wine."

"They'd talk?" Devine knew he sounded incredulous. "They discussed books?"

The tender nodded. "After a while, they'd go upstairs. Different people like different kindsa foreplay."

"What about the other guy?" Devine asked.

"Strictly business. She started undressing the moment he walked in."

"Those guys here now?"

The keep shook his head. "Haven't seen 'em for a few days. Ever since the story broke that she'd been murdered."

Jamie Quinn poked his head into the room and stared at the space like a kid who knew his parents were still hiding the biggest Easter egg.

"That's Jamie Quinn," the tender said as if he were embarking on a really bad acid trip.

"Friend of mine," Devine said. "Wanna be in his column tomorrow?"

"Fuck no."

"Is there a back way outta here?"

"Of course."

"Use it."

Devine ambled over to Quinn, who motioned around the room.

"Classiest bar I've ever seen," the columnist said as he took out his notepad. "Moldings in the ceiling. Gotta get that in."

"If Edith Wharton ever hung out in a bar," Devine said, "it woulda been here."

"That's why I like you, Terry," Quinn said as he scribbled. "For giving me stuff like that."

Devine peered into the coat room, which was dominated by wool jobs for men and leather ones for women, though he spotted an animal print at the far end.

"If we run through those pockets, we'll find some interesting IDs," Quinn said.

"We don't have time. Everyone's lawyering up already." Devine steered Quinn into the foyer. "I did some research on this place. J.P. Morgan had it built for his favorite mistress."

Quinn scribbled some more. "You're great, Terry."

Devine guided the newsman up the staircase while running his hand over the banister's smooth dark oak. Old Man Morgan must have loved that woman.

"When you think about it," Devine said, "the purpose of this house hasn't changed much."

"You missed your calling," Quinn said as he continued his jottings. "You're way better than any editor I ever had."

On the second floor women slumped against the walls in the classic bored-prostitute pose—arms folded across chest, jaws vigorously chomping gum, eyes cast upward or downward in search of something better than what they were facing. In a bathroom at the end of the hall, several men who looked like executives were struggling into their trousers.

"Those guys won't talk to you," Devine told Quinn, "but the girls will."

"What're you gonna do?" Quinn asked.

"Look around. Evidence and shit."

As Quinn approached the women, one of them asked if he was the guy on Channel Four News.

Devine entered the bedroom to his right: Four-poster bed; patterns of red roses on canopy, sheets and wallpaper; totally Newland Archer. On the other side of the bed was a door that Devine figured led to a closet, but when he pushed it open, he saw another bedroom. Communicating doors, he thought, and he began to speculate about the types of games J.P. Morgan liked to play with his mistress. Devine started yanking on drawers, and despite the Gilded Age decor, the contents were the everyday stuff he expected: condoms, cigarette packs, lacy lingerie, breath mints.

He pushed open another door. The rooms and beds were becoming progressively smaller, and he figured the place had a sliding scale, with the master fuckpad out front costing the most. The windowless room was plain, with scrubbed off-white walls, and Devine guessed this had once been the maid's quarters.

Beside the twin bed was a small closet that contained several negligees on hangers and a few pairs of heels jammed against the baseboard. Some johns liked it when the women kept their shoes on.

Devine swept his eyes over the closet's top shelf. Up in the corner, wedged so tightly into the wall and ceiling that it looked as if someone wanted to merge it into the masonry, was a handbag the color of ivory and made of glossy Italian leather. Devine stood on his toes and grabbed. It was a Gucci bag that had been purchased at the brand's boutique on Madison Avenue, and it was exactly like the one he had seen on Nadine LaFleur's bed.

Devine opened the clasp. Inside, he found rings and bracelets. He ran his hands over the lining, which was smooth and silky, but stopped when he felt a zipper. He tugged on it and stuck his fingers in the compartment, hoping for money, but instead pulled out a piece of folded-up notepaper. He smoothed it and read a long list of addresses in blocky, printed letters, with dollar values listed beside them. The ink was blue, and the writing was assured, and Devine had the feeling he should recognize it. Below, in a loopy hand that looked feminine, he saw the words "GET IN ON THIS!" in red ink, as if the writer felt the information on this page would free her from the bondage that defined her life. Beside the message was a small drawing of one of those smiley faces that always made him cringe.

He shut the bag. Shoved the notepaper in his pocket. Evidence and shit.

Tony Bennett switched to Bobby Darin on Clarke's jukebox.

"I found out something from those working girls," Quinn said.

"What was it?" Devine asked.

"Martha Owens, a.k.a. Nadine LaFleur, worked there sometimes."

"We know," Devine said.

Quinn's eyes lit up like a teenage boy who had just seen his first naked woman. "You stirring something up? That why you raided the place?"

Devine glanced at Lynch, who sipped his Courvoisier and gave the slightest of nods. He had not discussed the matter with the captain, but he understood the signal: Whatever you're doing, keep going.

Devine kept his voice neutral. "We can say nothing about that one way or another. The workers tell you anything about her?"

"Not much I didn't already know," Quinn said. "She kept to herself. They thought she was stuck up. She had a few regular customers but otherwise didn't mix with the clientele."

"That makes sense," Lynch said. "She was a call girl. Working in a brothel is a step down, even if the place was built by J.P. Morgan."

Quinn drummed his fingers on the beer-sticky table. "I should get something about Martha into the column."

For the first time in his life, Devine understood how an Alpine skier must feel when he loses control on a run. "What would you say?" he asked Quinn.

"That she worked there."

"Is that relevant to anything?"

"You sound like a goddamn copyeditor." Quinn downed a shot of Bushmills and a few swigs of Schaefer. "I got an idea. I'm gonna call the desk. They hate it when I change things so late, but sometimes I like to jerk 'em around. Just to show 'em who's important."

As soon as he left, Devine lowered his head a bit to make sure the wire would pick up everything. Before he could say anything, Lynch had a question: "We sure we want him to bring Martha into this thing?"

"He won't mention her by name," Devine said. "He doesn't have enough, at least not yet. He'll make a vague reference that only people like you and me will get." Devine drank some Harp. "Lemme tell you what else we found there."

"Go ahead."

"Finley and Burke discovered thirty thousand in cash. That place has the best gambling set-up this side of Monte Carlo."

Under the protocol Devine had devised when he began working in Public Morals, fifty percent of the money would be vouchered. Lynch was entitled to half the rest. Devine would then work out a split among Finley, Burke and himself.

"I'm not interested in the money," Lynch said.

"You sure?" Devine asked. "Not even a thousand, just for the aggravation?"

"I've been adequately compensated," Lynch said.

"DiNapoli told me he'd keep some of the girls around for you."

"Three of them. From different continents. That Vietnamese chick was really limber." He sipped more Courvoisier. "What happened to the goon?"

"He's outta the hospital. They patched him up. I knew it wasn't as bad as it looked."

Quinn sat down, grinning like a carnival barker who had just sold his last worthless raffle ticket. "They bitched and moaned, but I made 'em do it."

Lynch tried to sound politely curious. "What did you say?"

Quinn nodded at Devine. "I talked about that handbag you were carrying around after you searched the rooms. I said it looked like something that'd been bought at Saks. I said people would be surprised by the kinda dolls who work in a place like that, and the kinda guys who go there."

Chapter Nine

As she read the *Daily News* over breakfast, Gina looked at Terence Devine with eyes that were sleepy but glowing.

"You're mentioned by name in here," she said.

"What does it say?"

"You're one of the Four Horsemen."

She slid the paper toward him. They sat in the nook she had set up by the high arching window that fronted Peck Slip. Devine stroked her fingers, palm and wrist, then leaned back to read what Quinn had written.

The raid was presented in epic terms, with centurions from the NYPD—Officers Finley, Burke and Devine, under the dynamic leadership of Captain Adrian Lynch—storming a citadel of sin. Blood was shed, but that happens in all battles, and while critics might upbraid the unit for employing heavy-handed tactics, the ordinary people of New York should express gratitude that, at long last, some men in authority were taking decisive action to reverse the decline of a city that had been plummeting downhill for far too many years.

"A hooker with a handbag like that," Gina said. "Maybe I'm in the wrong line of work."

Devine went to his duffel, removed the bag, and brought it back to Gina, who looked it over as if she were an auctiongoer at Sotheby's about to bid on the most expensive item in the lot.

"I could use this in an installation," she said. "Alter it some and call it the Gateway to Gomorrah."

"Leave it alone," Devine said. "At least for now. But I want you to hang on to it."

She opened it up. "Looks like there's some stuff in here. Should I hang on to that, too?"

"Yeah. Evidence and shit."

The phones in Homicide rang more incessantly than usual as Devine sauntered across the room. He stopped at Mulligan's desk and tossed down the list Paco had given him. The detective's face was ruby red, and when Devine sat without being asked, the man's jaw began to work in a prelude to bellowing rage.

Devine pointed at the paper. Mulligan picked it up and blanched, but Devine kept quiet until he was sure the Homicide dick had absorbed all the names.

"Who ya gonna call first?" Devine asked. "The congressman? Or maybe the deputy mayor?" He smiled. Taunting Mulligan was fun. "I know—try these guys."

Devine jabbed at the names of a father-son pair of wheeler-dealers who dwelt professionally at the most lucrative residence in New York—the intersection of law and real estate. "If you breathe air in this city," Jamie Quinn once wrote, "the Grubb family makes money off it."

"Since they're in the private sector," Devine told Mulligan, "it won't screw up your career as much."

"You looked at this," the detective said in a voice that blended puzzlement with betrayal.

Devine ignored him. "Then there are the places she used. You should demand the front-desk records from the Plaza."

"Jesus Christ," Mulligan muttered over and over again as he opened the bottom drawer of his desk and shoved the list in it.

"You asked for that," Devine said. "You wanted names. Places. Now you've got 'em."

"Yeah, yeah, yeah," Mulligan said.

"Don't yeah, yeah, yeah me." Devine's voice rose. Heads turned. He wanted everyone in Homicide to hear. "Some deputy inspector comes around asking where that list is, I want you to tell him, I want you to tell him who's on it, and most of all, I want you to tell him that I gave it to you. Because if you don't, I will." Devine pounded his fist on Mulligan's desk for emphasis. "I am cooperating with this investigation."

"Maybe I should make the pimp for this after all," Mulligan said in a thinking-out-loud voice. "Whatshisname? Taco."

"How would you do that?" Devine asked.

"Blow a hole in his alibi."

"He said he was receiving personal attention in his apartment from two of his employees, and they backed him up. So did the concierge at his building. I read that guy's statement. He sounded jealous."

"Here's another possibility," Mulligan said. Devine recognized the tone of a detective throwing speculative spaghetti at the wall in the hope that one of the strands would stick. "I talked to the Puerto Rican guy across the street from her apartment. He peddles drugs, so he's on the block all the time. A well-respected businessman in the community. Mayor of West Seventy-Third Street."

Devine told himself not to react at all. He was just receiving information. There was no need to do anything about what he heard.

"I show him a picture of Taco. Just on the chance. He says, 'Lo reconozco.' So I ask if he saw the pimp the night the medical examiner thinks she was killed, and the dealer says, 'No, amigo. Lo siento.' So I ask if he saw the vic let anyone in that night, and he nods like he's got a spring in his neck and says, 'Sí, sí, señor.'"

Devine told himself to keep his voice flat and emotionless. He was just a policeman asking questions. "He get a good look at whoever it was?"

"Said he was a Caucasian. Said he looked like a cop. Said I probably knew him." Mulligan shook his head. "To scumbags like that, all white guys look like cops."

"Even if you find him," Devine said, "there's no guarantee he did it."

"The neighbors said they heard a struggle."

"But nobody called the police."

"Of course not. Crap like that happens all the time on the West Side.

Everybody hides in their apartments all the time 'cause the place is a hellhole."

"The dealer is the way out," Devine said with the adrenaline rush of inspiration. "He's on the street looking things over. Business is slow. He sees the vic in her apartment. We know she used drugs, so he probably knew it, too. Maybe she even bought from him."

"Makes sense."

"Anyway," Devine said, as if he'd witnessed what he was about to describe, "the dealer's getting lonely, and bored, and he figures she's the same way. So he crosses the street, rings her bell, and proposes a business exchange."

"His goods for her services," Mulligan said.

"And then something goes wrong." Devine shrugged. "Even if he didn't do it, the guy's a criminal. He should go away for something."

The vibe from the gay hustlers was even more hostile than usual.

I am not making you do this, Devine felt like telling them. If you dislike the life, leave it. I'm just trying to make some money in the little time I have left.

A few days earlier, he had called Da to say there was a good possibility he'd be quitting the force in the near future. He was deep undercover. It was likely the last thing he'd ever do in the department.

"So you're gonna move down here," Da had said.

"That's the plan."

"New York's dying. Florida's alive. We'll work something out."

Now Devine scanned the pier like an archaeologist surveying the ruins of a once-thriving civilization.

"Over here."

It was Erik, standing by a trashcan fire in a corner partly shielded from the wind.

"What happened to your digs?" Devine asked. "They were so nice."

"Big bull dyke muscled in. I was no match for her. Don't even think about shaking her down. She'll break you in half."

"I might like that."

Erik rolled his eyes while reaching into his leather jacket. One of its shoulder seams was torn, so he'd stuck in two big safety pins to keep the thing together. He thrust an envelope into Devine's palm. The cop began counting.

"Better be careful," Erik said. "My fellas get excited when they see all that green."

"I can deal with a bunch of pansies."

"You couldn't at Stonewall."

"Back then, you guys were appealing and energetic. Now you're this."

Devine waved his arm. Shafts of light crept through the partially collapsed ceiling. By the far end, where the open section of the dock extended into the river, two men wrapped thick rubber bands around their forearms.

"Where's the kid?" Devine asked.

Erik shifted his feet and blew on his hands. "Who are you talking about?"

"The Black kid I talked to last week. Randall."

Erik shook his head. "Not here. You know what it's like. Boys come and go all the time."

Society's flotsam, Devine thought, discarded and left to drift. Then people like me have to deal with them because nobody else wants to, and the do-gooders wonder why we take money.

A dark face poked through a hole that had been banged through the wall. Devine stuffed the envelope in his pocket and began striding that way.

"Where are you going?" Erik asked.

Devine moved faster.

"What are you doing?"

It grew colder with every step toward the river. Spring was late, and Devine never understood how these guys survived the winter. On the dock, the sun was blinding despite the chill. Devine screened his eyes. Near the end of the pier, he saw a slender, solitary form—a teenager who looked as if he wanted to keep going, but had run out of room.

Devine ran toward him as the wind whipped his body. The kid curled his back and head into his knees. Sludge lapped against rotted pilings, and in the distance Ellis Island and the Statue of Liberty mocked the city.

"Go away," Randall said.

"I wanna see you," Devine said.

"I'll give you a blowjob instead. Close your eyes and imagine I'm Diana Ross."

The kid let out a pained yelp as Devine yanked him to his feet. Randall's left eye was barely open because of the purplish bruise around it, his right ear was swollen, and his nose had shifted to the right.

Devine pushed him away, spun around, headed back.

"Don't."

The kid's voice sounded desperate and frantic. Devine heard the rapid footfalls of a youth who could run all day. Soft hands wrapped the cop's upper arm.

"It was my fault. I made him."

Devine shook him off and stepped over disintegrating concrete. Inside the enclosed part of the pier, a hustler stuck a needle into his pockmarked forearm.

"Where's Erik?" Devine asked in his don't-fuck-with-me cop's voice.

The hustler shook his head, but on the other side of the vast and crumbling space, a man ran out toward West Street and turned right.

Devine took off. From behind, he heard Randall begging him to stop. On the street, Devine saw Erik stumbling a hundred yards away underneath sunlight jangled by the crumbling latticework of the West Side Highway. The authorities kept saying they would tear down the road, but Devine knew it would remain standing until it collapsed on its own, just like everything else in New York.

Up ahead, Erik grabbed his side and stomach as he leaned against a lamppost.

If there is any justice in the world, Devine told himself as he jogged toward the pimp, a piece of rusty steel will fall from the road and crush that bastard's skull.

"Why do you care?" Erik asked.

"One life," Devine said. "Maybe I can save one life. Just once."

"They can't be saved," Erik said. "At least not by you or by me. You're the worst grifter I've ever met, and I have no idea why you're concerned about him because you've never cared about anybody except yourself."

Devine understood. He and Erik would banter and do business, but they would never respect each other.

"You wanna do something useful? For once in your miserable life?" Erik wheezed and panted before continuing. "Find out who killed Nadine. She was a pro, and she was careful, but somebody got into her apartment and murdered her, and now every hooker in the city, male and female, is scared shitless."

"She made a mistake," Devine said. "She opened her door."

"The rumor is she knew something that got her killed. In our line of work, we hear stuff all the time, especially from our clients. If we wind up getting killed because of what we know ... "

Devine sighed. He did not want to do what he was about to, but he had gone this far and needed to make his point.

In one swift motion, he reached for the ripped seam on the pimp's jacket and tore hard. The safety pins flew off, scraping Devine's palm and drawing blood. He balled his crimson fist and smashed it into Erik's midsection as hard as he could. The pimp caved in on himself and let out an "oof." Devine grabbed him by the collar of his jacket and half carried, half dragged him to the water's edge. By now, some of the queers had gathered, though they stood about fifty feet away, spectators unsure about sticking around for this drama's denouement.

"Next time I tell you not to do something," Devine said, "don't do it."

"I gotta run my business the way I see how," Erik said.

"You ruined the looks of one of your earners. That's bad business."

"Some of my clients like fellas who look beat up."

"Let's see how they like you after I'm done."

Devine lifted Erik off the ground and hurled him outward. The pimp hung in the air a moment, like Wile E. Coyote before he realizes he's run beyond the edge of the mesa, before falling hard and striking the Hudson with a sickening smack.

In the squad room, Devine kept his wire running while doling out the pad. Most of his colleagues told him how happy they were to see the cash, but a new guy named O'Shea grumbled that it made him sick to make money off homos. Devine reached into the envelope he was about to give the guy and removed five twenty-dollar bills.

"Whaddya doin'?" O'Shea said.

"You're making a contribution to the widows and orphans fund," Devine said.

"What?"

"We're all prejudiced, but it's bad for business. You need to learn that."

Devine put the bills in his pocket before heading to his desk, where he picked up a pink While You Were Out slip with a number from an unfamiliar area code. The operator had scrawled that the caller sounded like a woman who was intelligent and assured, though she didn't give a name or say what she wanted to talk about.

Devine considered ignoring it, but there might be a chance to earn, so he dialed and waited while the phone rang a dozen times. Out in America, a lot of those houses were pretty damn big.

"Hello?"

The voice was weary and brittle and belonged to a person who had given up everything, including sleep. Devine identified himself and asked what this was about.

"My name is Edna Owens," the woman said. "I got your name and number from Jamie Quinn."

Devine adopted the neutral but hurried tone of big city cop with a lot to do. "What's on your mind, Mrs. Owens?"

"Mr. Quinn suggested I call you. He thinks you have information about the investigation into what happened to our daughter. Martha. Some people called her Nadine. That Mulberry fellow won't tell us anything."

Mulberry, Devine said to himself. That's good. I should remember that.

"Well, ma'am, I'm sorry for what happened to Na—to Martha, but I'm not sure what I can do." He used a stiletto to open a letter from the union. "Detective Mulligan may seem gruff, but I'm sure he'll get to the bottom of it."

"I wish I could share your confidence," Edna Owens said.

Devine recognized the sound a velvet hammer made when it struck something vulnerable. In Dublin, New Hampshire, whenever Mrs. Owens or her husband, the doctor, called the authorities, the couple's concerns immediately consumed the community.

"Why do you say that, ma'am?"

"I talked to Mr. Quinn earlier today. He said the police still can't find the journal that Martha kept."

Devine thought of a number of responses, but he was definite about one thing—if Jamie Quinn said the NYPD didn't have the dead woman's book, they didn't have her goddamn book.

"Technically, Mrs. Owens, I'm not sure we should be having this conversation. Detective Mulberry—Mulligan—is in charge of the case, and you should be talking to him."

"I understand that," she said. "But Mr. Quinn said you get things done. He said New York needs more officers like you."

"I appreciate the sentiment, Mrs. Owens." Devine's mind began working: What's in that book that's so important? "And I'll tell you this—you've piqued my interest. I'll nose around and see if I can find something."

"My husband and I would be grateful," Edna Owens said.

"All of this is unofficial," Devine said.

"I understand that. And let me tell you something, Officer. You might find this useful."

"Go ahead, ma'am."

"Ever since she was a young girl, Martha was very good about hiding things. I realize that now. That book is probably in a place nobody thought of looking."

"She had secrets," Devine said.

"That's right."

"So even if we find this book, will we be able to figure out what she was saying?"

"That's an excellent question, and that's why my husband and I would like to look at it."

"Very good, ma'am. Now it's my turn to ask you something."

"I understand the way the world works, Officer Devine. Even if I do live in Dublin, New Hampshire."

Devine found himself liking Edna Owens. "Can you send me a sample of Martha's handwriting?"

Chapter Ten

Sheila came home with a note from Sister Immaculata that said, "We need to talk," so Devine and Bridget left the kids at home and wound up in their daughter's classroom, sitting in small chairs at a tiny table in a room dominated by imposing posters of Jesus and His Mother, the Virgin. Stick-figure drawings of Nativity scenes filled the bulletin board.

Sister Immaculata wore a pale blue dress and a gray headband that swept back flaming red hair. A crucifix hung from her neck, and wire-frame glasses rimmed her eyes. The nun's appearance surprised Devine, who expected the black-and-white penguin outfit he remembered from his days in a school much like this one.

Sister Immaculata opened a folder and slid a piece of construction paper toward Devine and his wife.

"What's this?" Bridget asked.

"That's what I want to ask you," the nun said in the brusque I-know-God's-desires-and-you-don't tone that Devine had heard from every member of a religious order he had ever encountered.

"I never saw this," Bridget said.

"I did," Devine said. "Sheila drew it."

"And you thought this was acceptable?" the nun asked.

"She did the assignment. I think she showed a lot of talent."

"This isn't about talent, Mr. Devine. This is about showing reverence for the Holy Family."

Devine considered smiling, but nuns were never charmed by anything. "Well, Sister, I did ask why she drew Jesus as a girl. And Sheila said that boys are icky, and Jesus wasn't icky. I believe that shows a great deal of reverence."

And then he heard his wife's voice in his ear, full of anger, despair and disbelief: "How could you let her?" Before he could respond, Bridget leaned forward so quickly she almost toppled, her arm stretched across the table so far she nearly touched the nun. "I am so, so sorry about this. I never woulda let this happen."

Sister Immaculata nodded. "I'm delighted to hear that, Mrs. Devine. Look at the way she drew the Blessed Mother."

Haggard features, drooping eyes—Sheila's version of Mary looked like every woman who had just given birth that Devine had ever seen.

"I know what you mean, Sister," Bridget said. "I promise it will never happen again."

"That's a start," the nun said, "although I don't know if I can ever forgive something so heretical."

"Is there anything we can do?" Bridget asked.

"She can make amends," Sister Immaculata said.

Amends? Devine said to himself. She's five years old, for Christ's sake.

"Sheila can start by drawing a proper Nativity scene," the nun said. "The Holy Family should have halos."

"Of course," Bridget said.

"A few angels would be nice. Sprinkled throughout. The way they were at Bethlehem."

"Absolutely. Nativity scenes need angels."

"And Jesus should be a boy. Obviously. He is the son of God, not the daughter."

"Consider it done."

"If all that is accomplished," Sister Immaculata said in a this-meeting-is-over tone, "then, in the spirit of Christian charity, we will try to put this unfortunate event behind us."

Devine expected her to give him the drawing. He intended to put it on his desk at work, but first he'd show it to Gina. He wanted somebody who knew something about art to confirm his belief that his daughter was talented.

With a fierce sigh, Sister Immaculata picked up the picture with both hands and tore it in half, then in quarters, then in eighths, and on and on until Sheila's Nativity scene was nothing more than bits of paper scattered on the table. Once all the pieces were arrayed before her, the nun swept them into a trash basket and then looked at her hands as if she were a nurse who had just touched the grossest form of refuse.

"What did you do that for?" Devine asked.

"It was blasphemous," Sister Immaculata said.

"She's a little kid. How can it be blasphemous?"

"I'll be the judge of that, Mr. Devine."

"Sheila likes to draw. She spent a long time on that picture. She put a lot of thought and effort into it—more thought and effort than any of your other students did, judging by the crap I see here—and you did nothing to acknowledge it. You just pissed all over it, and her."

Beside him, Bridget shrieked his name as he jumped to his feet. The pint-size chair clattered backward, and he regretted not being in the interrogation room, where he could have done what he wanted.

Sister Immaculata looked up at him. She did not blink. Devine reminded himself that nuns were the toughest people he had ever faced.

"My mission on Earth is to prepare these children to become followers of Christ. I assume that's why you want your daughter in this school."

"Of course it is," Bridget said.

"I want my daughter to become educated," Devine said. "I want her to think for herself."

"Then I'm not sure this is the right school for her," Sister Immaculata said.

Bridget stood and covered her husband's mouth before turning to the nun and adopting the pleading tone Devine had heard so often from skels trying to cut a deal.

"I am mortified about all of this, Sister. I apologize about Sheila, and especially about my husband." Bridget leaned close to the nun and dropped her voice, as if she were about to reveal her most closely guarded secret. "He's a police officer. There's a lot of stress."

"Jesus was under a lot of stress on the cross," Sister Immaculata replied, "and look how He handled it."

The argument began on their way to the car.

"How could you let her bring that piece of shit to school?" Bridget asked.

"She completed the assignment. She had to draw a Nativity scene. She drew a fucking Nativity scene."

"A moron coulda seen it was completely inappropriate."

"Sheila has a lotta talent. Maybe you'd notice if you didn't have your head up your ass."

The two of them got in the car and slammed the doors. Devine cut off a Camaro as he gunned the Lincoln out of the parking lot. When the Camaro's horn blared, Devine raised his middle finger.

"You're never home," Bridget said. "Out doing God knows what. I'm the one who has to deal with the kids until you swoop in like you're their guardian angel. Always being the good guy, while I hafta be the bitch." Bridget's fingers shook while she lit a Parliament. "That nun has figured out something, if you bothered to listen to someone else for once in your life. Sheila is willful, and you can't tell her anything. Just like you."

At dinner he drank two Heinekens but said nothing. Bridget stayed quiet as well, except for the angry noises the utensils made whenever she put one of them in a serving bowl. The chicken was baked to the point where it crumbled like dry paper, and he assumed she had overcooked it to punish him.

Bridget cleared the table as if she were a dervish and thrust the dishes in the sink with so much force Devine was afraid they'd break. Michael kept glancing between his parents. Sheila asked about dessert.

Bridget snatched two bowls of Jell-O from the fridge. Sheila smiled. The Jell-O was lime green, her favorite color and flavor.

"What did Sister wanna talk to you about?" she asked.

"Nothing important," Devine mumbled.

Bridget swiveled her head. "Did you say something?"

It's my house, Devine said to himself, and I'll talk to my children if I want.

He turned to Sheila, smiled as broadly as he could, and said, "It was nothing important, Sweetheart."

The next words exploded from Bridget's mouth with volcanic force: "How can you say that?"

The cords in her neck bulged, and Devine wanted to tell her that, for once in her life, she should keep what she was thinking to herself.

"Waddya want me to say?"

"Tell the truth for once! You've never told the truth in your life!"

Michael scurried from the table without asking to be excused. Sheila's eyes were big and round, but her horror at what she was seeing kept her rooted.

Devine swept his arm toward his daughter. "She's a little girl. Why are you doing this to her?"

"She could get expelled. Will that make you happy?"

It might, Devine thought. I wouldn't have to pay tuition.

Sheila burst out crying. "What did I do?"

"That Nativity drawing!" Bridget said. "How could you?"

"Daddy said it was okay."

"As usual, Daddy was wrong."

Sheila sobbed. Michael slipped out the back door with a baseball and glove.

Devine knew he was yelling, but he couldn't stop himself: "Why are you doing this? What's wrong with you?"

Bridget pointed at Sheila. "Do you want her to go to public school?"

I want her to be happy, Devine said to himself. Nobody I know is happy. I'm interested in seeing what it's like.

"I'd like her to do an assignment without turning it into a federal case," Devine said. "She made a nice drawing. Why can't everyone leave it at that?"

"What was wrong with my drawing?" Sheila asked.

Devine looked at her full. The girl's eyes were blue and darted with intelligence.

"Sister Immaculata didn't like it," he said. "I'm sorry. She wants you to do it again."

Sheila's face scrunched into a mixture of hurt and confusion. "Why didn't she like it?"

"She wants something more traditional," Devine said.

"What does 'traditional' mean?"

"Old-fashioned."

Sheila smacked her lips as she finished her Jell-O. The sugar had restored her equilibrium. "I don't like old-fashioned."

Bridget grabbed Sheila's empty bowl and shoved it in the dishwasher. "Draw it with angels. Give the Holy Family halos. Makes Jesus' mom look pretty."

Sheila frowned. Devine reached out and rubbed a bony shoulder. "Do what your mother tells you."

Sheila got permission to leave the table and started to walk away, presumably to begin a new Nativity scene, but then she turned and skipped back to her dad.

"Can I have my drawing?" she asked.

Devine worked his mouth, but nothing came out. He thought about employing the time-tested parental tactic of changing the topic, but Sheila was relentless once she latched onto something.

"Why do you want your drawing?"

"Because I really liked it. I worked super hard."

Devine began stammering.

"We don't have it," Bridget said.

"Where is it?" Sheila asked.

Tell her you're not sure, Devine said silently. Don't let her know what happened. That nun wrecked it, and she should tell Sheila about it herself.

"Sister Immaculata tore it up," Bridget said.

Sheila blinked her big eyes a few times. "What?"

"I said Sister Immaculata tore it up. And if she hadn't, I would have. It was inappropriate and offensive and disgusting, and it shouldn't have seen the light of day."

Sheila began stamping around the kitchen with the force of a small elephant. "How could she do that? How can you say that? I spent hours on it."

Christ, Devine thought, what's my life gonna be like when she's a teenager?

"You shouldn't have drawn it in the first place," Bridget said. "Drawing Jesus as a girl. Drawing His mother that way. What were you thinking?"

Sheila bawled that she loved that drawing. It was the best thing she'd ever done. Bridget replied that she didn't care. It was time Sheila started respecting adults instead of doing whatever she felt like.

"But I didn't even wanna do that stupid drawing," Sheila said. "That old nun told me to!"

"Don't call her old! And don't call something stupid!"

"But she is old! And it was stupid!"

"Stop it right now!"

"But it's the truth! All I wanna do is show the truth!"

Devine slid out the back door. The cool air cleared his head, and in the early spring darkness he discerned a form tossing a baseball against a mesh backstop. As his eyes adjusted he determined it was Michael, throwing as hard and rapidly as he could.

Devine walked close and watched him. Like most kids, he was pitching with his arm and not using all of his body, but he was left-handed, so in Little League he always had an advantage.

"Michael?"

"What?" The boy's tone indicated that, at this moment, he had no use for anyone.

"Wanna play catch?"

Michael continued hurling the ball as hard as he could. "You don't have a glove."

"I can handle it."

Michael motioned his dad to take a spot on the other side of the backyard about forty feet away.

"Baseball season starts soon," Devine said.

"I'm gonna try out for pitcher," Michael said. He played basketball in the winter, but baseball was his favorite sport. He was undersized, but he loved sports, and his father hoped he'd fill out into his ambitions.

Devine reached the spot his son had indicated and put his hands in front of him. Michael reared back on his left leg and used all of his skinny frame to fling the ball. Devine caught it flush with his hands. A vibrating pain ran through his wrists and up his arms.

"That was better," Devine said as he flicked the ball back. A tingling ache flashed in his shoulder.

"Waddya mean?" Michael asked.

"You used your back leg when you threw. That's how Ron Guidry does it. He's small for a pitcher, but only Nolan Ryan throws harder."

Michael paused before beginning another windup. This time, he considered every piece of his motion, and it took him ten seconds to release the ball, but it came in fast and straight and true.

Chapter Eleven

Jamie Quinn's latest column about Nadine was plastered over Page Three of the *Daily News*. Edna Owens and her husband, the doctor, were frustrated by the lack of progress in their daughter's case and by how the police ignored them whenever they called to ask about it. The department regarded Martha as a disposable creature who was less than human. Edna Owens said she realized her daughter had been reckless at times, but her punishment was fatal, and now the men in authority were doing nothing about it. As far as Mrs. Owens could tell, no one had even looked for Martha's journal. Was that too much to ask?

Toward the end of the piece, Quinn adopted the tone of righteous indignation that came easily to Irish Catholics whenever they believed powerful people were deliberately negligent:

"Martha Owens is dead, which counts for little in a city where murder is a spectator sport. But she was a human being, and her all-too-brief existence on this planet merits some respect, even if our officials refuse to dignify her passing with their attention. It's sad and offensive to think that this is what justice has come to in New York—whether the Police Department, in its infinite wisdom, decides your death is worth its time."

Devine pushed the newspaper to a far corner of his desk and reached into his top drawer. The envelope with the Dublin, New Hampshire, postmark sat atop a clump of paper clips, notepads and loose change. It had arrived in his mailbox the day before, but he had yet to open it because he was leery of what he might discover.

He tossed the envelope in his fingers a few times before slicing it open.

As he expected, Edna Owens' penmanship was flawless.

"Dear Officer Devine," the letter began.

She knows manners and etiquette, he thought. She will always be extremely polite as she gets people to do what she wants.

"As you requested, I've enclosed a sample of Martha's handwriting. In fact, this is the last letter she wrote to my husband and me. It struck us as anodyne, but perhaps there's something in it that you will find revelatory since you are, obviously, much closer to the investigation than we are.

"If there is anything further we can do to assist you, please let us know. We are pleased that at least one police officer in New York City is taking an interest in what happened to our daughter."

Devine smoothed out the letter that Martha Owens had sent her parents. The writing was loopy and covered both sides of a single sheet of paper. He was no expert, but it resembled the woman's writing on the notepaper he had found in the Gucci bag at the Murray Hill cathouse.

Devine cased the street to make sure the dealer was nowhere in sight, then hopped the gate outside Nadine's walkup and ran up the crumbling steps to the front door. He picked the lock in seconds and climbed the stairs inside. His shoulders brushed peeling paint.

Her third-floor apartment was marked with yellow tape that said it was a crime scene and no one could enter without permission. He pushed open the door and ducked under the marker.

The living room was more banged up than he remembered, which he attributed to Homicide dicks crashing around looking for stuff they could swipe. As he closed the door, he wondered where she had kept her journal. Someplace she could get to easily, he told himself, but nearly impossible for another person to find. He glanced around the living room. The closet by the door was filled with leather jackets and dark winter coats. He considered rooting around, but he heard the door to the street open and shut. Shoes clomped up the stairs. He decided to move away and reminded himself that women keep their secrets in the bedroom, so that was where he went.

Devine looked over the boxspring, mattress and coverings while asking himself if he'd left anything behind. He believed he hadn't, but he thought about what might occur if one of the detectives found an item that belonged to him. Cops usually protected their own, but he and Mulligan loathed each other, so all he could rely on was the department's desire to avoid shame and scandal.

He noticed the copy of "L'Etranger" still atop the nightstand beside Nadine's bed and figured that nobody in Homicide knew French. Her clothes hung in the closet. He was surprised Mulligan's guys hadn't taken them. Wives and girlfriends always needed dresses, blouses, skirts, slacks. Of course, Nadine had verged on the petite side. Maybe the sizes were too small.

A chain dangled from a bare bulb screwed into a socket on the ceiling. Devine yanked. He saw cocktail dresses at the far end and ran his fingers over the material. Silk. He priced out the cost of her apparel, most of which looked new, and concluded that Nadine LaFleur had expensive tastes that were almost certainly satisfied by a sugar daddy, or daddies.

Down on the floor, stacked against the walls, were several rows of shoeboxes. Devine also noticed a small folding stepladder, which would have given her access to the other shoeboxes on the shelf over the clothes rack. Above the rack was an indentation in the wall, partly painted over—most likely a badly installed fusebox jury-rigged into that spot when the townhouse was divided into apartments.

Devine asked himself: Do I have to open every one of these goddamn shoeboxes?

And then he answered his own question: No. You just have to keep opening them until you find what you're looking for.

He crouched to get a better look at the boxes on the floor. None had a marking that indicated it might hold a book, although a few seemed well worn, as if they contained particular favorites. He started with those.

The first box contained a pair of heels. He ran his hand around in hopes of finding some money, but all he felt was leather.

The second box contained a sensible pair of pumps. Devine reached into them and brushed his fingers against small and crumpled pieces of paper.

He took them out and smiled. Four twenty-dollar bills that he hadn't found the first time he was here, and he had just started looking.

He stopped. Years of often dishonest police work had made him sensitive to sounds, and he asked himself if his mind was conjuring noises because he was so alert to what he was doing.

But there it was again—the clunking thud of heavy footfalls on the landing just outside the apartment. Probably the guy he'd heard earlier when he was looking at Nadine's coat closet. Devine ran through who or what it could be. Perhaps it was Mulligan or some other schlub from Homicide, but they'd gone through the place a dozen times. It would take an order from the commissioner to make them search it again. The thumps could belong to a neighbor, and the sounds would fade as the civilian went about his business. Of course, the stranger outside could be one of those bizarre citizens who got a thrill from looking at places where people had been killed. In that case, Devine was confident he could scare the jerk by badging him.

The front door creaked open. Devine needed to hide. The space under the bed was too small, so he considered wedging behind the room's paneled door before realizing the intruder might catch his reflection in the vanity over the dresser.

Feet thumped around the living room. Devine turned off the light and eased the closet door shut. The space was tight, and he felt warm from his own breath. Devine was sure the intruder was a man and, from the sound of his steps, about six feet and two hundred pounds.

If it comes to a fight, Devine told himself, I'll have surprise on my side, at least in the first few seconds.

He reached into his waistband, took out his gun, and pointed it at the door. The stomping in the living room sounded like a bass line at a rock concert. Devine heard the man opening and closing doors, then flipping over magazines and seat cushions.

The sound of thudding shoes ceased. Devine hoped to hear the front door slam closed, but after a second the footfalls grew louder, and he told himself to remain calm and focused.

The bedroom door opened all the way. The mattress on the dead woman's bed was lifted, then allowed to fall back into place.

You have never searched a scene like this, Devine said silently to the other man in the room. She wouldn't have put anything she used regularly under the mattress—way too heavy and cumbersome.

Drawers were opened and closed with increasing force and anger. The new man was getting frustrated, muttering phrases that sounded like "What the fuck?" and "Where the fuck?" and "What a bitch."

Devine felt a strange surge of confidence. Open the closet door, he thought. I'm ready for you.

He held his revolver by the barrel. He figured he'd use it blackjack-style and wallop the intruder over his head. Devine would leave the man unconscious, ideally in a puddle of his own blood, before finding the nearest pay phone and calling Homicide and telling whoever picked up that he'd better check out Nadine LaFleur's apartment ASAP.

This schnook probably read Quinn's column, Devine told himself. He's afraid there's something here the cops can trace to him, and I bet there is. We'll make him for the murder and get this whole goddamn thing behind us.

The footsteps stopped just outside the closet door. A hand twisted the knob. Devine raised his gun and saw a head bobbing into the space. He whipped the pistol onto the intruder's skull and heard a cry that blended pain, anger and surprise. The head dropped down and Devine smacked it again. The guy fell face-first to the floor, and Devine was on top of him, ready to strike again, when the man turned his neck.

Devine rolled him over all the way. The man raised his hand to the back of his head while Devine hopped to his feet and put his gun back in his waistband.

"Looking for something, Captain?"

They needed a place to talk, so Devine and Lynch got into the last car of a No. 1 train heading downtown. The long and hard plastic bench was empty. The cops were alone with grime and graffiti.

"I knew her," Lynch said.

Devine was beginning to suspect that he was the only heterosexual man in New York who'd never had sex with Nadine LaFleur.

"What if something's there?" Lynch asked. "Christ, if Mulligan finds that journal and my name is in it … "

"Did you know she worked at that whorehouse?" Devine asked.

Lynch shook his head. "Never woulda raided the place if I had any idea. She was an interesting girl. But she had secrets."

The car's tires squealed as the train pulled into 66th Street. A dirt-encrusted junkie staggered into the car and fell onto the seat opposite them.

"You're not the first cop who's used a hooker," he told Lynch.

"I married Mulligan's kid sister. That asshole is my brother-in-law, and she's a lawyer who'd devour me in a divorce." Lynch reached up and touched the painter's cap that Devine had bought for him on their way to the subway. "Christ, my head hurts."

"If I'd known it was you, Captain—"

"Why were you there?"

Lynch's hundred-dollar loafers kicked at a floor sticky from dropped gum and spilled soda. At least Devine now knew why his captain didn't grift. Mulligan's kid sister made the money.

"Quinn gave my name to the mother. She keeps going on and on about that journal. I promised her I'd look." Devine shook his head. More subway squeals, even louder this time, as the train stopped at Columbus Circle. The junkie scratched his balls. "It was a rookie mistake. I should never make promises."

"You didn't find it?" Lynch sounded disappointed.

"The journal is mythical," Devine said. "Something the vic's parents cooked up to keep the pressure on. Dr. and Mrs. Owens always get their way in Horse's Ass, New Hampshire. They're not gonna let up, and they've got Quinn's ear."

Devine ran his mind over what he'd seen in Nadine's apartment. Something was missing, but he couldn't figure what it was.

"This case won't go away on its own," he told Lynch, "and Mulligan's in over his head. We've gotta clear it."

"Easier said than done."

"Something about that whorehouse is connected to her death. I can feel it."

Lynch shook his head as emphatically as he could, considering his condition. "Even if you're right, that would cause lots of problems. For both of us."

"Then try this," Devine said. "I told Mulligan something, but he blew me off. Maybe he'll listen to you, since you're related and everything."

Lynch snorted. Devine went on.

"The drug dealer across the street is our ticket outta this thing."

Chapter Twelve

Morning light brushed him awake. He wanted Gina to hang curtains or blinds, but she thought they were pointless. The nearby buildings were empty, and she liked to let in as much of the natural as possible.

Her dark hair sprawled. He considered playing with it, but before he could move, she pushed off the covers, plodded into the kitchen area, and reached for the coffee pot. In the morning she liked to walk around naked before taking a shower.

He pushed himself out of bed. Took out juice glasses and cereal bowls. Gina glanced at his waist.

"Not gonna happen," she said.

He was amazed he had anything left. The night before, they'd split a bottle of Chianti before humping like bunnies.

Devine sipped some Tropicana and grimaced. The first taste of the day was always bitter.

"Wish you'd seen it," he said.

"Seen what?"

"This drawing Sheila made. Nativity scene. It was really good, but the goddamn nun tore it up right in front of me. Called it blasphemous. I wanted to show it to you. I think my girl is smart and talented, but I'm her dad. I'd like your opinion."

Gina slammed a cupboard shut and stalked into the opaque shower stall. Devine watched her darkened shape while she cleansed herself. She came out with a towel around her torso and another around her hair, then began dressing hurriedly—panties, bra, stockings in a bland shade of neutral. Gina was temping all week in the DA's office. It cut into their sex, but Devine appreciated the assignments. She was inquisitive, and people told her things.

She brushed her hair so hard Devine expected it to come out in clumps.

"There's a lotta talk in the office," she said. "They're going after Public Morals. It's rotten to the core, and this time they're gonna clean it out."

She glared at him with a defiant gaze that said, I know everything that's wrong with you.

"One more thing," she said.

Devine stayed quiet.

"Don't ever mention your kids to me again."

She left. He went to the window and looked at the barren street and, in a minute, saw her striding west. When she was out of sight, Devine opened his duffel and removed the letter Edna Owens had sent. He brought it to the table in the nook and sipped coffee that had grown cold.

Martha told her parents that she felt her life was back on a good path after a long journey through the wilderness. She was serious about going back to school in the fall. She was also thinking about opening her own business. She realized it would be difficult to do both, so perhaps she'd have to choose one over the other, but in any event she'd need money no matter what, and she was trying to save some.

Toward the end of the letter, she said she had become acquainted with some of the men who made things happen in the city. They were powerful and heartless, and the public good was a joke because they were interested only in gaining influence and possessions. She was now persuaded that finance was the key to life, and these men were so determined to get their way she had grown convinced their wealth would push aside everything that might stop them.

After cutting a deal with the big bull dyke, Erik resumed running his shop from the crumbling warehouse near the piers. He coughed hard as Devine took the swivel chair next to his desk.

"She take pity on you?" Devine asked as he jerked his thumb behind him. The woman was six-foot-one if she was an inch.

"I was in the hospital three days after you threw me in the river," Erik said. "Doctors couldn't believe all the crap that was in me. Good thing my immune system's strong." He hacked up a wad of phlegm.

"Sounds like you should still be in the hospital," Devine said.

"This place fell apart without me. I'm gone less than a week, and half my workers get sick. Weird lesions all over their bodies. There's talk about a gay disease."

"Sounds like bullshit to me. I think you guys are just looking for attention."

Erik reached into his desk, took out an envelope, and threw it at the cop's face. Devine snatched it out of the air two inches from his nose.

"All your money is there. Now go fuck yourself."

Devine began walking away.

"You find out anything about Nadine?" Erik asked.

He's wearing a wire, Devine told himself. Jesus Christ, is everybody in this city working for an investigation?

"I heard she held out on Paco."

"So you think he did it?"

"He has an alibi." Devine hoped he sounded unconvinced.

"She was a pretty girl," Erik said, "if you like that kinda thing. Smart. Savvy. I had time in the hospital to think about this, and I'm more convinced than ever that she wasn't the kind of person who'd let a killer into her apartment."

"Maybe she let her guard down. Just has to happen once."

Erik shook his head. "I realize heterosexual sex is fraught with peril, but still ... "

"Speaking of homosexual sex—"

"We weren't."

"How's Randall?"

"Gone."

Devine worked his mouth a bit. "Waddya mean, 'gone'?"

"What part of 'gone' don't you understand?"

"How could you let him leave?"

"I don't chain my guys to a pylon." Erik sounded indignant, like a man convicted of murder who was guilty only of armed robbery. "When I got back from the hospital, he wasn't here."

Devine distributed the pad before stopping by Lynch's office to tell him what he'd done. Even if the captain wasn't part of the grift, he now had knowledge of it.

Lynch motioned Devine to close the door.

"It's about my brother-in-law." Lynch's voice was barely above a whisper. Devine moved closer to pick it all up on his wire.

"What about him?"

"I talked to him about Nadine. He's frustrated. Making no progress. Really has no idea who coulda done it, and he's catching all kinds of hell from his superiors."

"What did you say to him?"

"I mentioned the drug dealer across the street."

"How did your brother-in-law respond?"

"He's bringing the douchebag in. The guy is now officially a person of interest in Nadine LaFleur's murder."

The brass scheduled a presser at headquarters to coincide with the six o'clock news. The scene reminded Devine of feeding time at the Bronx Zoo. Sweaty reporters clutching notepads surged toward the front, where they were blocked by cameramen with cartloads of equipment and huge asses. All of them jostled and shouted except for Jamie Quinn, who leaned quietly against the far wall.

At the podium, the commissioner raised his hands in an attempt to quiet the clamor. The noise grew louder.

"May I have your attention, please?"

The commissioner was in his mid-fifties, tall and solidly built, with metal gray eyes that matched his hair. Despite his air of command, the reporters were acting like a class full of troublemakers who had just seen the substitute teacher walk in.

"I have a statement I'd like to read," the commissioner said.

This provoked more noise. Devine wondered how the act was playing on TV.

"Can I have a little quiet?" The commissioner sounded peeved.

"Hey!"

Quinn's voice, loud as a foghorn, cut through the ruckus like a battleship slicing a raft. Everyone turned to look at him, which he always enjoyed.

"Let the man talk."

As the room grew silent, the commissioner nodded at Quinn before clearing his throat.

"Earlier today, the Homicide Task Force, under the able leadership of Detective Francis Xavier Mulligan—"

Oh, sweet Jesus, Devine thought.

"—brought in a man for questioning in the murder of Martha Owens, a.k.a. Nadine LaFleur. The man's name is Geraldo Calderon. He has a number of aliases, the most common of which is his street name, Zaca. He is originally from Puerto Rico and has a long list of priors, mostly for drug dealing. He came to our attention—"

Because Mulligan finally figured out that he needed to do something, Devine thought.

The commissioner droned on until he said he'd take a few questions. This produced another explosion of sound as every reporter in the room began yelling. The commissioner raised his hands in another ineffectual gesture of begging for quiet.

"Wait a minute!" Quinn bellowed.

Stillness followed. The columnist separated himself from the wall and made a show of flipping through his notes.

"Let's cut to the chase, Commissioner," Quinn said. "Are you telling us that this guy Geraldo Calderon, street name Zaca, is a suspect in the murder of Martha Owens?"

The commissioner looked like he was having a root canal. "I, uh, I, uh, I—"

Devine closed his eyes. On television, stammering always looked evasive.

The commissioner found his verbal footing. "At this time, given the status of our investigation, I am only prepared to say that he is a person of interest."

This led to more noise, which subsided at the sound of Quinn besting everyone with cries of "Hold it! Hold it!"

Beads of moisture pooled on the commissioner's upper lip and temple.

"C'mon, Commissioner," Quinn said. "I'm a person of interest."

The reporters and cameramen laughed.

"Why'd you bring this guy in? You think he did it?"

"We don't need to tell you all of our reasons, Mr. Quinn. There are aspects of this investigation that even you don't know about."

This led to another cacophonous outburst, but once again Quinn's voice rode over it.

"Hold on! Hold on!"

There was an edge in Quinn's tone that Devine had rarely heard. The room acquired a nervous calm as every reporter and camera turned to the columnist. Most of the New York press corps hated his guts, but they all respected him.

Quinn slowed his usual rat-a-tat outer-borough cadence, taking extra nanoseconds to ensure his words could be heard clearly by the millions of people in the tristate area watching the six o'clock news.

"Do you have any evidence linking Geraldo Calderon, street name Zaca, to the murder of Martha Owens?"

The police commissioner looked like a man who wanted to swallow his lips. Quinn went on.

"Do you have any suspects at all?"

A drop of sweat trickled down the commissioner's cheek until it reached his chin, where it dangled for what seemed like hours. Devine looked to the wings, where the department's flacks wore the frozen looks of soldiers who couldn't believe a grenade had just rolled into their foxhole.

"This is an active investigation," the commissioner said, "and there are a number of leads we are pursuing."

The reporters roared again, filling the room with profane cries, the most audible of which was "Horseshit!" Devine realized what somebody had to do, and since no one else was moving, he strode up the center aisle and jumped onto the podium while keeping his back to the cameras.

"You have an urgent phone call," Devine murmured to the commissioner.

"Nice stunt you pulled there," Quinn told Devine as they strode from headquarters.

"It was like watching a man drown, and no one in the crew had enough sense to throw him a life preserver."

"I asked around before the press conference," Quinn said. "I found out something interesting."

"Go ahead."

"They dusted Martha's place for prints. Every inch. You know what?"

Devine suspected the worst. "Zaca's prints aren't there."

"Bingo."

Devine told himself to look stoic even if the most promising way to resolve the case had just evaporated like a puddle on a ninety-degree day. Quinn reached into a pocket inside his rumpled suit and took out a battered cigar, which he shoved into the corner of his mouth but did not light.

"The commissioner tried to insult my intelligence. Now I'm gonna go back to the newsroom and tear that schmuck apart."

The columnist stepped from the curb, flung up his right hand, and bellowed for a taxi.

"Before you do that—" Devine said. He told himself to keep his voice low. Quinn was relaunching his crusade, and Devine had to guide it in the direction he wanted.

"I'd never tell you what to write," Devine said.

"Not even my editors do that," Quinn said.

"And I suppose the commissioner has it coming. But I wanna tell you something about the Nadine LaFleur case. Just between you, me, and this broken streetlight."

Quinn chewed on the cigar.

"There's a list of her clients," Devine said in words so light they were blown east by the wind. "Mulligan has it. I'm not gonna name names. But it's really interesting."

It was too early for Clarke's, Gina was still pissed, and he didn't want to go home, so Devine kept walking west on Chambers Street. Night had swept the streets clear of people. Dingy stores lurked behind gates of steel and iron, while a few blocks south the empty floors of the Trade Center were bared by lights that could never be shut off. Near the Hudson, dilapidated buildings heaped into clumps of brick and cement. A block from the river, junked cars and ten-foot-high weeds filled a lot as long as a football field. Up ahead, the hulk of the West Side Highway loomed overhead. The plans to build Westway had put the area under eminent domain, so the road was frozen in decrepitude. Free-lance hustlers in leather jackets and torn jeans leaned against rusting pillars, but with no pimp protecting them, these men were in thrall to the whims of whoever was willing to pay.

Devine pondered his possibilities as the queers eyed him. When he started in Public Morals he rousted a few brothels, ran in streetwalkers and arrested some johns. Everyone he busted received a desk appearance ticket and walked away. His supervisors grumbled about low-level crap creating too much paperwork. After a month a deputy inspector called him down to headquarters.

We do not arrest johns, he said. We bring in the streetwalkers only if they're blatant and obnoxious. We're looking for pimps and madams, but barging into brothels and bringing everybody into the stationhouse is not the way to do it. Nobody tells us anything worthwhile. So cut it out.

"With all due respect, Sir," Devine asked, "what the hell am I supposed to do?"

The deputy inspector blinked a few times, as if he couldn't believe the question, before breaking into one of the biggest laughs Devine had ever provoked.

"If you ever figure that out, Officer, tell me."

So Devine organized the pad. He'd had his hand out from the moment he joined the force, taking whatever was offered in a haphazard way, but in this squad he realized he could make steady money if the take was run like a business. Every Monday morning, before heading to work for the week, he left an inch-thick wad of bills on Bridget's dresser.

Now Devine eyed the desperate tramps across the street. They had no money, so he couldn't shake them down, but arresting them was pointless. He was about to turn away when a boy stirred and moved. He had a lithe figure that was loose and limber and not yet grown into itself, and Devine recognized something about the physique and walk. The boy was with an older man, taller and filled out, the type of guy who'd get fat unless he exercised regularly. The two of them were close together, apparently in conversation, as they strolled onto the other side of West Street and into the darkness by the river.

Devine crossed quickly. The pack asked what he wanted—anything at all, every price and activity negotiable—so he flashed his shield, prompting cries of mock fear and faux respect.

He slipped through a hole in the chain-link fence that separated the edge of the road from the landfill beyond it. The ground underneath was debris from the Trade Center, sunk into the Hudson to provide a base for a string of high-rises that, Devine was sure, would never be built. There were plenty of plans to remake New York, but they were nothing but empty promises.

The boy and his companion were about twenty yards ahead. Their pace had quickened. Devine saw the outline of a bulldozer, and he had observed enough of these encounters to anticipate what would occur—the two would secrete themselves on the other side of the equipment where, surrounded by darkness and hidden from the city, their transaction would enter its most intimate phase.

As Devine eased around the bulldozer, he heard the older queer groan. The guy's pants were bunched around his ankles. His shirttail and jacket covered half his butt. The boy was kneeling, mouth and jaw working with the dexterity of a craftsman.

Devine took out a small flashlight and shone it onto the older man's face. "You should get a room."

The boy muttered something that sounded like, "Can't you leave me alone?" but it was the expression on the customer's face that left Devine confounded—crimson rage, as if the office pest had barged in while he was dictating an important letter.

"You're interrupting," the man said.

Devine badged him. "That's the point."

"Do you know who I am?"

Devine held the light closer to his face and wished he had brought a camera. "Councilman Dante Antonelli, head of the Public Safety Committee. You're a long way from your district."

"I'd advise you to get the hell outta here, Officer Devine."

"And I'd advise you not to talk like that unless you want me to describe what I just saw to Jamie Quinn later tonight while we're drinking beers at Clarke's."

Antonelli hitched his pants before gimping away with his unresolved erection. Devine shifted the light to the boy's face and told him to stand.

"You'll be sorry you did that," Randall said.

Devine took the kid to a chrome and Formica diner on West Broadway that hadn't been cleaned since Fiorello La Guardia was mayor.

"Where you from?" Devine asked.

"Pittsburgh."

"How much is the bus fare back?"

"Five bucks."

Devine tossed a wad of twenties onto the table.

"Here's some traveling money. Go to Port Authority and take the next Greyhound home."

Randall pushed the money back. "No way."

"How bad can it be there?"

"You have no idea."

"Broken home? Nobody loves you? Get in line."

"A broken home woulda been better," Randall said.

Devine brought the coffee to his mouth. Dregs lumped on his tongue.

"My dad whipped me," Randall said. "All the time, especially after he found out what I'm like. He thought I'd change if he hit me enough."

"What about your mom?"

"She's a God-fearing woman, so she supported him."

"If you stay here, you're gonna wind up dead."

"What if I do?"

"I deal with the scum of the Earth," Devine said. "They drift into New York, and most of them deserve what they get because they're screwed-up adults who made bad decisions and have nobody to blame but themselves. But you're a kid. I have kids myself. Your life shouldn't turn into a living hell because you made a mistake when you were sixteen."

Devine inched the money back toward Randall, who looked at it a long time.

"I don't wanna die," the boy said. "At least not the way—"

"The way what?"

"There are stories. Scary stories we all tell ourselves."

Devine tried to lift his shoes, but something sticky kept his feet on the floor.

"That woman who got killed," Randall said. "Nadine. It shook up everyone. Straight, queer, male, female, in between—"

"Why is that?"

"'Cause she was careful. That's what everyone says. She did everything right, and she wound up dead anyway. We're all afraid we're gonna wind up dead as it is, and then a pro like her gets murdered, and now guys are getting sick and dying for reasons nobody can figure out … "

Nadine did one big thing wrong, Devine felt like saying. She held out on her pimp.

Randall leaned forward and dropped his voice so low Devine could barely make out his words.

"Maybe it's the way it went down—offed in her apartment and everything—but all the working boys and girls say she died 'cause she knew something."

"I love a good conspiracy theory as much as the next person," Devine said, "but do you have any evidence to back this up?"

"In this line of work," Randall said, "you meet interesting people. Some are rich. Some are powerful. Some are both. You saw the man I was with. He likes me."

"I'm sure he does." Devine hoped he sounded sarcastic.

"Sometimes Dante tells me things, even if he doesn't mean to. He pays his money, and he wants to talk, so I have to listen. Every once in a while, he says stuff he should keep to himself."

A kid like Randall was the best confessor—much more forgiving than a priest.

"What are some of his secrets, aside from the one I just discovered?"

"I ain't sayin'."

"What about Nadine? What did she know?"

"I have no idea. But I bet she knew somethin'."

Devine pushed his money to the edge of the table. "All the more reason to go back to Pittsburgh. Since your mom's a holy roller, tell her you're the prodigal son."

"She disowned me," Randall said.

"You'd be surprised," Devine said.

"Surprised at what?"

"At how much parents will do when they're afraid of losing their children."

Chapter Thirteen

"Is Reggie Jackson really a jerk?" Michael asked.

Devine wondered where the question came from. Then he glanced at the back page of the *Daily News*, which was hyping a screed by grumpy columnist Dick Young that called Jackson, who had recently left the Yankees as a free agent, the most spoiled brat in all of baseball, which was really saying something.

Devine had read the back page for years and long ago concluded that Dick Young believed the only person who should make money off sports was Dick Young.

"Reggie is a jerk," Devine said. "He's also one of the best players in the game. Sometimes you just have to put up with things."

He smoothed the paper and resumed reading Jamie Quinn's piece, which had it on good authority that a list of Martha Owens' clients was circulating among officials at the highest levels of One Police Plaza. This list contained the names of men whose careers and reputations would be ruined if the information became public, so the department was doing its best to keep it secret.

"This is your police department at work," Quinn wrote. "A working girl has been brutally murdered, and the NYPD's biggest concern is making sure the names of her clients are never known.

"Which brings us to the matter of Commissioner McSweeney's performance at yesterday's comic opera of a press conference."

Devine read on. Quinn wrapped himself in self-righteous fury as he accused the commissioner of bumbling and dissembling, while noting how difficult it was to do both at the same time. He concluded by writing, "If Geraldo Calderon, street name Zaca, is responsible for killing Martha Owens, a.k.a. Nadine LaFleur, I will personally flap my arms and fly to the moon."

"I've been talking to my superiors," Fishman said.

The meeting had just started, and Devine already hated the direction it was taking.

"They say it's time to move on to the next phase of the investigation," Fishman said.

Devine felt tired and thirsty, and every time he sat in this windowless room, with its stale air and harsh lighting, he sensed the walls and ceiling creeping closer.

Fishman flipped through a yellow pad. "We've got enough here for indictments."

"You sure about that?" Devine asked. He had hoped to stay undercover a few more months. The longer the investigation lasted, the greater the chance it would unravel.

Powers jerked his thumb toward Devine while talking to Fishman. "For once, I'm on the same page as this guy. It's too soon."

"The mayor and the DA have both told me they wanna do this right now." Fishman looked pointedly at Powers. "So has your commissioner."

"It doesn't make sense," Devine said.

"Just between us," Fishman said, "the DA says it's about public perception. He wants people to think the city is making progress in its fight against crime and corruption."

"He'll make a lot more progress if he waits a while," Devine said.

"You got a memo on any of this?" Powers asked.

For the first time, Devine was impressed with the IAD dick. Like all savvy Civil Service survivors, he wanted his superiors to go on record about decisions he had to implement, but regarded as idiotic.

Fishman shook his head. "It's all verbal. None of them wanna go near this case until it looks like it's gonna succeed, and then they can swoop in and take credit for how well they handled it." He shrugged. "You know how it goes."

Keep kicking the can, Devine told himself. There's gotta be a way to string this thing along.

"Lynch mighta told some of his pals higher up in the department about that whorehouse," Devine said. "You could nab an inspector, maybe even a deputy chief. That'd make this investigation even bigger. But I'd need time to work on it."

Fishman brought pen to mouth. "I'll make that point when I meet the DA this afternoon."

The prosecutor opened his Gucci briefcase. He wore department store suits but toted his legal stuff in an expensive accessory. Devine had heard that even though the Fishman family was wealthy through real estate, Adam would stay on an allowance as long as his parents lived.

While the lawyer rooted through his stuff, Devine's eyes focused on a huge block of black type. Despite the prosecutor's disdain for the tabloids, a copy of that morning's *Daily News*, complete with a huge picture and headline about Martha/Nadine, rested atop his work papers.

It was nearly midnight, and Devine kept hitting the buzzer, and Gina kept yelling at him to go away, and finally he shouted: "Waddya gonna do? Call the cops? You're living here illegally, and I am a cop."

She rang him in. By the time he walked up the four flights to her space, his heart was pounding through his ears. Gina kept her back to him as she poured acrylic onto a canvas she had laid on the floor.

"Say something to me," he told her.

She sank down on all fours, leaned forward, spread paint around with palms and fingers. Once, when they were lying in bed after a furious copulation, she bit his ear and whispered that she stopped thinking whenever she got into the rhythm of painting or sex, and she loved that sensation because thought was the enemy of action.

"You're pissed 'cause I mentioned my daughter to you? I have children. They're a big part of my life. You knew that going in."

Gina sat cross-legged on the floor and finally turned to face him. The halogen lamps she had installed in the corners bounced the light, framing her face with the type of back glow he associated with old Hollywood movies. Her smock was a kaleidoscopic smear, her hair was pulled back tight, and dabs of purple and green paint speckled her nose. He had never seen a woman who looked more beautiful.

"I heard something this afternoon at the DA's office," she said.

Devine crashed onto the worn but comfortable sofa he had helped her carry the day they found it on a Mott Street curbside. After they brushed it off, she lowered his pants, climbed on top, and rode him as long as he could stand it.

"They're gonna move against Public Morals tomorrow," she said.

"Tell me more."

"They've rolled a lotta the pimps who've been making payoffs. All those guys have immunity, so they're gonna testify to the grand jury. But the most important thing the DA has is an undercover who's wearing a wire. People tell me he's as crooked as they come, but they've flipped him, and now they've got all kinds of stuff that'll blow the lid right off the squad."

She stood, then stretched her arms and back as far as she could. Devine walked over to look at what she'd done. Gina had grown up on the East End of Long Island in a family acquainted with Jackson Pollock—the weird guy down the road who drank way too much and made all those funny-looking paintings. Pollock had died before she was born, but she became familiar with his work and found that she liked it. Now that she was creating her own art she kept trying different techniques, though whenever she painted, she preferred smearing and throwing to dripping.

The canvas had bold streaks of red mixed with touches of black and gray, as well as the purple and green she had just tossed in. Lines, circles and blobs crashed into each other and separated. She was trying to capture her mood, and her mood was despairing.

She knows, Devine told himself. She knows it's me.

"I hear they might push the whole thing back," he said. "They'll keep climbing the ladder, go after even bigger names."

Gina looked at the canvas a long time.

"Adam Fishman took me out for drinks after work," she said. "He told me he has more than enough to get indictments, and they have to move now."

"Why did Adam Fishman take you out for drinks?" Devine asked.

"Because he wants to sleep with me."

Devine tried to respond but couldn't. Gina shook her head.

"Don't worry. He's tense and nervous, and I can't relax."

Devine went to his duffel to remove the letter Edna Owens had sent him.

"Where's that handbag I gave you?" he asked.

Gina washed her hands before walking to a corner of the loft where she kept her art supplies in a metal locker that reminded Devine of his high school gym class. She had repurposed it after finding it one day outside a shuttered Catholic K-12 on the Lower East Side.

She reached deep inside, brought the bag over, held it in her palm. "Evidence and shit?" she asked.

Devine reached for the note in it, then smoothed the paper on a Formica table Gina had reclaimed from a greasy spoon on Water Street that had been taken over by a celebrity chef doing a gut renovation.

Another dilettante wasting his money, Devine thought as he pointed to both note and letter.

"You're good at this stuff," he said. "Compare the handwriting in the letter to the writing at the bottom of the note."

"'GET IN ON THIS!'" Gina bent her head to look closer. "She seems excited. Almost orgasmic. Money will do that to a woman." She looked at Devine with the playfully inquisitive eyes that were the only weapon in the world that could disarm him. "What are you getting at?"

"I think that bag was Nadine's. Which raises the question of how it got in the whorehouse."

"Maybe she left it there after doing some tricks."

"Would you ever leave a bag like that behind?"

Gina shook her head. "You're good at police work when you put your mind to it."

"The woman who wrote those words put them underneath all these addresses that have dollar values beside them."

"Which were written by somebody else. Most likely a man."

"You're not bad at police work yourself. These addresses start in the West Village, at Jane Street, and run all the way down the Lower West Side to Vestry, Laight and North Moore. I've looked this over six ways to Sunday, and I can't figure it out. Most of that area's a moonscape."

"If it stops being a moonscape, all those properties will be worth a fortune."

"You sound like the mayor and the governor. They keep saying Westway's gonna turn everything around." Devine shook his head. "It'll never get built. The tree huggers have the road tied up in court, and these things always fall apart under their own weight anyway. It's just another pipe dream. That's all this city has. Pipe dreams."

He reached into his wallet and took out the crumpled paper he'd found in a nylon shell the night he went to Nadine's apartment.

"Then there's this. It's what led me to put the whorehouse under surveillance in the first place." He put the paper on the table beside the others.

"The handwriting matches," Gina said. She looked closer. "So you've got the address of the whorehouse, plus these phone numbers with initials by them. Stir that paper into the mix with the others, and the Sixty-Four Million-Dollar Question is, what does it all mean?"

Devine pointed to the phone numbers. "It's time to make some calls."

"I'll do it," Gina said.

"Why?"

"'Cause if you do it, you'll sound like a cop, and they won't talk to you."

She looked at him straight, and he felt like a man falling down an elevator shaft who was, at least for the moment, enjoying the sensation.

"You're in trouble, Terry," she said. "I wanna help."

Chapter Fourteen

he grand jury heard testimony from Paco and Erik and several other pimps, who took turns describing the exorbitant bribes they had to pay the leeches in Public Morals. Devine corroborated everything the whoremasters said, explaining what was on the tapes he had recorded and detailing exactly how much money he had doled out to various members of New York's Finest. He named every name he could remember.

After Devine was done, Fishman told him the indictments would be handed up just before the criminal justice system took a break for the weekend.

"It's all gonna hit the fan," the prosecutor said. "The papers will get hold of your name. You better change your phone number. Get something unlisted. But they'll find it anyway because they pay off people in the phone company. So put it in your wife's maiden name."

Devine thought this over. "When they figure out where I live, they'll camp out at the door."

"Is there any place they can go?" Fishman asked.

"My in-laws. They're in Tottenville. Staten Island's version of the ends of the earth."

"That's what you'll need."

"I can't stand my in-laws."

"Then you should hole up somewhere else by yourself. It could be better that way. If you and your family are separated, they might leave your wife and kids alone."

"I've got a bungalow down the shore," Devine said. "It's still off-season. Nobody's there."

"We'll send a couple of men with you. For protection."

"Protection? Who'd wanna kill me?"

"Just about everyone."

Gina wore a tight black T-shirt and ripped blue jeans. She pointed to the finished canvas, now propped against the exposed brick wall.

"Waddya think?"

"It's good. Waddya gonna do with it?"

"A gallery just opened on Franklin Street. I'm gonna ask them to look at it. Maybe they can represent me."

"An art gallery? In Washington Market? That place is a wasteland."

"They call it Tribeca now. It's all about branding."

"Doesn't matter. It's still a shit hole, and always will be."

She put her arm around him and leaned her head on his shoulder. "I wanna celebrate. Or mourn. Whenever you finish something, it's a little like death."

"You have something in mind?" he asked.

"CBGB's."

"I've never been there."

"Then there's no time to waste."

When they left the building Gina waved south toward the moribund docks at the Seaport.

"The city wants to build a mall," she said. "There goes the neighborhood."

"Never gonna happen," Devine said. "Who'd go shopping in a place like this?"

They walked north under the Brooklyn Bridge. Gina pointed out the dark image of a murder victim painted on the stones.

"Shadowman," she said.

Devine had seen his street art on the Lower East Side. "Somebody should stop him."

"Why?"

"He's defacing property."

"That's what property is there for."

They skirted Chinatown so they saw signs of human activity, but on the Bowery, every streetlight was burned out or busted and the night closed around them. An old Black guy in rags who reeked of reefer and apple wine heaved his guts into a doorway near Rivington. Junkies lolled outside boarded-up storefronts while drunks stumbled against garbage cans that had been turned upside down or tossed into the curb. A few winos warmed their hands over impromptu fires. One lowlife whistled at Gina and called out what he wanted to do. She laughed as she nibbled Devine's ear.

"What's so funny?" he asked.

"Decay inspires me." She swept her arm over the scene. "This is great."

"What's so great? The bums? The addicts?"

"Look." She pointed to the side of a crumbling building covered with graffiti. "It's the first new art form in generations. Every painter in the city is trying to figure out ways to use it."

"Visual pollution. It just proves the city has no control over anything anymore."

"Forty years from now, they'll be doing shows about graffiti in art museums."

Devine laughed. "That's like saying they'll still be listening to rap. You're just as crazy as I am."

She pressed her hand into his. "You keep saying you wanna leave New York, but you'll never be happy anywhere else. This place is fascinating, and you have no tolerance for boredom. Florida is for people who lack imagination."

Skinny white guys in torn leather jackets stood under the club's awning, and the front door vibrated from atonal waves of guitar, bass and drums. The place was violating every noise ordinance on the books, and Devine tried to figure out who was making money by looking the other way.

The inside smelled of beer, piss and sex. Chipped chairs and tables were strewn around. Photos and graffiti filled every inch of the walls, but the lighting was so dim details were impossible to discern. A battered bar lined the right side. At the far end of the room, the stage rose two feet above the floor. A four-member band was playing the loudest music Devine had ever heard and, in what he regarded as a major upset, the bassist was a woman.

Devine paid the two-dollar cover to a four-foot-eleven girl who weighed eighty pounds. He doubted she was legal but decided not to ask. Gina grabbed a table while Devine got two glasses of Heineken from the guy behind the bar. He wore a Mohawk. So did the woman working the tap at the other end. After Devine sat down, he tried to make sense of the band. The noise was furious and dissonant, the pace lightning quick.

"What's the name of the band?" he asked Gina.

"Sonic Youth."

"They are loud. What's their point?"

"There's no point. That is the point. Reagan's gonna get us all killed in a nuclear war, so nothing matters."

"Can't argue with you there."

Gina looked surprised. "You're NYPD. I figured you voted for him."

"I never vote. It only encourages them."

He looked around. A cop always did. Mostly a college crowd. Cigarette smoke fogged the air, but he didn't smell weed, and the patrons seemed reasonably sober, most likely bludgeoned into catatonia by the music.

"I made those calls," Gina said.

"Go ahead."

"The first one went through right away. The number belongs to the office of a city councilman named Dante Antonelli. DA."

"At first, I thought that might be the district attorney's office."

"I'll have something to say about that in a minute."

"Antonelli's queer."

"Queer strange or queer homosexual?"

"Both. Did you get through to him?"

"I had to come up with a story real fast, so I told his secretary that I was a friend of Martha Owens, and she had given me the councilman's number and told me I should talk to him in case anything happened to her. The secretary said she'd give the message to the councilman and asked for my number. She sounded kinda nervous. I said I was at a pay phone and I could wait a minute, but if he didn't talk to me, I'd reach out to Jamie Quinn. That was bullshit, but there was no way she could know that."

Devine brought Gina's knuckles to his lips, kissed them, told her to keep going.

"He came on the line a few seconds later. Sounded real smooth. Confident. You know how politicians are."

"A couple weeks ago, I caught him getting a blowjob from a Black kid who was hustling on the waterfront. He wasn't flustered at all. Just angry that I'd interrupted him."

"I stuck to my story and then said I was nervous because Martha was dead, and I was afraid I was gonna be next. He asked if she had ever told me anything about why somebody might wanna hurt her, and I couldn't think of anything, so I said No, she was just generally afraid for her safety. He chuckled and said lotsa people in New York were generally afraid for their safety, and then he told me not to worry my pretty little head. I felt like throttling him." Gina swigged some beer. "Then I asked why Martha had his number, and he said she'd called him a few times to talk about things that concerned her, but in the end he decided she was just a mixed-up young woman, and he hoped God had mercy on her soul."

Gina made the Sign of the Cross.

"Tell me about the second call," Devine said.

"It got picked up right away. Some really efficient-sounding woman said, 'Mr. Grubb's office.' Now, I dunno who Mr. Grubb is—I don't even know his first name—but I asked if he was in. She asked who was calling, and I gave her the same story I'd given the councilman's secretary."

"The Grubb family owns about half the real estate in the city," Devine said. "The old man started out building apartments in Brooklyn and Queens. A few years ago, he brought his son into the business. Since then, they've been buying real estate in Manhattan, which doesn't make sense because the city's falling apart, and all those properties are gonna be worthless."

"Unless they know something or can make something happen."

"Guys like them always think they can outsmart everyone else until they go bankrupt."

Onstage the bassist told the audience to go fuck themselves. The crowd cheered. Gina laughed.

"Let's do more police work," Devine said. "How did that call to Mr. Grubb go?"

"The secretary put me on hold and a few seconds later Mr. Grubb, whoever he is, came on the line."

"How old did Mr. Grubb sound?" Devine asked.

"He didn't sound like a guy who was on the verge of Social Security. About as old as you, I guess."

Devine passed on the invitation to discuss their age difference. "What did he say?"

"He started threatening me. Shouting into the phone. He said that if I called him again or talked to the media, he employed people who could track me down and sue me for everything I owned. Then he called me a cunt and hung up."

"Sounds like Grubb the Younger," Devine said. "His name's Aaron."

"Of course," Gina said. "AG."

"Tell me about the third call," Devine said.

"That one was the most disturbing."

"More disturbing than being called a cunt?"

"I felt I was getting somewhere. Like I was Nancy Drew or something. So I dial the number, and I'm ready with my spiel, and this time a guy answers, but as soon as he speaks, I hang up."

"Why?"

"Because it was Adam Fishman," she said. "AF. He woulda recognized my voice. But you were right to think Martha was in touch with the DA's office."

Devine leaned away. Three explanations came to mind:

1. Fishman was using Nadine in the investigation.
2. Fishman was a client of Nadine's.
3. Both.

Gina rested her head on Devine's shoulder, and he breathed in her perfume and perspiration before running his hands over her back. She kissed him on the neck and asked, "Who killed her?"

"I wish I knew."

Gina drained her Heineken. "I'm going to the bathroom."

"Okay."

"I want you to come with me."

As she led him through the room, the bassist looked at them with a "What the hell are they up to?" expression. Gina's head never turned while she headed down a narrow stairway before pushing open the door marked "Women."

Explosively colored graffiti covered the walls. Grime smeared the mirror over the sink. Gina locked the door. They embraced and tongued before she lowered his pants and took him in her mouth. After a while she stood, and he pushed her jeans and panties down to her ankles. She kicked them away. Spread her legs. He sank to his knees. Tasted her. She groaned softly at first, but as he went on, she got louder, and finally she shouted and shuddered and pulled him to his feet.

From upstairs, the music shook the room. Angry atonal guitars filled his ears. It was the end of the world, and he didn't care.

He turned her around. Her back was to him as she leaned over the sink. He slid into her as deeply as he could and glanced at his reflection. Even through the filth, he looked content.

She pressed against him. They could get no closer, and for the first time in his life, he understood what being joined with someone was like, and he wanted this sensation to last forever, but he realized what they both knew but had not said to each other:

This was their final time.

Chapter Fifteen

When he told Bridget about the investigation, she kept shaking her head and clicking her teeth and sighing. Devine emphasized that he'd keep his pension. When the whole thing was over, they'd move to Florida.

"What're we gonna say to the kids?" she asked.

"I'm on assignment. I have to go away for a while."

"That'll work. You're never here anyway."

Over dinner that night, Michael bit his lip at the news. Sheila cried and said she'd miss Daddy.

A day later, indictments were handed up against nineteen members of the Public Morals Division, most notably Captain Adrian Lynch. The politicians jumped in, with twenty-seven members of the City Council signing a petition that demanded an independent investigation into the vice squad, complete with televised hearings. The first name on the list was Councilman Dante Antonelli's.

By then, Devine was down the shore. Spring was late, so the days were gray. Hard winds barreled in off the ocean. He kept seeing the same six people. Two were muscleheads from the DA's office who watched his front door from an unmarked car. Once, desperate for conversation, Devine tried to talk to them, but their replies were monosyllabic, and he understood right away that they considered him a rat.

Fishman drove to see him and brought the city papers. The New York press never agreed on anything, especially the facts, but now they all called for a full-blown inquiry led by someone independent of the Police Department. As usual, Jamie Quinn's prose was the most purple.

"Asshole," Devine said as he tossed the *Daily News* into the trash.

"At least he's not writing about that girl Martha anymore," Fishman said. "Nobody is. Congratulations—you got him to change the subject."

That girl Martha had your phone number, Devine said to himself. He considered asking Fishman about it, but he was certain the man would lie, and he realized he couldn't pose that question until he knew the answer, which he would not discover while he was exiled on the Jersey shore.

"Don't get comfortable," Devine said. "Quinn will write about her again. Those All-American dipshits in New Hampshire will whisper something to him, and he'll do another column about her. He'll keep pissing all over us until somebody's arrested."

Fishman chewed on the cap of a ballpoint Bic. "I dunno if Mulligan has no information or too much. He can't make an arrest."

Devine looked over the prosecutor, a serious public servant filled with rectitude who was handling his first big case. A successful outcome would launch the political career everybody assumed he wanted.

"There's one thing I should tell you," Devine said in his trial balloon voice.

"What could you possibly tell me that I'd wanna hear?"

"I found out something interesting when we raided that whorehouse on East Thirty-Seventh."

"Go ahead." Fishman sounded like a father indulging a whiny child.

"Nadine, Martha, whatever you wanna call her—she worked there. Freelance. Her pimp didn't know."

Fishman blanched, but Devine could see the gears working in the legal mind.

"You think Almonte killed her, or was behind it?"

"I wouldn't rule it out," Devine said.

"Almonte's a big part of this investigation. Things could get complicated if it turns out he killed her, or was responsible for her death."

"Which makes it even better if you get in front of it," Devine said. "It shows you're a straight shooter who'll follow the evidence, no matter what."

Fishman's pinched face narrowed even further. He was quiet for a long time before asking, "What's your point?"

"I wanna go back to the city. I can't live with my family right now. I get that. I'll find a flophouse somewhere. I'll be all right. I can handle myself. But if you gimme a week, I'll figure out who killed her. If it turns out to be Paco, you hold a news conference and make the announcement."

Fishman laughed like an executioner who was about to hang his least favorite prisoner. "If you start going around New York unguarded, you'll be dead in five minutes."

Devine clenched and unclenched his fists. He had knocked around perps who talked to him that way. "You gonna do anything with this information?"

"I'll pass it along to Mulligan. But I won't say where I got it from. If I tell him it's from you, he'll ignore it."

Fishman glanced at the yellow legal pad he'd set in his lap. Like all lawyers, he was happiest working from notes.

"I've got something to tell you."

Devine braced.

"We're gonna do those televised hearings, and you're gonna be the star witness."

Devine stalked to the sliding door that led to the dock and beach. Sky and water were the color of ash.

"That wasn't part of the deal," he said.

"It is now."

"Maybe I should walk away. Just stop cooperating and tell you and Internal Affairs to go to hell."

Fishman rose to leave. "Then, instead of being the star witness, you'll be the star defendant. Works for me either way."

Reporters discovered that Bridget and the kids were staying with her parents, so when Devine watched the six o'clock news, he saw a platoon of journalists besieging the clapboard house on the dead-end street where he had spent so many unhappy holidays. Cameramen swarmed as his wife and children stepped out the door. Bridget threw her arms around Michael and

Sheila as they struggled toward the car. The shouted questions canceled each other in a cacophony, but Bridget's voice cut through, and it was especially sharp because she was protecting her young:

"Let us through. They have to get to school. Don'tcha have any decency?"

He stayed up waiting for the call. The phone rang just after midnight.

"I saw it on the news," he said.

"We're trapped," Bridget said. "We called the precinct. A blue-and-white came by. You know what the guys in the car did?"

Devine waited.

"They ate pizza with those animals, and after ten minutes they left. Everybody was laughing."

The next sound from her startled him, something between a gasp and a cry—the primal noise of a creature that had been wounded far more badly than it ever imagined it could be.

"How could you do this to us?" she asked.

The phone was tapped, but Devine had already admitted so many things.

"All that money I gave you over the years," he said. "Wads of cash tied in rubber bands. No explanation for them. Where did you think they came from? The Tooth Fairy?"

The line went dead.

In the morning the weather cleared. Devine took a long walk on the beach and noticed a flickering TV in one of the bungalows.

He went back toward the guy following him. The man was six-foot-four and built like a granite countertop. He was supposed to be a bodyguard, but Devine doubted he'd fight hard.

"I gotta take a leak," Devine said.

The guy raised his arm and motioned 360 degrees. "The great outdoors are all around you."

"There are laws against that down here."

Granite's jaw swung open. "Back in the city you're Al Capone, but down here you're an altar boy?"

Devine jerked his thumb toward the house where the TV was playing.

"Somebody's in there. She's watching a soap opera."

"How do you know it's a she?"

"Only old ladies with cats watch soap operas."

Devine rang the bell. Granite lingered twenty yards behind. The door swung open, and Devine was ready with a story, but the words stopped in his throat when the frame was filled by a sixteen-year-old girl tumbling out of the few clothes she was wearing.

"Waddya want?" she asked between ferocious chomps on a wad of gum.

Devine was tempted to ask why she wasn't in school. Instead, he said he was sorry to bother her, but he had to go to the bathroom.

"Why don'tcha go in the dunes?" she asked.

"What if a cop saw me?"

"Ain't no cops this time of year."

He had no doubt that this girl had been instructed to never let strangers in the house. It was the same thing he and Bridget had told Michael and Sheila. You just can't trust people.

Devine reached into his windbreaker for ID. "I'm a New York City police officer here on an assignment I can't talk about. Your local guys hate our guts, and they'll run me in if they even see me spitting on the ground."

The girl pointed beyond him. "Who's your friend?"

"My bodyguard."

"He's cute."

"I'll introduce you."

He beckoned Granite, who bounded toward them. Devine asked where the bathroom was. The girl pointed to a vague point inside the bungalow as she told Granite that she really liked bodyguards. They were so handsome and everything.

Devine found the phone in the kitchen, next to a refrigerator he was afraid to open because the room smelled like rotting fish. He dialed the number he wanted and prayed it was too early in the day for drinking.

"What is it?"

Devine smiled to himself. Of course Jamie Quinn couldn't answer a call like a normal person.

"It's me."

The newspaperman ran off a string of profanities before asking, "Where the fuck are you?"

"Down the shore. We should talk."

"I'm pissed at you. Extremely pissed."

"Take a number."

Devine heard the bark which meant Quinn had found something mildly amusing.

"There's a diner in Seaside called Vinnie's, even though it's run by Greeks," Devine said. "Be there at ten tomorrow morning and wait for me in the manager's office."

Devine, alone in his favorite booth, put the menu on the table before sidling over to Granite, who sat on a stool at the counter.

"Time for a dump," Devine murmured.

"I know way too much about your bodily functions," Granite replied. He wore the same suit as the day before. Devine detected faint odors of rotting fish and chewing gum. He patted Granite on the arm and asked how his wife and kids were doing, then walked past the pastries and made a sharp right, going by the bathroom and easing through the door to the manager's office.

A burly guy named Mikos wrapped his right hand around Devine's.

"Are you in a jam, my friend?"

"I've been in worse."

The Greek turned to Quinn, who sat in the comfortable chair usually reserved for men who needed an audience with the manager. The columnist's hand gripped a Styrofoam cup.

"This man and his family—" Mikos made a thumbs-up gesture. "Always treat me and my people with respect."

Quinn nodded like a straphanger humoring a crazy man on the subway. Mikos left the room, slamming the door with a finality that suggested they could use the office for hours. Devine put the latch in place anyway, then walked toward the deep leather chair behind the manager's desk. He felt

Quinn's eyes boring into him.

"I can explain a lotta things to you," Devine said.

"I know a lot already." Quinn started ticking off points on tobacco-stained fingers. "One, the long-rumored clean-up of Public Morals is finally taking place. Two, you're the star witness because you're the biggest crook. The crap I've heard about you—"

"Then why haven't you written about it?"

"'Cause I wanted to talk to you first. I'm in a bad position, using you as a source, but I'll come outta this better than you will. What kinda deal you pull?"

"Immunity, plus my pension for time accrued."

Quinn shook his head with the rueful admiration he'd show the mastermind of a diamond heist.

"C'mon, Jamie," Devine said. "I'm not public enemy number one. I got my hand caught in the cookie jar. I admit that. But I'm not doing anything thousands of other guys haven't done. And after all this is over, it'll be the same-old, same-old. You know that as well as I do."

The room went silent except for the sound of Quinn's breathing. The guy survived on cigars, cheeseburgers, French fries and alcohol, and Devine didn't give him more than a decade to live.

"You're a liar, Terry. D'ya know the biggest problem with lying?"

"I'll give you ten dollars if you don't tell me."

"You show contempt for the person you're lying to. You think he's so stupid he's not gonna figure out what the truth is. And you may be right— for a time. But after a while, he is gonna figure out what's what. And then he's gonna be pissed. Like I am now."

"This self-righteous act—I never liked it from priests and nuns, let alone from sinners like us."

"I've never pretended to be something I'm not. That bullshit with Lynch and the whorehouse—you set me up."

"Let me explain."

"I won't believe a word. I wanted to say that to your face."

"She worked there," Devine said. "Martha. Nadine. Whatever you wanna call her. You know that. She worked there, and I think there's a connection between that place and what happened to her."

Quinn plucked a booger from his nose. "Got any proof for this, Sherlock?"

"That bag I showed you? I'm pretty sure it's hers."

"Even if you're right, what does that prove?"

"There was a note inside it."

"Lemme guess—it reveals the name of her killer. I bet it was Professor Moriarty."

"It's a list of addresses on the Lower West Side, with dollar values attached to them. Why was someone like her interested in real estate?"

"Good question. Did you give the bag to Mulligan?"

"He'd just stick it up his ass."

"I can't disagree with you."

"I think we stumbled into something. Now that operation is up and running again a couple blocks away. If we do another raid, we could ask everybody who works there some precise questions about who Nadine's customers were. The barkeep told me there were two guys in particular who used her a lot. Maybe one of them became a stalker. Or maybe Paco found out what she was doing and decided to make an example of her. Whatever the explanation, I need to get outta here so I can—"

"You're grasping at straws, Terry. Nobody's gonna help you with anything. You haven't burned your bridges—you've napalmed them."

Quinn knocked back some coffee. Devine felt like a condemned man about to make his final request to a sadistic jailer.

"Then do me just one small favor."

"Christ, Terry, give it up."

"Talk to my wife. Write something nice about my family. Get the media dogs away from them. Bridget and the kids don't deserve what they're going through."

Chapter Sixteen

The column ran two days later with an enormous picture of Bridget, Michael and Sheila sitting together on the worn couch in his in-laws' living room and staring straight ahead with the sadly huge eyes that conveyed centuries of Celtic suffering. In the big, bold letters that Devine had assumed were reserved for wars and assassinations, the headline read: **"HIS SHAME, NOT THEIRS."**

Quinn started this way: "Bridget O'Mara married Terence Devine on Sept. 16, 1972, in Our Lady Help of Christians on Staten Island. Before God and the witnesses to the ceremony, she promised to love her husband and to honor him, and to cherish the life they would live together.

"She did not agree to go through hell because of what he did."

The columnist described the life she was leading—holed up in her parents' house, subjected to threatening calls even though they kept changing the number, her kids taunted at school by children who had once been their friends.

At least five times a day, Bridget told Quinn, Sheila said she missed her father and asked when he was coming home. "She's always been a Daddy's girl."

The column shifted to his son.

"'And Michael'—and here this strong woman gasped for air, as if her last breath were about to escape—'Michael has never been in trouble, ever. Now the nuns tell me he's getting in fights every day. If this keeps up, he'll get kicked out. I might even have to send him to public school.'"

At this point, Quinn wrote, Bridget wept.

The following Monday, in a hearing room at City Hall, Terence Devine placed his hand on a Bible and swore to tell the truth. As he sat at the long wooden witness table, he wished he could wear something that would shield his eyes from the klieg lights.

Ten yards in front, arranged in a semicircle on a six-foot-high platform designed to intimidate anyone who had to testify, were the seven members of what the press was calling the Clean-Up Squad. By virtue of his position as chairman of the City Council's Public Safety Committee, the panel was led by Dante Antonelli, Democrat of Canarsie.

Devine stated his name for the record before launching into his statement. He and Fishman had gone over it so many times he found the words meaningless. It was like the confessional—you made a rote recitation of your sins, received a rote response of absolution, and none of it meant anything.

But as Devine spoke, he became aware of being at the center of a riveted silence. The events he was so familiar with and that had seemed normal parts of life—the shakedowns, payoffs and robberies, the mechanics of how the pad worked, the favors he routinely performed for criminals— fascinated an audience that wanted to believe in the honesty of the people who were supposed to protect the city.

After a while, Devine began glancing up from the typewritten pages he was holding so he could look over the members of the committee. All were male, so they understood the urges that drove men to break the laws Public Morals had been created to enforce. Six were white; Devine was certain he had once rousted the Black minister sitting at the panel's edge from a brothel full of teenagers on Lenox Avenue.

At the end of his statement, Devine expressed the remorse Fishman had insisted upon, and for the first time in his life he understood just how badly words tasted when they were put in your mouth. When he was done, he took a long drink of water while Antonelli leaned his head close to a microphone.

"That was a remarkable opening statement, Officer Devine. While I deplore your actions, I appreciate your candor, and I look forward to your cooperation as we remove the cancer of corruption from Public Morals."

Devine wanted to roll his eyes like an adolescent schoolgirl.

In addition to Antonelli and the clergyman, the committee consisted of a banker, a lawyer, a college dean and the head of a good government group. (Devine felt like telling him: "Frankly, sir, I'm in favor of bad government. It's the only kind that's effective.") At the far end of the platform—sitting at the edge, Devine told himself, so he could rush into the wings the moment something went wrong—was Aaron Grubb, real-estate scion, publicity hound, and reputed client of Nadine LaFleur's.

Devine wanted to ask him about his relationship with the dead woman, but his mind snapped to his present circumstances when the clergyman asked if members of the Public Morals squad discriminated against the Black community.

"Not at all, Reverend. We didn't care who we took money from."

The crowd laughed. Fishman, who was sitting next to him, murmured that Devine should take it easy with the wisecracks.

Antonelli adjourned the hearing shortly after eleven. No matter the occasion, Devine marveled at the ability of the public sector to allow plenty of time for lunch. As he scanned the room, he noticed talking heads from the newscasts working their mouths in front of cameras. Off to the side, Jamie Quinn jotted something in a reporter's notebook. Devine kept looking around in the vague hope that Bridget would be there in reluctant support of the man she had married.

His eyes stopped. For a moment, he believed he had conjured her as a form of wish fulfillment. She was dressed in the style he liked to call total artist—torn leather jacket, ripped jeans, hair straight down her back, the body he craved filling out a black T-shirt that said "We're Not in Kansas Anymore." His eyes locked with Gina's, and he felt she was telling him that she didn't care what he had done—she wanted to be in his sight and to keep him in hers, even if they had to keep their distance.

Fishman made a dismissive motion in her direction. "She's a temp."

She's the hottest woman in New York, Devine thought. You want her as badly as I do.

"She's an artist," Devine said.

"You know her?" Fishman sounded surprised.

"We've met."

"What's she doing here?"

She loves me, Devine felt like saying. And, so help me God, I love her too.

In the afternoon, the committee members took turns excoriating Devine, who flashed back to tenth grade, when the Christian Brothers of Ireland would berate him for various violations of his high school's many rules. From those encounters he had taken away one great lesson: eventually, they get tired of yelling at you.

About four o'clock, the Black minister—he was wearing his clerical collar, which Devine assumed was for the cameras' benefit—cleared his throat and said he had looked through all the material the committee staff had gathered, and frankly there was one item in particular that troubled him deeply.

Devine stirred in his seat and tried to look interested.

"Correct me if I'm wrong, Officer, but it seems to me that you took money from just about anybody who was engaged in the activity that is commonly referred to as 'pimping,'" the minister said.

I'm sure that's how you refer to it as well, Devine thought.

He brought his mouth close to the microphone. "That's correct, Sir."

Black men loved it when white men called them "Sir." All that bullshit about respect.

"There are houses of ill repute throughout this city," said the minister, whose name was Bellows. "Places where men go to procure sexual favors from women. And you received bribes from the people who operate those establishments so they could remain in business."

"I've been candid about that with this committee."

"But there are other places as well," Bellows said. "I'm hesitant to talk about this matter in public because it disgusts me so. On the other hand, I feel, with every fiber of my being, that these establishments are the greatest blight New York is facing, and our toleration of these dens of the worst form of licentiousness is leading us down the same path that led to the destruction of Sodom and Gomorrah."

For a second, Devine considered asking the minister a question that had always nagged at him, but that he'd never had the nerve to ask a representative of Catholicism: Why does God insist on punishing people for having fun?

"I am speaking about places where men seek out pleasure from other men," Bellows said. "Where homosexual activity is tolerated, even encouraged. These beings—and I use that term loosely—engage in the most perverted acts imaginable, and you saw fit to profit from them."

Behind him, Devine heard a few mutterings about how awful those goddamn queers were. Bellows leaned away from his microphone, folded his arms across his chest, and shook his head slowly, as if he were a judge who believed his order of execution was too lenient.

Devine looked at the other members of the committee. He relaxed a bit because there had been no question, only pontificating, but the white men on the panel were all looking at the minister as if he had raised an important point they hadn't considered, and wanted him to continue.

Bellows suppressed a smile as he brought his head close to the microphone. This was probably the first time in his life that a group of Caucasians had encouraged him to browbeat a white man.

"What do you have to say for yourself?" the minister asked.

"I'll be honest about it, Reverend—I don't understand what your point is."

The clergyman's tone became thunderous, reaching back through centuries to tap into the fire and brimstone that had wreaked so much righteous destruction.

"You want to know my point?" he asked. "I think it's obvious what my point is, but I suppose I have to spell it out for you."

Devine reached for his water. Beside him, Fishman whispered, "You'll just have to take it."

"My point is that you took money from degenerates," Bellows said. "This type of decadence has done more to debase the city than anything I can think of. You encouraged sodomy, and now New York is a cesspool—all because of men like you."

As applause swept the room, Devine expected Antonelli to gavel the crowd into silence while issuing demands for order and decorum, but instead the councilman leaned back in his chair and flashed a smile so brief Devine was certain he was the only one who saw it.

Bellows pushed himself away from the microphone. Now it was Grubb's turn, and he pursed his lips before saying, "Where does this—" and here he almost choked on the next word—"homosexual activity take place?"

"The West Side piers, mostly," Devine said.

"The shipping companies and the city abandoned them years ago. Jet travel and containerization made them obsolete."

"But they're still there, and nature abhors a vacuum."

"What do you mean by that?" Grubb asked.

Devine rubbed his hands over his face. The TV lights were inducing a headache. "As long as those piers exist, someone or something will use them."

"They've been overrun by perverts."

"If it bothers you so much," Devine said, "why don't you use your influence to get the city to tear them down?"

"That's not the point." Grubb sounded peeved—a man surrounded by servants who'd never heard backtalk before. "Police officers should do what they're told. You guys have to make sure those places aren't being used for immoral and illegal activity."

I know more about you than you think, Devine felt like saying. You enjoy immoral and illegal activity just fine.

"Then that activity will just move someplace else," Devine said. "Right now, it's at the piers, so at least it's away from the main parts of the city. Nobody else wants to go there. You shouldn't, either, if you know what's good for you."

The audience laughed again. Grubb scowled. The members of the committee all looked to Antonelli to pick up their tattered banner, so the councilman lowered his distinguished face close to his microphone.

"Your attitude toward law enforcement is somewhat—" Antonelli dragged out his thought, as if he was rummaging through his head for the right word. "Fungible," he said at last.

"Why do you say that, Councilman?"

"Let's assume Public Morals truly cracked down on homosexual prostitution at the piers. How can you be so sure that activity would move somewhere else instead of being wiped out?"

Are you really asking me that question? Devine thought. You'll cruise for a gay hustler anywhere you can find one.

"It's the law of supply and demand, Councilman. They don't call it the world's oldest profession for nothing."

More laughter. Antonelli smiled with the air of a laidback professor conducting a meandering seminar out on the quad on a warm spring day.

"You're a witty man, Officer, and I'm not going to pretend I can trade quips with you. But I am wondering what gives you the power to decide which laws to enforce, and which ones to ignore?"

"We pretty much ignored all of them, Councilman."

Another round of laughter, but Devine clued in on Antonelli's eyes, which were steely gray.

"In certain ways, Officer, I'm like you," Antonelli said. "I went to Catholic schools, and I heard many sermons about the weaknesses of the flesh. But does that mean we should do nothing to stop behavior that most people in this city regard as depraved?"

Devine heard Fishman mutter that he better be careful about what he said.

"You ever walk around this city, Councilman?" Devine asked.

"All the time, Officer."

"Then why don't you do something about it?"

"Go ahead, Officer," Antonelli said. "Enlighten me about public policy."

"Most of the neighborhoods are falling apart," Devine said. "The men I work with go into sections of New York most of you haven't seen in years. Everything is dingy and broken, and nothing ever gets cleaned or repaired. Buildings collapse. Punks cover subway cars with graffiti. The piers have been left to rot. And you gentlemen—who have the power and the money and the authority to change things—you just sit there and tell yourselves you're doing a wonderful job, and it's all fine. But it's all going to hell, and the people of this city know it.

"In my first week in Public Morals, I busted a brothel in Harlem and arrested sixteen men for soliciting prostitutes, most of whom were high school students."

Devine stared directly at Bellows, who looked as if he was convinced his life was about to end.

"And do you know what happened to all those collars I made?" Devine asked.

His voice was rising. There were no other sounds in the room.

"They all walked. I was told by my superiors that we do not arrest johns. Two days later, that brothel was back in business, and the guys who ran it offered me money to let them stay open with no interruptions. 'Why bother?' they asked me. It was a good question. It still is.

"So, Councilman, maybe you can enlighten me. Maybe you can enlighten all the other police officers in this city, if any are left after the latest round of layoffs. Maybe you can answer the question we ask ourselves every single day as we put our lives on the line."

Devine paused. The room was dead quiet.

"What the hell is the point of enforcing a law if nobody's gonna be convicted for breaking it?"

Applause swept the room. The crowd stood and cheered. Devine glanced backward and saw Gina pumping her fist.

Chapter Seventeen

The DA's office stashed him in a sixth-floor efficiency in a building near the hospitals in the East Thirties. The room's tiny window looked over an alley where orderlies dumped medical waste. The guys who had guarded him down the shore now took turns sitting outside his door.

The Antonelli Commission heard new witnesses—madams, prostitutes and a few cops from Public Morals, including Finley and Burke, who had joined Devine in flipping. But Devine had no interest in watching on TV until the committee summoned Paco.

The pimp's hair was trimmed and combed. His blue blazer must have come from Barney's. He was dressed almost as well as his lawyer, the impeccably groomed Rolando Ortega.

"So Officer Devine wound up handling all your payoffs?" Grubb asked.

"That's correct," Paco said.

"And why was that?"

"A buncha different guys from Public Morals used to come around asking for money. Officer Devine said he could take care of everyone. I'm a businessman—I'm always looking to streamline operations and cut expenses."

"I understand entirely," Grubb said.

Paco said the pad worked on a schedule, and bribing the police was just part of his overhead. Devine knew all this, so he was about to switch over to "The Match Game" when he heard Paco say, with the urgency of a penitent trying to mitigate his transgressions, "There's one thing I wanna tell you."

The pimp leaned close to his lawyer. They almost bumped heads.

"The other day," Paco said, "this commission heard testimony about all the hustling by the maricons on the West Side piers. You were horrified, and I was, too. Everybody in the city felt the same way. That kind of behavior has no place in decent society. I'm not proud of what I've done, but I never went near nothing like that, and I hope this commission gets the city to clean that stuff up."

Antonelli let the ensuing applause drag on before bringing his gavel down in a perfunctory attempt at quiet. After the noise subsided, he said, "I certainly agree with at least some of your sentiments, Mr. Almonte. You only used women in your operation?"

"That's correct," Paco said.

"In fact, didn't your business supply what the media refers to as 'high-priced call girls'?"

"I had a top-flight clientele." Paco was a capitalist proud of his product.

"But your line of work wasn't free of danger," Antonelli said. "One of your workers wound up dead recently. Murdered, in fact."

Paco turned to Ortega with a furious what-the-hell-are-these-Anglos-trying-to-pull-on-me expression. The men whispered fiercely for close to a minute, and Devine picked up some muttered Spanish. With his shaky grasp of the language, he thought Paco was telling his lawyer that he was afraid these bastardos were trying to pull some bigtime mierda, and he'd talk about this matter only in private.

Ortega coughed into the microphone. "With all due respect, Councilman, my client can't figure out how this line of questioning is relevant to the commission's mandate."

"The Nadine LaFleur case has been all over the news," Antonelli said. "She worked for Mr. Almonte, and she was killed in a particularly brutal manner."

Battered body on a bed. Blood-smeared clothes. Ransacked apartment. No sign of forced entry.

Antonelli talked on: "If I don't point this out in public session today, the newspapers certainly will on their front pages tomorrow."

Devine recognized the look that Antonelli had fixed on Paco—the hard and satisfied gaze of a man with authority who was about to bring down all of it on a schlimazel, just because he could.

"Mr. Almonte," Antonelli intoned in a bass that seemed to suck all the air from the room, "do you have any idea who could have killed Ms. LaFleur, or why?"

Paco and his lawyer conferred again, this time with their hands over the microphones.

"Come on, Mr. Almonte," Antonelli said. "It's a simple question."

Paco swept his eyes over the commissioners with the aggrieved air that comes to criminals who feel they've been double-crossed. "I got no response to that," he said.

"I can compel you to answer my question," Antonelli said.

"If you do that, Councilman," Ortega said, "my client will invoke his rights under the Fifth Amendment."

"I'm not sure he's allowed," Antonelli said. "This isn't a judicial proceeding."

"Coulda fooled me," the lawyer said.

Antonelli flashed a plastic smile. "Your client has immunity."

"Not for this matter."

"Constitutional protections don't apply to foreigners," Antonelli said in a tone of confident one-upsmanship.

Ortega engaged in a quarter-hearted attempt to suppress a grin. Devine knew what was coming. Antonelli was one of those ambitious men who looked a lot more intelligent than he actually was.

"My client is a native of Puerto Rico," the lawyer said, rolling the R's in the island's name with extra flair. "That means he's a United States citizen, whether you like it or not."

Before the audience could react, Antonelli swung down his gavel and announced a ten-minute recess. The camera followed as he stalked offstage. Devine expected the councilman to hurry into the wings, where he could berate his staff, an action that always allowed politicians to regain their composure. Instead, Antonelli strode toward media row, where Jamie

Quinn stepped out from the pack. As the columnist put his hand on the councilman's back and drew him near for conversation, Devine suddenly understood where those questions about Nadine LaFleur had come from.

The knock at the door unnerved him. Devine was expecting no one, so he walked over noiselessly, wishing he had his service revolver, glancing around for something he could use as a weapon.

"Who?" he asked.

"Fishman."

Devine undid the chain and three bolts before pulling the door just wide enough to let the prosecutor slide through. Fishman wore his usual off-the-rack suit and fraying tie, and his thinning hairs were askew. Devine was still in his pajamas and didn't know what time it was.

The prosecutor held up the front page of the *Daily News*. "You see this?"

Devine shook his head and looked, although he had a good idea of what it would say. On the front page Jamie Quinn's logo was submerged by a huge headline that screamed, "**MARTHA'S PIMP STONEWALLS**". A sweet-looking picture of the dead woman, doubtless supplied by her parents, stared out at the newspaper's million-plus readers.

"We've gotta make this thing go away," Fishman said.

"I told you Quinn would come back to it," Devine said. "Let me outta here, and I'll pin it on someone."

Fishman sat on the battered brown couchette and unlatched his Gucci briefcase. Devine noticed a paperback copy of *Sophie's Choice*.

"You think we're gonna let the most corrupt cop in the history of New York roam the city to solve the biggest murder case in years? What're you doing when you're here by yourself at night—dropping acid?"

The prosecutor took out a yellow legal pad and riffed through its pages.

"The commission wants you back," he said.

"Why?"

"To rake you over the coals."

Devine remembered the priests and nuns talking about purgatory. The torments were as bad as hell, though the punishment lasted only an eon or two.

Fishman went on. "I have heard, unofficially, that they are extremely pissed at you. In fact, they're looking for a way to abrogate your immunity deal. We've told them to take a hike."

"But I've gotta jump through hoops again."

"They say they have new information. I suspect they just wanna berate you for a few hours."

Devine walked to the tiny window and looked down at a junkie scavenging the garbage for needles.

"I can't do it," he said.

"It's only one day," Fishman said.

Devine strode toward the prosecutor. Everything he kept trying to bottle up started to come out. "I gotta get outta here. Outta my life and outta this city. New York is dying. All that rot on the West Side, in Harlem, Brooklyn, the Bronx—it's all gonna spread until there's nothing worthwhile, even on Fifth Avenue."

"You don't know a thing," Fishman said. "There are plans to turn this city around. Great plans. My family is involved with them, and we're not gonna fail."

"Pipe dreams. That's the only thing guys like you can offer."

"Once the city and state get the go-ahead for Westway, they're gonna demolish the rest of the West Side Highway and clear out the piers and build a park that'll run all the way down the Hudson to the Battery," Fishman said. "The road will be underground, the whole thing will be beautiful, people will pay top dollar to live there, and the men with money will make it happen because they're gonna make even more money when the project's done. You think you know how the world works, but you don't have a clue. My family does real estate. Money always wins."

"You went to a goddamn prep school," Devine said. "I'm a street cop, so I know a shitload more than you do."

"And I know that one of the reasons the streets got so bad is because scumbags like you have been patrolling them. You've taken graft from every crook in the city, and all you do is whine about the lousy deal you're getting.

You brought all your problems upon yourself, Officer." He spit out the last word.

Devine balled his fists and stepped toward Fishman. He considered swinging his fist into the lawyer's nose.

"We'll clean up the streets, too," Fishman said, "once we get rid of vermin like you."

Devine was tired of taking it—from the press and from his wife, and most of all from the self-satisfied cretins presiding over New York City's decline and fall. He raised his arm, but before he could do anything else, Fishman clocked him in the mouth.

Devine fell backward over a glass-topped coffee table. Blood spurted from his lower lip. Shards from the tabletop sliced his skin.

Skinny bastard's stronger than he looks, Devine thought.

The apartment door burst open. Granite stood in the frame.

"What's going on here?" he asked.

"We had a disagreement," Fishman said.

Granite surveyed the scene and smiled. "Good."

A housekeeper cleaned the mess while Devine took a shower. The cuts were superficial, and although his lip was swelling, none of his teeth were loose. When he stepped out of the bathroom, he noticed an envelope lying face down on the floor. It must have been shoved under the door.

Devine looked at the thing a few minutes before fetching a pair of gloves from the cheap cardboard dresser, walking slowly to the spot where the envelope lay, and bending down as carefully as he could.

In a James Bond movie, he thought, this thing would emit toxic smoke the moment I touch it. I'd wake up in a private plane with the villain and his beautiful mistress, flying high over the Alps.

He paused his reverie.

No matter what those cretins have planned for me, he said to himself, it'd be a lot better than staying here.

Devine went to the pantry and took out a knife. When he returned to the envelope, he lowered himself as far as his knees would allow, then slipped the knife under it and flipped it over—and started to laugh because he recognized Da's handwriting immediately, as well as the return address in Clearwater. Da had sent the letter to Terence Devine, care of Police Headquarters, because the old man was still a legend in the department, and he knew somebody would make sure his message got through.

Devine brought the letter over to the table near the window. He wanted good light while he read. The envelope itself felt light, and he figured it contained a single page. Da had never been much for writing, but it would be good to hear from him.

Devine opened the thing and began reading.

"Terence—"

He was back home and little, and his father, who usually called him Terry or Kiddo or Sonny Boy with a tone of lilting affection, was in one of his black Irish moods when nothing and nobody could please him. His voice would grow ice cold, and he would refer to his son by his formal Christian name.

"I've heard about what you've done, and I am deeply ashamed."

Devine gulped. Of all the crippling emotions one could bring upon an Irishman, shame was by far the worst.

"You've dishonored a name that has been revered in the department for generations. Even worse are the feelings your mother and I have had."

Devine began a silent pleading: I can make it up to you, Da. To Ma as well. Once I talk to you, I'll explain why I did it, and you'll understand.

"The police force is a brotherhood. Whatever else happens, brothers do not turn on their own kind."

He found himself arguing with the words on paper: I was a target. They would have sent me to prison for decades unless I cooperated. Is that what you want? To visit me in jail?

"I thought I raised you better than this. I thought I taught you that, no matter what, an officer shields his brothers."

For a moment, Devine saw himself after all this was over, down in Florida at his folks' house on the canal, offering explanations as rapidly as his mouth could produce them.

"I'm trying to keep my hand steady, but my pen is shaking in anger. I cannot abide what you've done."

Devine saw himself in supplication, prostrated before his parents on the tile floor in their screened-off porch as he sought expiation. And then he realized it would be futile because his parents were Irish, so they belonged to a race that had never believed in forgiveness.

"I do not want to think of you ever again. And so I won't."

Chapter Eighteen

Fishman led him in through a side entrance to dodge the media. As they approached the hearing room, Aaron Grubb motioned to the prosecutor, and Fishman whispered that he had to talk to the guy. Devine slowed to watch them. They stood mouth to ear, almost as if they were lovers.

They're setting me up, Devine said to himself.

He straightened his back and walked into the hearing room alone. He had worn his best suit because he wanted to look good despite the bruises on his face. Flashbulbs popped. Lights from the TV cameras swiveled in his direction. For a moment he was blinded, but he told himself to keep moving forward, to look serious but not grim, although his eyes darted because he hoped she was there.

At the edge of the spectators' section, hair swept back in a ponytail, Gina wore the navy blue dress and a light smattering of makeup that indicated she was working in the DA's office that day. An animal print coat was draped over her shoulders, and he understood she might have to leave in a hurry, but he was grateful she had decided to show up, however fleetingly. Her lips were taut. Her eyes were narrow. He touched her mind, the way lovers do, and sensed she wanted to cry out a warning.

If I go down, he responded silently, I'm taking these bastards with me.

At the witness table, Devine poured a glass of water. Cameras clicked. Committee members had the look of Romans particularly anxious to release the lions. Councilman Antonelli banged his gavel and spoke into the microphone:

"What happened to you, Officer?"

"I slipped in the shower."

"I wish I could say I was sorry to hear that."

Laughs from the crowd, which had been packed against Terence Devine.

"I wanna introduce somebody to the audience," Antonelli said.

Cameras pointed toward the rear of the room. Devine turned. Mulligan, face more florid than ever, waddled toward him as quickly as his bulging middle would allow.

"Will you state your name for the record?" Antonelli asked.

"Detective Francis Xavier Mulligan, Homicide Task Force."

"And why are you here, Detective Mulligan?"

Mulligan stopped at the table. The room grew still as a tomb.

"I am here to arrest this man, Terence Devine, for the murder of Martha Owens, a.k.a. Nadine LaFleur."

Devine's ears filled with an explosion of noise that reminded him of an express train applying the emergency brakes. He couldn't see, and he couldn't think, and he couldn't even move as Mulligan reached into his jacket, brought out a pair of handcuffs, and wrapped them around his wrists.

Reporters and photographers swarmed. Somewhere in the distance, Antonelli banged his gavel and asked for order.

Devine tried to raise his voice above the din. "This is bullshit."

Mulligan ticked off points like a doctor delivering a fatal prognosis. "I've got an eyewitness who says you went into the victim's apartment the night of her death. I've got your fingerprints in her living room, bedroom and closet. I've got reports of a loud argument between the victim and a man the night you went in there. Most of all, I've got your buddy Taco."

Devine worked his jaw, but no words came out.

"It took a while to break him down," Mulligan said. "But we did. Taco told us he sent you to get money from her that night. After you got there, you beat that woman to death."

Devine felt his stomach drop the way it did when he was riding a rollercoaster with his kids. He flashed to the animal print Gina was wearing and to the coat he'd seen hanging in the Murray Hill brothel, and in a sudden awful epiphany, he thought he could piece together what had happened to Nadine.

"This is a fix," he said.

Mulligan snorted. "Why didn't you tell us you were in that woman's apartment that night?"

"I'm not a murderer," Devine said. Silently, he added, My children cannot see what is happening.

And then the reporters crowded around, screaming out questions that canceled each other while photographers and cameramen recorded the scene. Mulligan put his hand on Devine's elbow and leaned in close.

"Frankly," he murmured, "I don't care if you did it or not. I can make you for this, and that's what I'm gonna do."

II

Part Two

2022

Chapter One

She needed a project, so she found herself in a converted warehouse in Bushwick talking to an intense thirtysomething in a pantsuit.

Exposed brick, Sheila said to herself as she looked around. Big windows with an open floor plan and lots of natural light. I can do something with this.

"We get so many pleas for help," Pantsuit said. "More and more every day. We can't possibly handle them all."

Sheila nodded. Pantsuit was managing director of the Justice Project, a nonprofit that took on cases from prisoners who insisted they'd been wrongfully convicted.

Skepticism, Sheila reminded herself. Be skeptical of the system, but extend the same attitude toward the do-gooders. Almost all those people writing letters to this place have been incarcerated for a reason.

"We hafta do triage," said Pantsuit, real name Tara O'Bannon, one of those earnest liberals who thought she could change the world if people just listened. "We get thousands of requests a year, but we can only take the ones that have the best chance of success."

"If we do this … "

Sheila turned to the man beside her. Joel Moscowitz was chugging a ginormous latte with the fervor of a grad student who was convinced he'd have to stay awake five nights in a row to complete his thesis. He was skeletal and twenty-nine, and his curly hair clumped atop his head like a tumbleweed that refused to move. Sheila was Creative. Joel was Business.

"You should focus on a single case," he told Sheila. "From beginning to end."

Tara's shoulders sagged in disappointment. "We'd really like it if you focused on the thrust of our work."

Joel cut her off with a noise that sounded like a buzzer at the end of a basketball game. "Overviews are boring. People like stories."

Joel spent most of his hours navigating the new ways of distributing movies, which was a challenge because they changed every day.

"You got in touch with me because of the film I did about the Fergusons," Sheila said to Tara.

Sheila Devine's last documentary had focused on a Black family in Queens whose mom and dad were first responders. Early in the pandemic they worked double shifts, but their kids were home all the time after the schools went remote. With everyone cooped up in a small house in Springfield Gardens, they all got Covid, and the parents went from being heroic EMTs to desperate patients gasping for breath on ventilators.

"I coulda done a cosmic look at the virus," Sheila said, "but nobody woulda cared. You make the problem come to life by narrowing it down."

"We get so many cases," Tara said. "Picking one is unfair."

"Fair has nothing to do with it," Joel said.

Tara sighed and led them to her cubicle, which was adorned with a small poster that said, "HUMPTY DUMPTY WAS PUSHED."

"Here's one," she said seconds after booting her computer. "Guy was a janitor. Haitian-American. A woman who worked in one of the offices he cleaned was found dead at her desk. Bludgeoned with a blunt object. Cops never found out what it was. They brought in our guy for questioning, and he wound up confessing, but they never let him talk to a lawyer. He swears he didn't do it, and there was no physical evidence. We're trying to look at the DNA, but the State's Attorney is fighting us every step of the way."

"State's Attorney?" Sheila said. "Where's the case?"

"Orlando."

Sheila shuddered at the memory of taking her kids to Disney World. By the end of their trip to the Happiest Place on Earth, she felt homicidal.

"Florida is my least favorite state," she said. "And that's really saying something."

Joel squinted at the screen. "The guy has priors—two raps for assault and battery. You gotta do better."

Tara clicked her mouse a few times. "How 'bout this? Latino. Father of four. Cops say he set fire to his own house to collect the insurance money. Problem was, his children were asleep in their beds at the time."

"That's awful," Sheila said.

Tara went on. "He was convicted 'cause of the same thing you find in a lot of these cases—he confessed, but then he recanted. He made his confession after he'd been questioned for hours without talking to an attorney."

"Physical evidence against him?" Joel asked.

"None."

"You mentioned kids," Sheila said. "What about a wife?"

"She died a couple years before the fire."

Sheila felt suspicious. "How?"

"Cancer."

Sheila felt better. "Where did this happen?"

"Texas. Near Houston."

Sheila had never been there. She heard it sprawled.

Joel squinted again and pointed at something. "What's this?"

"A list of his meds."

"Meds?" Sheila asked.

"He has a history of depression," Tara said.

Sheila glanced at Joel and shook her head a bit.

"You'd be depressed, too," Tara said, "if you were on Death Row for a crime you didn't commit."

"Got anyone else?" Sheila asked.

Tara resumed mousing while muttering some words Sheila could not comprehend until she heard "agita."

"This came in yesterday," Tara said. "Snail mail. The intern typed it in, but we haven't had a chance to vet it."

"What is it?" Joel asked in a bored voice while he fished out his iPhone.

"It was the name," Tara said. She motioned to Sheila. "Devine. Just like yours."

Sheila froze.

"Happened in the early Eighties. I doubt there's DNA."

A vise gripped the base of Sheila's spine.

"Guy was a cop. NYPD. Convicted of murder. He says he was railroaded because he was cooperating with a corruption probe."

Sheila looked at Joel, whose eyebrows were knit in concentration. He was either playing solitaire or sexting his girlfriend.

"That's my father," Sheila said.

"No," she said as they stood in line at the coffee shop in Fort Greene.

"C'mon, Sheila."

"No fucking way."

"Hear me out."

And now she found herself channeling Sir Ben Kingsley's character in *Sexy Beast*—her all-time favorite movie performance—as she used a faux Cockney accent to shout: "No! No! No! No! No fucking way! No fucking way!"

The baristas stood at attention. They all knew Sheila was the boss's wife.

Joel ordered a latte. "You through?"

"Not yet." Sheila asked for espresso. Might as well get totally wired, she said to herself.

"Listen to me."

Sheila felt like covering her ears with her hands while making nonsense sounds. Sometimes she enjoyed getting in touch with her inner six-year-old.

"I met you at this place," Joel said as he pointed behind the counter. "I was working here while I was a film geek at NYU. Almost a decade ago."

"A lifetime in this business."

"We've had lots of success. The *Times* likes you, we do well at festivals, you even get high marks on Rotten Tomatoes. But there's one thing that's eluded you."

Sheila's body and spirit sagged. "A fucking Oscar."

"You've never even been nominated."

They took their drinks to a window table and glanced at a street lined with trees, strollers and well-scrubbed brownstones. Sheila pointed to his drink.

"You ever think you consume too much caffeine?"

"No."

Sheila sipped. The espresso blew some cobwebs out of her frontal lobes. "Do you have any idea how painful this is for me?"

"Great pain leads to great art."

"You don't believe that any more than I do."

She noticed her husband walking toward them with the rolling gait of the sprinter he'd been while he was growing up in Jamaica. Wesley McBride had dreads to his shoulders and the mischievous eyes of a man who was slightly bemused by just about everything. His apron bore the name of his microchain: CariBean.

"I'm tempted to ask you two to use your indoor voices." Wesley still spoke with the lilt of the islands.

Sheila jerked her thumb toward Joel. "This putz wants me to do a film about my father."

Wesley straddled the back of a wooden chair while his brown eyes looked deep into his wife.

He's gonna disarm me, Sheila thought. Bastard's been disarming me for twenty years.

"It's about time," he said.

At dusk, after everyone was home, Sheila went into the kitchen and began boiling water for pasta. She'd whip up a salad, too, using the last of the vinaigrette in the refrigerator. She prayed to Bacchus that a bottle of Chianti was stashed somewhere in the house.

She heard the kids upstairs, hoped they were doing their homework, realized she was kidding herself. Dylan thudded around his room with the heavy tread of the adolescent male. When he was up there with his friends, they sounded like a herd of elephants. A junior at Brooklyn Tech, he recently informed his parents that he was thinking about studying architecture. It was never too early to look at colleges, and Sheila blanched whenever she thought of the cost.

In the room next to his, Bethany moved with the light step of a girl who'd taken ballet classes for years. An eighth-grader angling for a spot at LaGuardia, her hormones were running rampant, so she sometimes shut herself in her space for hours while FaceTiming her friends.

Sheila drained the romaine, tomatoes, carrots and mushrooms that she had tossed into the colander. When the pasta water boiled, she dumped in the rigatoni, which she planned to top with an allegedly homemade marinara she'd bought at the food co-op.

Wesley's quick footfalls grew louder in the narrow hallway. He glided in, kissed her on the cheek, asked if there was anything he could do.

"You'll be my hero if you find a bottle of Chianti."

He returned in three minutes and reached into the cupboard for wine glasses. The sound of the popping cork was the best noise she'd heard all day.

"You look hollow-eyed," he said as he poured.

"I spent hours in front of the computer," she said as she put plates on the table.

"For your project," he said, only half believing it.

She slugged some wine and appreciated the way it dulled her brain. Sometimes she thought she thought too much.

"If I do it, I'll spend a lotta time mucking around in the early Eighties." She shuddered. "The hair, the clothes … "

During dinner, Sheila asked the kids ritualistic questions about their school day and received the standard noncommittal grunts. She gulped some Chianti, cleared her throat, and told her children she had something to discuss.

Dylan spoke first: "Dad texted me. He says you're gonna do a new movie."

Bethany next: "That means you're gonna get snarky and sullen."

Dylan asked: "It's that thing about the Justice Project, right?"

Sheila drank more and hoped there was another bottle in the house. "It's about my father."

She had expected an explosion of noise from her kids. Instead, Dylan glopped more marinara on his pasta, while Bethany broke off another piece of garlic bread.

"I was expecting more of a reaction," Sheila said.

"Why are you doing this?" Dylan asked, mouth full.

"Because of the Oscars," Bethany said.

"What?" Sheila hoped she sounded incredulous.

"Bethany's onto something." Dylan swallowed. "What did *The New York Times* call you? 'One of the best documentarians working today.' And you've never even been nominated."

"It's because you're a woman," Bethany said.

Wesley disappeared for a moment before returning with a second bottle of Chianti. Sheila congratulated herself for marrying the right man, but despite her feelings, she couldn't stop herself from sounding accusatory as she addressed him: "You said it was about time I did a film about my father."

Wesley moved head and dreads in assent while pouring more wine for his wife.

"Years ago," he said, "when we started seeing each other, after you told me about what had happened with your dad, I talked about him to some of my relatives—the ones who've been in this country a long time, even longer than I have. "

Sheila's eyebrows shot up. He had never told her this.

"They all believe he was set up," Wesley said.

"Did they have any special knowledge," Sheila asked, "or were they making an educated guess?"

"The latter." Now it was his turn to gulp Chianti. "I'm gonna make a point about white people. Don't get upset."

"I can't guarantee that."

Wesley went on. "White people tend to believe the things people in authority tell them. But since the people in authority in this hemisphere built their wealth and power by enslaving Black people, we tend to believe they're full of crap at best and malicious at worst."

"How is that relevant to what happened to my father?" Sheila asked.

"The successor to slavery is the so-called criminal justice system. White people think the wheels of justice turn in a proper and precise manner, and everyone in prison is there for a good reason. Black people know that the system exists to punish anybody who tries to disturb it."

Silence at the table. Bethany finally broke it.

"Waddya gonna do?" she asked her mother.

"I've made no commitments," Sheila said. "But I owe it to Joel to engage in due diligence."

"Where do you start?" Dylan asked.

"The prisons in this state are decades behind the times," Sheila said. "I have to write my father a letter."

Bethany looked puzzled. "What's a letter?"

Chapter Two

In the visitors' room, she stared at the inch-thick glass partition that separated her from the seat her father would occupy. She was afraid she might gasp or cry when she first saw him, swept away in an emotional surge that would destroy her ability to focus.

A few minutes later, an overweight guard in a stained uniform brought forward a prisoner in a short-sleeved orange jumpsuit who looked surprisingly good for his age: steel gray hair matted on his head, well-defined biceps and triceps from thousands of hours in the jailhouse gym, still-chiseled cheeks and jawline complementing the ramrod-straight posture of an ex-cop who never took shit from anyone. Terence Devine was defiant, not penitent, so she found it impossible to feel sorry for him.

Sheila picked up the receiver that would let them communicate. Her father grabbed the one on his side. He looked her over, taking her all in, but she couldn't tell if he regarded her as somebody he loved or as a possible perp.

"How have you been?" he asked.

"I'm okay," she said. No thanks to you, she added silently.

"Your letter didn't say much. You make movies?"

"That's right."

"Hollywood?"

"Documentaries."

"Oh." His face drooped in disappointment. "You said nothing personal in that letter. No word on what's going on in your life. One thing I found when I was a cop—you learn the most when people open up about the stuff that really matters to them." He pointed at to her ring finger, which was wrapped by a gold band with a small diamond. It was the only jewelry she wore regularly. "Tell me about him. Or her."

"He's a good man and a wonderful father." Unlike you, she thought. "He runs a small chain of coffeehouses in Brooklyn. He's also Black."

"You mean African-American." Terence Devine blinked a few times. "Or are they Black again? It's hard to keep up."

"His family's Jamaican. When they talk about American Blacks, some of them sound like the Klan."

"So you have kids."

"Two."

"Do you live in Brooklyn?"

"Fort Greene. We have a brownstone."

"Last time I was there was the Seventies, when I was still on patrol. My partner and I were in a blue and white, but we wished it was an armored personnel carrier."

"Things are different now. Or at least they were. Since the pandemic, everybody's become … " She searched for the word she wanted. "Wary."

"It's good to be wary. You make fewer mistakes."

"Are you wary?"

"Always. How do you think I survived so long in this hellhole? I'm sure they hoped I'd die from Covid, but I refused to give them the satisfaction."

"Who are 'they'?" Sheila asked.

"The bastards who put me here. The assholes who run the city. Politicians come and go, but the same crowd still calls the shots. It's dynastic. Nothing ever changes, and they manipulate everything for their own benefit."

"And you didn't?"

"I did some things I'm not proud of. I admit that. Have any of them ever admitted anything?"

"What should they admit to?"

It looked as if Terence Devine was smiling. "It's not gonna be that simple. It can't be that simple. I won't tell you everything right off the bat."

"I haven't even agreed to make the movie," Sheila said. "My producer/distributor thinks it's a good idea, but that's because it's not his family."

"You want it to be about our family?"

"That's what I'm thinking."

"Have you talked to your brother about this?"

"There's no point unless I commit."

"You two ever talk about me?"

"No."

"Both of you have done well for yourselves. I should be proud."

"Yes, you should."

Terence Devine leaned so close to the partition Sheila feared he'd smoosh his nose against the glass. The muscles in his forearm twitched, and he gripped the receiver so tightly she expected it to explode in his hand.

"I'm innocent," he said.

"You committed crimes," Sheila said.

"I did not do what they sent me away for," he said. "I'll keep saying that until the day I die."

Sheila glanced up as Michael wormed through the tables at their regular restaurant in Chinatown. They always sensed when the other was approaching. He was her big brother, and when they were kids he seemed so wise, a boy who'd figured out how the world worked long before he should have. Now he was the star prosecutor in the DA's office, and the media was full of hints that he was angling for the top job. His longtime boss had just cruised to re-election, but there were rumors he would retire before his term expired, allowing the governor to appoint Michael to the position. In the strange Kabuki of public life, none of this was official, but everyone knew it.

He wore the politician's uniform of navy blue suit, gleaming white shirt and flaming red tie, although instead of the usual American flag pin in his lapel, he wore one honoring first responders. Sheila was dressed in Brooklyn black. They looked like an odd couple, but there was no one in the world she trusted more except for her husband.

They shared steamed dumplings and kung pao shrimp. Since they had grown up deprived, they were always conscious of money, so they drank New York tap water.

"You look tense," Sheila said.

"I just fired a guy. Nelson Hernandez. He headed the Public Corruption Unit."

"I haven't heard much about them recently," Sheila said.

"That's why I fired him. How was Auburn?"

Sheila had said nothing to him about visiting their father in prison and was debating with herself whether she should bring it up. But Michael knew just about everything that went on in the criminal justice system, even if he kept most of it to himself.

"Depressing," she said.

"It's supposed to be."

"You've heard what I'm doing?"

"It's impossible to keep anything secret anymore, Sis."

"Everybody thinks I'm making this movie, but I haven't decided yet. I'm doing research."

"What's your angle?"

"What happened to our family."

Michael sprinkled soy sauce on the last remaining dumpling. "The man who married our mother used to file appeals all the time. A few years ago, he lodged a brief that he'd prepared himself because he couldn't find an attorney who was interested." Michael shook his head. "The judge threw it out and ordered him to stop making motions because he was making a mockery of the courts. She said the evidence against him was overwhelming, and he was, and I quote, 'guilty as hell.' I've never seen that in a judicial opinion."

"I'd like to look at his case file," Sheila said. "Due diligence and stuff."

"I'll ask Adam if it's okay. I can't imagine he'd object."

Adam Fishman had become DA at the height of the crack era. Crime had plummeted during his watch, although it was swinging up again, and everybody was getting testy about it.

"Are you sure?" Sheila asked. "He was involved in the case."

"It was a mess for everyone, but Adam never held it against me." Michael stopped. Sheila recognized his pause as a sign that he was thinking hard about what to say next. "I talked about our old man with him only once. Adam told me, 'You're just as driven as your father but a lot more honest.' I think he meant it as a compliment. Sometimes, with Adam, it's hard to tell."

"If I make this film," Sheila said, "I'll wanna talk to him."

"You're a big girl. Ask him yourself."

"I'll wanna talk to you, too."

"When the time comes, ask me."

"I'll ask you about Mom."

Michael chewed some shrimp. "She got a raw deal."

"It'd be good if you said that on camera."

Michael nodded, but the gesture meant nothing. Sheila's brother was extremely effective at being noncommittal.

"What's your next move?" he asked.

"I've been Googling, and I found out something interesting."

"What's that?"

"Jamie Quinn is still alive. Remember him—that windbag who used to write for the *Daily News*? I'm gonna reach out to him."

Michael patted his lips with a paper napkin. "I've talked to Jamie a few times."

"And?"

"Jamie Quinn loves causes. But do you know what his favorite cause is?"

Sheila shook her head.

"Jamie Quinn."

The old man opened the door to his sixth-floor loft in Tribeca before resting his forearms on his walker, then turning slowly, shoulders hunched, and pushing himself back one excruciating step at a time. The walker was equipped with a small oxygen tank, and Sheila heard him breathing through the tube that ran into his nose.

She wondered if he'd want to be seen this way before reminding herself that this largely forgotten journalist had an enormous ego. He would not care how he looked as long as people paid attention to him.

He lived on a full and open floor that had been renovated by his second wife, one of the city's leading interior designers. Soft light flooded the space, and Sheila began to think about where she could put him if it ever came down to an on-camera interview. She hoped he liked the highbacked chair by the window frame adorned with industrial moldings.

He motioned her to a couch whose color was on the border between tan and yellow. The color scheme was soothing, and Sheila wondered if his wife had used it in an attempt to keep him pacified.

"Thank you for seeing me, Mr. Quinn."

He eased himself into the highbacked chair and motioned for her to sit down.

"Terry Devine's daughter," he said. "Holy crap. We met once. You were a kid."

She recalled a large pale man with a loud voice asking Mom lots of questions. The *Daily News* ran a picture of Sheila with her mother and brother, and she'd been struck by the disembodied sensation of seeing herself on a printed page.

"You wrote a column about us." Sheila flashed her widest smile. Old men always enjoyed bantering with younger women. "My kindergarten teacher pointed it out to the class before warning us about the sin of pride."

"There's nothing wrong with a little pride, as long as you can back it up." Quinn wheezed, coughed, hacked up some phlegm. "I remember seeing a movie you did—the one about the school for delinquents."

"Nowadays they're called at-risk youth."

"Politically correct bullshit. Anyway, at the end credits, when it said 'A Film by Sheila Devine,' I asked myself, 'Is that Terry Devine's daughter?'" He shrugged. "I wasn't working anymore, so I didn't pursue it."

"I don't go around advertising it." She kept her smile going. It felt like Graduation Day. "At least until now. I'm talking to people who knew my father back then. I wanna know if you'll agree to an interview if I decide to go ahead with this thing."

"Sure, I'll talk to you. I've got nothing but time on my hands." Quinn coughed again. "I've met your brother. He likes putting people in jail. You don't need to be Freud to figure out why." He looked her over as if he were a lion eyeing the meekest creature on the savanna. "Don't tell me this is about closure."

"Closure is nonsense."

"I think I like you."

"My father sent a letter to the Justice Project. One thing led to another. I talked to him in prison a few days ago."

"The Justice Project gonna take his case?"

"I doubt it."

"I'm not surprised. He's guilty as hell."

"Some people are in prison for crimes they didn't commit."

"Your father isn't one of them." Quinn tried to smile. His teeth were the same color as his face and hair. "Had you been in touch with him before you saw him the other day?"

Sheila shook her head. "My mother cut off all contact. Never divorced him, though. She was a good Catholic."

"Your Ma deserved better," Quinn said. "Your father cheated on her, but what can you expect? He never told the truth about anything. Terence Devine is a pathological liar. I used him as a source, and it was the biggest mistake of my career."

"If he's so horrible, why did you use him as a source?"

Quinn's bushy eyebrows shot up. Like most reporters, he liked to confront people, but hated being challenged himself.

"Because I wasn't aware of how horrible he was until it was too late. A lot of the monsters in this world are charming, attractive, seductive. Your dad was that way. That's how he landed his mistress—Gina Something." He shook his head in rueful admiration, as if Terence Devine had embezzled money for decades without his employer catching on. "She was a good-looking woman. I'd have to look over my notes to remember her full name."

Keep him on point, Sheila said to herself. No old man ramblings. "So my father charmed, attracted and seduced you?"

Quinn's face brightened as Terence Devine's sins flooded his mind. Sheila was again reminded of how lovingly the Irish embraced their grudges.

"He always believed he was the smartest guy in the room, and everybody else was so stupid they'd never figure out all the scams he was running. He shoulda gone into politics."

"He had a swagger," Sheila said. "Still does, as a matter of fact."

Quinn nodded, conceding her point. "Every time he walked into a room, he acted like he owned the joint and everyone in it. Women enjoyed him. Men, too. He was that kinda guy."

Quinn moved his aging bulk toward the edge of the chair. The oxygen tank rattled. His wheeze grew louder.

"Back in the day," he said, "I never wrote dreck about what the goddamn mayor did during his useless workday. I did a street-level look at what was happening in the city. Cops, crooks, moms on welfare, guys sweeping the sidewalk—that's who I wanted to write about. Your dad was one of the people I used. I didn't mind if he played both ends against the middle. A lotta people did that. But I thought I could trust him, at least to a point."

"The night it all started, you met him at Clarke's. What did you talk to him about?"

"The new captain in Public Morals. Adrian Lynch. I wanted to know more about him."

"Why?"

"Because I'd heard the NYPD was launching a big drive to finally straighten out the vice squad. Lynch was the new guy in charge. I was trying to figure out if he was a sacrificial lamb or if he'd been sent there to clean house. I thought your old man could help me, but the whole thing turned into a clusterfuck."

"They straightened out the vice squad."

Quinn looked out the window, and Sheila thought his eyes were conjuring the New York of yesteryear that he had both loathed and adored—streets filled with hustlers and porn shops and squeegee men and open-air drug markets outside crumbling buildings, a story on every corner and all you had to do was ask.

"They did," he said with the sadness of a man who preferred to live in the past. "The city got safer, and way less interesting."

Chapter Three

At dinner that night, Sheila reminded her husband and children that she would return to Auburn State Prison the next day to interview her father. This time, she planned to bring a camera.

"I wanna go with you," Dylan said.

Sheila asked why.

"'Cause I wanna meet my grandfather."

Sheila thought of the things Terence Devine might say at the sight of this coffee-complexioned, 'fro-topped kid, so she turned to Wesley as he sipped some cabernet.

"Waddya think?"

He looked hard at the glass. Sheila expected him to say it was a terrible idea.

"I'm all for it."

She was silently pleased at the prospect of assistance and companionship on the trip to the upstate wasteland. She had considered hiring a freelancer, but that would cost money she preferred not to spend.

"Why are you for it?" she asked her husband.

Wesley thumped a large hand on his son's shoulder. "You should see what prison is like."

She was in bed, surfing the net on her laptop, when her iPhone began vibrating on the end table. She looked to see who was calling, then told herself it had been a mistake to give her number to Jamie Quinn. She was tempted to let him go to voicemail, but he was the type of curmudgeon who'd feel insulted if he had to leave a message, and he might have useful information. So she picked up her cell but employed her I'm-a-working-mom-who-is-really-tired voice:

"This is Sheila."

"Gina Galante."

"Huh?"

"That's the girl your dad was schtupping."

"Am I supposed to feel grateful that I know the full name of my father's mistress?"

"I told you I'd look through my files. I kept everything."

"That name doesn't help me much. I just Googled 'Gina Galante' and got 817,000 results."

"And none of them will help you, because she isn't Gina Galante anymore."

Sheila told herself to listen to the man.

"She goes by Regina Raimondo. She's out on the North Fork of Long Island."

"Raimondo Vineyards?"

"Bingo."

Sheila thought this over. "They make a good merlot. I usually don't like merlot."

In the interview room, Sheila pointed to the spot where she wanted the Sony.

"Always on him," she said. "From the chest up. He's still a powerful guy, and I wanna convey that."

"It's just a cinderblock wall behind him," Dylan said.

"It'll remind people he's in jail, not Club Med."

"The lighting's harsh in here."

"It's a harsh place. Work with it."

Dylan fiddled with the camera while Sheila ran over the notes she had printed out at home the night before. In its infinite wisdom, the State of New York refused to allow visitors to bring electronic devices of any sort into its penitentiaries.

"You think he did it?"

Sheila looked at her son. He had finished setting up, and now he slouched with arms folded across his chest in the classic pose of teenage tedium.

"Sure looks that way," Sheila said.

"We've been talking about the Bill of Rights in my government class. If somebody's convicted of something, they're supposed to be guilty beyond a reasonable doubt and stuff."

"I'm glad you're paying attention."

He shook his head. Hair swayed. "You could never pass those amendments today. They'd say you were soft on crime."

The door jarred open and Terence Devine, manacled, entered the room, with two obese guards behind him. His arms looked taut and toned from lifting.

Sheila nodded to Dylan, who began filming. Devine pointed at him.

"Who's this?" he asked in his cop voice.

"My son. Dylan McBride."

Sheila had given her father no warning. It was a stunt, but she was hoping for a reaction, and this tough man's blue eyes flashed with some sort of emotion, although she could not tell if it was surprise or yearning or perhaps even affection, before he motioned toward Sheila while asking the teenager, "She treat you okay?"

"Most of the time."

"That's the best you can hope for."

Devine eased himself into a plain wooden chair.

"There's a way out of here," Sheila said.

"Confess," Devine said. "Show remorse. All that bullshit."

"Why is it bullshit?"

"Because I'm innocent."

"No, you're not," Sheila said. "You committed lots of crimes while you were on the force, and they're all a matter of public record."

Devine jerked his hands in Dylan's direction. The cuffs clattered. "Is that why he's here?"

"Waddya mean?"

"I meet my grandson for the first time. I'd like to shake his hand. Hug him. Go outside and throw a ball around, then talk about girls and sports. But I can't do any of that unless I confess to a crime I didn't commit."

Devine turned to his grandson. Zoom in on him, Sheila said silently. Get as tight as you can. I wanna see the anger in those baby blues.

"I'm sorry you have to see me like this. I'm a bitter old man. I've spent forty years in here for something I didn't do. Imagine how you'd feel."

Devine lifted his head toward the ceiling.

Sheila spoke silently to her son: Go in even closer. Show the veins in his neck. They're pulsing.

"You accuse me of committing crimes," Terence Devine said to his daughter. "I never saw it that way. I performed services."

Keep going, she thought. Rationalize what you did.

"Public Morals was like the Wild West when I got there. The undercovers shook down pimps and hookers on their own. The cops felt the skels were stiffing them, and the skels thought they were forking over money all the time to the cops.

"So I created a system. We knew who operated where, so I went around every Thursday and collected money from the pimps. Then I'd go back to the squad room and dole out everyone's share so they'd have money for the weekend for their wives and girlfriends. It ran like a business. My Da did the same thing on the docks in Brooklyn thirty years earlier. That's when there were docks in Brooklyn."

"Now there's frappuccinos," Dylan said.

"Good one," Devine said.

"I've been talking to Jamie Quinn," Sheila said.

"That fat fuck is still alive?"

"He says you almost ruined his career."

"Too bad I didn't. I woulda done the city a favor."

"He told me that when all this happened, you had a girlfriend named Gina Galante."

Devine waited a few seconds before responding.

"I'm not gonna say anything about her."

"If I make this movie," Sheila said in the exasperated tone she used to employ when her then-small children refused to leave the playground, "I'll need to talk to people who knew you back in the day. Especially some women. In a perfect world, I'd ask Mom about you, but the world is far from perfect, so right now, your former mistress is the best thing going."

Devine kneaded his fingers. Forearm muscles twitched, and manacles clanked. He was summoning his strength, and it struck her that deep down, her father was like most criminals: Once exposed, he reveled in his misdeeds.

"Gina was a beautiful woman," he said. "And an unusual person."

"How so?"

"She listened. I told her things I never told your mother."

"Why was that?"

"In a way, I was looking out for Bridget. Internal Affairs and the prosecutors—those guys were bastards, and they woulda browbeaten her if she knew anything."

"Did they browbeat Gina?"

"I never told them about my relationship with her."

"But Quinn found out."

"He was a good reporter. I'll concede that point."

"Tell me about her."

"She was an artist, so she was broke. I thought she was talented, but she had to temp for the DA to make ends meet."

"So you two had a lot to talk about."

"I told her stories about my work. She told me about the gossip she picked up."

"Did you two talk about Nadine LaFleur?"

"We agreed the case was hinky. A lotta stuff didn't add up."

"Like what?"

Devine shifted in his chair. "I'll have to think about it. It's been a long time."

On the desolate stretch of Interstate 81 just south of Binghamton, Sheila motioned to Dylan to pull out his earbuds.

"What is it, Ma?"

She thought she heard "Next Year" by Macklemore and Windsor. She detested songs she regarded as mindlessly optimistic, but had vowed to never berate her kids about the music they listened to.

"What did you think about your grandfather?"

"He's holding stuff back."

Sheila gazed ahead. Wispy gray clouds skirted the tops of denuded hillsides.

"Why do you say that?"

"He's been in prison for decades, but he says he has to think about what he said to his girlfriend, and about the case that put him in jail?"

Dylan shook his head so forcefully Sheila thought his hair might brush against her cheek.

"I call bullshit."

Chapter Four

The vineyard she wanted was the last one on Route 25A before Orient Point. It meant another long drive, but at least the scenery was pleasant. As GPS guided her over the two-lane road toward the edge of Long Island, she glanced in the rearview and noticed a generic late-model black sedan about a hundred feet behind. She pulled her Toyota into the vineyard's gravel parking lot, but as soon as she stepped out, a pebble slipped into her flats. While she shook her shoe clear, she heard a car stopping behind her on the shoulder. When she turned to look, she saw a black sedan pulling away.

Beyond the parking lot, rolling rows of grapes stretched to Shelter Island Sound. It was almost noon, and the high sun reflected off the water, giving the scene the type of glow she associated with the early works of Botticelli. Now she understood why so many artists had settled on Long Island's East End before the hedge fund sharks sent real estate soaring into the financial stratosphere.

A sign outside the door of the faux-rustic building that served as the headquarters of Raimondo Vineyards said, "YOU STILL HAVE TO WEAR A MASK, DAMMIT." She pushed open the door and saw racks of wine lining the walls of a room that was airy and woody. See-through cabinets displayed glasses suitable for both white and red. Behind the counter sat a man in his twenties who had adopted the look she would never understand no matter how popular it got—crew-cut hair with a beard so bushy it could hide furry animals. A mask dangled from his elbow, and she wondered if he was illiterate.

He looked up from his iPhone, removed his buds, and reached for his mask.

"You're busted," Sheila said.

"Don't tell Big Mama," he said. "She'll expose me to Covid just to prove a point."

"Big Mama? Is that Regina Raimondo?"

"You know her?"

Sheila smiled, then realized being ingratiating was pointless because her mask was still on. She had hoped to find Gina in this room, just walk up to her and start talking, but now she'd have to go through an intermediary, and she wasn't sure how forthcoming she should be. She pointed to the guy's iPhone.

"What're you watching?"

"Well, ma'am—"

"Call me Sheila."

"I'm Victor." They bumped elbows. "I was catching up on 'The Cutting Room.' I missed it last week."

The fashion reality series was Bethany's favorite, so Sheila watched it with her. Mother-daughter bonding and all that.

"It's a good episode," she said. "I won't spoil it for you."

Victor wore a black T-shirt over tattered black jeans—a fashionista whose wardrobe was Salvation Army chic. His warm brown eyes glowed with contentment at making a connection, and Sheila found herself thinking, You'd be much better looking if you had more hair on top and less on your face.

"Did you see the one two weeks ago?" he asked. "When they kicked off Michelle?"

"I couldn't believe it. Her stuff was really creative."

"They can be cruel. Sometimes I think about going into fashion, but—" his head bobbed; facial hair flew in four directions "—I can't stand drama."

Victor confessed he had a crush on the show's newest judge, a Black designer named Tiberius Randle, whose esthetic blended hip-hop with MGM musicals from the Fifties. Sheila found him a bit over the top, but she kept nodding at Victor anyway.

"So tell me, why do you wanna see Big Mama?"

"Well, she was an old friend of my father's, and I'm in the area, and I've got a few questions I wanna ask her for a project I'm doing about him."

That was good, Sheila said to herself. I'm not lying, but I'm leaving it mysterious.

"What kind of project?"

"A film."

"Hollywood?"

"Documentary."

"Oh." His face fell as he tapped his iPhone. He brought it to his ear and said: "I've got someone up front who wants to see you. Her name's Sheila. She's making a documentary about her dad and says you were friends with him." He paused before lowering the phone and looking straight at Sheila. "She wants to know if you're Terence Devine's daughter."

"Now I'm the one who's busted."

Victor raised the cell and said, "Good guess."

This prompted a burst of sound from the phone, which Victor moved a foot from his head. When the noise ceased, he looked at the device as if it had harmed him.

"She says it isn't personal, but she doesn't wanna talk to you." He lowered his voice, afraid his boss would overhear even if she was laboring in the fields. "Now I'm intrigued. What's this about?"

"My father's life was … " Sheila stopped. She needed the right word.

"Complicated?"

"That's a good way to put it. He and Regina were lovers back in the day. I'd like to talk to at least one woman who knew him, and my mom is dead, so … "

Victor stared at his phone. He really wanted to stream that episode of "The Cutting Room."

Sheila stayed where she was. When people were bored, they often said or did things that were unwise, just to liven up the day.

"I shouldn't tell you this," he said.

Tell me, she thought.

"Go back on the road and make a right. About a half-mile down, there's a 'Deer Crossing' sign. If you park on the shoulder and head toward the water, you'll probably find her. She spends a lotta time there working on some new type of grape."

Deer Crossing, Sheila thought. Of course. Just about everybody who lives out here gets Lyme Disease.

The reflection from the high sun nearly blinded her as she walked down a slope that led toward the bay. She shielded her eyes and gazed at grapes that were green and plump. She kept turning in full circles until she saw two heads yo-yo-ing behind some vines. She walked like Quasimodo while slipping through the rows. Just a few yards from the water, she poked up her head and saw a woman working beside a man several decades her junior. Both wore floppy, wide-brimmed hats, and masks bearing the logo of Raimondo Vineyards.

You can brand anything, Sheila thought, and then she heard their voices as she tiptoed closer. Something about grafting.

"Are you Regina Raimondo?"

The woman raised herself to her full height of five-foot-eight. She was in her early sixties and her still-dark hair was swept back in a ponytail. Dirt caked her hands, in which she clutched a pair of heavy shears.

"Who are you?" the woman asked.

"Sheila Devine."

"Where's your mask?"

Sheila strapped a blue mesh job around her face.

"Have you been vaccinated?"

"And boosted. I'm not an idiot."

"That's debatable. I said I don't wanna talk to you. How did you find us?"

The young man beside her spoke up: "Victor couldn't keep a secret if his life depended on it. I keep telling you to get rid of him."

"You owe it to me," Sheila told the woman.

"I owe you nothing."

"You fucked my father."

It had been an unexpected benefit of the pandemic: When her mouth was covered, Sheila found it easy to speak the unvarnished truth.

Regina jerked her thumb at the young man beside her. "This is my son, Dominic."

He was dark-complexioned with wavy hair, six-foot-two and solidly built. Sheila figured he rarely lacked romantic companionship.

"Want me to get her outta here, Ma?"

He gripped a hoe. Sheila envisioned a rolling free-for-all that involved gardening tools.

"I'm considering making a movie about your former lover," she told Regina. "I haven't committed to it, but I'm doing some research. I've talked to him in prison. He insists he's in there for something he didn't do. I don't believe him, but maybe somebody who knew him back in the day can change my mind."

Sheila paused, then added: "You knew him intimately. In every sense of the word."

The air was chilly despite the sun. Regina Raimondo shuddered as she contemplated a dangerous part of her life that she had locked away for decades.

"I've seen some of your movies. I really liked the one about the abortion clinic. That took guts."

Sheila remembered the death threats from pro-lifers. "Thanks."

"I still don't wanna talk to you."

Sheila ignored her. "You temped in the DA's office when it was investigating Public Morals. You talked to my father about it."

Regina sighed. "The NYPD and the DA were determined to clean up the vice squad. They'd flipped a dirty cop who was wearing a wire and getting all kinds of stuff on tape. I figured out it was your father."

Dominic looked at his mother as if she had suddenly transformed into Wonder Woman. "You never told me you worked for the DA. I thought you were a squatter downtown."

"I was. Working for the DA paid my bills." Regina looked directly at

Sheila. "You really should leave now."

"How'd you feel when you discovered my father was the cop they'd flipped?"

"In a way, it was exciting. I knew things nobody else did, and it felt like a monumental event could occur at any moment. When you're in your twenties, you love to live that way."

"What was my father like, back in the day?"

"You sure you wanna hear this?"

"I'm sure I don't. But I drove a long way."

"A force of nature. Incredibly vital. Great in bed."

"Mom!" Dominic said.

Regina gave her son a look. "I had you when I was thirty-six. You think I lived in a convent until then?" She turned back to Sheila. "I hate it that your dad is locked up in prison. I'm amazed it hasn't killed him by now."

"His resentment keeps him going."

Sheila waited. She wanted Regina to say something to her, woman to woman, despite the presence of her son—an apology for having an affair with her father and an acknowledgment of how destructive her behavior had been. But then Sheila looked her over, head to foot, and realized that Regina Raimondo was the type of person who would never regret anything except, possibly, the hard reality that life hadn't worked out quite the way she intended.

Get back on track, Sheila told herself. Always remember that human beings love to talk about themselves.

"My father said you were an artist."

"That was then. After everything that happened, I left the city and came here. Back home, or close to it. I grew up in the Hamptons when real people could afford to live there." She jerked a dark brown thumb toward her son. "I've always liked wine so I got into the business, and that's how I met this kid's father. Pasquale. The kindest man I ever knew."

Sheila noticed the past tense. "What happened to him?"

Regina pointed to a row of vines twenty yards away. "About five years ago, he dropped dead of a heart attack right over there. I've been running the business since, but Dominic's gonna take over soon." She chuckled. "When I started here, they put me in the fields right away. I was working beside Pasquale for three days before I knew his family owned the place. It's that kind of a business."

She spoke with uncharacteristic tenderness. You never know what will move a person.

Regina went on: "Pasquale was fifteen years older than I was. I've always preferred older men. They've figured things out."

She grasped the shears as if she wanted to clip one of Sheila's extremities.

"And now, Ms. Devine, I have told you way more than you deserve about your father, and myself, and my business, and my son, so I must insist that you leave my property before I call the Suffolk County police—with whom I have a very good relationship, because I give them free wine every Christmas—to have you arrested for trespassing."

Sheila handed her a business card. "If you ever wanna talk about what happened—"

"I doubt it," Regina said.

"Would it kill you to go through the motions of being polite?"

After Regina told her son to take the card, which he forced into the pocket of mud-encrusted jeans, Sheila picked her way back toward the road.

Everybody's holding back, she said to herself. Which means that something really interesting happened all those years ago.

She passed the last row of grapes. Saw her car. Stopped still.

The Toyota rode low to the ground. On the asphalt, bits of glass shimmered in the sunlight. The windows had been shattered, the tires slashed, and a sledgehammer had smacked dents in the door, hood and roof.

Chapter Five

Michael told Sheila he had some bad news. She said she was used to it.

"Adam has reservations about letting you see the case file."

"You said it wouldn't be a problem."

"Now that I've talked to him, I understand his concerns. The man who married our mother is trying to get the Justice Project interested in his case. If they take it on, they'll be filing motions that we'll try to quash."

Adam Fishman had been district attorney through five mayors and six governors. He had lasted that long by being extremely careful about everything.

"I doubt the Justice Project will take the case," Sheila said.

"You sure about that?"

"If it'll make you and your boss happy, I'll shoot them an email."

"You do that. We can't."

Terence Devine's muscles bulged and twitched beneath the orange jumpsuit.

"I talked to Gina Galante," Sheila told him.

"How is she?"

"She runs a vineyard on Long Island."

"She always liked wine."

"She told me next to nothing."

Terence Devine scratched his nose. Manacles glinted under the fluorescent light. "It was a tough time for her. I'm sure she doesn't wanna think about it."

"She did say she figured out that you were the guy the DA had flipped."

"She's always been perceptive."

"Did anybody else know?"

"Not until it all went public."

"How did your colleagues react when they found out?"

"About what you'd expect. I was supposed to take one for the team. But I wasn't gonna do that. I had your mother and your brother and you to think about. I wasn't gonna go to jail."

"But you wound up here anyway."

"It's like somebody planned it."

"Did they?"

Devine shrugged. Sheila glanced sideways at Dylan, who frowned deeply, the expression he always used whenever he thought an adult was being less than truthful.

It was Saturday. Sheila had arranged for a weekend interview so her son wouldn't miss any more school.

"I wanna talk about Mom," Sheila said.

"What about her?"

"Did you love her?"

Terence Devine's eyes remained blank. Sheila wondered if this man had ever had any feelings for the mother of his children.

"I joined the police force because I was supposed to. I got married because I was supposed to. I had kids because I was supposed to—no offense."

"It's hard to take it any other way," Sheila said.

"All my life, I did things because people told me to do them, and I never had the chance to figure out what I wanted."

He was a cop, Sheila thought, but he's using the classic excuse of criminals: Society is to blame.

"Let me correct that," her father said. "By the end, there was one thing I wanted so badly I was willing to do just about anything. Which was why I acted the way I did during the investigation."

Dramatic pause. Now he's playing to the camera, Sheila thought.

"I wanted out of New York. The city was dying."

"Reports of its demise were premature," Sheila said.

"That fat fuck Jamie Quinn thought it was dying, too. But he loved what was happening. Gave him lots of material."

Terence Devine's eyes flashed, and Sheila suspected he was smiling, but the mask made it impossible to tell.

"Did he tell you that Nadine was one of the sources for his columns?"

This was news to Sheila, and she said so.

"That's why he was so bent out of shape over what happened," Devine said. "She gave him good information, and then she was murdered, and he took it personally. He wrapped himself up in righteousness, but he had a hidden agenda, just like everyone else."

Dylan stared out the windshield, and Sheila could tell her son was tossing around ideas in his still-developing brain as they cruised the two-lane blacktop that led to the interstate. She was driving Wesley's Honda because her Toyota was still in the shop.

"He keeps holding stuff back," Dylan said.

"Why do you say that?"

"Body language. He's coiled up."

"He's on tenterhooks. The interviews are stressful. Prison is a stressful place. A lot of bad people are in there, and they have nothing to lose."

"Maybe he's worried about what would happen if he tells you everything he knows."

"You sound like a conspiracy theorist."

"Sometimes conspiracy theorists are right."

"Here's my theory," Sheila said. "Your grandfather is an angry, bitter, lonely old man. Nobody has come to see him in years. He likes talking to me, and he thinks that if he keeps doling out information in dribs and drabs, I'll keep coming back."

She shook her head at the prospect of more long drives to the upstate barrens.

"Which I will."

Chapter Six

When Sheila checked her email on Monday, Tara O'Bannon's reply was waiting: The Justice Project had no current intentions of taking on Terence Devine's case. Sheila forwarded the information to her brother and considered how to get to Tribeca for the appointment she'd scheduled. The subway was filled with creeps, while Uber was expensive, and if she drove her husband's car into Manhattan she'd have to pay for parking.

So she took the subway because of money, but on the way to the Atlantic Avenue station, her sixth sense kicked in. When she glanced over her shoulder she noticed, about ten years behind, a guy who'd been loitering on the corner near her house—hands thrust in pockets; six-foot-one; 'roided; hoodie obscuring most of his features. From glimpses of his skin, she figured he was Caucasian. She couldn't tell his age, but he wore baggy pants and high-top sneakers, and nobody over thirty dressed like that.

She plunged down the steps and made her way through the warren until she wound up standing in the middle of the Manhattan-bound platform until the No. 2 train arrived. Hoodie Guy got into the same car she did. She took a seat near a door. Hoodie Guy did the same. Like some subway riders he still covered his face, and his black cloth mask had a skull and crossbones pattern.

The train lumbered under the East River. At Chambers Street the doors stayed open while a No. 1 train pulled in across the platform. Sheila scrolled her iPhone and noticed Hoodie Guy's eyes dilating. She pondered which pharmaceuticals were coursing through his system. When she heard a ping that indicated the doors were about to close, she bolted onto the platform and saw Hoodie Guy trying to scratch his way out of the car as it headed for 14th Street.

She rode the 1 to Franklin Street and zigzagged on foot past storefronts still shuttered by the pandemic fallout. Foot traffic was minimal, though she had to dodge the delivery guys on bicycles. Everyone ate at home, but nobody cooked. When she reached Jamie Quinn's loft, she sat in the same spot as before while her pulse and breathing returned to normal.

"You look rattled," the old man said.

"I was being followed."

"Why?"

"I think there are people who don't want me to make this movie."

"Who?"

"I'm not sure."

"Better find out."

Sheila took out her iPhone. "Mind if I film you with this?"

"No camera?"

"It'll look jumpy and edgy."

"Like that crap Godard used to do." Quinn waved his hand as if he were brushing away a gnat. "Go ahead."

Sheila adored *Breathless*, but let it pass. "I talked to my father over the weekend."

"How many lies did he tell you?"

"He said you used Nadine LaFleur as a source."

Quinn wheezed. Oxygen filtered into his nose.

"I had lots of sources. What of it?"

Sheila aimed the iPhone at him and used her interview voice. "How did you meet Nadine LaFleur?"

"I called her Martha. Her real name. She wasn't a streetwalker, like most of those girls. At Versailles, in the times of the French kings, women like her were called courtesans, and they were respected."

"You didn't answer my question."

"I met her downtown. At court. I was hanging around, looking for a story. She'd been busted for drugs. Possession. But she was an attractive woman. Didn't look like a junkie. And when she was arraigned, she made bail right away. She also had her own lawyer, not some dweeb from the public defender's office. News is what's unusual, and this was unusual."

"Do you remember who her lawyer was?"

"Rolando Ortega. Even then, he was expensive."

For many years, Ortega had been the most prominent criminal defense attorney in the city, which made him a frequent adversary of Sheila's brother.

"Given who her lawyer was, I figured she was involved in something that a guy with money wanted to keep under wraps. So I followed her when she left the courthouse. She was in Foley Square trying to hail a taxi, but back then cabbies wouldn't pick up women who were traveling alone. One hack told me, 'They tip like shit.'"

"We'd tip better if we were treated better."

"Point taken. Anyway, I stood next to her and yelled for a cab, and three of 'em came right away. She looked at me like she was really pissed, and I said, 'Do you know who I am?' and she said, 'I do,' and I said, 'I'm going back to my office uptown. If you're going that way, I'll pay your fare if you answer some questions.' She got in. Said it was the best offer she'd had in weeks."

"What did you talk about?"

"We started with Irish literature. Yeats. Both of us were fans. Then I told her Joyce was overrated, and she said I had to read 'Ulysses' again. I said I didn't have that kind of time, and besides, she wasn't my goddamn English professor. She laughed."

"That's a nice story, but you didn't make her acquaintance to discuss the Irish Renaissance."

Quinn shifted in his chair. Grimaced.

"Then I asked who her sugar daddy was—you know, the guy who was paying for Rolando Ortega. She just smiled at me and said, 'Let's call him "A."' She had a nice smile on those rare occasions she used it."

"She give you any inkling of who 'A' was?"

Quinn shook his head. "She did tell me that the men she slept with were at the top in government, business, finance, real estate—"

"Media?"

"TV. Print guys couldn't afford her."

"What did she talk about with her clients?"

"Plans. Money. Plans about money."

"Jesus Christ, Jamie, this is like pulling teeth. What the fuck did they do after they fucked?"

He smiled. "You are your father's daughter."

And you're a manipulative bastard, she thought. Everyone has forgotten about you, but now that I'm here, you're gonna turn this into the fifth act of "King Lear."

"Back then," Quinn said, "everybody thought New York's days were numbered. Lord knows my own columns reflected that. It was Martha who made me see things differently. She said these men had ideas to turn the city around, and they had the political and financial muscle to do it. But they had to let it all hit rock bottom. After that, they could do what they wanted."

Sheila imagined Nadine/Martha listening to the dreamy post-orgasmic boasts of New York's overlords as they tried to impress her with their machinations about ridding the city of its crumbling buildings, docks and highways, as well as the problematic people who went along with them.

"The city's bottomed out again," Sheila said. "I've been reading its obituary ever since Covid started."

Quinn shook his head. "Never bet against New York. The city will bounce back like a goddamn spaldeen. It always does. And the guys who made fortunes off the turnaround back then—they're still around, or their descendants are. Even as we speak, those bastards are figuring out ways to make more money."

"Those bastards must've freaked when Nadine was killed. Their favorite sex worker was murdered, and johns are always suspects in cases like that."

Quinn shrugged. His breathing apparatus rattled. "It was 1982. The Upper West Side was a hellhole, and the city kept setting records for murders. A prostitute's found dead in her apartment—they thought everyone would fuhgeddaboudit in a few days, and the NYPD would move on to the next homicide it couldn't solve."

"But you didn't let them forget," Sheila said.

"I owed it to her. She didn't tell me everything she knew, but she never lied to me."

"Unlike my father."

Quinn leaned forward. His eyes became rheumy with age and indignation.

"He ever tell you about the raid on the whorehouse?"

Back in Brooklyn, her landline's message light was blinking. She was tempted to erase it without listening because she'd been getting robocalls from the Chinese consulate, but she played it anyway because you never know. She was surprised to hear Michael's voice.

He was calling from home. He told her to get back to him. He emphasized that she should dial his landline, and when she did he picked up on the first ring.

"What is it?" Sheila asked.

"I forwarded that email from the Justice Project to Adam and told him we should let you see the case file. He still doesn't wanna do it."

Sheila chose the most benign possibility. "Over the years, your boss has been criticized for showing an overabundance of caution. He's been in office for decades because he doesn't rock any boats."

"The case is totally off the radar right now," Michael said. "I've looked at it from every angle, and I can't understand his decision."

Sheila felt like the little devil that popped up on the kid's shoulder after the girl passed out during the toga party in *Animal House*.

"You're the number two guy in the office," she said. "There's nothing to stop you from requesting the case file."

Chapter Seven

"I wanna talk about the whorehouse raid," Sheila said to her father.

"I raided lots of whorehouses and made a lot of money doing it."

"Murray Hill. You brought Jamie Quinn along."

Terence Devine nodded. "That was a good one."

"Quinn said you tipped him off, so he made a big deal about it, and both you and he found out Nadine LaFleur had worked there." She waited a few seconds to let him grasp the extent of her knowledge. "Why didn't you tell me any of this?"

"There are things you don't understand."

"Like what?"

"How precarious my position is. People die in prison all the time, and nobody cares."

"If you admit you killed her, you'll get out in a heartbeat."

"But I didn't kill her."

"Then who did?"

He worked his mouth. Nothing came out.

"Don't tell me you have no idea," Sheila said. "You've been here forty years for something you claim you didn't do. Thinking about who did it is your chief pastime."

Devine flinched as if he'd been slapped across the cheek. "I have suspicions, but I'm not gonna say anything until I have proof."

"The Justice Project won't take your case," Sheila said. "Right now, I'm the only person in the world paying any attention to you, so you better be straight with me even though you've never been honest with anyone."

Devine looked around the interview room like someone who was searching for a lifeboat after jumping off the *Titanic.* "Where's Dylan?" he asked.

"Sometimes he goes to school. Why did Nadine work in that whorehouse when she already had a pimp?"

Devine puffed out his cheeks and blew out some air. "To make more money."

"Did her pimp know about it?"

"No, and he woulda been really unhappy if he found out."

"Unhappy enough to kill her?"

"Good question. Lots of pimps kill the women who work for them. That's why prostitution is not a victimless crime, despite what all these new-age progressive dipshits claim."

"Did you find anything interesting in that raid besides scantily clad women?"

He looked at his daughter straight, and his eyes tried to bore through her head, and she sensed he wanted her to believe that, for once, he was being truthful.

"A couple things," he said so softly she was unsure the Sony would pick it up.

"Like what?"

"I saw a coat in the closet by the bar. An animal print. It looked like the coat I saw Nadine wearing when she went into her apartment."

"It was the Eighties. Animal prints were popular. That coat coulda belonged to any of the women who worked there."

"I shoulda taken it as evidence. My mistake. Because I mighta been able to tie it in with a handbag that was so interesting, Quinn mentioned it in his column."

"What was so interesting about the bag?"

"It was Gucci. I didn't expect to find something that expensive in a whorehouse. And I was certain I'd seen it before."

"Where?"

"In Nadine's apartment, the night I shook her down."

When she retrieved her stuff at the visitors' desk, the woman behind the counter pointed to her camera and asked, "Do you get tired of it?"

"Tired of what?" Sheila asked with downstate suspicion.

"Lugging that thing around."

"It's what I do."

"He likes seeing you. That's what I hear. He likes it when you come around."

The woman was middle-aged, with a pudgy face and round body. Her roots were showing, and she spoke with the guilelessness of rural America.

"I don't like it," Sheila said as she signed out, "but it is interesting. My mother cut off all contact when I was a kid." She shrugged. "It's a long story."

"He's had only a few visitors over the years."

"Who's come to see him?"

"I'm not supposed to reveal things like that."

Sheila glanced at the woman's nametag while summoning her red-carpet smile. "Well, Agnes, at the end of the movie I'll list the credits. I always slide in the names of the people who help me out."

"I don't want any trouble."

"I won't tell anybody what you did. Just thank you for your assistance."

"I've never seen my name on a movie screen."

"The first time it happens, it's a huge thrill. Almost orgasmic."

Agnes giggled. "The thing is, your father had no visitors for the longest time. But about a year ago, somebody started coming here to see him about once a month."

"Who is it?"

The woman looked away. Sheila dropped her voice and leaned close.

"C'mon, you can tell me. I am his daughter."

"I'll show you the name."

She took out a thick ledger and opened it to a page dated two weeks previous. When she pointed to the signature, Sheila had to stop herself from gasping.

I've turned into a goddamn stalker, Sheila said to herself.

She'd paid cash to rent a clunker for the day. On the Long Island Expressway, she exited and re-entered the road three different times to make sure no one was following. Now she was parked in dirt and weeds across Route 25A from Raimondo Vineyards.

At lunchtime, a charter bus disgorged two dozen tourists. She imagined Victor entertaining them with repartee about wines and fashion.

Regina's probably in there, too, Sheila thought. A savvy proprietress always takes advantage of a captive audience.

After an hour in the wine shop, the sightseers tottered out clutching recycled paper bags with the vineyard logo. The bus idled a minute before spewing away. When quiet returned, Sheila heard the caws of seagulls.

She emerged from the clunker to stretch her legs and back, then whipped out her iPhone to try to book a yoga session for the morning. The internet kept crapping out, and she began to swear until she heard a door slam across the road. She ducked behind the clunker, then peered over the trunk in time to spy a woman striding toward a late model Acura with the vanity plate WINELOVR. Sheila followed and tried to keep at least one vehicle between them as they cruised down 25A. Near Riverhead, the traffic thickened, and Sheila had an epiphany:

The outlets.

In the lot, she watched the Acura pull into a space outside the Williams-Sonoma store. Sheila parked the clunker, hurried into the shop, and spotted Regina Raimondo looking over a rack of wine glasses as if they had offended her. Sheila maneuvered through displays of tasteful home products and got ready to launch her spiel.

"So it was you," Regina said without turning around.

"Excuse me?"

"Loitering across the road all day. We were wondering who it was." She held a glass to the light. "Those goddamn bus riders broke three of these things. It's disheartening to realize how many people in this world can't handle alcohol."

"I know you've been seeing my father," Sheila said.

If Regina had a reaction, her mask hid it.

"What do you two talk about?" Sheila asked.

"That's between me and him."

"Why are you seeing him?"

Regina turned. Sheila had always been the biggest girl in the class and was unused to looking at a woman eye to eye.

"As I told you, my husband died a couple of years ago. Sometimes I get lonely."

"How did you reconnect?"

"I wrote him a letter. A totally out-of-the-box thing to do these days. He asked me to visit, so I did."

"He never told me you were seeing him. I had to find out for myself."

"It's none of your business."

"I'm making a movie about him. Everything he does, or has done, is my business."

"Then you can ask him, if you want, and if he wants to talk about our conversations, he can. But I'm not gonna tell you a goddamn thing."

"Have you told him he should admit he killed Nadine? Because if he did, the parole board would release him, and the two of you could start banging each other again."

"I know your father well enough to know this—I would never try to convince him to do something he didn't want to do."

Regina plunked the wine glass on the shelf with so much force Sheila feared it would shatter.

"And will you stop hanging around my vineyard? Cruising up and down the road all the time? It's annoying."

Is she gaslighting me? Sheila asked herself.

"Today's the first time I've been there since I talked to you and your son."

"It's not you?" Regina asked. "Black Nissan? Tinted windows?"

"I drive a Toyota, and it's in the shop."

Chapter Eight

Sheila wanted to slap Terence Devine the moment she saw him but forced herself to stay still while he arranged himself in his chair. Ramrod straight. Unblinking. Jaw square and unmoving. Despite four decades in prison, he would never stop being a cop.

Sheila glared and waited. She wanted him to speak first.

"Where's your camera?" he asked.

If I brought my camera, she thought, I'd stick it up your ass. But I'd never do that. Cameras are expensive.

He had another question: "Waddya so angry about?"

Everything, she felt like saying.

After her father and the money he made disappeared from their lives, her mother had to sell the house on Staten Island, the bungalow down the shore, and the boat that went with it. Bridget Devine moved with the kids to Freehold Township, where they rented a garden apartment near a junkyard. Mother and daughter shared the bedroom while Michael slept on a fold-out couch. Bridget proceeded to run through the shitwork of service-sector America: cashier, waitress, saleswoman, cleaning lady. Nothing lasted.

One night over dinner—they were eating franks and beans again, Sheila recalled, and if her memory was correct she was eight years old—she asked her mother what had happened to Daddy.

Bridget winced as if she'd been struck by a bullet. Sheila kept looking at her. It was an honest and simple question, and she didn't understand why answering it was so difficult.

"Don't you ever," Bridget said, the words escaping one excruciating mouthful at a time, and she left it at that.

"Don't I ever what?" Sheila asked.

"You know what I mean."

Sheila felt like saying that she didn't, but she recognized the resentment that always simmered inside her mother, so she focused on using the beans to make patterns that reminded her of rain clouds just before a storm.

After dinner, the kids sat on the edge of the sofa watching "Family Ties." The couch had already been turned down so Michael could sleep. Bridget had gone to bed because she needed to get up at four in the morning for her latest job. Michael would make sure Sheila got to school. He was always super responsible.

During a commercial, he shifted close to his sister and dropped his voice as low as it could go. They often murmured to each other in the apartment. Bridget slept on pins and had ears like a rabbit's.

"Never talk about Dad to Mom," he said.

"Why not?"

"He did something really bad."

Bridget Devine's cigarette habit eventually reached three packs a day. She smelled like an ashtray, and so did the apartment, and by the time they became teenagers the kids kept telling her she had to quit or at least cut down, but Bridget said tobacco was the only thing that comforted her. The coughs that wracked her body became more intense every year, but she put off seeing a doctor because it cost so much. By the time she was diagnosed, the cancer had crossed organs, and she died when she was fifty-four. Her kids told each other it was slow-motion suicide—the woman hated life, so she made a conscious decision to smoke herself to death.

Now Sheila sat only yards from the man responsible for destroying her mother. Bridget Devine was flawed, but her fate was undeserved.

"What do you and Regina Raimondo talk about when she comes to visit you?"

"The old times."

"She told me you were great in bed."

Sheila's father smirked. "We had a good physical relationship."

She summoned all her self-control to resist slapping him. Through gritted teeth, she asked, "What about the rest of it?"

"Why are you asking me this?"

"Because you and that slut were together all the time, and you couldn't have spent all those hours just fucking each other's brains out. I was a kid, and you were home maybe two days a week. Did you ever think about how much I liked being with you? How sometimes a little girl needs her father? Have you ever spent a second of your life thinking about somebody other than yourself?"

"That's unfair," he said.

"Unfair?" Sheila was shouting and didn't care. "Unfair is what happened to Mom and Michael and me. You got what was coming to you."

Terence Devine sprang to his feet. The chair clattered to the floor as the guards stepped toward him.

"This is pointless," he said.

"Yes, it is," she said. "You never told me you'd resumed contact with your old lover. You're playing games with me just the way you've played games with everybody who's ever been unfortunate enough to meet you, and I am beyond being tired of it. I do not work with people who lie to me."

She left.

Dim sum, Sheila said to herself. We should do dim sum sometime, just to mix things up.

"I've got some news for you," Sheila said to her brother.

Michael dipped a spring roll into a pool of duck sauce. "You're abandoning the film."

"How'd you know?"

"I hear things. It's part of my job."

"Did you know his ex-mistress has been visiting him in prison?"

"I knew a woman had been seeing him. I didn't realize it was her."

"She's in her sixties, but she's still a harlot."

Sheila sprinkled soy sauce over her General Tso's. I can't believe I'm eating fried food, she said to herself. I've just given up.

"Waddya gonna do now?" Michael asked.

"I have to tell Joel. He'll be upset with me, but that's our usual state of affairs." Sheila chewed her broccoli and hoped it negated the effects of the chicken. "Maybe I'll go back to the Justice Project and see if they have anything else. I'd like to do a movie about someone who's at least a little bit straightforward."

"Nobody who's been in prison a long time is straightforward," Michael said. "That's how they survive."

Sheila looked over her brother as closely as the restaurant booth would allow. As usual, he wore the politician's uniform. Michael Devine always paid attention to the rules, especially when he didn't play by them.

While they were in high school, he and Sheila began going into Manhattan together without getting their mother's permission. Sheila liked the art museums and galleries and quirky movies that never came to the multiplex. Michael felt energized by the crowds, and one day he told his sister that this was where they should live. Jersey was dull and stifling, but as he walked around the city, he felt alive because the place was filled with possibilities.

He received a baseball scholarship to Fordham, but it paid only a portion of his bills, so he hustled his way through college on a combination of odd jobs, loans and bravado. The Jesuits liked him, so after he graduated, he got a spot in the law school. That cost even more money; he took up bartending, which consumed most of his weekends. Hanging around drinkers at a young age made him wary of alcohol, and nowadays he limited his consumption to red wine at dinner.

Sheila recalled the day he revealed his career plans. She was almost out of film school and was eying an unpaid gig with a guy who kept hitting on her. Despite her revulsion, the man knew Ken Burns, and it was before #MeToo, and she had to start somewhere.

"I'm gonna look for a job with the DA," Michael told her at a greasy spoon in the East Village.

Sheila looked at her cheeseburger. She ate a lot more red meat back then. "Why do you wanna do that?"

"I wanna put bad guys in jail."

Sheila had to address the elephant in the diner. "Adam Fishman's the DA. How you gonna deal with him?"

Michael drank some tap water. "I'll ask him not to judge me because of what the man who married our mother did. Just give me a chance. I wanna be a prosecutor, and I wanna do it in Manhattan. This is the big leagues."

The meeting must have gone well, because Michael thrived. Sometimes, Sheila watched him in court. He had taught her to play chess when she was seven, and he always beat her because of his ability to anticipate her moves. The trait worked well in the legal profession. He rarely lost a case, and his assignments became more prominent, and Fishman kept promoting him until he was named the office's top deputy.

"The thing is, Sis, you piqued my interest," Michael said.

Sheila snapped back to the present. "What did I pique your interest about?"

"I keep thinking about the case file you wanted to get."

"Is there anything in there?"

"I still haven't looked at it. But as I run through the possibilities, I always engage in the lawyer's ultimate conceit."

"Which is?"

"Whenever we look at a cold case, we think we're gonna discover something everybody else overlooked."

Chapter Nine

Since they were engaged in subterfuge, Michael told Sheila it was important they operate in a manner that seemed aboveboard. If anyone asked questions, they'd say she was there to interview him for her film, and they wanted to do it when the place was nearly empty so there'd be fewer distractions.

Michael made a show of greeting Sheila in the lobby of the DA's office just off Foley Square, getting her a visitor's pass, signing her in, and leading her to his office. On his desk, she noticed photos of his wife, his kids, and Bridget Devine.

Michael pointed to an end table wedged into a corner of the room. On top of it was a manila folder that looked awfully thin.

"That's it?" Sheila asked. She'd expected more.

"That's it."

Sheila unzipped her backpack, took out her laptop, and held up the folder. On its cover was a fading case number written in magic marker.

"Have you read this?" she asked.

He shook his head. "I'd have a conflict of interest. But you're not subject to the same rules I am, and if you see something you think I should look at …"

Sheila glanced out the window at the fading daylight. The utilitarian room had a sweeping view of downtown and the Hudson, and whenever she was in Manhattan at dusk, she was astounded at how beautiful New Jersey looked while the sun went down.

With a sigh she hoped was dramatic, Sheila booted her computer and opened the folder. The case against her father was laid out in dispassionate bureaucratic prose:

Early in the morning of February 28, 1982, the body of a sex worker named Martha Owens, a.k.a. Nadine LaFleur, was found in the bedroom of her walkup apartment on West 73rd Street. The official cause of death was strangulation. Her windpipe was crushed, so her neck was bruised, but she also had been hit repeatedly on the arms, face and torso. Her nose had been broken, so blood splattered her clothes. Although there was no sign of sexual assault, traces of semen were found in her vagina. Neighbors had heard sounds of a struggle and an argument about money, but of course, nobody had done anything.

The medical examiner determined that the victim had been dead about seventy-two hours before her body was discovered. Suspicion immediately fell upon her pimp, Jose Almonte, street name Paco, who spoke to counsel before he could be questioned and produced an alibi backed by two women who worked for him. The lead investigator, Detective Francis Xavier Mulligan, obtained the victim's client list, which was lengthy, but all the men on it who were interviewed by investigators could account for their whereabouts on the night of her death.

After several fruitless weeks, Detective Mulligan brought in Geraldo Calderon, street name Zaca, as a person of interest in the investigation. A known dealer in narcotics who worked on West 73rd, Zaca denied committing the crime or ever setting foot in the victim's apartment. His fingerprints were on file, but they failed to match any of the prints in her lodgings. Calderon gave the police only one shred of information—on the night the medical examiner determined that Martha Owens had died, Zaca saw her open the door to her walkup and allow a Caucasian man to enter the building.

Mulligan and the detectives working with him tried to establish the man's identity, to no avail. Then, one day, while he was eating lunch at his desk, Mulligan picked up a call on a hotline that had been set up to receive information about the death of Martha Owens.

"You watchin' TV?" the caller asked.

"Who's this?"

"Zaca."

"What the hell do you want?"

"Don't talk to me like that."

"You're a scumbag, I'm a cop, and I'll talk to you any way I want."

"Turn on Channel Five," Zaca said.

Mulligan flipped on the portable black and white TV in the Homicide room.   The local stations were airing the hearings of the Antonelli Commission, which Mulligan had no desire to watch.

"The guy who's testifying," Zaca said.

Mulligan felt like punching the screen while Terence Devine bragged about his crimes.

"What about him?" the detective asked.

"That's the guy I saw go into that puta's building. I told you he looked like a cop."

Devine's prints were on file—SOP for every employee in the department— so Mulligan ordered another round of dusting in the apartment, and the lab responded quickly: Terence Devine's fingerprints were found in the living room, bedroom and clothes closet of Martha Owens' apartment.

Devine had never said anything to anyone about being in her place. In fact, he had never mentioned having any contact with her at all.

Mulligan called Rolando Ortega, lawyer for the pimp Almonte, saying he still had a few questions about the death of Martha Owens and would they please come around to Homicide as soon as possible.

They used a private room. Mulligan asked if they had any objection to him recording the conversation. They said they didn't. As soon as the detective flipped on the machine, Ortega said he couldn't understand why they were there. His client had cooperated with both the murder investigation and the probe into the corruption in Public Morals.

"I wanna talk about the night Martha Owens was killed," Mulligan said.

"My client has an alibi."

"Terence Devine went to your client's apartment that night."

"There's no secret about that."

"He had money for your client. Where did he get it?"

The pimp and his attorney exchanged some words in Spanish. Mulligan really wished people would speak English all the time. What was so hard about that? Finally, Paco said: "Some people owed me. He collected the jack, and I gave him a cut. Me and Devine did a lotta work together."

"Some people?"

"That's right."

"You remember their names?"

"Tom, Dick and Harry. No, I don't remember their names."

Mulligan smiled. He was enjoying this conversation. "Devine got that money from Martha Owens, a.k.a. Nadine LaFleur. You sent Devine to her apartment that night to collect for you, which he did, but he also beat her to death, and you never told us jackshit about it."

This produced a rapid explosion of Spanish from Paco and his lawyer. Mulligan talked over them in English.

"I've got a witness who says the victim opened the door and let Devine into the building. Even better, I've got Devine's prints in her apartment, which he ransacked because he was looking for the cash she owed you. I have people nearby saying they heard a loud argument about money in her place that night, and we have you on tape accepting money from Devine a couple hours later. A three-year-old can connect the dots. Now I've got you for aiding and abetting a murder, obstruction of justice, and lying to the police. I don't care what kind of deal you made with the DA—this is murder, and you don't get away with it."

They spent the next thirty minutes negotiating Paco's surrender. In return for a suspended sentence on the obstruction of justice charge, the pimp agreed to testify against Terence Devine. Paco emphasized that, whenever they discussed the matter, Devine had never admitted killing Ms. Owens— although, to be honest, the pimp had suspicions.

The indictment was handed up, Devine was arrested, the trial was a slam dunk. Given the physical and eyewitness evidence, Devine admitted being in the apartment and shaking her down, but he insisted she was alive and conscious when he left.

"She was swearing at me like crazy," he told the jury. "I've never been cursed out like that by a woman, and believe me, I've had plenty of experience."

Nobody laughed.

Sheila dropped the folder on her brother's desk and said, "Your turn."

Michael was standing. He had one of those gizmos that allowed him to raise or lower his monitor.

"You see something?" he asked.

"Consider the conflict of interest resolved. As a citizen, I am calling a prosecutor's attention to a potential problem with a murder conviction."

Michael began to read. He had looked at thousands of files like this, so he went through it quickly before putting it down.

"I've convicted plenty of perps on way less than this," he said.

Sheila punched notes into her laptop. "The bathroom puzzles me."

"They didn't find anything in the bathroom."

"That's what puzzles me."

"Waddya mean?"

"No fingerprints."

"So?"

"They found the fingerprints of the man who married our mother in the living room, the bedroom and the clothes closet. But not in the bathroom. And he had to use the bathroom."

"Why?"

"To get rid of the blood."

"What blood?"

Sheila kept her voice even. Michael was usually much sharper than this.

"The blood that must've been on him, considering the way that woman was beaten. Her nose was broken. Blood was all over her clothes and would've been all over his, too."

Michael blinked a few times in a sign of incomprehension. Sheila slowed her words, the way she did with her kids when they zoned out, and began counting off the sequence of events on her fingers.

"He goes to her apartment. Then he goes to Clarke's to drink with Jamie Quinn. Then he goes to the pimp's place to give him the money. After he did all of that, he planned to see his mistress."

"You'll notice it didn't dawn on him to go home to you, me and Mom."

"I did notice that. But I also noticed that nobody said anything about seeing blood on him until after he gave Paco the money and beat the crap out of him. Think about it. After busting Nadine's nose, he would've needed to use her bathroom to wash off as much of her blood as possible. Even in New York in the Eighties, somebody covered in blood would've attracted attention."

"It's entirely possible the cops overlooked the bathroom," Michael said. Years in the courtroom had given him the ability to explain away problems. "Stuff like that happened a lot more back then. There's one big upside to all those Dick Wolf shows—the police take procedures a lot more seriously than they used to."

"What if they didn't overlook it?" Sheila asked.

Michael lowered his monitor, sat in his chair, kicked his feet onto his desk.

"What's your next move?" he asked.

Sheila finished typing and shoved the laptop into its bag, which she zipped shut with the fury of a woman who was angry at all the incompetent men in the world who refused to admit their mistakes.

"I don't wanna go back to Auburn and talk to that man unless I absolutely have to," she said. "Is Detective Francis Xavier Mulligan still alive?"

"He's in Breezy Point."

The last Irish enclave in the city, Sheila said to herself. I'm heading into a den of unreconstructed micks who spend all their time bitching about the government while they collect civil service pensions.

Mulligan lived alone in a bungalow at the end of a cul-de-sac. Sun glinted off the water. Homes were packed close. Salt air blew crisp and fresh.

When the door opened, a dark square form filled the frame. Sheila entered after hearing a gruff "Come in." Once her eyes adjusted to the indoors, she saw a florid man with a shock of white hair, a protruding gut, and the tall-as-I-can-make-myself posture of a police officer.

Sheila flashed her widest smile. "Thanks for seeing me, Detective Mulligan."

"I got nothing better to do." He led her toward the back. "I have a deck outside. It's cool today, but it's a nice place to sit. You like the water?"

Sheila avoided beach vacations because sand got into parts of her body she hadn't even known existed. "Sure."

"My wife loved the ocean," he said. "This place belonged to her family for decades. But then ... "

His wife had died years ago. Michael provided Sheila with a theory: "She wanted to."

The deck had a view of Jamaica Bay. Birds swooped and gurgled. Mulligan pointed Sheila to a plastic chair by a wobbly table before taking a seat near the railing. Sheila whipped out her iPhone.

"Mind if I record you on this?"

"Why should I mind?"

Mulligan reached into the pocket of his windbreaker and took out a cigar, which he proceeded to light by cupping the tip against the wind. Sheila abhorred cigar smoke but appreciated the visual.

"I've worked with your brother," he said. "Some people call him Ming the Merciless because he's such a good prosecutor. Never woulda figured Terence Devine's kid was gonna turn out that way."

"Michael's always been a straight arrow," Sheila said.

"And you're a filmmaker?"

"That's right."

"Hollywood?"

"Documentaries."

"Oh."

"Let's talk about my father."

"He's guilty as hell. He never let anyone in Homicide know he'd been there the night that hooker was killed. Believe me, it woulda been useful to learn that right off the bat. So we're spinning our wheels, and the newspapers are going batshit, when finally an eyewitness comes to us saying he saw the victim admit your father into her building that night."

So far, Mulligan's account jibed with what Sheila had read in the case file.

"Why do you think my father killed her?"

"I don't have to prove motive."

"Speculate."

"Things got outta hand. Happens all the time."

"How well did you know my father?"

"I'd run into him a few times."

"What did you think of him?"

"Total asshole."

Takes one to know one, she thought.

"He was cooperating with the investigation into Public Morals," Sheila said.

"I didn't know that at first."

"How did you feel when you found out?"

Mulligan blew out a long stream of cigar smoke. "Mixed, to tell the truth. Only cops know what we go through every day, so we're supposed to have each other's backs all the time."

"The blue wall of silence," Sheila said.

"There's a reason it exists. Almost every day, we ask ourselves, 'Do you follow the rules, or do you put the bad guys in jail?' A lotta times, you can't do both."

The wind picked up. Mulligan sank a few inches into his jacket.

"But Public Morals was a cesspool," he said. "The city had to clean it up."

"Were you happy to pin the murder on my father?"

He shook his massive Irish head. "Murder never makes me happy, but I was satisfied with the way things turned out. The case was rock solid. For a while, he had douchebag lawyers who filed appeals, but the courts always knocked them down because we had the evidence."

"He still denies killing her."

"He's a liar. Maybe you've noticed that."

"I wanna go over what you did after that drug dealer dropped the dime."

"We dusted the place again. I told the lab what we were looking for and said it was a top priority. They got back to me PDQ. Your father's prints were all over the place."

"In the bedroom—" Sheila began.

"And the living room and the clothes closet. He was everywhere looking for money."

"But you didn't find any prints in the bathroom."

Mulligan blinked a few times. "What's your point?"

"Did you dust the bathroom?"

He jabbed the cigar toward her in what Sheila regarded as a phallic gesture. "We weren't amateurs. We went over every goddamn inch."

"Don'tcha think my father woulda used the bathroom?"

"What for? Men don't need to take a leak every fifteen minutes the way women do."

"He woulda had blood on him after he struggled with her, right? Her nose was broken. Blood covered her clothes."

"I'm not following you."

Because you don't want to, Sheila thought. This was the most high-profile case of your career, and you'll never admit you might have goofed.

"Nobody saw any blood on my father when he went to Clarke's later that night. How did he get rid of it if he didn't use her bathroom to clean himself up?"

"He musta wiped it down."

"Then why didn't he wipe down the rest of the place? He was a cop. He knew his prints were all over her apartment."

"Maybe he didn't realize how badly she was hurt. We never determined if she was dead before he left her apartment. In terms of getting a conviction, it didn't matter."

"And what about his clothes? He never changed them."

"He wore a leather jacket. He took it off while he was there and then kept it on the rest of the night. His pants were dark, and he was in a bar. Nobody woulda noticed."

Mulligan nodded as if he were pleased with himself, but then his face grew grim as he recalled all the indignities Terence Devine had inflicted upon him.

"If your father didn't do it," Mulligan asked in a voice clipped with annoyance, "why did he make us jump through all those hoops? He kept saying, 'Look at this,' or, 'Look at that,' but he never came out and told us he was in her apartment that night until we confronted him with the eyewitness and the fingerprints."

"What was he supposed to tell you?" Sheila asked. "'I was in her apartment shaking her down for the money she owed her pimp, but I didn't kill her.'"

"If that was the truth, yeah." Mulligan chuckled without mirth. Sheila marveled at how cops could go through the motions of humor without feeling it. "He coulda told us he was screwing her. We woulda believed it." Mulligan puffed on his cigar in a sign that he was pleased with himself, then let out a long plume of smoke. "I understand sticking up for your old man—"

"I'm not sticking up for him."

"Coulda fooled me. The evidence points to him. Are there loose ends?" Mulligan shrugged his wide shoulders. "There are always loose ends. That doesn't change the facts. And the fact is, he's guilty. He shoulda come to us right away. Maybe we coulda done something."

"Waddya mean by that?" Whenever Sheila talked to cops, her tristate accent kicked in all the way.

"He coulda cut a deal. Manslaughter. She was a whore."

"Sex worker."

"Whatever. If he'd just played it straight, he woulda been out in three years."

Mulligan took a drag on his cigar. The ash glowed blood red.

As the guards gripped Terence Devine's upper arms, Sheila observed that every time she saw her father, his biceps seemed a bit bigger.

"I'm surprised you came back," he said.

"We're gonna talk about the night you went to Nadine's apartment."

Devine rolled his eyes like a school kid facing a demand from his most despised teacher. "It's all in the trial transcript and in the appeals I filed. Why do I have to talk about this again?"

"Because I said so."

He puffed his cheeks. "That night, I got a call from Paco, the dickhead, asking me to get some money from one of the women who worked for him. I'd get a cut. Thirty percent. I went to her place, talked my way in, and asked for the money. She said she didn't have any. I knew she was lying, so I got angry. You should never lie to a cop."

"Did she try to seduce you?"

"Yeah, but I wasn't interested. A lotta guys in Public Morals used hookers, but I never did. All the prostitutes I ever met were monumentally screwed up. Pun intended."

"You got angry at her. Then what?"

He breathed deeply. "I threw some of her stuff around. I knew where whores kept their money."

"Did you take out your gun?"

He waited a second. The intense fluorescent lighting bore down on her brain, and Sheila wished she'd worn shades or at least a baseball cap because she felt the start of a headache.

"I did," he said. "But I never took off the safety, and I didn't hit her."

"It still sounds violent. Coercive."

Devine's voice rose. "If she'd just fucking paid fucking Paco what she fucking owed, I wouldn't've spent the last forty fucking years of my fucking life in this fucking hellhole."

Eventually, Sheila thought, every criminal winds up blaming the victim. "Did you get the money?"

"I did. But I was there a lot longer than I thought I'd be. I needed a drink. I needed several drinks."

"So you got the money. Then what did you do?"

"I went to Clarke's and drank some Bass and ate a cheeseburger and talked with that fat fuck Jamie Quinn."

"Then what did you do?"

"I went to Paco's to give him the money. I thought about asking him for more than six hundred because it'd been such a pain to get it, but we'd made a deal, and I always honored my agreements."

Sheila licked her lips. She was about to pose her most important question, but she wanted it to sound like a throwaway.

"Did you use the bathroom?"

He stared at her as if she'd just upbraided a mass murderer for leaving a mess.

"What?"

"Before you left Nadine's apartment, did you pee or wash your face or anything?"

He shook his head. "I just wanted to get outta there. If I felt like arguing with a woman, I woulda gone home to your mother."

Sheila waited a minute, and when she resumed talking, her voice was low and even. "I'm gonna give you one last chance on this film. But you've gotta be honest with me. No more games, no more bullshit. If I catch you in one single lie, I am walking away from you and the movie forever. You can die in prison, and I won't even go to your funeral. Capeesh?"

Devine glared at her. He'd once been a cop, and he was used to giving orders. Now he was being told what to do by his little girl, and resentment oozed from every pore in his body.

"Do I have a choice?"

"No. Now tell me everything that happened during the investigation. And I mean everything. Hold. Nothing. Back."

Chapter Ten

As she drove the two-lane road that led back to the interstate, she told herself to suppress her exhilaration. Happy to be back in her Toyota, because she knew where everything was, she reached for the satellite radio button. Bob Marley always juiced her.

A late model Acura with the vanity plate WINELOVR passed in the other direction.

She braked fast, made a highly illegal U-turn, hoped no state troopers were around. She gunned the Toyota and thanked the bastards who had smashed her car for sparing the engine. When she saw the Acura in the distance, she slowed to match its speed.

As she approached Skaneateles, a few cars merged onto the road, and Sheila feared losing the tail, but when they reached town she saw the Acura angle into a parking spot in front of a wood-framed Starbucks.

Of course, Sheila thought. It's a long drive, and the prison visit will take a while. She needs a caffeine rush.

Sheila pulled in, slung her purse over her shoulder, and strode into the shop. The scene looked comforting—baristas behind the counter, metal machines grinding beans, millennials staring at laptops. Sheila saw the woman she wanted sitting at a rickety table by the wall, as if she wanted to blend with its faux rustic decor. She sipped her coffee with one hand, fingered her smartphone with the other, and looked up as Sheila got near.

"We've gotta stop meeting like this," Regina Raimondo said.

Sheila sat without being asked. "My father says he gave you a Gucci handbag. Maybe you can discuss it when you see him."

"What makes you think I'm going there? I could be checking out the local wineries. Studying the competition never hurts."

"The wineries around here suck, and you're on the verge of retiring. Stop jerking me around."

"I'd heard you abandoned the project."

"I've reconsidered."

"Over the years," Regina said, "I've accumulated lots of handbags. It's hard to keep track."

"Let me refresh your memory," Sheila said. "My father found it in a brothel he raided with some other crooked cops. They snowed Jamie Quinn into thinking what they'd done was legit, and he wrote a glowing column about them. My father said the bag resembled one he'd seen in Nadine's apartment, and he couldn't figure out how it got there."

"It's possible the bag wasn't hers," Regina said. "Some other woman sees the bag, likes it, then goes out and buys something similar."

"My father said he found some notepaper in the bag that had a long list of addresses with dollar values beside them. Below them, someone had written the words 'GET IN ON THIS!' He believes a woman wrote those words because the handwriting was loopy, and in this case I'll go along with the sexist assumption because she also drew a smiley face, and men never do that. To top it all off, my father said the writing resembled a sample of Nadine's that he obtained from her mother."

Regina chugged her drink. "The addresses, as I recall, were all on what was then called the Lower West Side before the developers and real estate people broke up that part of the city into trendy micro neighborhoods. In those days the area was down at the heels, just like the rest of New York."

"What did you do with the bag?"

"I keep it on my nightstand at all times, so it's next to me while I sleep."

Sheila suspected sarcasm.

"It was decades ago," Regina said with the clipped tone of a preschool teacher who had run out of patience with an annoyingly inquisitive student. "It's someplace, but I have no idea where."

"I wanna look at it," Sheila said. "Evidence and shit."

She rose to leave. Regina told her to get her butt back in the seat.

"There's a reason I left New York. There's a reason somebody smashed your car. Above all, there's a reason your father's been in prison all these years." Regina shook her head. "I don't know exactly who did what to whom, and even if I did, I'd keep my mouth shut. But some powerful men are quite happy with the way everything worked out. In fact, knowing the way things work in Sodom-by-the-Hudson, I bet they're ready to make another killing."

"Metaphoric or literal?" Sheila asked.

"Probably both. The pandemic cratered the city. Offices, apartments—everyone who could get out did, and now a lot of businesses are shuttered. Just like 1982. 'Escape From New York' and all that."

"It's a good movie," Sheila said, "in a guilty pleasure kind of way."

"In those days, Chicken Little was screaming that the sky was falling, and lots of people believed it. Your father certainly did. But what was happening was this: the men who could make things happen were gathering up all the eggs while the hens just stared stupidly at the clouds. Now those guys are ready to add to their fortunes because the city is gonna make a comeback just like it always does, and, believe me, they're mighty pissed that some cineaste from Brooklyn is calling attention to what happened."

"I'm making a movie," Sheila said. "I'm not a prosecutor."

"Your brother is."

Terence Devine had told his daughter that the former pimp once known as Paco was now pastor of a storefront church in Corona named Temple of the Redeeming Spirit.

"He could spend eternity repenting." Devine spat out the words. "It still wouldn't be enough time."

The website said the church held services every evening, so as night fell Sheila stood under the el near the 111th Street station, watching Hispanic families squeeze through a narrow entrance across Roosevelt Avenue. After the door closed, she began to hear ecstatic sounds of singing, shouting and clapping. She checked the time on her iPhone and wondered how long worship would last. She planned to talk to the pastor, who now went by his real name, once he concluded the rites. In the meantime, she checked her messages and voicemail before playing Spelling Bee on her *Times* app.

She looked up from the screen. Down by the corner was a figure she'd seen before. At first, she couldn't quite place it, but as it moved toward her, she remembered:

Six-foot-one. 'Roided. Hoodie obscuring most of his features. Hands thrust in pockets. Skull and crossbones on his mask. He'd once trailed her from house to subway.

She glared in an effort to shoo him, but he kept approaching with zombie remorselessness. Posture rigid. Arms still. He exuded the utter calm of a sociopath.

Former Army, Sheila said to herself. Possible PTSD. Can't hold a steady job. Doesn't want one. Prefers freelance gigs where he can use the lethal expertise he acquired at taxpayer expense.

Cars sped past, and the el rumbled overhead, but aside from the church all the storefronts were either boarded up or secured behind metal grates. Sheila considered how easy it would be for Hoodie Guy to grab her, clamp his hand over her mouth, drag her someplace where no one could see or hear them. Just like Nadine, she'd be another luckless victim of a violent city.

Sheila snapped his picture with her iPhone, but the hoodie and mask obscured his features. She thought of calling 911 but doubted the cops would arrive in time, so she headed for the curb while keeping him in her peripheral vision. He veered to stay parallel. Sheila wriggled through a gap between two parked cars and looked both ways. The lights were green, so cars, trucks and vans rushed by, and she remembered something she had told her kids long ago when they kept asking why they couldn't dart out into oncoming traffic the way everyone else in New York did:

You are crossing the street. You are not making a midnight dash to freedom across the border.

Hoodie Guy was two vehicles away and trying to wedge through the parked cars at the curb, but he was bulkier than Sheila and had to stand on tiptoe to lift his butt over the bumpers. Sheila swiveled her head and noticed a gap in the traffic because a city bus was lumbering up to speed. She pressed her bag against her side and sprinted into Roosevelt Avenue.

Do not look, she said to herself. If you look, you'll lose your nerve.

She heard blaring horns and squealing tires, but she kept her eyes focused on a fire hydrant directly across the street. She leapt to the curb, landed on the cracked sidewalk, sprinted toward the storefront church. Euphoric noises of rapture grew louder with every stride. She pulled open the door, stepped inside, and breathed again.

A sudden and complete silence came over the space as every head turned toward Sheila, who suddenly remembered that she hadn't set foot inside a church since her mother's funeral.

She looked toward the pulpit, which was closer than she expected. The pastor's gaze indicated he had been expecting her all his life.

"Hola, Señora," he said.

"Hola," she replied.

"Cómo esta?" he asked.

"Preocupada," she replied. "Y usted?"

"Salvado." He lifted his eyes toward the ceiling, raised his hands to the heavens, and shouted, "Alabanza a Dios!"

Sheila thought about this a second before responding, "Sí. Alabanza a Dios."

After the service, the pastor embraced his flock as it filed out, chatting in Spanish and paying special attention to los niños and warning los madres y los padres about los peligros de homosexualidad.

Sheila stayed in the folding chair she had occupied the entire service. When he was done with his flock, the pastor strolled over with his hands clasped in front of him.

"If you don't mind my pregunta, Señora—"

I might mind, Sheila thought.

"—what brings you here?"

"My father," she said.

The pastor lifted his eyes to the popcorned ceiling. "He brings us all here."

"My biological father," Sheila said.

The man looked at her blankly.

"You did business with him many years ago."

She reached into her bag and handed him one of her cards, which produced an expression of unhappy realization.

"It's no secret that I am a sinner," he said. "Although I've never told my parishioners exactly what those sins are."

"I'm making a film about my father."

"Hollywood?"

"Documentary."

"Oh."

Sheila thought it was time for a little intimidation, so she rose to her feet. She was three inches taller than he was, but the man seemed unperturbed.

"I do not wish to go on camera, Señora. Lo siento."

"Then let's talk unofficially."

He rocked on the balls of his feet and tilted his head back. Maybe he's praying, Sheila said to herself. Maybe this religion thing isn't total bullshit on his part.

She pointed outside. "I was followed here by a psycho on steroids. That's why I ran into your church the way I did."

"What do you wish me to do, Señora?"

"Walk me to the train station."

They stepped outside. A night chill had settled, and the zigzag lights under the el reminded her of the framings and compositions of a Fritz Lang film.

"My father swears he didn't kill Nadine LaFleur," she said.

"You'll pardon me for saying so, Señora, but the evidence against him was quite strong."

"How did he seem when he came to see you the night she was murdered?"

"Angry. Upset. But that was normal for him."

"Did you notice anything unusual about his appearance?"

"No, but I was more intent on making sure my wire was working. Your father was a big target of the DA's investigation."

"Did you notice any blood on him?"

"No, but I assumed he cleaned up before he saw me."

"That's a good assumption, but they didn't find his fingerprints in her bathroom, he swears he didn't use it, and the cops claim they dusted every inch of the place."

Jose Almonte shrugged. "I turned to the Lord, Señora, when I realized there are many things in life that cannot be explained."

The stairs leading to the station were a block ahead. Sheila slowed. She needed to keep the conversation going.

"How did you wind up working for the DA?"

"The police arrested one of my workers. She was streetwalking—stupido. I didn't want the ladies who worked for me to do that. I always told them to make appointments, like a regular business."

"Why was she streetwalking?"

"She was a junkie. She needed money. The cops found heroin in her purse, and she was looking at a long time in jail if she didn't cooperate, so she told them about me and that I was paying off your father and his colleagues. The narcs relayed that information to the Internal Affairs department, and that's how the whole thing started."

"Did they arrest you?"

Jose Almonte shook his head. "My lawyer, Señor Ortega, was confident I'd beat any charges related to prostitution that were filed. Then the DA began talking about bringing my business dealings to the attention of the IRS. That's when Señor Ortega urged me to cooperate."

They stopped at the street corner and waited for the light to turn. Sheila realized she had only a few minutes left with the man once known as Paco.

"Nadine was your best," she said. "High-end clientele. She'd gone to college, studied literature, knew French. She could keep up with the movers and shakers if they wanted to talk."

"Many of them liked that. They asked for her specifically."

"You gave my father a list of her clients."

"For the murder investigation. I squawked, but I understood he was doing his job."

"My father said there were a lot of interesting names on that list. Like Aaron Grubb. He's still around. Still making deals. Still ruining the city for his benefit."

"You'd have to talk to him about it, Señora. I left those concerns behind long ago."

"Grubb's father was on that list, too."

"As far as I know, they used her separately, but you can never tell. When I was in that line of work, I discovered that men often behave in ways that are extremely dispiriting."

"My father got a lot of attention when he raided a brothel in Murray Hill."

"I remember that."

"Nadine worked there."

"Without my knowledge."

"Should I believe you?"

Almonte stopped and turned to face her. His voice grew clipped—whoremonger pique overcoming pastoral placidness.

"As soon as her body was discovered," he said, "I knew I would be suspected in her death. But I had an alibi for that evening. Two of the señoritas who worked for me swore to the police that they were giving me their full attention."

"Were they?"

He tried to suppress a smile. "They were in my apartment most of the night. As they were leaving, the men from the Internal Affairs division arrived to fit my wire. I made introductions, and everyone was extremely cordial."

Almonte turned toward the station. Sheila had withheld the question she regarded as the most crucial, but now she posed it casually, as if she were confirming the time of a flight.

"How did Nadine know Adam Fishman?"

The pimp-turned-pastor sucked in some air. "We kept that quiet, for understandable reasons."

Sheila had watched Michael handling witnesses who wanted to avoid the topic. "Answer the question, please."

The man once known as Paco puffed his cheeks.

He's not Catholic anymore, Sheila said to herself, but he must've been raised as one. If he's like me, he has never lost the need for confession.

"I shouldn't tell you this," he said.

Tell me, she thought.

"It was my doing. During the investigation, I introduced her to Señor Fishman."

Sheila stepped in front of him to block his way.

"Holy crap." Her astonishment was genuine.

Paco pointed toward the entrance to the 7 train. He wanted to get rid of her, but as a disciple of the Lord, he had to be polite about it. They resumed walking.

"You ever tell the police about that?" Sheila asked.

"Of course not."

"Did you ever talk with Fishman about what happened to her?"

"I didn't have to. We both knew silencio was muy importante. Talking about Nadine, and what happened to her, would have opened a can of gusanos."

"Why did you introduce her to him?"

"I thought his investigation would gain a great deal of insight if he talked to one of the women who worked for me. And Nadine was, as you said, my best."

"An educated young woman," Sheila said.

"Correct."

"A courtesan, not a streetwalker."

"Correct again."

"So they had a physical relationship," Sheila said.

"I'm not sure of that," Paco said. "I never asked either one of them about it. But whatever she was doing with Señor Fishman was helpful to me as the investigation proceeded. He always treated me with, as the expression has it, kid gloves."

"There were a lot of things you never asked about." Sheila hoped she sounded accusatory.

"Over the years, Señora, I've learned that when you ask preguntas about sensitive topics, you usually receive respuestas you dislike." He lifted his eyes toward the el. "The answers to everything lie with Him."

"Let's get back to Earth. How did you introduce them?"

"Over dinner. I broached the idea to Señor Fishman, and he was intrigued. When I told Nadine about it, she didn't want to. But when I said that Señor Fishman's family had money, she became more interested."

Sheila pictured them—Nadine LaFleur, real name Martha Owens, courtesan with a drug problem, tired of the life; Adam Fishman, homely and socially awkward, product of a well-heeled family, rising force in politics and the law. During their meal, while she provided revelations into the world he was investigating, Nadine may well have started to think: Some woman has to wind up with this man. Why not me? At least for a while?

The el's tracks shook. Sheila heard the rumbling rattle of the 7.

"Your train, Señora. We should hurry."

The traffic light turned. Sheila and the former pimp set foot in the crosswalk.

"Let's talk about this dinner," she said.

And then she heard squealing tires making a hard right turn. In a spasm of instinct she sprang back as quickly as she could, but a second later her senses were filled with the sickening splat of a man's body being struck full speed by an SUV.

Chapter Eleven

"**I** want out," Sheila said.

Despite the cold they sat outside CariBean so Joel could vape. Eyes locked on tablet, he puffed before swallowing two gulps of espresso.

"You can't," he said.

"Why not?"

"Sundance wants to look at your movie once it's done. So does the Tribeca Film Festival. I haven't told you any of this because you should focus on making the project. Selling it is my job."

"Somebody's trying to kill me," she said.

"Who?"

"I dunno. But I've started carrying this around."

She opened her bag and pointed to a can of Mace.

"Nowadays, they should give one of those to everybody who rides the subway." Joel sucked some more, then said, "We might get sued."

"What in the world?"

"I got a certified letter from one of Aaron Grubb's lawyers the other day. Who the hell sends certified letters anymore?"

"What did it say?"

"It said that if the quote, Unnamed Film Project by Sheila Devine, unquote, defamed Mr. Grubb in any way, shape or form, he and his attorneys reserved the right to sue us for everything we own."

"What did you do with this letter?"

"I wiped my ass with it."

Wesley came out of his shop and jerked his thumb at Joel while directing his words to Sheila.

"Did you tell him?"

She nodded. Joel shook his head.

"It'll look real bad if we back out," he said. "National Endowment for the Arts is thinking of sending money our way. PBS wants to air it after the theatrical release. Netflix, Hulu and Amazon could get into a bidding war over the streaming rights. Then there's the Oscars."

"What about them?" Sheila's voice sounded far away in her ears.

"Last week," Joel said, "outta the blue, a guy high up in the academy calls and says: 'I hear Sheila Devine's working on something good. Could blow the lid off a lotta stuff.' And I say I haven't talked to her about the details 'cause I wanna give her space to operate, yada yada yada, and he says: 'Just let her know that all the former New Yorkers out here really wanna see it.'"

Sheila wanted to slink down to the sidewalk and merge with the groundwater, but she straightened when Wesley put a large, firm hand on her back. After all these years, she still thrilled to his touch.

They met at a party in Alphabet City just after she left film school. She had stopped smoking pot, but her friends hadn't, and Wesley was the only sober guy in the room. She enjoyed their conversation and went back to his place, and everything was terrific, but when she woke in the morning, she was alone.

Great, she thought. Another guy who just leaves, even when it's his apartment.

But then she heard whirring in the kitchen, so she investigated. Wesley (naked) stood at the counter, pouring coffee beans into a grinder. Sheila (naked) sat in a chair in the breakfast nook and watched.

"Whatcha doin'?" she asked.

"My morning ritual. The coffee people drink in this city... " He grimaced. "Swill. I get these beans from my auntie. They grow in my hometown."

When he flipped on the coffeemaker, a strong but sweet aroma filled the room.

Best smell in the world, Sheila thought. Much better than perfume.

"Go back to bed," Wesley said. "I'll bring you a cup."

A girl could get used to this, Sheila thought.

Now here they were, outside Wesley's store. Married. Kids. Mortgage. Business loans. Still in love, she said to herself. But it's different now.

Wesley ran long fingers over her shoulder.

"I encouraged Sheila to do this," he said to Joel. "But that was before I realized how dangerous it was. We should pull the plug. I would like to grow old with my wife."

Joel vaped again. "If we pull the plug, it'll look like we're afraid of something."

"We are afraid of something," Wesley said.

"I suppose I should think about my father ... " Sheila let her voice drift.

"What about him?" Wesley asked.

"I'd be abandoning him."

"He abandoned you," Wesley said.

"That still wouldn't put me in the right." Sheila tried to smile but couldn't. "I hate being noble."

"There's something else I should tell you," Joel said.

"Uh-oh," Sheila said.

"You said you were looking for your dad's old supervisor, but he'd fallen off the face of the Earth."

"Adrian Lynch. What about him?"

"You mentioned that the guy had literary pretensions. So I raised his name with some people I know in the publishing industry."

Joel bit into a half-eaten energy bar that he'd found after rummaging through his Channel 13 tote bag.

"Yesterday, I struck paydirt. An editor with a mystery imprint told me that Lynch writes a series with a partner. They do it under a pseudonym. The editor says the partner looks like a squid, so they use Lynch's picture on the dust jackets. Lynch comes up with the ideas and a synopsis. His partner writes the first draft. Then the two of them start arguing and revising."

"What's the pseudonym?" Sheila asked.

"Bill Darcy."

Adrian Lynch is a Jane Austen fan, Sheila said to herself. You never know.

"Where does he live?" she asked.

"Florida. St. Pete Beach."

"I hate Florida," Sheila said.

"You're welcome," Joel replied.

She hated driving into Manhattan, but Hoodie Guy was loitering at the corner, so she took off in her Toyota. Hoodie Guy snapped a picture with his phone and then started talking into it. She got in the left lane, sped for the Triborough, took the Harlem River Drive to the Henry Hudson, then cruised south with the water on her right.

The long way around, she said to herself.

She exited at 72nd Street and debated looking for a spot by the curb but figured it'd be better to put the car in a garage despite the cost. She could always expense it, but Jesus, her taxes were getting complicated. The attendant at a place on West End Avenue asked how long she'd be, and she said she had no idea. She slung her bag over her shoulder and walked fast, ignoring the panhandlers, until she stopped across the street from the walkup where Nadine LaFleur once lived.

Sheila conjured the scene forty years earlier. Dirty, she reminded herself. Garbage everywhere. Crumbling brownstones with graffiti-smeared walls. A drug dealer did business in the open. Mayor of the block. He saw everything and watched Terence Devine talk his way into Nadine's apartment.

A stroller-pushing mom on a BlueTooth barked that she needed to get through. Sheila stepped close to the curb and noticed a cute young lesbian couple, arm in arm, heading up the steps of the brownstone where the deed had been done.

In the early Eighties, in a pathetic attempt to keep out the criminals, the building had a gate in front. Now it was open to the street, and in this Seinfeldian yuppie paradise the tenants' biggest problem was takeout guys clogging their mailboxes with menus.

Sheila waited for a delivery guy on a mountain bike to pass before crossing the street and taking the steps. She looked at the buzzer for 3A.

Maybe her ghost is there, she thought. If I ask it some questions, I'll resolve everything.

Voice on the intercom: "Hullo?"

Masculine. British accent. Sheila looked at the name on the slot over the buzzer and saw the word "Robinson."

Brits love mysteries, she reminded herself. Sherlock Holmes, Miss Marple, Inspector Morse—maybe all that nonsense I've watched on PBS will finally prove useful.

She leaned in close and said, "Mr. Robinson?"

"Not here, I'm afraid."

She ran through her Britishisms—bloody hell, rubbish, bugger. She brought her lips near the intercom again. "Let me explain why I'm here, sir."

No response. She feared he might ring off, so she started speaking quickly.

"I'm a filmmaker."

"Hollywood?"

"Documentaries."

"Oh."

"Something happened in that apartment years ago that's important to my movie, and I was hoping to take a look at it. You don't have to buzz me in right now. We can discuss the matter out here. I'll wave up, and you can take a look at me. I swear I'm harmless. Eccentric, maybe, but harmless."

She bounced down the stairs, turned, waved. She glimpsed a form in the window, but then it was gone, and she wondered how long she should wait. She'd understand if the guy blew her off, but the British revered idiosyncrasies so she decided to follow the advice she had heard for years from those self-help gurus on late-night TV: Visualize what you want actually occurring.

He will come out of the building, she said to herself. He will approach me, and we will converse, and I will talk my way into that apartment, just as my father did all those years ago.

She stared at the stoop for what seemed like an hour. When she was on the verge of walking away, she summoned one last big thought: Open the goddamn door.

It opened.

I should try that more often, she said to herself.

The man was lanky, with a rumpled thatch of reddish hair. His thin face was clean-shaven, and he approached with wary interest. Sheila opened her bag, took out her card, flashed her best smile. He scrutinized the card the way Howard Carter must have looked at the hieroglyphics in King Tut's tomb.

"You're subletting?" she said.

"Perhaps." He sounded upper crust. The playing fields of Eton and all that.

"As we like to say in this country, let's cut to the chase. Forty years ago, a murder took place in that apartment. A young woman—a sex worker—was killed in her bedroom. A man was convicted, and he's still in prison, but now there are questions about whether he did it, and I'm making a movie about the whole thing."

The man held up her card between his index and middle fingers. "May I keep this?"

"Certainly."

He put the card in his shirt pocket. "Tell me more."

"There's the official version of what happened," she said. "Then there's the account the convicted man related to me. I'd just like to look in the space and see which one makes more sense. Shouldn't take more than five minutes."

He pointed to her bag. "You don't have a gun in that thing, do you?"

She took the bag off her shoulder and zipped it open. "My laptop. An N95 mask, just in case. Some other stuff. See for yourself."

He peered in and pointed. "What's that?"

She reached for the spray can and lay it flat in her palm. "Mace. A woman can't be too careful."

He told her to follow. As they walked up the front steps, he twisted his neck around.

"My friends all warned me that everyone in America owned a gun and liked to use it."

"Sorry to disappoint you."

Inside the building, the stairwell zigzagged.

"The victim—was she shot to death?"

"Beaten and strangled."

"Too bad." The Brit sounded disappointed as he unbolted the door. The living room was dominated by a 55-inch hi-def TV mounted on the wall. A beige area rug covered most of the floor.

"How long have you lived here?" Sheila asked.

"About a month."

"What do you do?"

"Consultant and entrepreneur."

He's unemployed, she thought. Then she spun 360 degrees and swept her arm around. "It started here. The man talked his way in. Then he demanded money. He was collecting for her pimp." She pointed to the bedroom. "They went in there."

She walked in. The Brit followed. She saw a double bed with a comforter that vaguely matched the area rug. Plaster flaked from the ceiling. A MacBook teetered on the edge of the night table.

"They argued," she said. "It got loud. She owed two thousand dollars, but she was determined to keep as much of it as she could, so she handed over bills in fits and starts. The man admits pulling a gun on her."

The Brit nodded in satisfaction.

"But he insists he didn't kill her," Sheila said.

She looked around again. The bathroom was just to her left. After it was over, as Nadine lay dying, it would have been easy to walk in there, take a piss, and wash away the blood.

"Who was the perpetrator?" the Brit asked.

"My father."

The man's eyebrows arched nearly into his hairline. "Was he a collector for the Mafia?"

Sheila puzzled out his pronunciation of Mafia, then shook her head. "He was a New York City cop. Back then, there wasn't much difference."

The closet door had a narrow glass mirror. Sheila wondered how old it was. Perhaps Nadine had primped before it.

"He came back here a couple weeks later," Sheila said. "The victim's parents kept talking to the press about the case. They said the police weren't doing enough to solve it. They told a newspaper columnist their daughter kept a journal that might shed light on what happened. The dead girl's mom talked to my father about it, and he agreed to look, even though it violated procedure."

"Covering his arse?"

"He thought there was something hinky about the case, and that he might find some evidence the guys in Homicide had missed."

"'Hinky'?"

"Not quite right."

"I love American slang."

She pointed to the closet. "He wound up rooting around in there. Because that's where women keep their secrets. Do you mind?"

"My wardrobe is your wardrobe."

Sheila opened the mirrored door. Most of the Brit's clothes were black, so he had adapted to New York. The space smelled musty, as if nobody had sprayed air freshener since Bush the Elder was president.

She held her breath and stepped in. The closet felt cramped. Definitely not a place to linger if you're claustrophobic, she said to herself. In fact, it kinda feels like a prison cell.

She began talking to the wall. "My father came in here and started his search, but he heard something. So he closed the door. Another man had entered the apartment, so my father waited. When the guy finally reached the closet, my old man clocked him."

"Who was the man your father clocked?" The Brit clucked in approval. "Another wonderful word."

"His superior. A police captain named Adrian Lynch. It turned out that Lynch was one of the dead woman's clients, and he was afraid his name would pop up in that journal her parents kept talking about." Sheila shrugged. "When they got around to discussing it, my father and Lynch decided all that stuff about a journal was mythical. Something the parents concocted to keep the heat on the department."

Sheila shuddered as she stepped out of the closet. This place is speaking to me, she told herself. But what is it trying to say?

The Brit pointed to a painted-over indentation near the closet's ceiling that looked as if it could be pried open if a handyman needed to get to it.

"What do you think that is?" he asked.

"Probably the fuse box. The wiring in these converted brownstones can get really funky."

"The fuse box is in the kitchen."

Sheila pointed to the indentation. "Can you open that thing?"

The Brit reached up with long and slender fingers. Decades of dust and grit caked off. He coughed as the gunk hit his nostrils, but he clawed deeper, and finally, a small metal door swung open.

"Can you see in there?" Sheila asked.

The Brit shook his head. "I keep a step stool in the kitchen. For the cleaning lady. A Latin woman who's about four-foot-two."

He disappeared for a moment before coming back with a riser. He put it in the closet, stepped up, and peered inside.

"Hullo." He stuck in his hand and came out with a wad of dirt-encrusted bills. "You said your father was looking for money."

"So that's where she kept her stash." Sheila laughed. "If only he'd known. He coulda been out of here in two minutes."

The Brit blew some crud off the bills. "You're not going to take any of these, are you? With that gun you don't have?"

"I could Mace you, but finder's keepers. Anything else up there?"

He extended his arm. His face brightened.

"Hullo again."

Chapter Twelve

he journal's cover was filthy, and the pages were dry as sand. She feared they'd crumble as she turned them. Reading slowly, careful with every movement, she made notes on a Word doc. When Dylan came home from school, he helped her create a PDF that she stashed in a dozen digital hiding places.

In the early evening she texted Michael that she'd found something he should look at. He texted back that she could swing by his office. He was working late. When she was ready to head to Manhattan, she peered out the front window. No Hoodie Guy. For the second time in the day she drove into Manhattan, but this time she headed straight to the Brooklyn Bridge.

At the DA's building, she got a visitor's pass in the lobby. In the nearly empty space, her flats echoed on the linoleum floor. The door to Michael's office was halfway open. Sheila poked her head in and saw her brother standing at his desk.

"Waddya got, Sis?"

Warm but noncommittal. Classic politician tone.

Sheila put the journal on his desk. "Nadine LaFleur's diary. Be gentle when you open it. The pages rip easily."

Michael wet his fingers, held the leather cover in his left hand, and turned the pages with his right.

"I'm not sure this changes anything."

"Read it all the way through."

"Even if we reopen the case, the burden of proof rests on the man who married our mother and whoever represents him. The courts will assume that his trial was fair and the correct verdict was rendered." Michael shook his head. "It's not enough for him to establish reasonable doubt. For him, that ship sailed decades ago. Now he has to prove his innocence, and we both know he's anything but innocent."

Just after seven a.m., in the midst of her family's morning rush, Sheila's iPhone pinged with an incoming text. She silently cursed whoever had sent it but looked at the message anyway.

It was from Michael. Adam Fishman wanted to see her.

She put on a blue dress from Bloomingdale's and a pair of low-heeled wedges before leaving through the front door. When she saw Hoodie Guy leaning against a lamppost, she headed straight for him. His slitted eyes widened as she approached. When she was ten yards away, he turned and headed for DeKalb. Sheila used her strongest accent to call out: "Hey you!"

He kept moving. Sheila lengthened her stride. In a few seconds, she was beside him.

"I'm gonna tell you exactly where I'm going."

No reaction. She imagined a rock-hard body covered with tattoos underneath a tight T-shirt. Some women liked that kind of thing. So did some men.

"I'm heading to Manhattan to talk to my brother. He's a prosecutor there, but you probably know that already. I'll also be talking to the DA. Who hired you to follow me?"

Hoodie Guy stopped and turned. Now that she finally had a chance to look at him up close, she noticed an inked image of a snake circling his neck.

"You're crazy, lady." A Lawn Guyland accent spewed through his skull and crossbones mask.

"Why?"

"For thinkin' I'm gonna answer a question like that."

Adam Fishman's office was dark and paneled and had a sweeping view of the city, but the walls were bare of photographs and mementos except for one framed shot of him with his father on the night he was first elected.

He nodded at Sheila as she entered, but they made no physical contact. Sheila had met the DA a few times and he was always correct but distant and she reminded herself that public officials were like actors—they created a persona they eventually had to live with, and Adam Fishman was the serious man of probity who got things done.

Fishman pointed her to a leatherbound chair. Michael was already in an identical one six feet away. Fishman opened a drawer in his oak desk, which was the size of a small barge. He slid something toward her, and as it got closer, she could see it was the journal she had given Michael the night before.

"Normally," Fishman said, "I'd wear gloves so my fingerprints wouldn't contaminate something like this. But even if it's authentic, there's no chain of custody, so it would never be admissible."

Sheila slipped the journal into her bag. "You don't think it's authentic?"

"Your brother and I have developed a metric we call the Ortega Rule. After Rolando Ortega, our frequent nemesis. When we're developing a case, we always try to think of how he would attack a piece of evidence."

Fishman's words were robotic but fast, an affectless cadence that had become familiar to New Yorkers over the decades. Now, he counted off points with long and bony fingers.

"One, there's no way of knowing how long that thing had been there. For all we know, somebody could've planted it last week. Two, if it is real and it's been there for decades, who knows who's had a chance to get in there and alter it? Three, can we be certain the victim wrote all those things herself? We have no way of knowing, and no way of verifying it."

"I'm not making a legal case," Sheila said. "I'm making a movie."

"And you can keep making it," Fishman said. "But that journal is a lot less persuasive than you think it is."

Sheila's jaw moved, but no sound came out until she blurted, "How can you say that?"

"A lot of it is cryptic," Fishman said. "Martha refers to a man named 'A.'

That could be anybody."

Sheila shook her head. "'A' had money and influence. He talked to her about how things got done in New York. Who owed favors to whom? Who was in bed with each other, figuratively and literally. 'A' also made promises to her. From what she wrote, he didn't treat her like just another sex worker."

"Do you have any idea what 'A' stands for?" Fishman asked.

"His name probably starts with it," Sheila said.

"First name or last? Was it even his real name?"

Sheila told herself she should have expected a cross-examination. "The victim was handling a high-end clientele," she said. "Some of the men were prominent. She was an intelligent and curious woman, so I bet she knew their real names, even if they didn't tell her."

"That's a good guess," Fishman said. "But it's just a guess, and judges don't allow that."

Paco told me he introduced you to Nadine during the investigation, Sheila said to herself. My father told me she had your phone number. What kind of a relationship did you have with her?

She glanced at her brother and remembered something he had told her years ago, when he was beginning to acquire his reputation as the city's most relentless prosecutor:

Whenever I ask a witness a question, I already know the answer.

Sheila realized she wasn't there yet.

She leaned back in her chair, an impressive piece of furniture that looked comfortable but wasn't.

"I wanna talk to Aaron Grubb," she said. "He's threatened to sue me and my distributor, but I think we can clear things up. I've sent him emails, but he hasn't replied."

"Aaron Grubb has never sent an email in his life and has no interest in learning how to do it," Fishman said. "The people who handle that stuff for him are probably ignoring you."

"Can you put in a word for me?"

Fishman and Michael exchanged glances. They both knew Grubb, who had helped finance Fishman's campaigns. In fact, Michael's wife was a distant step-relative of Grubb's extended family.

"I'll mention it to Aaron," Michael said. "He threatens to sue all the time, but rarely does. He hates to spend money, except on his mistresses."

Sheila walked into Foley Square with the unsatisfied feeling she had experienced after her first sexual encounters. She sat on a bench and typed in notes on her laptop while pigeons and squirrels circled and beggars pleaded for money. As she looked over what she'd written, she told herself there had to be a move she could make. When she realized what it was, she linked to Expedia.

Chapter Thirteen

Wesley insisted on driving her to the airport. They left at three in the morning. She kept checking all around but didn't believe anyone had followed. At the curb, she embraced her husband. They kissed long and hard, and she enjoyed the stares of bleary-eyed white people taken aback by her P.D.A. with a Black man.

"Be careful," he told her.

Too late for that, she felt like saying.

Sheila went through the airport rigmarole and was reading *The Testaments* in the boarding area when her sixth sense kicked in. She bolted to her feet and spun 360 degrees.

Am I imagining something? she thought. Am I paranoid? Or is paranoia the sensible default option these days?

She was about to sit down when she thought she saw a familiar form duck into the men's room—a blur of a 'roided guy in a hoodie, skull and crossbones mask covering his nose and mouth, facial features that looked Caucasian. She stared at the bathroom entrance, waiting for him to emerge, but when she heard the boarding call for the flight to Tampa, she was afraid she'd get bumped if she lingered a nanosecond. As she took her seat on the plane, she reflexively reached for her iPhone before reminding herself to keep it turned off. Instead she stared at the gangway door, waiting for Hoodie Guy. But there was no sign of him, and she wondered if she was becoming prone to hallucinations. When the doors closed, the captain's voice came on, calm and flat. The flight would take two hours, he told everyone, and he expected no turbulence.

At the airport's Avis counter she paid cash to rent a convertible, then drove over bridges and causeways toward the beach. She did not know the address or phone number of the man she was seeking, so she'd have to nose around, but first she needed to eat, so she stopped at a Waffle House. A middle-aged waitress with a magnolia voice took her order and asked if she wanted coffee.

"A big pot of the highest-octane stuff you've got."

"You planning on a long day, Honey?"

"I woke up before dawn, and I have no idea when I'm going back to sleep."

"You poor thing. I'll bring that right out."

Sheila took out a notebook. She had to stay off the grid. At home the night before, she had printed out information from Bill Darcy's website, which struck her as deliberately sketchy, although the blurb was honest about the name being a pseudonym. It did say one of the authors had once been a high-ranking officer in a big-city police department who now lived in Florida. The site also contained a moody and airbrushed picture of a man fighting hard against the effects of age and gravity.

The other writer looks like a squid, Sheila reminded herself. The airbrushed guy has to be the one I'm looking for.

The coffee was strong. Caffeine always made her think better.

How do I find this dude? she thought. He's around here somewhere, and I've got only a few hours before they—whoever they are—figure out where I am.

She looked up from her notes as the waitress got near with her order of strawberry waffle, country ham on the side. Sheila realized she shouldn't overlook the obvious—horndogs never stop prowling.

"I've got a question for you," Sheila said as the woman slid plates in front of her.

"Sure thing, Honey." Her nametag said her name was Betty.

"I really like this guy's books," Sheila said as she pointed to the picture she'd printed out, "and I've heard he lives around here. You know anything about him?"

Betty stood straight as a board and backed up a step. "Wellllllll … "

Sheila poured syrup on the world's largest waffle. "Does he ever come here?"

"Not anymore."

Sheila looked over Betty from head to toe. Her hair was dyed, and her face was made up, but she was not wearing a wedding ring, and a once-desirable body was surrendering to midlife sag. Her eyes flashed with the hard glint of betrayal, and Sheila had a strong sense of why Adrian Lynch no longer patronized the Waffle House.

"You know where he goes?" Sheila asked.

"There's a bar about a mile down the road called the Captain's Quarters. He's usually there for Happy Hour." Acid crept into Betty's voice. "Be careful, Honey. He likes to buy drinks for the ladies."

With a few hours to kill, Sheila went to a mall and bought tees for the kids and a tropical shirt for Wesley before ducking into a bookstore to purchase a Bill Darcy paperback and a print edition of *The New York Times*. She paid cash for everything, found a seat in the food court, and leafed through the newspaper while drinking a liter of Aquafina. She usually read the *Times* online, and in the digital world each story existed discretely. Laying the paper on the table in front of her and viewing the articles in toto provided relentless documentation of just how thoroughly the world was fucked.

She left for the Captain's Quarters shortly before four. A sign outside said, "Masks Prohibited Under All Circumstances," and she realized she had entered an alternate reality. The bar itself was spacious and rectangular and frigid from air-conditioning. Behind the counter, a tattooed and ear-ringed guy in his twenties concocted a frothy drink in a metal shaker. The sound system blasted "Margaritaville." Sheila cringed but took an empty seat anyway.

The barkeep asked what she wanted. Sheila knew she'd have to drive away, so she ordered chardonnay, which she did not like. As the tender filled her glass, she looked around. The men stared as if she were an oasis in the middle of the Mojave. For the first time all day, she considered her appearance and demeanor. Her only makeup was a bit of eyeliner, she was dressed in Brooklyn black, and she kept glowering because she thought Florida was the armpit of the United States. In a land of bright floral clothing and sunny dispositions, she was as exotic as a geisha.

When the barkeep put the wine down, she motioned with her index finger, and as he leaned in, she could hear his mind working: I know you're older than I am and potentially dangerous, but a one-night stand with a woman like you might be memorable.

"I have a question," she said.

"Go ahead." He sounded like a boy who enjoyed playing with matches.

Sheila opened her bag, took out the Bill Darcy paperback, pointed to his picture, and said: "I'm trying to meet this guy. I understand he comes here a lot."

The barkeep tried to hide his disappointment as he looked at his watch. "He should be here in a few minutes."

Sheila put her stuff on the stool beside her and slid a twenty across the counter. "Make sure he sits next to me."

The barkeep's face brightened as he put the bill in his pocket. Sheila ran her eyes around the room again and, this time, she focused on the women. They were roughly her age, and all of them had had work done—eye lifts, tummy tucks, boob implants, liposuction, the human equivalents of Chevys souped up for Nascar.

The man she wanted to see walked in at four-thirty. He was an even six feet and tan, with wavy gray hair and the ramrod posture cops never lose. The regulars hailed him the way the barflies once greeted Norm in "Cheers." He looked over the surroundings the way personal shoppers glance over the half-price bin. A few women batted their eyes, but his gaze swept past them as if they were familiar landmarks on his highway of life. Instead his stare settled on Sheila, who flashed an opening-night smile while the barkeep leaned toward the ex-cop and whispered something. Lynch nodded like a gambler who'd been told the fix was in before heading straight toward Sheila as she lifted her stuff off the stool.

"Buy you a drink?" Lynch asked as he took the seat.

Sound seductive, Sheila said to herself. This guy thinks he's God's gift to women, and for a few minutes you should let him believe it.

She motioned toward her chardonnay. "I've already got one. But thanks anyway."

The barkeep set a Courvoisier on the rocks in front of the ex-cop, who lifted his glass and said, "Here's to you—what's your name?"

"Sheila."

"Sheila. I like it. I like it a lot."

She reached into her bag, took out the paperback, and said, "If you could sign this, I'd really appreciate it. I'm looking forward to reading it."

She slid a pen toward him. He scrawled a few words on the title page.

"If you don't mind me saying ... "

"I doubt I'd mind anything you say, Sheila."

Do women really fall for this shit? she asked herself.

"You look really good for a man your age." Lowball him, she thought. "You're about sixty, right?"

Lynch grinned. "I take care of myself, Sheila. I exercise, watch what I eat, drink in moderation, get the right amount of sleep. All that stuff is important, and everything is still working." He grinned. "And I do mean everything."

He probably has a lifelong Viagra prescription, Sheila said to herself. A four-hour erection. Jesus Christ, what's *that* like?

She put the book and pen back in her bag and said in the tentative tone so many men seemed to like, "I don't mean to pry ... "

"Go ahead."

"Where do you get the ideas for your books? That bio says you used to be a police officer in a big city."

"That was a long time ago, Sheila."

"What did you do there?"

"A little of this, a little of that. Cop stuff."

"It must help with your books."

"It doesn't hurt."

Sheila sipped her chardonnay. I've never been good at playing dumb, she thought. How long can I keep this up?

"You sound like you're from New York," she said.

The ex-cop's eyebrows shot up. "I've been here a long time. I thought I'd lost my accent."

"Not all the way."

"You sound like you're from Jersey."

Sheila flashed another smile. "I grew up there. I live in Brooklyn now."

"Brooklyn…" Lynch shuddered like an atheist trying to avoid a horde of Jehovah's Witnesses. "I haven't been there in years."

"It's changed."

"That's what I hear."

"Ever think of going back?"

"Not until a minute ago."

She resisted the urge to smack him over the head with her bag. "What was it like in the old days? The mean streets and all that?"

"It was a hellhole. Everything was boarded up, and everyone had a bad attitude. Crime was rampant, but we could do nothing about it because we got zero support from the politicians, who just kept laying us off." He sipped his cognac. "Sorry about the rant. I'll get off my soapbox now."

"Is that why you left the force? You'd had enough? Couldn't take it anymore?"

The ex-cop smiled in an attempt at looking rueful. "Well, Sheila, let's just say that my superiors and I decided that a parting of the ways would be best for everyone."

Sheila nodded with grudging respect. That's not even a lie, she said to herself.

"I don't wanna talk about the past," Lynch said. "I'd rather focus on the present. What do you do? In Brooklyn?"

"I'm a filmmaker."

His eyebrows rose in pleasant surprise. "Hollywood? My agent would love to talk to you."

"Documentaries."

"Oh."

"In fact, I'm working on one right now. Lemme give you my card."

He took it with an air of pleasant acceptance, but as he gazed at her name, his sunshine face morphed into a Big Apple scowl.

"That's right," Sheila said as softly as she could. "I'm his daughter."

Lynch rearranged his face into an impassive cop expression as he slid the card into his shirt pocket. "You tracked me down 'cause you wanna talk to me. Congratulations. Terrific work. But I've heard about that movie you're making, and I've been an idiot for talking to you."

He pushed his stool away from the bar, grabbed his drink, rose to his feet.

"I think you'll keep talking to me." Sheila flashed a mirthless cop smile. "You've made a nice life. Low profile, but you make a good living. Nobody really knows anything about your background, and your author bio keeps it vague. But all it takes is one tweet, one blog post, one entry on Facebook …"

She let the possibilities hang. Nothing tortures a person like their own worst imaginings. Sheila patted the stool he'd been sitting on.

"Sit down and talk to me."

"Not here." Lynch swallowed the rest of his Courvoisier. "Let's walk on the beach."

He established ground rules before they set foot on the sand—everything was on background and she could never reveal where he lived and, above all else, she could not film him.

"My father insists he didn't kill Nadine," Sheila said.

"The DA had enough evidence to convict him. That's all that matters."

"How well did you know her?"

"Well enough."

The sun was falling toward the water. Sheila felt it burning the corner of her eye.

"When did you meet her?" she asked.

"About six months before she died. At Chumley's. Some john had stood her up. I could tell she was a call girl."

"Why were you at Chumley's?"

"I knew some people in the writing game who hung out there."

"What did you say to her?"

"I pointed her out to the people I was with. I told them I could get her into a situation where I wound up arresting her."

"Did you?"

Lynch sighed like an acne-ridden schoolboy longing for a cheerleader. "She wasn't what I expected. We started talking about books."

"What happened after you stopped talking about books?"

"She knew a place near the river in Chelsea. The area was desolate. That meant we weren't gonna run into anybody. So we took a room."

"Did you tell her you were a cop?"

"In the morning. She laughed and said: 'Arrest me. After a night with you, I can use a break.'"

"But you didn't arrest her."

He shook his head. "We'd get together a couple of times a month. Always in that place in Chelsea. The things she could do ... "

"You never went through her pimp?"

"It was just between us. I figured she pocketed all the money, but that wasn't my concern."

"She ever talk about her pimp?"

"They never like their pimps."

"She was holding out on him."

"They all do."

"But he found out."

"So he sent your dad to collect the money he was owed. And we all know how that worked out."

Sheila was conscious of the information she was withholding. As if he could read her mind, Lynch said, "You'll save us both a lot of time if you lay all your cards on the table."

She ignored him. "What was Nadine like?"

"Good-looking, obviously. Smart as a whip. She had a wicked sense of humor when she felt like using it."

"But ... "

Lynch shrugged with the helplessness of a man who had thrown a life preserver to a woman intent on drowning herself. "She kept going on coke benders. That was how Paco kept her in line."

Doling out blow to his biggest earner—the deceased pimp/pastor had kept that nugget to himself.

"She wanted to get out of the life," Sheila said.

"They all do."

"But if she did, what would she do?"

Lynch stopped walking and turned to face her.

"You're playing games with me, and I don't feel like going along. You know a lot more than you're letting on."

"Answer my question."

Lynch made a face. "She had a few things in mind. For openers, she talked about opening a boutique."

"Was that realistic?"

"She needed money. That's one reason she was holding out on her pimp." The ex-cop shrugged. "She might've made a go of it. She had good taste and a head for business. She liked some locations on the Lower West Side. She saw the area's potential long before most people did. Her biggest problem was staying sober."

"She also had literary aspirations. Just like you."

"We discussed that. Pillow talk. We threw out ideas about books we wanted to write. She asked me about being a cop, and I asked her about the life."

"And she put that stuff in her journal."

"The infamous journal." Lynch sneered. "Bullshit her parents came up with to keep the heat on."

"I found it."

The ex-cop's jaw worked up and down a few seconds. "Can't you just put all your goddamn cards on the table?"

"Let's keep walking."

Lynch fell in beside her. They headed south.

"What's in it?" he asked.

"The well-written observations of a profoundly unhappy young woman."

"Sounds like every chick-lit novel I've ever read. What did she say about me?"

"Hard to tell."

"Waddya mean?"

"There was a man she referred to as 'A.' He seemed to have money, influence and connections. He talked to her about the machinations that were going on in New York at the time."

"I never had money. Still don't. I like nice things, but I'm careful about every dime I spend." Indignation crept into Lynch's voice. "You're here on a jihad on behalf of your father, who hoovered up every illegal cent he could get his hands on. I have my flaws, and I made mistakes, but I never grifted."

"You didn't have to. Your wife had money."

"She was a lawyer with her own practice, and she didn't want kids, so we made out all right. But we weren't rich."

"Then let's talk about influence and connections."

"Influence? I was a police captain. That counts for only a few watts on the power grid."

"Connections?"

A pause. "I heard things."

"Like what?"

"In New York, everyone always has a hustle going on. Nadine had hers; I had mine; your dad had his—"

"What kind of hustles did you hear about?"

"Real estate, mostly. The conventional wisdom was that the city was dying. But there were visionaries—people who saw that the city wasn't dying, just underachieving. It's like buying stock—if you get in when it bottoms out, you make a fortune. But a lot of visionaries don't have the money to make that initial investment."

Like Nadine, Sheila thought.

Lynch kept talking, a professor wrapping his tongue around his favorite topic. "Your dad accepted the conventional wisdom, which is always a mistake. He believed the city was gonna collapse, and he was intent on cleaning out every last penny, shekel, drachma and farthing before he bailed out. He thought he was the smartest man in the room, the guy who figured out all the angles before everybody else did, but he could never see more than five feet in front of his face. All that money he stole—if he'd sunk it into real estate on the West Side of Manhattan, you'd be living like Melinda Gates."

They walked on.

Now he's the one who knows more than he's letting on, Sheila told herself.

"I've seen pictures of New York from that time," she said. "Lots of neighborhoods looked bombed out, like Berlin after World War Two."

"Not a bad analogy."

"Today it looks abandoned. So many stores and offices closed during the pandemic."

"It'll come back. It always does. The only people who lose money in New York real estate are the ones who panic. I've learned that you should never underestimate the city or the men who run it."

"Jamie Quinn told me the same thing a few weeks ago," Sheila said.

Lynch looked at her with genuine surprise. "That fat piece of shit is still alive?"

"I've talked to him a few times. Another person who isn't telling me everything they know."

"You have no right to know everything. Nobody does."

"Quinn says a lot of men who made a killing back in the Eighties are still around, and they're gonna make even more money when the pandemic's over."

"Money is the only thing the men who run the city ever think or care about." Lynch shrugged, then grinned. "Well, sex, too."

Sheila looked over the Gulf of Mexico. The sun glowed dull orange just above the waterline.

"I despise Florida," she said. "But when it's like this, just for a moment, it all seems beautiful."

"My favorite part of the day," Lynch said. "But the sunsets are fast. You have to be careful around here. Darkness comes quickly."

I've overlooked something, Sheila thought. What is it?

"In the journal," she said, "Nadine wrote about the brothel you raided with my father."

Lynch let out a half-whistle that reminded her of air escaping a punctured tire. "Let's turn back," he said.

They headed toward the bar. Night began to blot the sky.

"Sounded like quite a place," Sheila said. "Every illegal activity you can think of, under one roof."

"It was like the Garden of Eden," Lynch said, "and your dad was the serpent."

"Did you know Nadine worked there?"

He shook his head. "I never would've raided it if I had."

Sheila began thinking out loud: "A spot like that is awash in cash. But the money's dirty. So the guys who run it have to make it clean somehow."

"Dirty money is the Achilles' heel of organized crime," Lynch said. "That's why the feds went after Al Capone for tax evasion."

"The brothel's money would've gone into a business that at least seemed legitimate." She thought some more. "So where did it go?"

"That's a good question."

"Where do you think the money went?"

"I'd be speculating."

"Go ahead."

"People are always trying to sell projects in New York," Lynch said. "The money could've found its way to one of them. Back then, banks charged fifteen, twenty percent interest. You could get a better rate from loan sharks." He flashed another humorless cop smile. "You make documentaries. Do some research."

They neared the Captain's Quarters. The bar was on stilts and the lights were on, the place was full, and the drinkers were trying to talk over the Jimmy Buffet songs.

"My father has theories about who killed her," Sheila said. "Sometimes he thinks it was Paco. Sometimes he thinks it was you."

Lynch turned to face her, and even in the fast-developing darkness she could see splotches of red that signaled his anger. He was three inches taller and sixty pounds heavier, and Sheila remembered the Mace in her bag.

He spat out his question: "And what do you think?"

"I think Nadine knew something that somebody wanted to keep hidden. And when I figure out what it was, I'll know who killed her."

"I think she died because she opened her door to somebody she shouldn't have." Lynch jerked his thumb toward the bar. "I've got two hours before the magic pill wears off, Sheila, so I'm heading back in."

"Go fuck yourself."

"Here's hoping."

Chapter Fourteen

She used her laptop for the first time all day as she tried to book an immediate flight out of Tampa. Nothing was available until morning. While she ate at a strip-mall Chipotle, she quick-texted her family that she'd be landing at JFK around noon. She turned off the device, finished her salad and drove around, changing directions several times, before pulling into the parking lot of an airport motel. She paid cash, took her bag into the room and bolted herself in. Before she went to sleep she put her Mace on the nightstand within easy reach, then scattered pages of *The New York Times* on the floor between the bed and the door.

Let's see the internet do that, she thought.

Her eyelids surged open as soon as she heard the crinkling sounds. Two a.m. Pitch black. She reached for the light but a large, strong hand forced her arm down. She wriggled her other arm free and tried for the Mace, but another hand pinned that arm, and she wondered if there were two of them. She hated seeming helpless, but she cried out for help as loudly as she could.

"Shut up, bitch."

Male voice. Sandpapery rough. She smelled tobacco and expected something to hit her, but two hands were confining her arms, and she sensed a heavy form on the bed hovering inches above her backside.

Only one guy, she said to herself. Gotta roll over. Gotta get my arms free.

She called out for help again and felt something cold and metallic in her ear.

"I told you to shut up."

She imagined the shot going off. When the cops came, they'd find signs of a struggle in a pillaged room. The woman had been the victim of a robbery. Just another victim of America's resurgence in violent crime.

But now her right arm was free, and with a powerful burst she swung it up and rolled her body and felt her forearm hit something that felt like the side of a head and heard the voice, still male but less rough, yell out with surprised hurt.

Men have no tolerance for pain, she thought.

She sensed the intruder wavering on the side of the bed, trying to avoid falling to the floor, and in one motion she kicked off the covers, sat up and grabbed the Mace. He thudded to the floor, and she considered turning on the light, but her eyes had adjusted to the dark. She saw him rise to his knees and aim the gun, so she dove off the bed just as he fired.

"He's shooting at me," she yelled out. She heard stirrings in the rooms beside hers. She reached up and wrapped her hand around the Mace and hoped to God it worked.

On her feet now. The guy was two feet away. He wore dark clothing and a balaclava. She lunged at him and aimed the spray at his eyes.

"Bitch! You crazy fucking bitch!"

The gun went off again when it crashed to the floor. The TV screen shattered, and as sparks flashed across the room Sheila got a look at the intruder—over six feet, solidly built, race uncertain, but from the glimpse of skin around his eyes she guessed he was Asian.

She had gone through a kickboxing phase when the kids were small, and she hoped muscle memory was a real thing as she extended her foot toward the intruder's kneecap. Her sole connected with bone, and the guy's leg buckled, and he cried out again and bent over in pain. Then she raised her foot as quickly as she could and smashed it into his face, and he screamed, "Oh fuck, my nose, my fucking nose, you insane goddamn bitch."

He backed away. Blood seeped into his balaclava and dripped onto the floor. Sheila heard people in the adjoining rooms saying, "Que?" and "Como?" and "Estan loco."

The intruder slipped on newspaper pages stained with red droplets. He yewled in pain, scrambled upright, and reached for the doorknob. Sheila wished motels still allowed smoking so she could hurl an ashtray at him.

He opened the door just wide enough to stumble out. Sheila yanked it the rest of the way and saw a late model Toyota with tinted windows idling in the lot. A driver sat behind the wheel. As the intruder gimped to the passenger side, Sheila thought about rushing out to get the tag number, but then the driver's window lowered.

All she could see was the gun pointing at her.

She hurled herself back into the room, slammed the door and dove to the floor just as the driver fired. Something tore through the door and then the wall, and she heard shrieks from the next room. For a moment she feared the driver would come after her, so she rose to her knees, locked the door, then lay flat on the ground while gripping the Mace.

Tires squealed. An engine revved. She listened to the fading roar of a car speeding away.

While Sheila lay there, she recalled Winston Churchill's line about the exhilaration of being shot at with no effect. After a few minutes she heard a muffled conversation in Spanish outside her room. When she opened the door, a man and a woman looked her over. They seemed astounded to see her alive and uninjured.

The man and the woman were short and thin and in their early thirties. The door to their room was ajar, and four small children poked out their heads with the wide-eyed wonder of kids who still thought the world was endlessly interesting.

"Que pasa?" the man asked Sheila. "Por qué te dispararon?"

"No se," Sheila replied.

The man shook his head. "I think you do."

She returned to New York after nightfall. Wesley picked her up at the airport and fought the traffic back to Brooklyn. He asked what had happened and she said she wasn't ready to discuss it. They were silent a while, and finally he said that Dylan and Bethany were worried about her.

She had talked to the Tampa cops, telling them what had occurred as best she could remember.

"You really think it's connected to this movie you're doing?" the lead investigator said. His nametag gave his name as Menendez. His neck was as wide as his head.

She told him to check out Adrian Lynch, but when the cops found him, he had an alibi—shacked up all night with a fortysomething pharmacist named Doris who confirmed that he hadn't left her sight since they hooked up at the Captain's Quarters.

At home, Sheila shared Indian takeout with her family. Nobody said anything. After dinner, she went to her workroom and called her brother on the landline.

"The deputy state's attorney in Hillsborough County called," he said. "Professional courtesy."

"What did you tell him?"

"Her. Nothing much. It seemed like a good time to play my cards close to the vest."

You always do that, Sheila thought.

Michael went on: "Nobody got the license plate, but the car was probably stolen anyway. The cops will run ballistics on the bullets and try to trace the gun the assailant left in the room, but I figure the weapons they used were stolen, too. There is some blood, so they can do DNA tests on the guy who attacked you, but that's likely to take weeks."

Sheila kept shrinking lower in her chair. One thought kept running through her mind:

I can't go on like this.

The room was familiar and the scene so ritualized it seemed like Kabuki—a ripped Terence Devine being led in by guards who lived on a diet of Dunkin Donuts. His eyes narrowed as he sat.

"Where's the camera?"

"I didn't bring it."

"Why not?"

"I'm quitting the project."

Devine sucked in air as if she'd just hammered his solar plexus. "I've been straight with you."

She told him about the motel, and about what had happened to Paco.

"You're getting close," Devine said.

"Close to what?"

"The truth, whatever it is."

"I'd prefer to stay alive."

He shook his head. "You don't have a choice."

"Waddya mean?"

"They—whoever they are—can't be sure of how much you know, or don't know. So they're not gonna take a chance. They'll keep coming after you until they succeed." He paused. "Unfortunately, they need to succeed only once."

"You mean I have to keep doing this—"

Devine nodded.

"—and I have to figure out who killed Nadine—"

Devine nodded again.

"—and I have to do it before they kill me."

Devine finished nodding.

"I don't like my odds," Sheila said.

"They'll do something stupid," Devine said. "In fact, they already have."

"How so?"

"They tipped their hand. They've got something to hide. Nobody would be bothering you if everything was on the up and up."

Sheila sighed. A mounting body count never troubled people with power. She silently cursed the day she'd set foot in the Justice Project.

"You could end it today," she said.

"How?"

"Admit you did it. You're a pain in the prison system's ass. The parole board would be happy to release you. Then, as soon as you're out, recant the confession."

"There are cases like that. You know what the state does?"

Sheila shook her head.

"They charge the guy with perjury. Throw him right back in."

Sheila shut her eyes. She rarely cried, especially in front of men, but she was close.

"There's gotta be a way outta this," she said.

"The best way out is always through," Devine said.

"Robert Frost," Sheila said. "I never liked him. Saccharine New England shit."

"You need to talk to all the scumbags you haven't talked to already," Devine said. "Antonelli, Grubb, Fishman. Especially Fishman. He's a gutless bastard who'd snatch a baby out of a cradle to take a bullet for him."

Chapter Fifteen

Alarm at three-thirty. Wesley still asleep. Sheila kissed him on the cheek and checked on the kids before slipping out. It was still dark, and she felt grateful for the cover as she walked toward the subway. She had thought about Ubering into Manhattan, but if she'd been hacked she could be followed, so she kept her phone off.

She got on the No. 2 train and glowered at the skeeves while swaying on her feet by a door. She remembered what Michael had told her decades ago when they first began coming into New York:

"A lotta people think they're gonna get mugged the minute they set foot in the city. You'll be fine as long as you stand up straight, walk fast, and look pissed off."

She got off at Times Square and strode through the passageway that led to the Port Authority bus terminal. She paid cash for her ticket to Cape Cod and felt relieved that most of the passengers were Black or Latin. She tried to doze but failed. When the bus was well into Connecticut, she turned on her device and texted a two-word message to her family: EN ROUTE. As soon as it was delivered, she powered down and took out *The Testaments*.

The bus stopped in Providence and Fall River and New Bedford—hollowed-out cities with the living dead of America lurching along their sidewalks. After the bus pulled into Hyannis she rented a car and told the clerk she'd return it in New York. She paid cash. Then she ducked into the ladies' room and put on a blond wig, kerchief, N95 mask and dark glasses.

While she drove, she feared she'd rear-end somebody because she spent almost as much time glancing in the rearview as she did looking at the road. Near Wellfleet she made a sudden right without signaling and headed toward Marconi Beach. She sped nearly a mile before pulling to the side to see if anyone was following.

She heard seagulls.

Back on Route 6, she drove past the windswept dunes of Truro before making a left at the sign for Provincetown's commercial district. She left the rental in a municipal lot. It was nearly eleven, and she'd had little to eat, so she was getting hangry.

I do my best interviews when I'm hangry, she said to herself.

The B&B she wanted was called the Standish Inn. Tasteful Olde English lettering was painted on the white trim just above a heavy oak door that Sheila pushed open. She stepped into a foyer filled with framed portraits of Pilgrims. A big book that looked like a guest ledger was open on a writing desk. She peeked at it; the most recent name had been entered three days ago.

"Anybody home?" she called out through the mask.

Her words reverberated off wood and plaster. A minute later she heard a footfall on the stairs that led to the second floor. When she glanced up, she saw a seventy-something Italian-American man who was aging as gracefully as genes allowed.

Pilates, Sheila thought. Yoga. Tai chi. Bike riding and barbells. Maybe I should do Pilates.

"I wasn't expecting anyone," he said. "Can I help you?"

He had a mellifluous voice and the easy smile of a man who wanted everyone to like him. Sheila's Google search the day before revealed many things about Dante Antonelli. In the mid-eighties he was one of the first politicians to take a vigorous stand in favor of AIDS prevention and education. It was a gutsy position for an outer-borough councilman from a heavily Catholic district; although his views gained favorable notice from Manhattan liberals, his constituents believed he was coddling perverts and deviants. He was in a tough race for re-election when the *New York Post* came out with the story that ended his political career—City Councilman Dante Antonelli, Democrat of Canarsie, father of three and lector at Holy

Family Church, kept a boyfriend in a studio apartment at the rent-stabilized Independence Plaza a short walk from City Hall. Adding to the scandal, the boyfriend was Black.

Routed in the primary, divorced by his wife, disowned by his children and abandoned by the boyfriend, Antonelli moved to Provincetown and wound up opening a bed and breakfast on Commercial Street. He headed the Chamber of Commerce, befriended Norman Mailer and settled into a long-term relationship with a portrait photographer. The two of them were married on Race Point Beach in the summer of 2017; Sheila found a write-up about their wedding online in the *New York Times* archive.

She extended her arm toward him and said, "My name's Bridget."

"Dante."

He wrapped a warm hand around hers. Once a man engaged in political life, he never entirely shed its habits.

"What can I do for you, Bridget? Do you need a place to stay?"

"Actually, I had a few questions I wanted to ask. For a project I'm working on." She swept her arm around. "This is a wonderful place you have here."

"I've got a few minutes. Why don't we step inside?"

He led her into the lounge, which had a fireplace, a sofa and several high-backed chairs. It looked like the type of room where tea was served every afternoon at four during high season.

He motioned her to the sofa while he took a chair near the fireplace.

Geez, I'd like to film this, she thought. Logs and andirons always look good.

"You can take off your mask, Bridget. I've been vaxxed and boosted."

"I'm sorry, but I'd prefer to keep it on. I'm immunocompromised."

"I understand. What's this about?"

Sheila's stomach growled as she glanced around. The wood was burnished, the furniture antique. On the inn's website, the guest rooms were displayed in elaborate schemes meant to invoke Provincetown's nautical past.

"How do you get the money for a place like this?"

"Loans. I got some favorable terms. And don't discount sweat equity. You wouldn't believe how much work it took to bring this place up to code."

"I would believe it. My husband and I bought a fixer-upper in Brooklyn."

"I'm from Brooklyn," he said. "Haven't been there in a long time, though."

"Why did you leave?"

"It was time for a fresh start."

"Have you worked in the B&B business before?"

"No, but it seemed like a good line of work to get into in this town. Are you interested in starting your own place?" He chuckled. "I'm not sure I should help someone who sounds like a potential competitor."

"My husband and I like staying in B&Bs, but we'd never want to run one. He owns some coffee shops back home, and he's always looking to expand."

"That's another good line of work. If you and your husband want to scout locations around here, I could put you up, and we could work out the price. It is the slow season."

Sheila knew that Wesley would be amused to walk around town with a white woman in a blond wig.

"Of course," Antonelli said, "we already have some terrific coffeehouses. There's always room for a good one, but nowadays, in the caffeine business, you need a shtick."

"My husband imports all his beans from home. Jamaica."

Antonelli looked puzzled. "Queens?"

"Caribbean."

Something clicked in Antonelli's mind. The creases in his forehead grew deeper, and he leaned toward Sheila, stared at her head, and realized he was talking to a woman who had disguised herself.

"Why are you here, really?" he asked in the Inquisition-like tone she had heard on the YouTube videos of the commission hearings.

Time to fess up, Sheila thought, so she removed the mask, glasses and kerchief, then stuffed the wig in her bag.

"What makes you think I'm gonna talk to you?" Antonelli asked.

"Because you were once a politician, and they love to talk."

"I will say this—I really liked that movie you did about the trans kid at high school in Bay Ridge. My husband and I cried. We were surprised it wasn't nominated for an Oscar."

So was I, Sheila thought. To Antonelli she said, "My father told me he once caught you receiving oral sex from a Black teenage hooker named Randall."

"I've been open about my sexuality for decades. How is that relevant to anything?"

"My father thinks you had it in for him. He says if he had it to do over again, he would've mentioned the incident at the commission hearings."

"And I would've ruled him out of order before he got two words out of his mouth."

"You're not denying it."

"We were hounded in those days," Antonelli said. "Made to feel like freaks and psychopaths."

"You weren't in a relationship. You went cruising, and you picked up a boy."

"Randall and I developed a relationship. I admit he was vulnerable, and there was an age gap, but we were together a while, and I helped him get out of hustling."

"By taking advantage of him?"

"I set him up in a new place."

"Waddya mean?"

"I couldn't help him out financially. I was a father of three living on a city councilman's salary and, unlike your dad, I never took a dime in graft."

"My father gave him some money to go back home."

"Randall told me about that. Terence Devine's one act of kindness in an otherwise despicable life. Randall used that money to find a cold-water flat in Hell's Kitchen, but I knew I could get him something better. Tribeca was still off the beaten path, so I pulled strings to get him into a studio at Independence Plaza. We kept seeing each other, and he got a job in the fashion industry."

"But then the *Post* broke the story about you two."

Antonelli puckered his lips at the sour memory. "I had to leave the city, but Randall wouldn't come with me. Nobody falls in love with New York the way starry-eyed out-of-towners do."

"I'd like to talk to Randall."

"I've had no contact with him in decades. I don't even know if he's alive."

"Then there was that stunt you pulled the day my father was arrested."

"One of my best moments in public service."

"Why did you arrest him in front of the cameras? The NYPD could've hauled him in any time."

"If you wanna talk about stunts, let's start with that lecture he gave us. We're dealing with one of the most corrupt cops in the city's history, but he comes across as Robin Hood, and we take it like putzes."

Antonelli licked his lips. He was warming to the story.

"Aaron Grubb said we shouldn't take it lying down—we had to hit back at that shitheel, and hit him hard. At the time, I was getting information about Nadine's murder, and Jamie Quinn told me the cops were leaning on her pimp. That's why I asked Almonte all those questions about her."

"You didn't get far with that."

"He'd lawyered up, but later that day I got a call from Detective Mulligan. And he said—"

Here the former councilman did a passable imitation of the Homicide dick's voice.

"'Don't feel too bad, Councilman. You're barkin' up the right tree. but at the wrong squirrel.'"

"So Mulligan told you my father had been in Nadine's apartment the night she was killed?"

Antonelli nodded. "I got all the commission members together at my home for a meeting that night. Grubb came up with the idea of bringing your father back before us. I was afraid he'd make us look like idiots again if we questioned him, and Aaron said: 'We don't question him at all. We bring him in and then let the cops arrest him. Put that fucker in jail where he can't bother us anymore.'"

"The arrest was dramatic," Sheila said.

"It was."

"It was also prejudicial."

"What of it?"

"The way he was arrested made it impossible for him to get a fair trial."

"That was the point."

Time to shift gears, Sheila said to herself. "Why did Nadine LaFleur have your phone number?"

"What are you talking about?"

"Your phone number was found in her handbag shortly after the murder. A woman who claimed to be a friend of hers called you and said she was scared, and you told her not to worry her pretty little head."

Antonelli glared. "If that conversation ever took place, I don't recall it."

I think you recall it goddamn well, Sheila thought.

He stood. Loomed over her. "And now, Ms. Sheila Devine, it's time for you to get off my property."

She glanced around again. The furnishings gleamed. The B&B's website made a point of saying the house had been in disrepair when Dante Antonelli purchased it in 1987.

"The first question I asked you was better than I thought," she said as she got to her feet.

"Which question was that? I lost track."

"It takes lots of cash to renovate and operate a place like this, and when you came here, you must've been broke or close to it—disgraced and divorced after years on a civil service salary. How did you get the money? What did you use for collateral on those loans you took?"

Antonelli ran his hand through his still-impressive head of hair and set his jaw so tightly his lips barely moved.

"You're not the IRS. I don't have to tell you a thing."

Sheila slung her bag over her shoulder. Antonelli was going to call people, so she had to leave quickly.

A hand wrapped around her wrist.

"I've reconsidered," he said with mock solicitude. "Stay a while. I know people who'd like to talk to you."

They were right by the water. Hundreds of boats were docked only yards away. A thug could bundle her body on board one of them and then motor out to the sharks. People disappear all the time.

She elbowed Antonelli's ribs and heard a soft oof, and then she remembered the free karate lessons her mother had made her take at the Y, so she chopped at his neck. He yowled and took the Lord's name in vain. She grabbed one of the metal rods near the fireplace and swung it at his stomach. Antonelli gagged before sinking to his knees. Sheila kicked him on the side of his head. He toppled over and lay on the floor. When she checked his pulse, she had mixed feelings that he still had one.

Back home, Sheila was dog-tired, but Bethany wanted to watch that night's episode of "The Cutting Room" while it aired. The judges had to kick out one more designer before the final three reached the season-ending show at Hudson Yards, and Bethany was afraid she'd find out who'd gotten the ax on social media.

Sheila nuked a bag of low-fat Newman's organic popcorn and brought it out to the couch, where she sprawled with her daughter while the TV flickered on. Sometimes Sheila thought Bethany should take up fashion in case dance didn't work out. You always need a Plan B, and the apparel industry will survive until nudists rule the Earth.

Usually it was easy to tell who was about to get bounced, and on this episode the judges had their scissors out for a Russian girl named Nadia, who was talented but antagonistic. Her hair was dyed three different colors and fell in four different directions. After the designers displayed their wares, Nadia stood before the panel with the fatalistic air of Captain Dreyfus at the court-martial that sent him to Devil's Island. The chief inquisitor was Tiberius Randle.

"Listen, Honey," he told Nadia, "and I say this with all due respect—"

Which meant, of course, that he didn't.

"—but right now your clothes, your presentation, your whole *aura*, are all about attitude instead of attire."

The other judges nodded in agreement.

"You need to lose the 'tude and gain some tools, you know what I'm saying?"

Nadia looked stoic. That's one thing about Russians, Sheila thought. Horrible news never fazes them.

"Now, in my younger days, I confess to having just as much 'tude as you do. Maybe even more. And some of the stuff I did when I came to this city …"

He shook his head and his hand, as if both of them contained information he would be happy to shed.

"It was the early Eighties, honey, and you survived by doing whatever was necessary. Back then, I spent a lot of time on the piers, and those things were so decrepit I was afraid they'd fall into the river and take me with them. It was like *The Hunger Games*, 'cept nobody was as good-looking as Jennifer Lawrence."

The other judges laughed.

"Now, darling, I received some help and, unlike you, I was ready to accept it. We offer constructive criticism, and you react like we're sending you to the gulag. But sometimes you need to rely on the kindness of strangers, which I have done because I am the Black and queer Blanche DuBois. Back in the day, I got some good advice and even better money from an older man—a police officer, truth be told—who damn near ordered me to leave New York and go back home. Of course, that meant Pittsburgh, and no way in hell was I heading there."

He shivered before he resumed talking, but Sheila stopped listening as her jaw swung open and a piece of popcorn fell from her mouth.

Bethany passed her hand in front of her mother's eyes.

"Ma?"

Another pass of the hands and the same word, a little louder: "Ma?"

One more time, with an urgent question: "Ma, you okay?"

"Holy crap," Sheila said.

Chapter Sixteen

Her iPhone was ringing and she looked at the time—6:03—and her first thought of the day was, Who the hell calls somebody at this hour?

She didn't recognize the number. She wanted to go back to sleep. But the damn thing kept going, so she unlocked it and grunted her name.

"This is Aaron Grubb's office." The voice was female and officious. "Mr. Grubb understands from your brother that you'd like to talk to him."

Sheila considered the possibility that she was being punked before saying, "I would."

"Be at Mr. Grubb's office at seven-thirty. He can give you fifteen minutes."

As she walked up the Sixth Avenue power canyon, she noticed the dearth of activity. She'd last been in the area several years before to see the Christmas show at Radio City. The kids were twelve and nine, and the tourists jammed the sidewalks so tightly it was almost impossible to move inside the music hall. Dylan just kept staring at the Rockettes' legs. That was when she knew for sure that her son was straight.

Now she feared those shuttered storefronts would never reopen. The potentates in business and politics kept saying things were returning to normal, but Sheila felt like responding that the world had changed.

After passing through the lobby's security theater, the elevator whisked her to the forty-ninth floor, home of Grubb Rosen Gould LLC. Dark wood absorbed every sound. Sheila walked toward the reception desk, but before she could say anything, the woman behind it—stern-looking outer-borough type, Caucasian, a little too much makeup, gray hair that looked as if it hadn't moved since Rudy Giuliani was mayor—glanced up and asked, "Are you Mr. Grubb's seven-thirty?"

"I am."

The woman shifted her eyes to her computer screen. Sheila took out her phone again. Seven twenty-two.

"He'll be with you in eight minutes."

Sheila sat on a vinyl sofa with no give to it. As she glanced around, she sensed that this was a workplace where everyone had been ordered to return to the office five days a week, whether they liked it or not.

After seven and a half minutes, the receptionist said, "Mr. Grubb's secretary is at the fourth desk on the left."

A Black security guard built like a linebacker opened a ponderous oak door. The space beyond it was open, but the wood paneling was even darker, with each side lined by smoky glass that obscured the offices behind. The fourth desk on the left looked about a half-mile away, and as Sheila walked over the carpet, her feet sank deeper than she'd anticipated. Although she wanted to add height, she regretted wearing heels.

She stopped at the desk. Aaron Grubb's secretary was a fierce-looking white woman of about sixty with pinched cheeks. Sheila assumed her blond hair was dyed. Before she could say anything, the woman spun from her desktop and took three steps to her boss's door, which she cracked open two inches.

"Go in."

Aaron Grubb stared out the window, which faced south and offered an IMAX view of midtown and lower Manhattan. Far away and slightly to the west, Sheila detected the harbor and the Statue of Liberty, which she had last visited when she was in middle school.

Grubb whirled in his chair and motioned for her to take a seat on the other side of his desk, which was as big as his ego.

"Why are you doing this shit about your father?" he asked.

"Because I wanna win an Oscar."

Grubb blinked a few times. Candor was the only thing in the world that surprised him.

"You think this'll do it?"

Stay cool and confident, Sheila said to herself. This guy is an apex predator who will leap at your throat if you show the slightest doubt or weakness.

"It's a real-life mystery. The academy will eat it up."

"There's no mystery. He killed that whore. The jury said so."

"He says he was wrongly convicted, and I think he's right."

Grubb ogled her as if she were a prospective mistress. Apparently, women who put up a fight turned him on.

"We've met," he said.

"My brother's wedding. His wife is related to your family somehow. I never did figure it out."

He nodded. "Rachel is my step-niece or niece-in-law or niece by marriage or some bullshit like that. There are cousins and divorces involved, and I've got more important things to think about."

She took out her phone. "Can I record you with this?"

"Hell no."

"Let's talk about the Antonelli Commission anyway."

"We did good work. Most of it was my doing, but I let Antonelli take the credit. After that, he owed me a big one. Too bad he's queer. He woulda been mayor."

"My father laced into you guys when you testified."

"Your father's a schmuck who got what he deserved."

"Because he told you off?"

Grubb's face scrunched into a series of furrows. "What are you up to?"

Time for the drone strike, Sheila said to herself.

"During the murder investigation, my father forced Nadine's pimp to produce a list of her clients for the Homicide detectives. Your name was on it."

"So what?"

Sheila had expected him to deny everything, plead memory loss, or at least get defensive.

"You used a sex worker?"

"'Sex worker.' Politically correct horseshit. She was a prostitute, and it's none of your goddamn business if I used her or not."

"Your phone number was on a piece of paper my father found in Nadine's apartment."

"Lots of girls had my phone number. Still do."

"Did the cops ever interrogate you about Nadine?"

"Nobody's ever interrogated me about anything."

"You didn't answer my question."

"The police never talked to me."

"How long have you known Adam Fishman?"

"Practically forever. Our fathers did business together."

New York's leading real estate families were America's version of the Bourbons and Hapsburgs, right down to the feuds and intermarriages.

"He married your sister," Sheila said.

"Stepsister."

"And you've contributed to all his political campaigns."

"I've asked you this before—what's your point?"

Sheila straightened her back and moved her butt to the edge of the chair. "The day my father was arrested, Adam Fishman brought him to the hearing room. But you stopped Fishman just outside the room, so my father walked in there alone."

"What of it?"

"Did you warn Fishman about what was gonna happen?"

"Goddamn right I did. I wasn't gonna let Adam look like a schnook while the NYPD arrested your father for murder."

"Did Fishman have any inkling that my father was gonna be arrested that day?"

"Not until I told him."

"And what was his reaction?"

"No reaction at all. Adam's a great poker player."

"So my father took the fall for Nadine's murder, and everyone else went on with their lives."

"It worked out well."

"Not for my mother."

Grubb waited a second before asking, "What do you see behind me?"

"The bottom half of Manhattan. It looks like a postcard."

"It looks like a postcard because men like me worked our asses off. You remember 9/11."

"Of course."

"After that day, everyone said downtown was dead. It was gonna be a ghost town. Nobody would live or work there." He shook his head. "Morons. Pussies. But I wasn't surprised they said that, because most people are afraid of their own shadows. So prices hit rock bottom in the financial district, I went all in, and downtown came back just like I knew it would."

"That's a nice business lesson for Management 101," Sheila said, "but how does that relate to what happened to my father?"

Grubb paced to the window, where he gazed south like a medieval lord surveying his lands. Without turning, he made a motion with his hands. Sheila joined him while wondering if she should bring along her bag with the Mace.

Grubb nodded toward the buildings as if they existed at his sufferance.

"Your father thought he was the only guy around who knew the score, but he didn't even know what the game was. I could point in any direction and show you a site I bought for peanuts back in the Seventies and Eighties because everybody thought the sky was falling." He shook his head. "The sky never falls, but nobody ever learns that lesson."

"My husband owns some coffee shops in Brooklyn," Sheila said. "After the pandemic scrambled everything, he renegotiated his leases. Then he rented some other spots where he'd been looking to expand. Landlords are desperate, so he locked up those spaces for next to nothing."

"Disaster creates opportunity," Grubb said. "I remade the city before, and I'll do it again."

His eyes shifted west toward the Hudson River, and Sheila remembered her father talking about the piers that were kept together only by the will of the gay men who hung out on them. Now a park ran along the shoreline, and West Street was lined with brand-new glass condominiums and nineteenth-century warehouses rehabbed into luxury digs. Aaron Grubb's company had supervised the transformation.

"The area turned out fine, though we hit a few snags," Grubb said. "It would've been better if the city had built Westway, but the goddamn tree-huggers found a judge who took them seriously."

Sheila recalled that they were actually fish lovers, but she decided not to correct him.

"What's your next move?" she asked.

"Tech's coming in," he said. "They're smart people, so they're taking advantage of the downturn. Whenever I find out where they're going, I buy the land around it."

He turned to face her. Even in heels, she still had to look up to him.

"Above all else," he said, "I don't let anyone get in my way."

She took the D train to 14th Street before transferring to the L. The office she wanted was on Gansevoort across from the entrances to the Whitney Museum and the High Line. In her film school days, she often came here when the Meatpacking District lived up to its name, so she could shoot videos of blood dripping off the carcasses of slaughtered cows.

She cursed her shoes as she wobbled over the cobblestones and trudged up to the second floor of a gut-renovated building that had once housed New York's largest porn emporium. A small sign outside the office she wanted reminded entrants that masks were okay as long as they looked fashionable. When she opened the door, she was assaulted by bursts of noise, color and activity—people shouting over one another, framed posters lining brick walls, the blip blip blip of incoming calls. Although the space was open, her way was blocked by a marble slab staffed by a young Black man with dreadlocked hair that stretched past his waist.

The company was called Pitts, in what Sheila guessed was a nod to its owners' roots. She nodded at the receptionist. Got nothing in return. His mask was purple, which she considered an interesting color choice.

"I'm looking for Mr. Randle."

"Do you have an appointment?" The guy's tone was affectless. He could have been from Iowa, or Mars.

"I saw him last night on 'The Cutting Room.' He said some things that struck a chord."

The receptionist shook his head. Watching the dreads move was like seeing waves roll in. "We've been inundated because of that."

Sheila took out her business card, wrote a few words on the back, and handed it to the receptionist. "Can you see that he gets this? I can wait."

The receptionist looked at the card as if she'd just pulled it out of a landfill. "Filmmaker, huh? Tiberius has lots of deals in the works."

"Nothing like this," she said.

Sheila sat, checked messages and voicemail, looked over email, sent a few replies and settled in to work on Spelling Bee. She had just become a Genius when the receptionist came back.

"Tiberius says it's nothing personal, but there is no goddamn way, in this life or the hereafter, that he will ever talk to you."

Wind gusted off the Hudson, but she refused to move from the outdoor table that gave her a head-on view of the building where Tiberius Randle worked. She was glad she'd worn her heavy winter coat, which covered the power outfit she'd worn for her meeting with Aaron Grubb. She pulled oversized shades and a knit cap out of her bag, then lowered the headwear close to her eyebrows. To complete her hiding-in-plain-sight look, she kept her mask on.

Sheila spotted her quarry shortly before noon when he stepped onto the sidewalk with his head bowed toward his iPhone as if he were in prayer. He was smaller and thinner than he appeared on TV, his close-cropped hair was dyed orange, and he wore granny glasses. His mask was pulled down under his chin, so when he smiled at something on his screen, he revealed the signature gold tooth that was mentioned in every article that had ever been written about him. His skin was smooth as a calm sea; Sheila assumed plastic surgery.

He knew the way to Chelsea Market so well he never looked up. Sheila followed. A profile in New York magazine had described his midday ritual—

a solitary lunch at Takumi Taco, where he ordered a bento box of two tacos (spicy tuna and chipotle shrimp) with a side of Asian slaw. He told the writer that even though he regarded it as me time, he liked being surrounded by people as long as they maintained a proper distance. Yes, Tiberius Randle proclaimed, I am a man of contradictions.

Sheila got behind him in line but stayed a few feet away. The woman at the counter asked the designer if he wanted the usual.

"You know it, honey."

As the help started whipping together his lunch, the woman asked Sheila for her order.

I'm dubious about this Japanese-Mexican mix, Sheila thought. What do you call it? Japican? Mexinese?

And then she turned to Tiberius Randle and blurted that this was her first time here, and it sounded like he was a regular and did he have any recommendations.

He smiled at her. The gold tooth was blinding.

"Darling," he said in the jolly cadence she recognized from TV, "everything here is good. Now, to my eyes, you look like a salad person."

Is it that obvious? Sheila asked herself. Even underneath all the stuff I'm wearing?

"So, if I were you, I'd go for the salad bowl. And if I were you, I'd be good-looking if I ditched the mask and the shades and the coat and the cap. You're a long way from Aspen, sweetheart."

He smiled again, and Sheila wondered what it was like to go through life saying outrageous things all the time. She ordered a salad bowl with grilled chicken and noticed Randle taking a counter seat with nobody around. She sat six feet away and put her bag on the stool between them before removing her mask. When she bit into her salad, she jazzed on the ginger dressing.

"This is delicious." She kept her voice low. Just two people having a conversation.

"Told you. But what's with the witness protection gear?"

"I have a confession."

"The things I could tell you about priests, dearie ... " He shook his head.

"I've seen you on 'The Cutting Room.' I love the show. My daughter and I watch it every week."

Randle thanked her while chewing one of his tacos.

"She's thirteen," Sheila said. "It's one of the few things we still do together."

Randle muttered something about family values.

"Sometimes, I think she might be interested in fashion. You never know. She's still so young."

Randle mumbled that she had plenty of time to figure things out. Sheila ate more salad and took a long swig of water.

"If you have any ideas about that," Sheila said, "I'd love to hear them. Lemme give you my one of cards."

She rooted around in her bag. Randle chomped on some slaw as she slid over the card she had given the receptionist. At first he glanced at it distractedly, but then his eyes went wide, and he turned it over and reread the message she had written on back.

He put down his taco and shifted his body around so he faced her. Sheila removed cap and glasses but kept her coat on. She still felt chilly.

"My assistant told you to get lost," Randle said.

Sheila patted her mouth with a paper napkin. "I hate taking 'no' for an answer."

"That is an annoying trait in people," Randle said. "What part of 'no' didn't you understand?"

Sheila was undeterred. "My father gave you the money that turned your life around. You owe your good fortune to a corrupt cop. I could tweet about it. I've got more than five thousand followers, and so far today I've been quiet."

"Your dad is toxic."

"Why do you say that?"

Randle seemed ready to say something before wagging a long and blingy finger.

"Uh-uh, honey. I know a trick when I see one. You're just gonna keep asking me questions because you think I'll start yakking, and I'll forget that it's actually in my best interests to Shut. The. Fuck. Up."

Bethany and I have watched you an entire damn season, Sheila thought. Talking about yourself is your favorite activity.

She brought out her iPhone. "Mind if I film you?"

"Goddamn yes, I mind." But he couldn't resist a smile. "This is the first time in my life I've turned down an interview request."

Sheila surreptitiously engaged the record conversation app before putting the device back in her bag.

"Your real name is Randall Jones. Why'd you change it?"

"Because a name like Randall Jones is so pedestrian it won't get you anywhere in fashion. When I joined the industry, I shifted my first name back and changed the spelling, then started calling myself Tiberius because it sounded Roman and regal and shit. One thing about being African-American: you can give yourself an outrageous name, and nobody will think anything of it."

Randle stopped and shook his head.

"You're good. Too good. I gotta be careful around you. Maybe I should demand to see my lawyer."

"My father insists he was set up."

"I dunno nothin' 'bout that, honey."

"But you knew Dante Antonelli. You two were together for a while."

"I would not use the word 'together.' Dante had his place, and I had mine."

"But sometimes he stayed with you."

"Those City Council sessions could go on a long time, and Canarsie was far away."

"You two must've talked about my father. He told me about interrupting your encounter on that landfill off West Street."

Randle laughed. "Poor Dante. He walked away from that like he'd just finished riding a horse a hundred miles."

"My father thinks Antonelli had it in for him because of that."

"A lot of people had it in for your poppa."

"Waddya mean by that?"

Randle looked up at the ceiling. He seemed ready to scream.

"Why am I even talking to you?" he asked, more to himself than to Sheila. "There is no way this conversation can benefit Tiberius Randle, or Randall Jones, or whatever the hell I'm calling myself today."

Sheila pointed to his plate. "You're still here because you haven't finished your lunch. People who grow up poor never waste anything."

Bridget Devine always forced her children to eat every last bean, or noodle, or grain of rice.

Randle picked up the remaining taco. "I'm gonna wolf down this sucker and get back to my office, where I don't have to deal with nosy white ladies."

"What was my father like, back in the day?"

"What kind of dumbass question is that?" Pieces of tuna dribbled from the corner of his mouth.

"I was a little girl when he went away. I had no contact with him for forty years. I didn't really know him. Still don't, to tell the truth."

Randle stared into the distance as if he could dissolve the food court's walls and the years that had passed and re-create the decaying piers that once lined the river only a block away.

"Your pop had an aura, honey. When he walked into a room, everybody, and I mean everybody, paid attention to him."

"Were you afraid of him?"

"Everybody was afraid of him. You never knew what he'd do from one minute to the next."

"Do you think he killed Nadine?"

Randle snorted. "I ain't going near that one."

"You worked for a guy named Erik. I'd like to find him."

Randle shook his head. "Erik was an early casualty of the plague. Died of AIDS in Eighty-Seven."

Sheila considered this before tossing out a question in a thinking-out-loud way: "Do you believe my father was the kind of man who could've killed Nadine?"

"If there's one thing I've found over the years, Ms. Sheila Devine, it's this." He faced her, and his eyes grew narrow and resolute. Tiberius Randle was a gay icon with a prominent spot in the rag trade, but Randall Jones had grown up hard. "Under the right circumstances, anybody is capable of anything. For good and for bad."

Sheila dropped her voice as low as it could go. "He always treated me like a princess. I can't believe he killed anybody."

Randle smiled at her. The gold tooth gleamed.

"One night Dante and I were arguing—it was a big fight, one of our worst—and he threw all the bad things your old man had done right in my face and said I should be ashamed of myself because I'd taken money from one of the worst men in the world. I said at least somebody had given me money when I needed it desperately, and I didn't have to give him a blowjob. Well, that pissed off Dante, and he tried to slug me, but I was young and quick and agile, so I slid away and grabbed a chair to protect myself. I was angry, and I didn't even know what I was saying, I just pulled it out of my butt and yelled: 'I bet he didn't even kill that girl. You helped set him up. I know you're that kind of man.' And he just laughed and said: 'What if I did? And what if I am?'"

Sheila's mouth felt as dry as the Mojave. She had finished her water and desperately needed more.

Randle stood up. "I should've walked away the minute you sat next to me. But I can never resist gabbing my brains out to a cunning female."

"This conversation has been … " She needed the right word. "Helpful."

"Helpful for you, honey, but not for me. I was warned about you. Dante sent me a text from a hospital bed saying you were nosing around and I should be careful in case you contacted me. I tried to keep my mouth shut, but instead, I just started yakking because that's the way I am."

He walked away, shaking his head. Sheila ate the last of her lunch and put her bowl in the garbage and her empty water bottle in recycling while she thought over what Tiberius Randle had told her.

Holy shit, she thought.

She swiveled her head, but he had disappeared. As she hurried from the market, she cursed her heels before turning south on Ninth Avenue. She hustled across 15th Street against the light and heard cars honking at her. She saw him at the corner of 14th, bouncing on the balls of his feet and texting while waiting for a chance to cross.

The signal changed. Randle stepped into the crosswalk without looking up.

"One last thing," Sheila gasped when she caught him on the sidewalk on the south side of 14th.

Randle looked at her as if she were a piece of gum that refused to come off the bottom of his shoe. "Who are you? Lieutenant Columbo?"

"You said you got a text from Dante."

"It's the twenty-first century, sweetie. People do that sort of thing."

His stride picked up length and pace. Sheila struggled to keep up.

"He told me he'd lost contact with you. That he had no idea what happened to you. He didn't even know if you were still alive."

Randle looked at her with the open-mouthed expression her kids displayed whenever she caught them in a lie.

"There's one thing I'm dying to know," Sheila said. "How did Dante Antonelli get the money to open that B&B?"

Randle gritted his teeth. "If I ever lay eyes on you again, I'm gonna scream 'Rape!' and tell the authorities I have an order of protection against you because you're pulling stalker shit on me. You know how long it's been since I thought about all this crap?"

Chapter Seventeen

She was in the Toyota before daybreak because of the slog she faced while driving across Long Island. She saw no sign of Hoodie Guy or his Asian sidekick. She drove surface streets a while, changing direction several times, before merging onto the Brooklyn-Queens Expressway. She kept checking the rearview, segued onto the Long Island Expressway, got on and off it several times before shifting to the Northern State Parkway when she was in Nassau County. She returned to the LIE near the Suffolk County border, merged into the left lane as soon as she could, and did 75 until she reached the end of the road in Riverhead.

By the time she hit 25A, the strip malls had yielded to wineries. The digital clock on the dash said it was just past nine. Sunlight glinted off Long Island Sound.

I wonder what she'll say when I show up, Sheila thought. Maybe just hand over Nadine's bag without a word. She must have found it by now, dammit.

Traffic crunched to a standstill near the vineyard. A line of cars whizzed in the opposite direction. Sheila realized part of the road must be closed so she took out her iPhone. A few clicks and swipes revealed police and fire activity in the area.

She lowered the window despite the morning chill and smelled smoke. Traffic stopped and started. Wasting time always irritated her. She wanted to get back home by the afternoon. Ahead, she saw flashing police and fire lights. She rolled forward and was about to switch lanes when a state trooper raised a gloved paw.

Wooden barricades lined the middle of the road. The eastbound lane was blocked as far as she could see.

Sheila silently ran through all the profanities she knew. She was growing claustrophobic in the car, so she put on her mask and approached the trooper, who wore tinted aviator glasses.

"Get back in your vehicle, ma'am."

He had the flat voice of cop-speak, a tone that expected immediate and unconditional obedience.

"What's going on?" Sheila asked.

"You really should get back in your vehicle, ma'am."

The smoke stung Sheila's eyes, which began to water.

"Where's the fire?"

"Just ahead, ma'am. Get back in your vehicle. That's an order."

I'm not in the military and neither are you, Sheila thought.

"I was gonna stop at the winery. Will I be able to do that?"

The trooper's back stiffened. "The fire's at the winery, ma'am."

She barely got out the question: "How bad?"

"It's burned to the ground, ma'am."

"I know the owners. How are they?"

"We've been unable to reach anybody, ma'am. It's the worst fire we've seen around here in a long time."

On her way back to Brooklyn, she listened to the news. An inferno had raged across Raimondo Vineyards, one of the North Fork's oldest wineries. The fields were scorched, and the offices were cinders. So was the nineteenth-century farmhouse where the owner, Regina Raimondo, lived with her son, Dominic. Investigators suspected arson and were pessimistic about survivors.

She was picking at a salad at her kitchen table when the doorbell rang. She grabbed the Mace from her bag, crept forward through the house, peered through the peephole, and gasped at what she saw: crew-cut hair, black T-shirt over tattered black jeans, bushy beard sprouting underneath a black mask.

Victor clutched a packing box tight to his abdomen.

Sheila threw open the door. "I am so happy to see you. Wanna come in?"

He shook his head so vigorously his beard swayed. "I am going as far away from New York as possible." He thrust the box toward her. "They canned me yesterday. Regina and her son. But just before I left, Big Mama gave me this thing and said I had to hand it to you personally. So I am."

He sprinted down the steps and around the corner. Sheila carried the box to her kitchen, where she placed it on the counter before slicing it open with a sharp cutting knife. An object inside was encased in bubble wrap and packing material, with a handwritten note on top.

"Your father said I should give this to you. And so I am. Regina"

Chapter Eighteen

ichael was at her door a half-hour later, accompanied by a man Sheila did not recognize. Michael introduced him as Brendan Haggerty, the head of the detectives' union and a guy he had worked with for years on the district attorney's most sensitive cases.

Sheila wanted to protest, but before she could utter a word, Michael spoke up: "We need a third party. You know how people are. If it's just you and me, we'll be accused of collusion and conspiracy."

She filmed both men, who stated their names for the record. Then she handed her iPhone to Michael and told him to film her. She described how Victor had delivered the box and what she suspected it contained.

"You think it's potential evidence," Michael said, "but even if we prove it's the victim's handbag, the thing has been out of circulation for forty years, and any defense lawyer with a pulse will be able to exclude it."

"Understood," Sheila said. "But I don't want anyone saying I manipulated it." She pointed to Haggerty. "Open it. I'm gonna record you while you do."

Sheila handed the detective a pair of food handlers' gloves. He removed the bubble-wrapped object from the box and used Sheila's kitchen scissors to cut the Scotch tape that kept the wrap in place. A few seconds later, he displayed a Gucci handbag for the camera.

Michael began to talk. "That bag has been in the possession of Regina Raimondo since 1982. It was originally found that year by Police Officer Terence Devine during a raid on a bordello in Manhattan. The bag is suspected of belonging to Martha Owens, a.k.a. Nadine LaFleur, murder victim."

"Open the bag," Sheila said.

Haggerty undid the clasp and said, "I see a piece of notepaper." He sounded like Archie Bunker. The guy was a throwback.

"What does it say?" she asked.

"It has a list of addresses with dollar values next to them. Below the list are the words 'GET IN ON THIS!' along with a smiley face. The message and the smiley face are in different ink. The handwriting looks different, too."

He held up the paper for the benefit of the iPhone. Sheila took a closeup before handing the device to her brother. When he started recording, she said, "We're heading to my office, where I believe I'll find something significant."

Michael filmed her as she led them through the brownstone's ground floor. In her office, Sheila walked straight to a bookcase stuffed with manila folders. On the top shelf was a recently purchased paperback novel. She opened the book to the title page, where the author had written his name and a few words:

"Sheila—hope I get to know you better."

Be careful what you wish for, she said to herself.

She looked at the phone and said, "My father told me there was a note in the bag, but he couldn't figure out what it meant. He also said the man's writing looked familiar, but he couldn't quite place it. I'm taking an educated guess here—I wanna compare the writing on this page to the writing on the note."

She lay the book and the notepaper side by side on her desk. "Thoughts?" she asked the men.

Michael and Haggerty scrunched their faces as if they were Biblical scholars examining the Dead Sea Scrolls.

"Could be the same guy," Haggerty said. "But the note was written forty years ago. Handwriting changes."

"It's suggestive," Michael said. "It doesn't prove anything."

"You've looked at Nadine's journal," Sheila said to her brother. "So have I. Do you think the writing at the bottom compares to hers?"

"It does," Michael said. "Of course, this case has been closed for decades, so the objects I'm looking at are not, in a technical sense, evidence." He paused. "Keep the journal in a secure place, Sis. I'll take the bag. I can do something with it."

She stopped recording and put the iPhone next to her monitor. Once the men left, she'd upload the footage to her computer and stash copies all over the cloud.

"One more thing," she said to her brother.

Michael glanced at Haggerty. "I told you she could be demanding."

"Velvet hammer?" Haggerty asked.

"Usually, it's just the hammer."

"I need to track down two men who've had extensive encounters with the criminal justice system," Sheila said. "I'll Google them, but both of you are way more likely to have access to the information I want."

She began her search by entering the name Geraldo Calderon, a.k.a. Zaca, but the entries petered out after Terence Devine's murder trial, where the witness testified that he saw the victim allow Officer Devine into her building shortly before she was beaten to death. Prosecutors pointed out that Officer Devine never admitted to being in her apartment that night until confronted with fingerprint evidence that placed him at the scene. On direct questioning, the prosecutors made sure that Zaca acknowledged his drug dealing. On cross-examination, the defense tried to make a big deal about his criminal past, but after a while the judge told Officer Devine's lawyers to move on. Badgering the witness and all that.

The last story she found about Geraldo Calderon, a.k.a. Zaca, was dated 1994, when he was sentenced to a long stretch in Dannemora for buying and selling crack cocaine. The article's final paragraph noted his connection to the notorious case of Terence Devine.

Sheila turned her attention to Angelo DiNapoli, the poised mobster who ran the brothel where Nadine LaFleur once freelanced. The man kept running in and out of jail on prostitution charges, but in 2012 he was busted on a New York State rap for masterminding a heroin ring out of a high-end pizza shop in Nolita. His priors looked bad to the judge, who sentenced him to fifty years in Sing Sing.

Craigslist ruined the sex business for guys like him, Sheila said to herself.

She turned her attention to the PDF she had created showing the addresses on the notepaper in Nadine's handbag. She accessed a city database and hoped the records went back to 1982. The addresses were all on or near West Street, beginning in Chelsea and slithering down to Battery Park. The properties had been purchased by something called Shenandoah LLC, and they'd been flipped in short order to a variety of real estate firms that Sheila suspected were shell companies. She further suspected that most of the transactions had been in cash.

Her cell rang. It was the NYPD Detective Bureau, so she picked it up.

"We found Zaca," Haggerty said.

She risked the subway because she knew she'd be making multiple stops. An Asian kid with purple tattoos on his arms and neck trailed as she walked to Atlantic. Sheila noticed bruises on his face and a bandage on his nose under his sagging mask. Even from six feet away, he reeked of tobacco. She boarded a Coney Island-bound Q train but slipped out just as it was leaving, and she waved bye-bye to the Asian kid as he pounded the doors while he headed deeper into Brooklyn. She switched lines, took the 4 to Manhattan, exited at City Hall. She used the last working pay phone in the city to call Michael. A few minutes later, her brother and Haggerty met her outside Tweed Courthouse. Michael told her they'd Uber uptown. As Haggerty summoned a car, Michael filled her in on what had happened to Geraldo Calderon, a.k.a. Zaca:

The prisons grew crowded, and the drug dealer grew old, so despite his lifetime sentence as a three-time loser, he was released from prison under the condition that he report to his parole officer once a week forever. Zaca now worked as a maintenance man in a grimy apartment building near the George Washington Bridge.

When the car came, they crowded into the backseat. Sheila and Michael wore masks. Haggerty didn't. Sheila considered asking him about his vaccination status but decided against it.

"Zaca saw the man who married our mother enter the building that night … " Michael let the thought linger.

Sheila: "Did he see anything else?"

Michael: "Nobody ever asked him."

The car dropped them off in Washington Heights at a building crud-encrusted from decades of fossil fuel exhaust. The names on the buzzers were illegible, so Michael pressed the button beside the word "Oficina."

"Hola?"

A man's voice, middle-aged and strong. Michael put his mouth close to the intercom.

"Hola, señor. Estamos buscando Geraldo Calderon."

"Are you from the parole, señor?"

"I'm from the district attorney's office, sir. I'm here with a detective."

The man muttered something that sounded like "ay Dios mio" as the intercom clicked off.

Seconds later, the front door was opened by a guy who looked older than the glaciers. His back was hunched and his body drooped, but what struck Sheila most was his gray and ravaged face.

I'll show his picture to my kids, she thought, and tell them that this is how you look when you get old and you've done a lot of drugs.

"Señor Calderon?" Michael asked.

"Sí. You're from the district attorney?" His voice rasped from all the crap he'd inhaled over a lifetime.

Michael showed ID. The ridges in Zaca's face surged upward with surprised respect.

"Chief deputy," he said. "I'm honored."

Michael jerked his thumb at Haggerty and identified him as his lead investigator, then said, "We have some questions for you."

"I should call my lawyer," Zaca replied. "He'll tell me I shouldn't talk to you at all."

He moved back toward the building and put his hand on the door.

"You like going to your parole officer every week?" Michael asked.

Zaca stopped. "El cabrón? What do you think?"

"I'm in a position to cut your visits to once a month. Maybe even end them altogether, if you make me really happy."

The parolee motioned toward Sheila. "Who's she?"

"My sister."

"She don't look like no DA person. More like some moderna from Brooklyn. They started moving in here a few years ago, and I said, 'There goes the barrio.'"

Zaca's smile revealed that his few remaining teeth were the color of his weathered skin.

"I'm a filmmaker."

"Hollywood?"

"Documentaries."

"Oh."

"My name is Sheila Devine."

Zaca pointed to both of them and said: "I get it now. Su padre. The cop who killed that puta."

"We've got some questions for you, Zaca," Michael said.

"It's been a long time since anybody called me that." He smiled again, revealing scabbed gums. "My life was a lot better then. I had Money. Drugs. All the women I wanted."

He made a grinding motion with his hips. As she took out her iPhone, Sheila reminded herself of how much she hated dealing with criminals.

"Mind if I record you?"

"I got nada to lose," Zaca said.

You'd be surprised, she thought.

Michael began the questions: "You testified that on the night of February 24, 1982, you saw Martha Owens, a.k.a. Nadine LaFleur, open the door to her apartment building and allow entry to my father, Police Office Terence Devine. Do you stand by that testimony?"

"That's what I saw."

"Did you observe him leave the building?"

"Sí."

"How long was he in the apartment?"

"Between thirty minutes and an hour."

"How did he look when he came out?" Sheila asked.

"Pissed off. Like something had gone wrong."

"You see any blood on him?" Sheila asked.

"No."

Haggerty took over the questioning: "Let's talk about what happened the rest of the night. Did you see anything happen in her apartment? Any movement? Anything at all?"

Zaca shook his head. "The shades were drawn. The lights stayed on. Everything looked normal."

"So what were you doing all that time?" Haggerty asked. "Hanging on the street waiting for customers?"

"Pretty much." Crooks loved telling the police about their illegal activities once the law could do nothing about them.

"Any buyers that night?"

"I was busy. I made a nice living." Zaca raised his hand, ready to swear on a metaphorical holy book. "Lots of dealers cheated people, but I never did. I was a good and honest businessman, always gave my clients a fair deal, so I had a lot of repeat customers."

Great, Sheila thought. New York's only ethical drug dealer.

"How long did a transaction usually take?" she asked.

"I knew what my customers wanted," Zaca said. "I'd duck into my apartment, come back out in a couple minutes."

"So you were in and out of your apartment all the time?" Sheila asked.

"Sí."

"So you might not have seen somebody else enter the building?"

"That's possible. You think another hombre got into her apartment and offed her?"

"I'm not ruling anything out. Maybe she left the apartment, and you didn't see her."

"How could she have left the apartment? She was muerto."

"Let me ask you this—how did it work when someone you didn't know approached you?"

"I had to be careful," Zaca said. "They might be cops."

"You deal with anybody you didn't know that night?"

"Sí. Some guy I'd never seen before came by late. Real late."

"How late is real late?" Sheila asked.

"About three in the morning. Said he wanted to talk to me. It was muy frío, and chico listo was grande like a moose."

Zaca was cold, the streetlamp that illuminated his favorite spot on the sidewalk had just burned out, and he was thinking of knocking off for the night. That was when he heard heavy footsteps that sounded like they belonged to an animal instead of a man. A guy twice his size was walking toward him with the zeal of a Marine who'd been ordered to take a hill or die trying. He was about twenty-five, his features were swarthy, and he looked far healthier than Zaca's regular customers.

Zaca felt nervous as the guy got near, and Zaca never felt nervous about anything. He'd grown up on the streets and knew how to handle himself, but Jesucristo this muchacho was enorme.

The moose stopped a foot away and said, "I'm interested."

"In what?"

"Buying."

"Buying what?"

"I hear you got everything."

"Who sent you?"

"Is that important?"

"Es muy importante, amigo."

"A guy named Ange," the moose said. "He's connected."

Zaca knew wise guys, but he had never allowed them to get involved with his business. Once they did, they sucked out all the money.

"Dunno, man," Zaca said. "Dunno what I got. Dunno if I can make him happy."

"This is a one-time thing," the moose said. "Ange needs some stuff right now, and there ain't a lot of people still doing business."

Zaca considered his options. The riskiest one was telling this guy to get lost.

"What's on your mind?" Zaca asked.

The moose insisted on walking because he felt creepy just standing there in the dark. They went to West End Avenue and strolled north toward 74th Street. Zaca didn't want to cross it because that area belonged to an hombre named Chava. He and Zaca had negotiated their boundaries a few years back.

Zaca heard sounds coming from 73rd —car doors opening, a trunk slamming shut. He was afraid of missing something.

"Ange runs a place," the moose said. "Y'know what I mean?"

Zaca did.

"Some high rollers are in from outta town, and they're with some girls, and it's a swell party. Gonna last till dawn. Maybe longer. Ange is keeping tabs on things, and they're starting to run low. He needs to restock, and he can't wait."

"How much you looking at?" Zaca asked.

"Half-pound of pot. Three ounces of coke. Can you handle it?"

Zaca whistled. "I'll look, amigo. But if I have all that, you'll just about clean me out."

"We'll make it worth your while."

They haggled about the price a few minutes before heading back toward 73rd, where a black Lincoln Continental was parked across the street from Zaca's place. The dealer looked up and down the block. All the lights were off except the ones in the puta's apartment, which had burned low all night but now were brighter.

Zaca pointed to the Continental. "Friends of yours?"

"Go inside and get the stuff," the moose said.

Zaca's home was in the basement. He could look onto the sidewalk and street, so while he assembled the merchandise, he kept glancing outside. The moose was still there, and the Continental was across the way.

Zaca needed a few minutes to put the package together. The moose's order came close to exhausting his inventory. He'd spend most of the next day getting resupplied. That was a pain, but it was the price of being an independent businessman.

He gave the moose what he wanted in exchange for a large wad of cash. The moose said it had been a pleasure, walked across the street, and disappeared into the Continental. When the car pulled out, Zaca glanced at the puta's apartment. The lights were out. At first, he assumed she'd been recruited to join the party.

"But she couldn't have been with them," Sheila said to Zaca. "She was dead in the apartment."

"Sí, Señora."

"Why didn't you ever tell anyone about this?" Michael asked.

"I did."

Haggerty toughened his cop voice. "There's nothing in the case file about it. It should've been noted, even if nobody followed up on it."

"I talked to a prosecutor," Zaca said. "I told him what I told you."

Michael's voice dropped to a level barely above a murmur. "Christ Almighty, that's an enormous oversight. I've got to tell Adam about this. Maybe something got misfiled. Adam's been around forever. He'll know where to find it."

"Señor," Zaca said.

"What?" Michael sounded like a stressed-out parent handling a toddler's nine-hundredth request of the day.

"You say you're going to talk to Adam."

Michael bit out the next words. "Adam Fishman. The district attorney. My boss."

"No estoy el stupido. I know who he is." Long pause. "That's the man I talked to. He told me to keep it quiet. If I said anything, I'd louse up the investigation."

Chapter Nineteen

They rode the A train downtown because the subway provided blend-in-ability, and besides, you never knew what an Uber driver might overhear. Sheila created a mental checklist: Upload the interview as soon as I get home, make copies, stash them in digital hiding places.

She glanced at Michael and Haggerty, slumped on the seats beside her with the dazed looks of seal pups who'd just been clubbed by one of those crazy Newfies. Michael leaned toward her.

"Here's my issue," he murmured.

Sheila waited.

"I dunno what my next move is, and lawyers hate it when they don't know what to do next."

As the train pulled into West 4th Street, Sheila had an epiphany.

"Get out here," she told the men. "I've got to tell you something, but I'm not gonna do it on the subway."

She did a 360 after they set foot on the platform. No sign of Hoodie Guy or his Asian sidekick. They took the stairs two at a time and walked past the basketball courts on West 6th before turning down West 4th. As they approached Washington Square, Sheila anticipated the skunk smell of marijuana.

"Mind telling us what this is about?" Haggerty asked.

"Zaca saw lights on in Nadine's apartment when the moose came around to buy the drugs. They'd been low all night, but then they turned brighter."

"Right."

"Then, after the moose left in the Continental, the lights were out."

"What's your point?"

"She was dead, and my father had left her apartment hours before."

"So?"

"Who was turning the lights on and off?"

Michael and Haggerty returned to the DA's office to write their report. Back in Brooklyn, Sheila emailed Michael a dupe of her interview with Tiberius Randle, then resumed researching the Lower West Side properties listed in Nadine's handbag. Real estate transactions were public records, but the people who made their living in that racket knew how to make their affairs as opaque as possible. Still, she ascertained that the comptroller of Shenandoah LLC was a guy named Paul Siragusa, who had scrawled his name on all the necessary legal documents.

She Googled Shenandoah LLC and found many lovely property listings in the hills and valleys of Blue Ridge country. Then she Googled Paul Siragusa and pursued several threads. The one that most intrigued her described how the body of a member of the Gambino family with that name had wound up stuffed in an oil barrel on a loading dock in Red Hook in 1991. The cops said he had run afoul of John Gotti by violating one of the mob's many unwritten rules.

She knocked off at two a.m. Slept a few hours. At breakfast she drank a cup of Wesley's latest strong blend, looked over her family, and considered what her mother would think. Bridget Devine was not a prejudiced woman; she disliked everybody. Sheila had begun dating Wesley when her mother was in terminal decline. He was always solicitous of her. In response, she was gruff and aloof.

One day, near the end, after Bridget had been sent back home to die in her apartment in the wastelands of Central Jersey, Wesley went out to run an errand for her. After a few minutes of rasping and wheezing, Bridget said to her daughter, "That fella you're seeing."

Sheila waited for a racist diatribe. The woman is in her last days, she told herself. Just let her say what she wants.

"I see why you like him," Bridget said.

Sheila suspected a trick. She waited for more.

"He puts you on a pedestal," Bridget said. "That's what you want. Your father treated you that way, and you've been looking for the same thing ever since."

It was the only time Sheila ever heard Bridget Devine mention her husband.

The caffeine surge engaged the gears in her brain. She had to talk to Angelo DiNapoli at Sing Sing. After that, she said to herself, maybe I'll contact the Justice Project after all.

Dylan's face clouded as he looked at his cell.

"No phones at the table," Sheila told him.

"I just got an alert," Dylan said.

"I don't care."

"I think you will."

Dylan handed her the device, which showed a series of urgent tweets from New York One:

Michael Devine, chief deputy in the Manhattan district attorney's office, had been mugged outside his home on Central Park West shortly after three a.m. Apparently, he'd taken an Uber after a late night at the office. Initial reports said he was in a coma. It was the latest and most vivid reminder that the scourge of violent crime had returned to the city.

Sheila hurried past the media scrum outside New York-Presbyterian Hospital without answering questions. At the information desk, she asked a Black woman in a hijab about Michael Devine. The lady said he was in intensive care. Sheila showed ID and asked if there was someplace she could wait. The woman directed her to a waiting room.

As soon as Sheila walked in, she saw Rachel Meyer, Michael's wife, trying to look stoic as she sat by the swinging doors that led to the I.C.U.

"How is he?" Sheila asked.

"You know what it's like trying to get information out of doctors."

Rachel was a lawyer. She and Michael met while they were working for the DA right out of school.

Sheila heard footsteps behind her.

"He was sandbagged," Haggerty said.

Sheila swore he was in the same clothes he'd worn the day before.

"I'm looking for that Uber driver," Haggerty said. "Most of those guys are scum."

Haggerty was a cop. He believed most guys were scum.

Rachel shifted her gaze from her sister-in-law to the detective. "Michael told me he'd just started working on something with both of you. But he wouldn't give me the details. That's unlike him."

"Knowing the details could get you in trouble," Sheila said.

Rachel motioned toward the I.C.U. "Is that what caused this?"

Sheila's stomach churned. "Probably."

People stirred. Sheila turned in time to see Adam Fishman striding toward them. The DA had always been bone-thin, bordering on gaunt, but now he looked cadaverous.

"How is he?" Fishman asked.

"Hard to tell," Rachel said.

"I can't figure out why he was working so late."

"He texted that he was gonna be at the office 'til all hours." Rachel shrugged. "You know how it goes."

Fishman tried a smile. Attempts to show humor never worked for him.

"He should've sent me an email about what he was doing, and he didn't." He turned to Haggerty. "Were you with him last night?"

"We knocked off about two-thirty. I went back to Queens."

"What were you investigating?"

"A cold case that's warming up. We're still investigating it."

"Wanna tell me about it?"

"Lotta loose threads right now. When we tie them together, you'll be the first to know."

Fishman turned to Sheila. "I keep hearing different things about that project you told me about. You still working on it?"

Sheila considered the dozens of ways she could answer his question.

"Yeah."

Fishman motioned toward the I.C.U. "Is that what caused this?"

"I don't have to answer that."

"It's funny," Fishman said.

"What's funny?"

"You demand that everyone answer all of your questions, no matter how uncomfortable they make people feel. But if I ask you one thing you don't like, you clam up like a mobster taking the Fifth."

Fishman and Haggerty left. The women waited. Sheila looked at her phone. Some Twitter feeds said Michael Devine was close to death. Others said he was expected to make a speedy recovery. Wesley and the kids sent anxious texts, and Sheila replied that she had no information. Above all else, they should believe nothing they saw on the internet.

Close to lunchtime, a male nurse came out of the I.C.U. He was Black and bald and burly. The women stood.

"Your husband is alert," he told Rachel. "He wants to see you."

The women embraced. Sheila thought about leaving. She had so much to do.

"Will you stay?" Rachel asked.

"Of course."

Rachel disappeared with the nurse. Sheila sat down and texted Wesley and the kids, who all responded with bursts of happy emojis. She then tweeted that Michael Devine was talking to his wife in the I.C.U. Within three minutes, New York One, the *Post* and the *News* had all updated their stories. It took the *Times* half an hour.

She looked around. Hunger and fluorescent lighting had induced a headache. Sheila considered heading to the cafeteria. She had last eaten hospital food when her mother was in the cancer ward, wasting down to ninety pounds. The mystery meals were another awful memory.

Something in front of her. She glanced up.

"He needs to talk to you," Rachel said.

Michael's left eye was purple and nearly shut. His lips were swollen. Bandages covered nose and forehead. Sheila threw her hand over her mouth to prevent herself from crying out.

"Do I look that bad?" His voice was surprisingly strong.

Sheila nodded.

"Rachel told me I looked okay. I knew she was lying."

"What happened last night?"

"I took an Uber. It was weird. The driver never said anything, and when he let me off, it wasn't in front of my building. We were at the corner. I told him where to take me, and he just sat there, and after a couple of minutes I figured he didn't speak English. Asian kid. He wore a hoodie and a mask."

"Tattoos?" Sheila asked.

"On his neck and hands. He smelled like tobacco. Bruises on his face. Friend of yours?"

"Sounds like someone I've encountered. Keep going."

"I paid him and got out of the car. It's only thirty seconds to my door, right?" He winced. "That's when another guy jumped me."

"Did you see him?"

Michael winced again. "He came at me from behind. It was dark. He was in a hoodie, too, and masked, so I didn't get a good look. I put up a fight, and when I yelled out, the doormen on the block realized what was going on. A couple of them called 911 right away."

"I thought you were in a coma."

"I never lost consciousness. The goddamn internet—"

"What did he take?"

"My phone." Another wince. "I'm like most people—I carry around, at most, forty dollars in cash. That's why hardly anyone gets mugged anymore."

Sheila's cell pinged with an alert. "NYPD is saying the Uber that picked you up was stolen. Original driver was beaten up and left in an alley near South Street Seaport."

Chapter Twenty

The next morning, Haggerty picked up Sheila in a dark sedan that screamed unmarked police vehicle. At the hospital, the detective used a funky side entrance before badging his way into Michael's room. Once they got what they needed, they headed to Sing Sing.

Sheila and Haggerty took chairs at a small table in the visitors' area and waited until a white-haired man flanked by guards approached. The prisoner wore the inevitable orange jumpsuit, but looked more suited to Versace.

"Thank you for seeing us, Mr. DiNapoli."

He glared at Sheila. "Your father was a shakedown artist."

"And you weren't?"

"He was a cop. I never pretended to be anything other than what I was."

"You claimed to be a businessman."

"The services I provided were illegal at the time. Now the government makes money off them."

"I'm doing a movie about my father."

DiNapoli nodded. "Word gets around. Even in here."

"My brother has been helping me."

"I heard what happened to him. How's he doing?"

"Much better than the internet would have you believe."

"Your brother sent me away. Stone-cold bastard. I mean that in a positive way."

Why do men enjoy baiting women so much? Sheila thought.

"He's prepared to make you an offer," Haggerty said.

"Go ahead."

"Time served, if you talk to us."

"I'm supposed to believe that?"

Haggerty reached into his pocket. "Here's a signed affidavit."

The detective handed the paper to DiNapoli.

"If I talk to you, there's a real good chance I'll wind up dead."

"You'd rather die in here?" Sheila asked.

DiNapoli's eyes clouded.

"You're never getting out unless we give you a break," Haggerty said.

"I should talk to my lawyer."

"If we walk outta here," Haggerty said, "we're not coming back."

Sheila was willing to haggle, but when the detective began to rise, she did too.

DiNapoli patted manacled hands on the table. "Sit down."

They sat.

"What do you know?" he asked.

"Nadine worked in your brothel," Sheila said.

"I dislike that word. The place was a retreat. My customers included a lot of wealthy and powerful men. They needed an oasis where they could forget about their cares for a while."

In Sheila's dealings over the years with people who had authority, whether legal or illegal, one unassailable fact had become clear: Eventually, all of them wound up believing their own bullshit.

"Why did Nadine work for you?" she asked.

"I made her kick back a lot less than her pimp did," DiNapoli said. "Plus I offered protection. I never let any of my clients hit one of my girls. Anybody who got out of line wasn't allowed back. And once a man came to my place, he wanted to return."

"You did a cash-only business," Sheila said. "In the eyes of the government, the money you made was dirty. How did you turn it clean?"

"That gets into a sensitive area."

"Sensitive areas are why we're having this wonderful conversation."

DiNapoli's eyes narrowed. Sheila realized he was considering how much he should tell her.

"There were a number of legitimate businesses we could steer our money to," he said. "A lot of my clients welcomed our investments, especially when they were having cash-flow problems. Back then, inflation was high, the economy kept tanking, and the Fed had raised interest rates through the roof. So everybody had cash-flow problems—except for me. Sex is recession-proof."

Time to shift gears, Sheila said to herself. Guys like DiNapoli get way too guarded when you pursue the same line of questioning.

"When my father raided your business," she said, "he found a Gucci handbag in one of the rooms. He believes it was the same handbag he saw in Nadine LaFleur's apartment the night she was killed."

DiNapoli blinked a few times. "Your point is?"

"How did it get there?"

"I have no idea."

"I think you do."

He shrugged. "I assume she brought it over."

"She couldn't have."

"Why not?"

"She was dead."

They stared hard at each other. DiNapoli spoke first.

"Believe it or not, Sheila, I was running a business, and I couldn't spend all my time paying attention to one worker. It was also forty years ago, and I haven't thought about this stuff in decades. So maybe you can enlighten me about what happened."

She ticked off points on her fingers. "My father goes to Nadine's apartment to collect for her pimp. The endeavor goes badly, but he finally gets the money and leaves. According to the police and the prosecutors, he's choked her and beaten her really badly. If she isn't dead, she's close to it." Sheila paused. "So how does the handbag he saw on her bed wind up in your place?"

DiNapoli stared at her.

"There was a note inside the bag," Sheila said. "It was a list of addresses along what was then called the Lower West Side. Now it's some of the most expensive residential real estate in the world. We think that list was written by Adrian Lynch."

"One of my most enthusiastic customers." DiNapoli looked at Haggerty. "We had to comp him, since he was a police captain and everything."

The detective's face flushed.

"There was another note at the bottom that we believe was written by Nadine," Sheila said. "In big, underlined letters, it said, 'GET IN ON THIS!' Like she was really excited."

"Without seeing the list of addresses," DiNapoli said, "it's as cryptic to me as it is to you."

"My father also saw a coat with an animal print pattern in the closet of the first-floor lounge. He saw Nadine wearing a coat exactly like it earlier that night when she was heading into her apartment."

"It was the Eighties. Lots of women wore animal prints back then."

"I think Nadine was at your brothel at some point that night."

"You don't have enough to prove anything in court," DiNapoli said.

"I've got more than enough to put in my movie," Sheila said.

DiNapoli stared at his fingernails. They were gnarled and bitten—his last manicure had been years ago.

"When they threw me in here," DiNapoli said, "I could've said some things. But I kept quiet because nobody would've believed me, and then I'd wind up dead in prison."

"What could you have said that was so dangerous?" Sheila asked.

DiNapoli squirmed. "This is why I want to talk to a lawyer."

Haggerty stood and motioned toward the door. "C'mon, Sheila."

She wanted to stay seated because they needed to talk to this guy, and she resented the way Haggerty was ordering her around as if she were a cadet at the police academy.

On the other hand, she said to herself, we've got to show DiNapoli we're not screwing around.

She rose to her feet.

"You can talk to your lawyer all you want, but I'll tell you one thing." Haggerty pointed to the socially distanced groups of guards and inmates and prisoners clustered around the room. "Everybody here has seen you talking to us, and nothing stays secret in jail, so once word gets out … "

He headed for the door. Sheila followed, silently pleading for DiNapoli to say something.

"Detective!"

They stopped and turned. DiNapoli stood with chest pumped out and shoulders back, trying to look as distinguished as the orange jumpsuit would allow.

"We have things to discuss," he said.

Sheila and Haggerty took a few steps back.

"Like what?" the detective asked.

"Total immunity," DiNapoli said.

"You got it."

"Protection."

"You got that, too."

DiNapoli looked them over from head to foot, as if he were a commander about to send two of his least favorite soldiers on a suicide mission.

"You may be sorry you said that," he told them.

Angelo DiNapoli always kept his head clear while he was working, so he was sipping ginger ale in the first-floor lounge and making small talk with the clients and girls when the door slammed open, and Martha Owens strode in. She was fantastic in the sack and extremely smart, but she also liked drugs and was, in general, off-the-charts high maintenance. When he saw her animal print coat, he figured she'd skinned the beast herself.

"I've had it, Angelo," she said.

Her voice was loud. He smiled anyway. "It's good to see you, too, but why are you here? You're not on the schedule."

"I'm quitting. As of tonight."

"That's fine. I don't hold anyone prisoner. It's been a pleasure."

He waved her toward the door.

"That's not what I mean, asshole."

"Then what do you mean?"

"I'm tired of being ripped off by men. I've been fucked over, literally and figuratively, and tonight it all comes to an end."

DiNapoli glanced around. The people in the lounge were staring. He told Martha to hang up her coat and come into his office. He instructed the barkeep to comp drinks for everyone.

He waved her to a chair as he sat behind his desk. He was surprised when she refused a drink.

"What's your problem?" he asked.

The words poured out. She'd been in her apartment minding her own business when a cop named Terence Devine came by, and at first she thought she was gonna be busted, but actually he was collecting for her pimp. Devine wound up cleaning her out of two thousand dollars that she'd saved because she wanted out of the life.

"If you need to make money," DiNapoli said, "I can give you more shifts. My clients like you."

"Did you hear a word I said? I'm done doing tricks."

"Then I fail to see how I can help you."

"I want a piece of this place."

He wasn't sure he'd heard correctly. "What?"

She waved her arm around. "This retreat, as you like to call it, is a money machine. You have to steer that cash into something that looks legitimate, and you have to do it fast, or else the government will ask you uncomfortable questions. Nobody in your line of work wants to end up like Al Capone."

DiNapoli silently cursed himself for hiring a woman who had attended Barnard.

"You've figured out my business model," he said. "Congratulations. But the cash moves in and out very quickly. It's not like I have two thousand dollars lying around that I can just give you."

"That's not my point."

She reached into her Gucci handbag and produced a piece of notepaper.

"I have a list of addresses on the Lower West Side. Some of your customers mentioned them to me, so I discussed them with—well, let's call him a friend."

DiNapoli smirked. "One of your many … friends."

Her eyes flashed with rage. He expected her to start cursing again.

"If we're gonna talk business, Martha, we better be frank with each other."

"Nobody can get loans right now because the Feds have jacked up interest rates to levels even you mob guys won't charge." She waved the paper around before shoving it back in her bag. "But your customers are getting the cash to buy these properties for pennies on the dollar, which raises two big questions."

"Enlighten me."

"One: Where are they finding the money? Two: Why are they investing in such a crappy area?"

"The answer to the second one is easy. Once the city builds Westway and demolishes the piers, you'll have a fantastic park with wonderful views. It'll be the new Millionaires' Row. The commercial landlords along the river lack imagination. Once all the industry left, they couldn't think of another use for the area. But some of my customers are in residential real estate, and they have vision."

"What about the first question?"

DiNapoli grinned like the Cheshire cat. "They all like talking to you. Why don't you ask them?"

Martha grinned back. "I think I know the answer, but let's call Aaron anyway. He's horny every waking moment. He'll be glad to see me."

DiNapoli had the number for Aaron Grubb's pager. The protocol was simple—whenever Martha was on duty, DiNapoli was supposed to alert the guy. So the proprietor of the pleasure palace reached out to him before swinging by the front door, where he told Paulie to escort Mr. Aaron (as he was called at the retreat) to the back office once he arrived.

The townhouse had five stories, so there was plenty to supervise. DiNapoli made his rounds, and fifteen minutes later he was on the third floor, talking to Judge Roper at the roulette table, when Paulie barged in, saying there was something that needed his attention right away. DiNapoli excused himself and went downstairs. As he walked through the lounge, he heard the sound of two people arguing and stuff being thrown around in his office. When he opened the door, he saw blood dripping from the side of Martha's mouth as if she were Lady Dracula. Shards of two smashed brandy snifters glistened on the floor.

"I'm not gonna give you a goddamn cent for anything but a good hard lay," Grubb told her. "If I gave you two thousand bucks, you'd just snort them up your nose."

Martha grabbed books off the shelves and threw them at the men while screaming obscenities even DiNapoli found objectionable. Then she said:

"I'm gonna tell Jamie Quinn about the scam you shits are pulling, and then you'll be all over the goddamn *Daily News*. Is that what you want?"

DiNapoli fetched Paulie, who asked, "Want me to take care of her?"

DiNapoli nodded, then resumed his tour of the building. A half-hour later he was on the fifth floor, making sure everything was ready for Judge Roper, who always hung out with the boys after roulette.

Paulie came up the stairs. He was winded from climbing, but between breaths he said they had Martha in a room on the second floor, but she was still out of control.

"I'm out of ideas," DiNapoli said.

"I got one," Paulie said.

"I'll listen to anything."

"That guy she likes. The skinny one who's going bald. Let's get him over here. Maybe he can talk some sense into her."

When DiNapoli stopped talking, Sheila wondered if this was what priests felt like in the confessional. The penitent had described his sins more or less truthfully, but she was convinced he was withholding the most important information.

"For the record," DiNapoli told her, "I never felt sorry for your father. In the end, it really was his fault. Even if he didn't kill her."

"When the cops investigated Nadine's murder," Sheila asked, "did anyone from Homicide ever question you?"

"No."

"Where is Paulie these days?" she asked.

"St. Peter's Cemetery on Staten Island."

Sheila felt like a five-year-old who was solving her first math equation. "Was his last name Siragusa?"

"Yeah. What of it?"

"You better tell me about Shenandoah LLC. And that guy you called to talk sense, as you put it, into Martha Owens."

Chapter Twenty-One

Haggerty told the warden that Angelo DiNapoli needed to be put in protective custody right away. The warden looked at him as if he had Tourette's, so Sheila demanded they find a private office where they could call her brother. They talked by speakerphone. Michael sounded tired, but he told the warden that if Detective Haggerty said Angelo DiNapoli needed protective custody, the prison had better provide it.

In the parking lot, Sheila noticed that the sun visor on her side of the unmarked police vehicle was down. She was sure she'd left it up. Haggerty advised her to keep as far from the car as they could. He aimed his keys and hit the button as they ducked behind an SUV the size of an Abrams tank.

The doors unlocked. Nothing else. Sheila and Haggerty walked to the sedan. When she opened the glove compartment, she saw that her phone was gone.

On their way back to the city, Sheila kept turning her head.

"You can stop doing that," Haggerty said.

"Why?"

"The bad guys found what they were looking for."

They stopped at the hospital to see Michael, who had been moved to a private room in a far-flung wing. He winced as they let him know what DiNapoli had told them.

"I wish I could get outta here," Michael said.

Haggerty looked at Sheila. "I've got plenty to do. How about you?"

"I think I should take this thing to the Justice Project," she said.

Michael asked why.

"To force the issue. But I'll need the convicted man's permission." She tried to smile. Failed. "This was his idea in the first place."

She had backed up all of her device's data on her desktop, then scattered the information throughout the cloud, so the iPhone theft was annoying but not devastating. After calling Apple to disable the thing, she bought a burner at a storefront on Atlantic.

Early the next morning, she flew standby out of LaGuardia. Within an hour, she was at the Avis counter in the Syracuse airport. A pleasant white woman with a flat upstate accent said she wasn't used to dealing with walk-ins who paid cash. Sheila said she was trying to simplify her life. She rented a Sentra and kept looking around. The absence of pursuers bothered her.

In the visitors' area of Auburn State Prison, she had ten minutes to kill before meeting her father. She glanced around at the usual rabble, but her eyes stopped when she saw a Latino in a Brooks Brothers suit. He was in his late sixties and his salt-and-pepper hair was slicked back, so he stood out like a Mormon at Mardi Gras. She felt she should recognize him, and after a minute it hit her:

Rolando Ortega, long considered the best defense attorney in New York City.

And then a second thought:

What the hell is he doing here?

Ortega shifted in his seat, looked at his Rolex, tapped Italian wingtips on the linoleum floor.

I could speculate, Sheila said to herself, or I could go over there and talk to him.

Ortega glanced up as she approached.

"Señor Ortega?"

"Sí."

"Me llamo Sheila Devine. Soy una cineasta."

"Your documentary about the first responders was brilliant."

"Gracias."

She didn't tell him that she'd gotten Covid herself during the filming. The case was mild—headache, cough, loss of taste and smell, fatigue and, her favorite, diarrhea. But the illness took a few weeks to shake, so in a setting like this she tried to keep her distance.

"I am acquainted with su hermano, of course."

"Claro. Can I ask you una pregunta?"

"Sí."

"Why are you here?"

"Legal work," Ortega said. "A client."

"An appeal?"

He shook his head. "I received a call early this morning on behalf of a man named Octravian Murray. I've never met him, but I have done some work on behalf of his associates."

Gangbangers, Sheila thought. All those guys deal drugs. They're paying Ortega in cash or crypto.

"What did Señor Murray do?" Sheila asked.

"Apparently, he has been accused of assaulting another inmate. But I need to find that out officially."

"What happened to the other inmate?"

"I've heard he may have died. But I have no word about that from the people who run the penitentiary. I expect them to tell me the details shortly."

He looked at his Rolex again.

If the guy killed another prisoner, Sheila thought, Octravian Murray is up to his eyeballs in excrement. It could be an interesting story to follow once I finish the film about my father.

The room stirred. Sheila looked to the door. The warden entered, flanked by the public information officer and a man in a clerical collar. Their demeanor was grim, and Sheila understood the reason: A prisoner had been attacked and might be dead, and a particularly harsh spotlight was going to be aimed directly at all of them.

She stepped away from Ortega so they could speak to him.

"Ms. Devine," the warden said.

"Yes?"

"I have bad news."

She hadn't expected them to talk to her. She wondered what this could be about.

"Go ahead."

"It concerns your father."

A premonition: He's gonna tell me something I don't wanna hear. Her mind raced: They won't let me see him. The rules have changed. The case is too hot, so the authorities are turning the screws.

"Okay."

"I'm afraid … " The warden looked at the floor.

I'll give him credit, Sheila thought. He doesn't wanna do this. He knows how rotten it is.

The warden yanked up his head and gazed straight into her. "I'm afraid your father is dead, Ms. Devine. I'm terribly sorry."

At first she suspected a macabre practical joke. They have cameras all over this place, she thought. Maybe they just wanna see how I'll react.

The public information officer spoke up: "There was an altercation early this morning at breakfast. Your father got into an argument with another inmate. He was stabbed."

The cleric leaned close to Sheila and murmured something about God's plan, but she broke away and felt her breath getting short and hot and quick.

Think clearly, she said to herself. Whoever's behind this wants you to lose it.

In her peripheral vision, she noticed Rolando Ortega rising to his feet. A prison flunkie was talking to him, and the lawyer swiveled his neck and adjusted his tie. Sheila suddenly understood exactly what his client was accused of doing. She took three long steps toward the attorney before barking, "He did it, didn't he?"

Ortega looked at her as if she were a toddler on the verge of a tantrum.

"What are you talking about, Ms. Devine?"

"Your client killed my father."

"I know nothing of the sort, Ms. Devine."

"That's why you're here. They want him to lawyer up before he says anything."

"Who are 'they,' Ms. Devine?"

"Whoever's behind this."

"You are upset, Ms. Devine. I understand completely. You have my deepest condolences."

If there's one thing I don't need right now, Sheila thought, it's mandescension.

"How did you know?" she asked.

"Know what?"

"That Octravian Murray would need legal representation?"

"As I told you, I received a phone call quite early this morning."

"And you dropped everything and came right up here?"

Sheila sensed the prison staff inching her way, as if they were ready to tase her.

"That's correct," Ortega said. "The people who called me said it was a matter of the highest urgency." His eyes flashed with inappropriate mirth. "I am on retainer."

Keep your voice down, Sheila said to herself. Sound cool and clear and detached—the way these pricks think men would react in a situation like this, even though they rarely do.

"How did they know?" she asked.

"What do you mean, Ms. Devine?"

"The people who called you. How did they know Octravian Murray would need legal counsel as soon as visitors were allowed today?"

"I did not ask, Ms. Devine."

She took the next flight to LaGuardia and grabbed a yellow cab to Jamie Quinn's loft. She paid cash and punched in his number on her burner.

"Go fuck yourself, unknown caller."

"It's Sheila Devine. I'm downstairs. Open the goddamn door."

Quinn was waiting when she got out of the elevator.

"I thought you were a telemarketer," he said. "I love telling them off."

He pushed his walker toward his favorite chair. The afternoon sun angled in on the far side of the room. He plopped in a chair that caught the dying rays.

"I'm not sorry about your father," Quinn said.

Sheila remained standing.

"You met Martha Owens in Foley Square the day she walked on drug possession charges. Rolando Ortega was her lawyer."

"What are you getting at?"

"I just saw Ortega. He's representing the gangbanger who killed my father."

"Lucky break for the gangbanger."

"I found Martha's journal," Sheila said.

Quinn's eyes sparked with the mischief of a man whose greatest joy came from instigating trouble. "Fuck me."

"I'd rather not. She kept referring to a man named 'A,' and she mentioned him to you. Some kind of high roller. It could be Aaron Grubb. She ever say anything about him to you?"

"She never named any of her clients to me. This 'A' could've been a composite. She might've been making notes for that book she kept threatening to write." He hacked a booger into a handkerchief. "I'll let you in on something—a lot of characters in my columns were composites."

Sheila almost said, That's no secret, Shithead.

Quinn went on. "She studied literature, so she used a device. Most likely, 'A' is a combination of some of the men she knew, Aaron Grubb among them."

"Let's go back to the night she was killed," Sheila said. "My father goes to her place, roughs her up, gets the money. Then he goes to Clarke's to see you. Then he goes to Paco's, beats him up, finds out about the investigation."

"None of that's a mystery."

"The mystery is who killed Martha Owens. My father couldn't have done it."

"You sound awfully sure of yourself."

"Angelo DiNapoli told me and a police detective that she was at his brothel that night after my father left her apartment."

Quinn let out a whistle. "That's a big piece of dynamite. When are you gonna light it?"

"I dunno, but I've got very little time to put this all together." She glanced at the ceiling and told herself the moldings were lost on Jamie Quinn. "Aaron Grubb was there that night. Martha told him and DiNapoli that she was gonna talk to you about the scam they were running."

"Rich guys running a scam with mobsters? I would've listened to her. I'm listening to you. Keep going."

"The brothel took in tons of cash that DiNapoli had to launder. Remember that handbag my father found in the raid on that place?"

Quinn nodded.

"It was Martha's. And it had a list of addresses the men she slept with told her about. They were all near the Hudson—in Chelsea, the Village, SoHo, Tribeca, FiDi, all the way down to the Battery."

"Back then, the state and the city were trying to build Westway, but it was tied up in the courts, so construction and demolition were frozen all along the West Side. If you were willing to gamble, you could buy into those areas for next to nothing."

"What if they weren't gambling? What if they knew exactly what was gonna happen, or could make it happen themselves?"

Quinn breathed hard, as if the effort of inhaling and exhaling took all his strength and concentration. "Your father was a good investigator on those rare occasions he put his mind to it. You inherited some of those genes. What else ya got?"

"Much of that land was purchased by something called Shenandoah LLC. I believe it was a shell company for the city's real estate families."

"Shenandoah?"

"DiNapoli was behind it. A winking nod to Stonewall."

Quinn's eyebrows shot up. "Civil War buff—who knew?"

"That company steered lots of cash to the real estate families."

Quinn nodded. "And never underestimate the power of eminent domain. Those families could make it happen, and they could afford to wait a few years. They also had the power to get those areas rezoned—or not rezoned, depending on which option worked out best for them."

Sheila paced. "But I still haven't figured out who killed her. It's the last piece of the puzzle, and DiNapoli swears he doesn't know. He says he never asked the question because he didn't wanna know the answer."

She heard a ping that signified a news alert. Quinn reached into his pants pocket and shakily removed an iPhone.

"The only reason I have this thing," he said. "To get the alerts. I love news. Always have. Always will."

"What happened?" Sheila asked.

Quinn squinted at the phone. "Some fashion guy fell to his death from the balcony of his apartment in Chelsea. Splattered all over a bunch of tourists on the High Line." A grim smile. "At least the tourists are back. Never thought I'd say that."

Every muscle in Sheila's body began to cramp. "Tiberius Randle?"

"How'd you know?"

Sheila grabbed the remote from the armrest on Quinn's chair and clicked on a sixty-inch hi-def TV pinned to a wall of exposed brick. On New York One, the anchor said they were breaking away from the High Line tragedy to bring the latest on Michael Devine. A correspondent in front of the hospital said the chief deputy in the DA's office was expected to make a full recovery, though his convalescence might take weeks.

In the background, Sheila glimpsed a form she recognized heading into the hospital: Six-foot-one. Caucasian, skull and crossbones mask, 'roided. Hoodie pulled far over his head.

Chapter Twenty-Two

She bellowed for a cab as soon as she reached the sidewalk. While the driver barreled crosstown, she called Haggerty on the burner and left a voicemail telling him where she was going. When the taxi sped up the Henry Hudson Parkway, she phoned New York-Presbyterian and asked for Security. The call was disconnected. She tried again and said it was urgent and finally got through after ninety seconds of recordings that thanked her for her patience. She asked whoever it was if Michael Devine's room was guarded, and the person said they had received a call from the DA's office saying it was no longer necessary.

"You better get somebody there now," Sheila said.

"You're not authorized to do that, ma'am."

At the hospital she strode past the information desk and marched through a pair of swinging doors while a nurse said visiting hours were over. Sheila half expected security guards to follow, but as she walked down the hall and made a right, then walked some more before making a left, the hospital noise faded, and she heard her steps clicking on the tiled floor.

The door to Michael's room was closed. No guard. She reached for the knob.

Locked.

Sheila thought of calling out, but that seemed pointless, so she opened her bag and straightened out a bobby pin that she slipped into the tumbler.

Click.

She dropped the pin into her bag, gripped her Mace, and pushed open the door.

Michael on the bed. Eyes closed. Strapped to machines monitoring his functions. IV clipped into his forearm. Blips, beeps and lines all seemed normal.

Two men, neither in medical gear, hovered on either side of him.

Closer to Sheila, with his back to her, was an older man—tall, thin, almost bald, wearing a business suit. A Gucci briefcase rested on the floor within grasping distance. On the other side was a hulking guy who clutched a six-inch-long hypodermic.

Of course he knows how to use a needle, Sheila thought. He cycles through 'roids the way Taylor Swift goes through boyfriends.

Sheila stepped toward them and pointed her Mace. The men froze, baffled by the sudden appearance of a woman who seemed intent on vengeance. She spun the older guy around.

Adam Fishman.

She squirted Mace in his eyes. He howled and doubled over. She shoved him toward the door and turned to Hoodie Guy, who aimed the needle at the exposed skin on Michael's left arm.

Sheila chopped at Hoodie Guy's wrist. He let out an oof. The needle wobbled. She tried to hack him again, but he wrapped her forearm with his left hand and tightened his grip on the needle, so she leaned over her brother's bed and used her free hand to push at the needle as hard as she could.

The hypodermic flew toward the wall. Sheila reached for the phone on the nightstand, but Hoodie Guy's right paw encircled her wrist. They were inches apart, but she got her finger on the Mace and sprayed.

"Shit!"

He reeled. Sheila grabbed the phone. A bored-sounding nurse on the other end asked what it was.

"Emergency in Room 268. We need people here. Stat!"

Something crashed into the back of her head. She fell on top of her brother. The same object hit her again and again, and it felt like leather with something inside it. She rolled over and saw Fishman raising his briefcase over his head. Sheila kicked him in the kneecap. Fishman clutched his leg, yelled in pain, crashed to the floor.

She slid off the bed. On the far side of the room, Hoodie Guy picked something off the floor. Sheila rushed toward him and shoved him into the wall as he straightened. The syringe in his hand was filled with air. If he injected Michael, her brother's death would look like an aneurysm.

Hoodie Guy swung at her. Sheila tried to kick him but failed to connect. She still had the Mace, so she raised it, but he swiped at her wrist. The can clattered to the floor. He approached her slowly. She backed up, but in her peripheral vision she noticed Fishman still writhing on the floor, so she grabbed his briefcase and held it in front of her as if it were a shield.

Hoodie Guy lunged. Sheila blocked him with the briefcase and raised her knee until it slammed into his groin. He yowled and doubled over, but all she could think was:

Tiny testicles. That's what 'roids'll do to you.

Sheila shoved him to the ground. Kicked him in the face. Blood spurted from his nose. Doctors and nurses surged into the room. Haggerty was with them.

The detective commandeered a conference room, posted guards at the door, and instructed everybody, for God's sake, to say nothing to the media.

Fishman rubbed his knee. "You gonna tell me my rights?"

"You know them," Haggerty said.

Sheila motioned toward Hoodie Guy. "You find out anything about him?"

Haggerty looked at his phone. "Name is Tad Wojciehowicz. Used to be Special Forces. Four tours in Iraq and Afghanistan. Since his discharge, he's been dealing designer steroids. Three raps on that, but they've all been dismissed." He glared at Fishman. "I suspect the district attorney can enlighten us on why that happened."

"Anything else?" Sheila asked.

"In 2019," Haggerty said, "Mr. Wojciehowicz spent four days in Rikers. One of his cellmates was Octravian Murray."

All eyes on Hoodie Guy.

"I ain't sayin' nothin'."

Haggerty went on. "A few weeks after their time together at Rikers, members of Mr. Murray's gang in the Bronx began to get arrested for peddling PEDs. Interesting coincidence, no?"

"Who told you to approach Octravian Murray?" Sheila asked.

Hoodie Guy said he wanted to talk to a lawyer.

A groggy-sounding Michael spoke up. "You can do that. But if we unravel this without your help, you'll be looking at multiple charges of conspiracy, attempted murder, aiding and abetting a murder, and obstruction of justice. By the time you're out of prison, Miami will be underwater."

"When I looked through your wallet," Haggerty said to Hoodie Guy, "I found two business cards from people in the Grubb Organization. Given the circumstances, I could get a court order right now to examine your phone."

Hoodie Guy mumbled something. Sheila thought she picked up the words "didn't know nothin'."

Haggerty told him to speak up.

Hoodie Guy shouted, "I said I didn't know nothin' 'bout killing nobody in prison."

Sheila tried to parse all the negatives.

"Mr. Grubb aksed if I knew anyone in Auburn, and I said sure I did, and he told me to get in touch with him. There was a guy there they wanted to scare. Old guy. I didn't know nothin' 'bout killing him. Nobody never said nothin' 'bout that, least to me."

Hoodie Guy put his elbows on the table and rested his drug-swollen head in his hands. The room was quiet for a long minute.

"You've got the floor, Sis," Michael said.

Showtime, Sheila thought.

She stood and paced. Height always conferred an advantage.

"After reading the police report on the death of Martha Owens, I began to doubt she'd been murdered in her apartment. It all fell into place when Detective Haggerty and I talked to Angelo DiNapoli."

Pause for dramatic effect. Sheila had learned a few things by doing theater in high school.

"Ms. Owens was killed in the brothel in Murray Hill. After my father ripped her off that night, she went there because she needed cash, and she knew the place was a money machine. But the men refused to share, she got pissed off, and eventually DiNapoli called the one guy she might listen to."

Sheila glared at Fishman.

"That guy was you."

Fishman's back straightened. "Now, wait a minute."

Sheila reminded herself that the most essential quality in public life is shamelessness.

"DiNapoli told you she was at the brothel and, even for her, she was in quite a mood."

Sheila spoke fast and forcefully but reminded herself not to shout. Men never took women seriously when they shouted, especially when they were right.

"Paco had introduced you to Martha during the investigation into Public Morals. At that point you were a regular customer at Murray Hill, so you suggested she work there. You liked her, and she liked you, in a left-handed way, so the two of you were able to hook up in surroundings straight out of 'The Age of Innocence.'

"Now, DiNapoli claims he has no idea what happened after you got there that night. I think he has a really good idea of what happened, but he never asked about it because he didn't want to lie to the cops when they came around asking about her. The strange thing is—they never did."

Sheila took a swig of water from a paper cup she'd filled at a fountain.

"Nadine kept a journal, and she kept referring to a man she called 'A.' She had a literary bent, and the character was a composite, but he mostly resembled Adam Fishman. She seemed to think you two might even have a future together. We all have our fantasies … "

Sheila let her voice trail off, then resumed.

"When you got there that night, she was in a room upstairs with Aaron Grubb and Paulie, the goon. She was demanding a skim from the brothel because she'd figured out that DiNapoli was laundering the cash through his holding company. The money was being loaned out to the real estate companies, who were buying as many underpriced properties as they could on the Lower West Side. They knew how much that land would be worth once Westway got built. They were wrong about Westway, but they were right about the land."

"Making money isn't a crime," Fishman said.

"Killing people to do it is. The argument in the brothel persisted. The confrontation got physical. Martha struck you. My father said the first time he met you, you had cuts and bruises on your face. He thought you'd shaved in a hurry, but that wasn't it. Martha had scratched and slapped you because you wouldn't help her out."

"Baseless speculation," Fishman said.

"I'm still not sure exactly who killed her—you or Grubb or Paulie—but since you were there, you're guilty of murder."

"The goon was a professional," Haggerty said. "It would've been his job."

"Unfortunately," Sheila said, "Paulie is no longer with us because he ran afoul of John Gotti, but he was the comptroller of Shenandoah LLC, Angelo DiNapoli's holding company, and I'd be amazed if he ever took an accounting class."

Sheila drank more water. She hoped her adrenaline rush could last a few more minutes.

"The room where Nadine was killed was scrubbed down. That's why it looked so clean when my father raided the joint. But on that night, the killers were faced with a big problem—taking care of her body. So Adam Fishman saw a way to turn a mountain of lemons into lemonade."

She turned to the DA.

"You were leading the investigation into the Public Morals squad, and by then you understood just how rotten an apple my father was. At that point, he was your big target. All of you knew that he'd ripped off Martha that night, and you figured he'd never admit being in her place. If you got her body back into her apartment, eventually somebody would pin her death on him. He was crooked as hell, and it wouldn't take much to make everyone believe he was a murderer as well.

"But then he flipped and started cooperating with your investigation. It must've unnerved you because now he was your star witness. So you sped up the probe into Public Morals. You told my father you were under pressure to close it quickly, but there's no record any of your superiors ever told you to do that."

"My instructions were verbal," Fishman said.

"Sure. Nobody in a bureaucracy ever writes a memo."

Haggerty chuckled. Sheila went on.

"You played a hunch that proved correct: When my father testified to the Antonelli Commission, Zaca dropped a dime on him. That was bad for you in the short run, but in the long run everything worked out. Public Morals was cleaned up, my father was convicted of Martha's murder, and you became district attorney. Your family made money buying properties on the West Side. So did Aaron Grubb, and over the years Grubb has helped you out plenty—you've never had to worry about financing a campaign."

Michael's phone pinged with an incoming text. He glanced around the room.

"I dipped into my discretionary fund," he said, "and asked a private lab to do some forensic analysis on the bag my father recovered in the raid on the brothel in Murray Hill. Now, there's one thing about being a member of law enforcement—your fingerprints and DNA are always on file. Just in case. So I asked the lab to check if Adam Fishman left any traces on it, and they found fingerprints and hair that match. There are also prints and hair from other, unidentified individuals. It would be interesting to get some samples from Aaron Grubb and Adrian Lynch."

"You can't use any of that as evidence," Fishman said. "There's no chain of custody."

"I can use it in my movie," Sheila said to him. "And here's one more factoid I can dwell on. My father told you that Martha worked in the brothel. You said you'd pass that information on to Detective Mulligan."

She glanced at Haggerty, who was happy to speak up.

"I just called him," Haggerty said. "He says he never heard anything about it. That's why he never questioned anybody at the brothel in connection with her death."

Sheila stared at Fishman. Say something, she silently yelled at the man.

"How did you know I knew her?" he asked.

"She had your phone number," Sheila said. "And when we talked about her, you called her Martha. Almost everyone else called her by her professional name: Nadine LaFleur. Then there was the handbag. Gucci. She said it was a gift. It was a gift—from you." She pointed to his briefcase. "The brand has always been your biggest indulgence."

Fishman drummed his fingers on the table.

"Did you love her?" Sheila said.

"What kind of dumbass question is that?" Fishman said.

"The kind of dumbass question a woman asks," Sheila said.

Fishman took a few seconds. "She was … interesting."

"Barnard and all that," Sheila said. "Great sex coupled with sophisticated pillow talk."

Fishman's pasty face reddened.

"But you told her too much," Sheila said. "You and the other men she slept with. Information is the most potent weapon anyone can have, and when she threatened to use it, she was killed."

No sounds at all in the room. Sheila felt like a diva about to launch her final aria.

"And so, Mr. Fishman, you and Aaron Grubb and Paulie brought Martha back to her apartment to plant the body. The city never sleeps, but sometimes it dozes, and it was the dead of night. So you and Aaron Grubb put her back in her bed while Paulie distracted Zaca.

"Martha was a good source for Jamie Quinn, so he played up her murder. That was good for you. It was a high-profile case; the pressure to solve it was intense, and you knew the Homicide cops would eventually find my father's fingerprints in her apartment.

"But Adrian Lynch figured out what happened. He's a slut, but he's good at police work, so he could sniff out a crime when he put his mind to it. He was also a client of Martha's, and they had long conversations where he found out about what you guys planned to do on the West Side. He was the one who wrote down those addresses my father found in her handbag. He wanted in on it, but that scam was a closed opportunity. Nevertheless, after the scandal died down, you and Grubb gave him some money to head off to Florida to start a new life."

Fishman's face had turned scarlet. Sheila was reminded of a tomato ripe for picking.

"Dante Antonelli figured out what had happened, too. He was the head of the Public Safety Committee, and Martha was savvy about the way things work in the city, so she contacted him as the investigation into Public Morals got underway. You were a rising young prosecutor, and you wanted to impress her, but she let Antonelli know that you were one of her clients. He kept it quiet at the time. But you knew he was gay, so you two had weapons against each other. A few years later, when Antonelli was run out of town, you and Grubb did the prudent thing by giving him the money to open that oh-so-cute B&B in Provincetown."

Sheila looked around the room.

"Am I wrong about any of this?"

Michael turned to Fishman.

"All these years we've worked together," he said, "and you knew what happened to that woman, and you never said anything to me."

"You were estranged from your father," Fishman said.

"Because I thought he was an unrepentant murderer."

"Your father was the dirtiest cop in the history of New York. He got what he deserved. I'm not sorry about him in the slightest."

The district attorney rose to his feet and looked at his Timex before turning to Haggerty.

"I understand the situation. There are a few things I need to take care of at home. You know where I live—come by in two hours. I'm not going to run away. Everything will be ready."

Michael lay propped in his hospital bed while his wife stroked his hand and arm. Sheila wanted to film the tableau, but decided against asking if she could.

"How did you know?" Rachel asked.

"Martha was beaten up, and there was blood all over her, but the report on the crime scene said there were no stains on the sheets or bedcovers. In fact, there was no blood anywhere in the apartment except on her. I started asking myself how that could possibly happen."

"And if you put that together with the handbag … " Rachel let the thought hang.

"What is it about women and their bags?" Michael asked.

"I would never leave my bag behind," Sheila said.

"Especially if it's Gucci," Rachel said.

Michael leaned back as far as he could. "Haggerty's gonna call when he arrests Adam. Your friend in the hoodie is talking, and NYPD is swearing out warrants for Aaron Grubb, Adrian Lynch and Dante Antonelli."

"What happens to you?" Sheila asked.

Michael shrugged. "The governor will appoint a new district attorney. It might be me. It might be somebody else. Either way, I'll run for the job."

Michael's cell rang. He listened for a minute, grunted, then looked at his wife and his sister.

"Adam Fishman jumped to his death. He left behind a note saying he was recently diagnosed with incurable health problems."

The room was quiet except for the blips and beeps of hospital machines. After a minute, Sheila spoke up.

"Daddy said he had no guts."

Acknowledgements

This book has been in the works for a long time, and I apologize to anyone who made a contribution to it whom I am overlooking. In particular, I received useful editing advice from Charles Salzberg, Steve Kasdin and Esmond Harmsworth. I'm indebted to the team at Level Best Books, particularly Harriette Sackler, Verena Rose, Shawn Reilly Simmons and Deb Well, for taking on this book and shepherding it through the publication process. Although I've lived in New York City most of my life, some books about the dark days of the 1970s and '80s helped in my research, especially *New York, New York, New York*, by Thomas Dyja; *Varnished Brass: The Decade After Serpico*, by Barbara Gelb; *They Wished They Were Honest: The Knapp Commission and New York City Police Corruption*, by Michael Armstrong; and *Vice Cop: My Twenty-Year Battle With New York's Dark Side*, by Bill McCarthy and Mike Mallowe.

Most of all, though, I need to thank my wife, Jill, and our daughter, Skyler, for their patience while I wrote this thing and shopped it around.

About the Author

Tom Coffey is a longtime journalist who has worked for some of the leading news organizations in the country, including *The Miami Herald, The Los Angeles Herald Examiner, Newsday, New York Newsday,* and *The New York Times.* He grew up on Staten Island, where he went to Catholic schools. A graduate of the Newhouse School of Public Communications at Syracuse University, he later attended film school at the University of Southern California. His first novel, *The Serpent Club,* was published in 1999. A member of Mystery Writers of America, his other titles include *Miami Twilight, Blood Alley* and *Bright Morning Star.* Tom lives in Lower Manhattan with his wife and daughter.

SOCIAL MEDIA HANDLES:

I have an active presence on both Facebook and LinkedIn. Look me up! https://www.facebook.com/tom.coffey.311

AUTHOR WEBSITE:

www.bloodalleynovel.com

Also by Tom Coffey

The Serpent Club (Pocket Books, 1999)

Miami Twilight (Pocket Books, 2001)

Blood Alley (Toby Press, 2008)

Bright Morning Star (Oak Tree Press, 2015)

9 781685 125189